The Ring of Disaster

The stranger passed the ranks of courtiers and halted before her. "I am Leith, Prince of the Isles."

"I am told you have found my ring," Kess declared.

He drew the golden circle from his smallest finger. He had rather large knuckles, and the ring stuck fast for a moment, making him struggle while Kess contemplated the expediency of having his finger struck off with the first handy blade. Finally he held the circle up for her inspection.

Kess did not deign to lean forward to receive the jewel. Movement would have spoiled her poise. "Yes, that is my ring."

The witnesses sighed happily. Well they might—for them, it was the hero tale sprung to wondrous life. Kess reminded herself that only she saw the tableau as an unmitigated disaster . . .

By Susan Dexter
Published by Ballantine Books:

THE RING OF ALLAIRE

WIZARD'S SHADOW

The Warhorse of Esdragon
THE PRINCE OF ILL-LUCK
THE WIND-WITCH*

* *Forthcoming*

THE PRINCE
OF ILL LUCK

Book One of
The Warhorse of Esdragon

Susan Dexter

A Del Rey Book
BALLANTINE BOOKS • NEW YORK

This book is for:

Mr. Richard Shaffer—the white knight unawares of my fourth-grade class, who picked up the pieces halfway through 1964.

Veronica Chapman—possibly an angel unawares, certainly an editor of taste and discernment.

Cost-Plus Imports English Breakfast and Apricot teas, without which this book could not have been written.

A Del Rey Book
Published by Ballantine Books

Copyright © 1994 by Susan Dexter

Library of Congress Catalog Card Number: 93-90712

ISBN 0-345-38065-7

Manufactured in the United States of America

First Edition: March 1994

Author's Note on Names

A note on names: If the Isles were those of Scotland, the name would be *Lĕth*, but Leith isn't Scottish, so he prefers *Layth*. The other names present no confusions that I'm aware of.

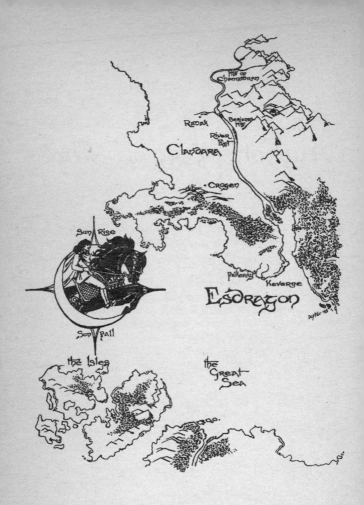

Prologue

LONG AGO, ERE wizards banded together to build their city of Kôvelir on the bank of the River Est, ere ever the Maristan Kings landed as conquerors upon Calandra's shore, when what was to become the kingdom of Calandra was yet a quilt of petty kingdoms and threadbare principalities, her neighbor Esdragon was already a land united under hereditary dukes— albeit a small and relatively poor land, bounded by sea and hills, with much that lay between untamable moorland, naught but bog and heather.

On that wild pasture, a horse was bred and foaled, and grew to fame. He was black as the night—a night when neither moon nor star was to be seen. His name was Valadan.

The Begetting

"THAT IS DARKSHINE," Duke Symond said to the cloaked figure standing at his right hand.

They observed the little band of mares from a distance, but the horses were perfectly aware of them—had been from the instant the duke's men pulled aside a half dozen of the palings to admit their master into the enclosure. Most of the mares had resumed their grazing in short order, but one—a dark bay—stood with head still lifted and ears yet pricked, her nostrils flaring wide to pull in the intruders' scent as the breeze carried it to her.

Hooves drummed the ground.

" 'Ware the stallion," the duke said, turning about toward the sound. The pasture was all hills, and the red war-stallion crested the nearest to appear before them as abruptly as if conjured, snorting and tossing his head to threaten them. He trotted between the intruders and his band of mares, back and forth, arching his neck to demonstrate his vigor, lowering his head and snaking it side to side to warn them off. Not satisfied, the stud then rapidly circled the mares and drove them away over the hill—all save the bay.

She ran the opposite way, nimbly evading the stud, aiming a kick or two at him till he ceased his efforts to turn her, forced to choose between letting her go or losing control of all the others. She squealed derisively at him as he departed.

"And you say he cannot get her in foal?" the cloaked man asked blandly.

"He can't get near her!" the duke explained, producing a sack of grain from inside his cloak, bait to lure the mare close. "Nor any of my other stallions. It makes no difference which stud I choose for her—she shows them each her heels, and if

2

by chance one manages to corner her, she marks him. She kicked my best destrier lame last season, when he pressed his suit too ardently for her taste. This year promises no difference."

The bay mare was walking tamely up to them, interested in the grain. She allowed the duke to handle her without protest, to slip a halter over her fine head whilst she lipped oats from his familiar hand. The stranger circled her, slowly so as not to alarm, his dark eyes busy.

The mare's form was compact, supported by legs delicate of appearance and tough in actuality, with no coarse hair upon the fetlocks to obscure their sculpturing. Her shoulders sloped, her loins were strong, her heart-girth was deep. Her neck was both arched and gracefully tapered. Darkshine was by no measurement tall, but she was neither pony nor crossbred scrub. Her conformation bespoke careful breeding, refined over a score of matings.

Fierce as she had been with the stallion, the mare was yet gentle with her master. The grain was gone, but still she rested her small muzzle upon his palm, while the duke rubbed the fingers of his free hand between her dark eyes, playing with her raven-black forelock, scratching between her wide-sprung jawbones—an attention Darkshine seemed especially to enjoy, in a spot a horse is hard put to find means of scratching.

"Proud she is, but she likes you well." The inspection was concluded.

"Truly said," Symond agreed. The mare behaved like a pet. "But *I* cannot get a foal upon her, though that foal is my dearest desire. I want her sons and daughters in my herd. So, I have turned to you—for the skills rumor says you possess."

The stranger had put up the hood of his cloak, against the freshening wind and the spatter of rain it inevitably carried. He had been some weeks at Esdragon. The duke could see no more of his face than a bit of chin, the tip of his nose. Nor, Symond found, could he recall the precise cast of those features. The man's expression was unreadable even when his face was visible, his voice mostly expressionless.

"There are ways," the wizard said, "to obtain your heart's desire."

The bay mare grew restive as the storm drew near. She trotted with anxious frequency from one side of her pasture to the other, her steps springy, as if she misliked to touch the earth.

She was alone, bereft of the herd, which increased her unease, and she called out often, but by design no other horse was near enough to answer her.

"Should we not remove her to shelter?" the duke fretted. The incoming weather had him nigh as nervous as the mare— his every sense warned of danger, though storms were a common occurrence in Esdragon and a soaking part of every day spent outside the walls of his fortress of Keverne.

"No," the wizard answered, calm. "She is where she must be."

The whole expanse of the sunward sky was dark as a bruise. Thunder rolled, so low it could be felt more than heard, and vague glows fitfully lit the gloom of the massed clouds. Yet 'twas the wind that reached the mare first, far in advance of any rain and surprisingly strong. It swept past her roughly, circled about her like a small cyclone. It had a wild scent, more akin to the crackling lightning than to the wetness of rain.

The mare greeted the wind angrily, lowering her head, flattening her ears. She squealed a warning to companion her threat and clamped her tail tightly to her hindquarters. She was prepared to mete out further justice with her heels, though no target for her fury could be seen. She squealed again and snaked her head, showing her teeth.

The wind responded with a shrill whistle. It circled her again, playfully lifting a strand of her dark mane, letting it drop into place once more.

Still not a drop of rain fell, though the blackness overhead had reached the pasture and the mare could scarcely be seen by the two watchers. Dust, wind-whipped, veiled her form. She looked to be standing at the precise center of a tiny dust devil—when she could be seen at all.

Suddenly Darkshine's heels slashed out, kicking at nothing. The mare bucked once, spun, and raced away into the night, fleet as the wind that pursued her. The duke saw nothing more of her for many anxious moments. His ears told him that she was racing about, for the sound of her hoofbeats waxed and waned as she advanced or retreated. Their tempo never altered, being always rapid, galloping. He began to fret that the mare might crash into the palings in the darkness, blinded by storm and panic. The wooden planks were stout; she'd injure herself, perhaps fatally.

The duke wanted, then, to call off the venture he'd begun, but his throat seized up when he tried to bespeak the unheeding wizard, and the words could not be forced out. The mare still raced, her hooves hammering the ground. The pitch of the wind increased, till it filled the whole of the world, and the duke knew that whatever power he boasted in Esdragon was inconsequential before it.

Spent, turned back in her every attempt at escape, the bay mare halted at last.

The still-circling wind whispered endearments, enticements, to her. The mare pricked her ears. She called softly, a tiny unfamiliar welcoming sound inaudible a yard off. The storm wind, gentler yet, pranced about her, flicking at her mane, at her flowing tail. Thunder crashed, all about.

The rain never did fall.

Come first light, the duke hurried anxiously to his favorite's side. He found her grazing placidly, her mane wind-snarled into elf locks, bits of straw and twig caught fast in the silky hair. It appeared the storm had brought no harm to Darkshine, for the brown satin of the mare's coat bore no mark. A wonder, that, considering the mare's panic, the violence of the storm winds. There had been crops flattened not far off. But the mare was well, none the worse for any fright.

Finished with his inspection, the duke turned and looked a question at the wizard, who had spoken not a single word. The man smiled at the duke's uncertainty.

"I would not ask you to believe if I could not offer you proof, but you will have to wait for it, my lord. A year less a month, as with any horse.

"Then you shall behold that which was wrought last night."

"She's been in foal a year now," Duke Symond said, concern shading his reasonable tone. "A full month over term. Something must be amiss—"

The wizard lifted his ear from Darkshine's rounded flank. "One more day," he pledged, smiling away a worry he had, unannounced, begun to share. "All's well, my lord. I misjudged, when I led you to expect that such a mating would be normal in all other respects, but the time has come. You shall have your foal by sunrise."

The wizard ordered the mare loosed in a small pasture, lest confinement within a stable hamper the birth that was about to take place. There might be other surprises in store, beyond the unusual length of gestation, though he said nothing of his guess. He allowed the duke to keep grooms at hand, but ordered them held out of sight unless their aid should be required. Foaling mares were touchy creatures, oft resentful of interference and likely to delay birthing if they could not have privacy for it. The unusual nature of Darkshine's mating might be assumed to add other factors to those expected.

By the last watch of the night, the duke had fallen into a doze where he sat against the fence, and the wizard had veiled himself in shadows until he could scarcely be observed at all. It had been some while since the bay mare had lowered her head to graze. She had slept, or at least stood quietly—but now she was restive, shifting her weight often, turning her head about to gaze at her thickened flanks. The signs were plain. Her time was upon her.

The foaling proceeded unremarkably. It was difficult for the wizard to scry out precise details—a black night, a dark mare lying wrapped in it—and the foal, when it slid free of its mother, revealed only by the pale birth sac, the glitter of its eyes when it raised its head. Daylight would show its color—whether 'twas dark bay like the mare or black like its sire. And whether 'twas filly or stallion foal. Werelight would have provided the answers on the spot, but would have been an invasion, and the wizard tactfully eschewed that folly. Dawn was not far off.

The mare was back on her feet quickly, nosing at her foal, encouraging it tenderly to try out its own long legs. Suddenly she lifted her head, staring fixedly into the wind, which was rising. Such winds herald storms, though there had been no earlier sign of a shift in the weather. There was a wild scent in the air, of rain and lightning.

The wizard took a pace toward the mare, reckoning it was time to remove the treasured one to shelter, now that her work was done—and all at once he was thrust back as if shouldered by an unseen beast, jostled so roughly that he stumbled and nearly fell to the ground before he recovered his footing. The mare's mane lifted, floating on the air as the wind circled her. She called softly in answer to its shrill whistling and began to move after it as it retreated. Her foal struggled frantically to rise, aching to follow a dam it had scarcely had time to know. She did not so much as turn her head back, but trotted straight into the wind's embrace.

Dust filled the air. Tree branches waved, and limbs cracked at the sudden stresses put to them. Torn leaves swirled like snowfall. The grass flattened, sprang up, flattened again. The wizard grabbed an oak bole as he was pushed against it, and clung fast to safety till the whirlwind died away. The duke, wakened, fought his way to his feet, calling questions and Darkshine's name while leaves and wind-flung pebbles assaulted his face and the gale took his words beyond reach of mortal ears.

In the sudden calm and unnatural quiet the cyclone left behind it, there was no sign of the bay mare. Only her colt foal, on his wobbly legs too late, skirling his despair at the stormy sky as the wind retreated to the far horizon.

The wizard felt the hairs on his head lift, though the whirlwind had died. All his skin prickled. He realized he was fortunate to be left alive. Magic consented betimes to answer to a sorceror's will, but sometimes by ill chance one woke more than one required or anticipated. He had just been forcibly reminded that magic could escape the sternest control, could easily become more than was requested or desired. The wind stud had returned to claim the mare, and there would be no getting her back. They were lucky he had taken no interest in the foal.

A nurse mare would need to be found.

The awed wizard slowly closed in on the foal, whilst the duke blundered about under the trees, searching in vain for his vanished mare. The little creature stood splay-legged, ears a-flop. Its eyes sparkled in the gloom, flashing colors quite foreign to normal-begotten horses. Ruby, emeraude, topaz, sapphire, peridot, adamant. Those eyes, and his black coat, were the only visible marks his stormy sire had stamped on him, for the little colt was otherwise unremarkable and in truth rather small, undersized. Whatever the wizard had expected to see, it was not this, a foal like any other foal.

The wizard stretched out his hand. The foal sniffed, then tried to suckle at his fingers.

"I suppose you are hungry," the cloaked man observed. "Let us see to that, then. All the rest, in its own time."

Reived Away

THE ACCEPTED PRACTICE for rearing foals in Esdragon was to let them roam free upon the moors once they had been weaned from their dams. At the duke's stud, records of coat colors and markings were kept, and neck brands high under the manes of those without distinguishing markings made eventual sorting an easy matter. Filly foals would be gathered in again after a year had passed, lest they be chance-bred too early, but the young stallions were allowed their freedom for three winters, untroubled by any man's hand. The weather and the country tested and tried them—they grew strong, developed speed and stamina both. The rough grasses nourished them, the ground, rocky and boggy by turns, taught them to be clever and sure-footed.

The duke rode out often to inspect his herds, so mounted men were no novelty. The arrival of a larger retinue in the springtime did not alarm the young horses, and being bunched together and chivvied along was no cause for concern amongst them. It was indeed a fine thing to run as a herd across the treeless moorland, racing the wind and one another. Dark-shine's black colt, though still smaller than his herdmates, was ever in the lead, head and tail both lifted high as he galloped joyfully on his strong legs.

There were holding pens constructed, where the colts could be kept and gentled before being sent on for their training, and gelding done on such of them as were judged not suitable for war or future breeding. The bright-coated colts milled about, testing the limits of their confinement and in some cases the strength of the pens. It was always an exciting event, to see the young herd brought in, and the duke's pleasure was evident as he sat his well-trained courser, his young daughter by his side on her own sleek palfrey. A smile split his dark beard as he directed his men at their work, when he called a particularly well-made horse to his daughter's ready attention

He picked out Darkshine's orphaned colt easily. The young stallion had his lost mother's refined head—broad between the eyes and through the jaws, tiny at the muzzle—with ears whose tips pointed in at one another whenever the colt pricked them. He was doing just that, watching the duke intently from the far side of his herdmates, oblivious to the jostling and the calling as a dozen colts raced between them.

The attention he showed was rather beyond the ordinary, but perchance that was illusion; likewise the impression that the colt's eyes sparkled with jewel colors. It was sheer nonsense—horses have brown eyes or, rarely, blue—and however wild the night of his birth had been, this colt was a horse like any other.

A pity he had not grown taller, the duke mused. His proportions were sound, but he was a hand lower at the withers than any of his pasture-mates, and they made him look a runt. There might be a spurt of growth yet to come, but Darkshine had not been overtall, and it seemed her son took after her in that. The nurse mare could not be faulted—she had kept her charge fat as a prize bullock.

The duke noticed the colt had closed the distance between them while he mused—only the side of the pen now separated them from one another. His courser stretched out its neck, nostrils fluttering as it whickered a greeting. Some of the colts were still immature enough to mouth when confronted by an older, strange horse, opening their jaws to demonstrate their youth and harmlessness, to beg that no harm be done them on that account. Darkshine's colt boldly returned the courser's snort, tossed his shapely head, and reared, spinning as he landed upon all fours once more, trotting away a few high-stepping strides, seeming to dance. Again he halted, again pricked his ears and fixed his attention on the duke.

He seemed to want something.

The duke smiled at his fancy and pointed the colt out to his small daughter. Most of this young stallion's wants—save for a comely mare or two—were met already. The only thing he could conceivably be said to lack was a name.

Yes. Why not give him one, then?

The black colt still watched intently. His eyes flashed, a swirl of ruby mingled with sapphire—surely a trick of the sunlight, which was overbright that day, a wonder for well-watered Esdragon.

"Your name is Valadan!" the duke called to him all at once, then spun his horse and rode away.

A horse fair was held at the edge of the moorland, where all the young bloodstock was proudly displayed, and those colts the duke chose not to retain for his own herds were annually sold off. With the past year's results in view, the next season's matings were arranged.

It had become an occasion for the selling of horses of all ages and descriptions, grown up around its original purpose of exhibition, attended by folk hailing from every corner of the duchy and many of the principalities beyond her borders. Far-famed was the duke's stock, and even his culls were desired greatly in lands less blessed with fine horses.

A city of pavillions sprang up about the colt holding pens. Picket lines were thrown up, row upon row of horses were tethered to them. There were races held on the moors, and never was there an hour of the day when some trader was not showing off a steed's paces to a hoped-for buyer, with a crowd of onlookers enjoying the spectacle, calling compliments or deprecations.

Those young stallions the duke reserved for himself were quartered on the fringes of the fair, where they would be least upset by the unaccustomed noise and activity. Their quality being so far-famed, they had plenty of visitors despite not being offered for purchase, no matter how remotely they were housed. One such visitor came in the darkest reach of the night, and all alone.

He had observed his quarry carefully and knew precisely what he sought. The black stud colt, one of the boldest, came right up to him, unafraid, curious at the intrusion. All the duke's colts had been taught to accept a halter ere the fair commenced—there was no difficulty in slipping a rope restraint over the black's head. It suffered itself to be led away from the pen, and the mare the thief had left waiting a little way off ensured that the colt was not tempted to return to the pen and his old companions.

By dawn the man and the two horses were leagues distant from the fair, moving at a steady pace over the moors, under a low pewter sky. A rainy morning removed the few traces left of their passage early on, and the moors—though in no wise so vast as they appeared to human eyes—were adequate to protect them from pursuit.

Valadan was not especially unhappy to be on the move once more—the time in the pen had been tedious despite the novelties of the strange horses and men. There had not been room to stretch his legs—he was weary of ever being turned from his course by the side of a pen. So he was content to trot alongside the strawberry roan mare and never once fought the rope that kept him tethered closely to her. The mare was polite, and patient, good company on the journey. Her rider seemed content with their pace—for the most part—and did not annoy the horses overmuch. It was pleasant to range over the moor, to see new sights.

By the third day, matters had begun to alter. The ground underhoof was rising and drying out, its rock bones thrusting through with increasing frequency. The mare was no longer so young as she once had been, and the pace her rider insisted upon was hard for her to maintain day after day. A steady trot is an easy gait for a horse over a distance, but the mare was tiring all the same. They halted at intervals to graze, but the mare no longer returned to her work refreshed afterward, as she had at the outset of their trek.

By the fourth day, a bruise on the sole of her off forefoot was making itself painfully known. They were at a walking pace by then, for they were climbing into hills, but that was no help—the mare was dead lame by sun-high.

Still her rider urged her onward, and the roan bravely tried to obey. She limped along painfully while her rider scanned the backtrail, frowning. Whatever the thief saw or did not see never prompted him to grant the mare the mercy of more than a brief rest. They went on haltingly till nearly twilight.

Finding a flat patch on the general upslope, the thief drew rein and dismounted. He inspected the hoof again, shook his head, cursed. He eyed the dimming sky, hastily climbed to a high place, and scryed the trail again, both ahead and behind. Upon returning to the flat, he swiftly untacked the mare and flung her gear piece by piece onto a startled Valadan's back.

The unfamiliar sensations came so rapidly, piling one atop the other, the young stallion could scarcely register them, far less decide about objecting. There was a weight pressing on his back, saddle and padded blanket. The wide band of a girth was tightened against his tender belly. Stirrups dangled and clattered against his sides when he moved, no matter how he squirmed. Worse, a bar of cold hard metal was knocked against his teeth and shoved rudely into his mouth. Leather straps were forced over his ears ere he could fling his head up, holding the distasteful metal in place. The colt strove to spit the bit out, but 'twas no use. Held fast by the straps, it could not be budged.

His back was burdened, his head restrained and strapped about—and just then the man vaulted into the saddle and jerked on the reins to demonstrate to him how the bit could bite into his tender mouth at a rider's pleasure.

Valadan's reaction was tempered by amazement. He scarcely stirred a step as he strove to comprehend the fate that had befallen him. The unaccustomed weight on his back threatened to alter the very way he moved. He *wanted* to move, to keep his balance under the load. But the pull on his mouth ordered him to stand still, and that response seemed to be correct. Valadan tucked his chin and found that was better still. The pressure on his mouth eased, though it did not go away altogether.

The man had a leg on either side of him and was squeezing his sides with them. Valadan shifted his weight uncertainly, fearing for his mouth, then dared a step forward, to get away from the squeezing. The pressure was released for an instant, then repeated. The colt took another step, trying to decide how to carry his head, how best to balance the load atop him. After a moment it grew easier, he learned the knack of it. A squeeze meant move, a pull on the mouth meant stop or slow. A pull to one side turned his head, and his body followed. He quickly learned that if he turned toward the pull, his head was not yanked so far.

They began to cover ground, step after step. There was more squeezing, a kick or two, and Valadan suddenly accelerated into a trot. A hand patted his neck, assuring him that he did well, though the touch startled him, and he flinched and flung his head till the bit brought him up short.

The mare was on the tether now, constrained by it to follow them and keep their pace. The loss of her load had not much eased her plight—she was still lame and struggling to keep up, the rope jerking her head when she failed.

Valadan could hear her gasping for breath. She did not cry out with her pain—horses seldom do—but her ragged footfalls told the tale of her suffering in broken cadence, plain as any minstrel. He tried to slow his pace, but insistent kicks refused his mercy. Finally the mare was hobbling three-legged, unable to touch the injured hoof to the earth for more than an instant's balance. And she was slowing their progress markedly as night came fully on, no matter how the thief cursed and kicked and jerked the lead rein.

Valadan dropped back into a walk. The slope was steep, covered with cruel stones that the mare could likely not manage, brave as she was. Again he was kicked hard in the side— and the thief hauled viciously on the tether rope, dragging the mare after them. She staggered, her hurt foot striking the hard ground, and the man pulled the rope again, forcing her to stumble onward. Only the rope kept her from falling to her knees. She groaned, tried to catch her balance.

The thief did not quite slacken his hold on Valadan's reins, but Valadan was past caring whether the bit hurt him. The stallion dropped his head, arched his back, and bucked like a siege engine. The unwary horse thief went over his head, sailed through the air for a little distance, and thudded onto the rocks of the trailside gully.

Valadan snorted, dancing to keep his footing, feeling light as a breeze. He stepped on one of the trailing reins, and the heavy bit dug into his mouth. He flung his head back from the sudden pain, and the leather rein snapped like an old twig.

The mare stood shivering beside him, her knees both bloodied, her flanks sweat-soaked. Valadan nosed her neck gently, offering what comfort he could.

They each kept an ear cocked toward the rocks, but no sound issued from the gully. Night fell, and after a time they moved slowly away, letting the mare set a pace she could manage.

Leith of the Isles

TWO HORSES ROAMED free, and soon enough neither bore any sign that the hand of man had ever been upon them. All tack was gone—girths had loosened, leather had torn, and the gear had been shed. The mare's pulled mane grew out, and the hair of her dainty fetlocks was thick and long.

The black stallion and the red roan mare wandered the mountain slopes for a season, growing sleek on the sweet mountain grasses, which they shared only with the wild deer. The mare's bruised hoof healed, but in the end soundness proved useless to her—a mountain cat took her unawares at a watering place one evening, surprised and slew her before she could take flight. Valadan, arriving just moments after the mishap, found the deed done, and though he charged at the cat furiously, he was still alone, and no vengeance could bring his companion back.

The red deer that frequented the mountain meadows would permit a lone and lonely horse to graze close by them. It was not entirely the companionship he longed for—the deer were not his own kind—but it was all there was, and Valadan availed himself of it. Accepted as part of the herd, he ranged with the deer through the mountains and descended the slopes with them when winter came, sheltering in the fringe of forest that cloaked the foothills.

The shy deer were little inclined to venture out onto the moors, but Valadan would happily race the shadows of the clouds as they swept across the heather—or the wind itself, when he chose. Sometimes it seemed to him that he outpaced the gales, but there was no way to be sure of an opponent that remained ever unseen. Valadan ran and, if he ran well, claimed the victory, his head and his tail carried high.

When spring returned and the land greened, the deer climbed to their high pastures once more, following the fresh grasses that sprang up on the lower slopes and in the forest glades as they had done for centuries. Valadan trailed along, observing their custom.

Just past the mid of summer, when the days had imperceptibly begun to shorten once more, an intruder came to the forest.

The deer fled at once, as was their instinct, but even they quickly laid aside their fright and returned to their browsing. The stranger had done nothing untoward save to appear. Now he sat upon a mossy boulder and could be mostly dismissed, unless he should arise and make some threatening move.

He was young, this stranger, but looked to have been hard-used by his brief life. His garments were threadbare and stained, his boots were broken down, his dark hair was tangled, and his hands were stitched with cuts and bramble scratches. He had limped when he was walking, and there was an old scar on his left cheek, which he rubbed at absently as he sat. He had the face of a chessboard king—narrow, sculptured—with a ragged growth of beard blurring the long line of his jaw.

His right eye was deepest brown, very nearly black—the same shade his hair would likely be when it was clean. The left eye did not match its fellow, being green as a young willow leaf in sunlight.

He was Leith, Prince of the Isles, but he was more apt to style himself Prince of Ill Luck, and for good cause. Some of the stains on his clothes were sea stains, and he had come to the coast—Leith had no idea just *what* coast—the sole survivor of a shipwreck.

For three days he had been walking steadily inland—because the coastline had reminded him unbearably of his salty ordeal—and he had seen no human soul. He recognized that ill fortune was having at him once again—he had made a bad choice and now faced starvation in the wilderness, whereas beside the sea he might eventually have found a village, and food. Suddenly there was this wonder—a fine horse, ranging free with the deer. He had no notion what this betokened.

Leith had sat himself down as much to stay out of harm's path as to rest his legs. He had turned one ankle or the other times past counting on sticks and rocks hidden by the leaves of the forest floor, had more than once ducked insufficiently under a low-hanging branch and had his scalp twig-raked. He had tripped over every vine he had come upon, and fallen into streams, rocks, and bramble patches. The deer—and the horse—seemed to accept him if he sat still, and Leith was pleased to oblige them, while his thoughts spun and tried to sort themselves into sense.

His right hip ached from too much walking—though it nagged at him most of the time, to varying degrees, pangs Leith ignored with the fortitude lifelong practice lent. He shifted on his boulder, finding as easy a position as he could, and fingered the raised scar on his cheek again, tracing its curve by memory as much as by touch.

He was the third son of the King of the Isles, got upon that ruler's cherished queen. His birth—so Leith had been told—had been joyfully awaited. Though the king already had a brace of heirs in robust health—Leith's elder brothers—he had nonetheless lifted up his latest son proudly, rejoicing in the babe's vigor and his lady's safe delivery. Then—at the tender age of one hour—the first disaster of Leith's life commenced. He had opened his infant eyes.

The king, looking into the tiny red face, beheld not the milky blue eyes common to infants, but a mismatched pair, black and green, known to be possessed by the demon-born. There was no cure for odd eyes, and only a single remedy against such a demon. The king, a brave man who had never shirked a duty however unpleasant, acted swiftly.

He cast the demon down, stabbed it with his cold iron sword, crushed it with his nail-shod boot, and carried his sobbing queen from the birthing chamber, while priests chanted incense-bolstered incantations to ward away further evil and tidied the room with cloths and blessed seawater.

They soon feared sterner measures would be required. A thin cry rose from the chilly stone floor, where the little body lay in its blood and a silver patch of the full moon's light. The demon was not quite laid to rest. Other remedies were hastily considered.

Because of the moonlight, the underpriest of the moon goddess felt a closer observation was unlikely to harm him—his Lady could be relied upon to shield him from the demon. The other priests—who served the greater light of the sun—feeling less secure by night when their master's great Eye was veiled, hung back, making dire predictions.

The underpriest leaned close over the wailing infant—

though not so close that a demon hand might clutch him. What he saw made the close-shorn hairs rise on his nape. The king's aim had been faulty, due no doubt to his distress. His sword's point had but nicked the babe's cheek beneath the sinister green eye, before chipping at the slate floor. The no-wise-fatal wound still bled, but its *shape* was what set the priest's neck prickling. The cut was in the form of a new-moon crescent, and there was no greater mark of his Lady's favor to be shown, even though She washed the child in Her own full light for extra measure lest he mistake the signs.

At once the underpriest exercised privilege and, gathering the babe up in his silver-white cloak, took the infant away to be fostered by his brother priests—no longer a member of the royal house, but given a higher favor.

Leith, scarred and lame in his right leg from the traumatic first hour of his life, grew toward manhood in the Lady's great temple, Her willing servant. He learned the chants for greeting Her upon each moonrise of every month of the year. He read the holy books full of the wisdom She had chosen to reveal to Her priesthood. He tended the menagerie of white animals She had sent—like *him*!—into the keeping of Her priesthood. He went to sea with his fellow apprentices and the senior priests, hauling in netloads of night-running silver pilchards, calling out thanks for the moonglade She spread across the water from Herself to Her servants, to guide them on their way.

Leith's ill luck was more of a joke in those early days—a compedium of the scrapes all boys know. His clothing might be more ragged and stained than that of any other young priest-in-training's, but he had learned to mend his things thriftily, a useful skill. His shins were generally bruised, his toes stubbed, but those hurts were trifles. Leith led an active life, working much with the white horses the moon priests bred and trained and sold—a bruise or two was in no way inconsistent with his career.

When Leith was sixteen the time came—long looked for— for his ordination as a priest of the Lady, the time when he would enter Her service in full dedication, for the rest of his life. The ceremony was lavish with meaning if it was not endowed with the worldly goods a prince might have been expected to bring to it. Leith's birth family had never acknowledged that they knew aught of his survival.

Midway through the ceremony—as the Lady's silver light made the desired perfect column from the central piercing of

Her temple's dome through the incense-smoked air to the mo-
saic floor below where Leith stood in his plain moon-white
robe—an earthshake brought the building right down to the
ground. The temple was a total loss.

The other priests gave Leith to know—as he recovered from
the injuries got in the disaster—that they did not hold him re-
sponsible for a mishap whose timing was surely naught but
awkward coincidence. All the same, they must accept it as a
sign—and so must Leith—that the Lady did not desire his ser-
vices as Her priest. They therefore sent him back to the
palace—and to a father Leith had not seen since the day of his
birth.

The King of the Isles was far from pleased at Leith's reap-
pearance. His queen had borne him other sons—both before
and after Leith—and he had no need of this tainted, all-but-
forgotten scion. Even if the prince was in truth no demon, he
was a reminder of an unchancy event, an embarrassment.

And ill fortune dogged the boy, sluffed off onto those about
him. On the very night of his arrival, ere Leith had even laid
his head upon the pillow in the stuffy chamber he had been
grudgingly assigned, lightning struck the top of the palace's
highest tower and set its wooden roof alight. The fire was put
out, but the roof had been consumed, and a year's store of
wool was spoiled by the rain that followed the lightning. The
king packed Leith off to one of the smaller islands in his
realm, where buildings were all made of stone, immune to
lightning. A plague of black-leg carried off all the local cattle
within two months. Sent hastily to a yet more remote spot,
Leith watched as half a fishing fleet was sent to the bottom by
a freak storm within sight of the harbor's safety.

Plainly, disaster attended his every step, even if Leith could
not himself be proved of any fell intent. After a year of many
moves, of mistrust and held breath, he was packed farther
afield—into a foreign marriage. Let other lands suffer in place
of the Isles, the King of the Isles reasoned. Strangers would
never suspect the source of their troubles. It was sound policy,
sparing the king the loss of another son he actually cared for,
by way of a dividend. Leith replaced his second brother on the
chancy venture. Wearing a new suit of clothes, clutching a
painted wooden panel portrait of his bride-to-be, he left the
Isles behind.

When Leith's ship, far from any shore, was storm-tossed and
dismasted by a gale, the mariners knew full well who to blame

for their foul luck, and cast fate's lodestone overboard with hardly an instant's pause over the morality of drowning their prince. Mayhap his death would appease the gods of wind and wave. Let the ship be spared—that was moral enough for the sailors.

But as ill luck would have it, Leith had been taught to swim in his earliest childhood—it had been a means of strengthening the leg left crippled at his birth. The cold seawater burned his eyes, chilled his blood, but he was swimming still when the ship went down, broached by mountainous swells. The sailors met quick deaths in the waves, but Leith found no such ready mercy. He struggled and suffered for twenty cruel hours in the cold water before he was wave-battered to shore, washed up on an unknown and deserted beach, all alone.

Now, salt-crusted and near starved, the castaway had chanced upon a marvel—this horse dwelling placidly with the deer.

Leith compared in memory the moon-pale horses he had learned and practiced the arts of war-training upon—sacred by their color, valued for the martial skills the moon priests gifted them with. This stallion was dark, where the moonsteeds were light, grays aged to white ere they had completed their schooling—but was he less a horse than they? His bloodlines might be unknown, but his conformation was superb. The slope of his shoulder made Leith's heart ache. Could he not be trained as the Lady's purebloods were?

Leith had the skill to train a horse. He had, in fact, a knack for it. If he could capture this one, tame and train it—he could sell such a horse for gold enough to live a decent while, wherever precisely he *was*. It was a certainty. At the least, the horse could take him to inhabited parts far more swiftly than his own legs. He was most weary of walking.

Leith had been cast out—or had he perhaps been cast *into* something? However he had arrived, this was a new land, where his birth and his curse might mean nothing—or less than his skill at crafting a battle steed. A forlorn hope fluttered in his breast, like a moon moth. Leith tried to push it away, to resolve that he'd catch this horse aiming to increase its value for resale—nothing more than that. To dream beyond that would surely tempt his curse, which might not yet have been entirely satiated by the shipwreck and was perchance yet hovering near him, waiting to strike.

* * *

Catching the stallion was a matter of walking slowly and looking harmless. The deer all fled at Leith's closer approach, but the horse was docile and seemed unafraid of him. Likely the deer had been hunted by men a time or two, and the horse had not.

Leith's belt was crafted of braided strips of leather, dyed in three colors. After removing it, he undid the weaving and used the thin strips to makeshift a bridle, adding the belt's silver buckle—its tough wire twisted to a new shape—to serve as a bit. He tore narrow lengths from the bottom of his cloak and made a short rope out of the woolen cloth, but it was scarcely needed. The horse stood watching alertly as he advanced innocently upon it, but made no attempt to retreat.

He approached a little from one side, keeping the bridle hidden behind his left leg as he walked. He was close enough to count the whiskers a-quiver on the stallion's muzzle. Still the horse showed no sign of alarm. Leith closed the last pace between them and put his right hand out to rub the side of the horse's neck. Horses nuzzled one another in that spot by way of courteous greeting, it was a friendly action. And he wanted this horse to regard him as a friend.

The stallion turned his head, sniffing at Leith's hair, at the sea scents still caught in his clothing. Leith slid his right hand casually over its neck, gently easing a leather strap over the small ears, tying another into place beneath its jaw, a third under its chin. The bit, leaving his left hand, went into the horse's mouth so easily that Leith was hardly more aware of that success than the stallion was. The animal mouthed the metal curiously. Silver might taste different from the more common iron, Leith supposed.

So the horse was no stranger to a bridle. All to the good. Leith patted the dark neck approvingly, smoothed the sable mane over it, removing a burr. This was a *fine* horse, worth a bit of silver just as a reward for discovering it, had it merely strayed from its home. Perchance his mastery of it might earn him a position in some great lord's stable—there were many futures spreading before him, of a sudden. Foremost, however, was the promise of the pleasure of having a good horse moving under him, of covering ground without bruising his feet and breaking blisters. It had been such a long, miserable while since he had known that feeling . . .

Leith took a double handful of the black mane, so that he'd be unlikely to jerk the reins should he slip, and vaulted lightly up onto the stallion's back. He nearly went clean off the other side—he had supposed the horse taller. He felt the stallion shift its weight to answer to his own as he settled himself, but else the horse did not stir. That confirmed the matter for him—if it had been taught to stand for a rider, then being ridden was not strange to the animal. He was not dealing with a wild creature, but with one that had spent perhaps most of its life under a man's hand.

What on earth was it doing, then, grazing there with the wild deer? Had it wandered away after some great battle, its master dead and none left to claim it? He gave the glossy black sides a gentle squeeze with his calves, asking the horse to step forward. Built as it was, its paces must be smooth as water.

Leith was in no wise prepared for the mighty bunching of the stallion's hindquarters beneath him—certainly not for the forward leap that ignored bridle and bit as if they were last year's cobwebs. He almost went off over the horse's lashing tail, and had no leisure for noting the way the scenery went whipping past at awe-inspiring speed.

Just go with him, Leith ordered himself sternly. *He'll stop when he gets to the trees.* The little meadow had been crossed between one heartbeat and the next, the forest loomed like a wall of shadow. Had there been time, Leith's nerve might have failed him, but they were upon it in an eyeblink.

The forest's edge did make the stallion swerve and slacken his pace as he turned. Leith regained his seat, found his balance, and was ready to ask for another run back across the greensward—perhaps ready even to laugh with the delight of the speed—when the stallion planted all four of his hooves and stopped dead under him.

Leith stayed with that too, barely, by sitting deep. *"What a horse!"* he cried, leaning over to pat the dark shoulder in front of his left knee. The stallion's agility was impressive, and it scarcely seemed to draw a deep breath, even after its exertion. It was strong, fast, supple . . .

The reins burned through Leith's fingers as the stallion's head plunged downward. Its back arched as if it intended to bend itself double beneath him, its hooves thrust the earth away.

Some things weren't worth riding out. Leith hastily scissored his right leg back to join his left, gripping the horse's mane for purchase as he slid to safety. He wanted to keep hold of the reins, though, to keep control—

He was too late, not having sufficiently valued the lesson

that the horse could explode under him after having lulled him with seeming calm. An instant before Leith's boots reached the ground, he was flung forcefully backward, assisted by the stallion's shoulder thrusting against his chest.

An oak stood a little in advance of its fellows at the meadow's edge. It received Leith roughly.

Valadan snorted, furious. He had rid himself so easily of his uninvited passenger, yet he could not remove the harness the man had put on him. He recalled belatedly the difficulty he'd had in getting the thief's gear off a year earlier—rubbing at trees to break the leather and tear the girth, scraping his tender skin and jerking the iron bit against the sensitive bars of his mouth. He had been tortured for days. At least this time there was no saddle. His back itched where the man had been.

He shook his head, sending the thin reins whipping, and ran a few yards when the ends stung him unexpectedly. He paused to buck again. The reins tangled this time, and he managed to plant a hoof squarely upon the snarl.

Good. Having captured the foe, he would now proceed to destroy it. Valadan flung his head up and back, pulling the leather taut.

Instead of snapping, the twisted straps slid up over his off forehoof, caught tight about his pastern. Now a second forceful toss of his head pulled his leg, startling him. He swung the leg, hoping to free it. That was worse—too great a motion with the trapped leg jerked the bit in his mouth. The stallion's eyes showed a rim of white. He might walk a short-stepped walk. But he could not run.

No matter what he tried, Valadan could not win free of the bridle. Struggle promised only a choice of disasters. He would rip his mouth—or risk a fall that would leave him lying helpless, prey for one of the mountain cats, if he yielded to the panic that rose up in his heart like a black wind.

Valadan snorted and strove to bite the leather. His teeth were made for tearing grass. Well-tanned leather was beyond their capacity. He could scar the leather but never part it.

Perchance the man could undo what he had done. Valadan, sweating, pointed his sharp ears toward the lone oak. At distance, he trusted his other senses far beyond his sight.

He could make out breathing, along with the calls of birds among the leaves above, the sigh of the wind. But there was no sign of the man stirring. No groans, no curses. By small, delicate steps, almost dancing, so carefully did he move, Valadan ventured closer. He stretched out his head and neck as best he could manage, to further investigate. There had not been breath sounds after, when he had rid himself of the last man who'd dared sit upon his back. No breath, no life. This he had learned.

The man's tangled mane had fallen across his face. Valadan's questing breath shifted a few strands. The odd-colored eyes were both closed. Valadan remained all caution, but after a long moment he ceased to fear the sudden snatch of a hand on his bridle and boldly nosed the man's shoulder.

There was no response.

He might not be able to raise his head without tugging on both mouth and leg, but he could still graze comfortably. Pretending that naught was amiss, Valadan began to crop the long grass.

Leith floated in the dark sea a long, endless while. He was aware that he was cold, but as he drifted and lazily spun about 'twas difficult to fix his wandering attention firmly on the temperature—the sensation of motion overwhelmed nearly all else.

He struggled betimes to direct, to control his course, and thus come to some warmer shore. The effort seemed futile—and risky, like to shove him clean under the dark waves if he proceeded recklessly. Not unlike those dark hours he had spent drifting in the true salt sea, save that struggle now made no pretense of saving him and he somehow sensed he was in no danger of drowning. Still, he wanted to keep his head out of the water, or at least his face, as he floated . . .

All at once he came ashore with a jolt. The rocking motion ceased, the world itself seemed to hold its breath. Leith tried to leap to his feet, and discovered he could not command the smallest of his toes. Even his lungs refused to fill, though they were painfully empty. His heart hesitated between beats.

Almost the dark waves dragged him back under. Leith bit his bottom lip against the pain and found thereby that he actually could move. As if released from a witch's spell, he could of a sudden breathe also—and doing so cost pain. Leith discovered that his eyes were open, and looked about for a distraction.

He was lying against a tree. Its gnarled branches arched overhead. Its rough bark scraped at his back when he pushed himself up. That he had not broken his back and stoved in all of his ribs instead of merely driving the breath from his body was a marvel.

And quite astounding bad luck, to fall against the only tree within spitting distance, with plenty of safe open meadow all about, free for the tumbling everywhere he looked. Leith tasted blood and wondered whether his nose had been bleeding, or if he'd only bitten through his lip. So much for the tiny hope that his curse might not have trailed him to this foreign land, that he'd lost it in the waves. He'd been a fool, to think that finding a horse meant anything had changed for him.

Certainly the beast of fortune was long gone. Leith moved his legs cautiously, testing them, uncertain whether he had been trampled when the horse bolted. It seemed not—he hurt from his head to his toes, but he could not isolate any pain great enough to have come from a horse's careless hoof. No bones felt broken.

Still, the activity sent the forest's edges dancing around him, a gavotte of sky and leaf. Leith closed his eyes and put his head down on his drawn-up knees, waiting for the world to settle once more. A snort nearby disturbed him, made him open his eyes and sit up in a panic to see what had come upon him while he sprawled helpless. A boar? A panther? Bandits? A dragon ready to break its fast?

None of those. He was surrounded instead by horse legs. It was a long dizzy moment before Leith ascertained that there were no more than four of the legs—and therefore but one horse.

A black horse.

After a gray interval, Leith sat up once more, leaning weakly against the inconvenient tree. Getting the rest of the way to his feet seemed unwise for the moment. He watched the horse, since that required nothing but that he keep his eyes open. The stallion was unconcernedly grazing, but is ears tracked Leith's slight movements with interest—it was keenly aware of him. The knotted leather straps of the makeshift reins were snarled together, and the horse had a foreleg through them—doubtless explaining why it had remained close by instead of fleeing. It couldn't run, probably could barely walk.

He regretted having trapped the horse—Leith almost felt worse about that than he did about his own hurts. If it couldn't get free of the bridle, it might die ensnared, a disaster he had never intended but might be helpless to prevent. He had known horses to strangle on their own tether ropes, if left too long untended.

Leith didn't think he could pursue the horse—even hobbled as it was—successfully. He was by no means certain that he could stand without fainting. Chasing a horse for hours was probably out of the question.

Wetting his lips, Leith whistled. The fine-boned head came up, till the knotted reins checked it. The stallion didn't fight the restraint, surely a sign of sense. It respected its situation. Maybe it would let him help it, after all.

"Come here," Leith bade it.

He was fey enough—having been so nearly parted from his body—to fancy that the horse would understand him. That it would heed him. "Do you want that off?"

Yes.

The horse had hobbled right up to him, within arm's reach. Leith blinked at it, amazed. Its eyes were most unusual—full of colored sparkles, spinning almost as rapidly as his head did. He'd never seen such eyes in any horse—indeed in any animal. Was it cursed as he was?

Well, cursed horses weren't his problem, and he had surely sufficient of his own. "All right. Hold still," he begged it.

He was mad, sure as sure. His wits were hanging on that damned tree. But the horse held still while Leith hauled himself to his feet, clinging to its mane. He kept a good hold, thinking all the while that if the horse bolted again he'd probably be killed. He'd fall under its hooves, like as not, get kicked in the head. But the stallion did not stir, even during the worst part of Leith's struggle to get his wobbly legs firmly under him.

Upright for a moment, Leith applied himself to the knots. Most had been pulled tight as the horse struggled. Unpicking them seemed to take him hours, and required more concentration than he could expect himself to have. Finally he got a critical one untied and was able to slip the headstall off. The makeshift bit dropped out of the stallion's mouth, into his hands.

Thank you. Warm breath on his fingers. Bright sparks within the black eye, rubies and diamonds.

"Don't mention it." Leith bent to free the reins from the stallion's forehoof. The action was ill advised. The green meadow upended, and Leith toppled over into it.

The Wild Bull

VALADAN HAD NO notion of why he remained in the meadow, near the man he had been at such pains to rid himself of. He would have followed the red deer, but they were hours gone, and he lacked the knowledge that would have guided him to them. Panic at the sight of the man had begun their flight. Their habit of seasonal migration had extended it, and he had not yet learned where all their pastures lay. They could have been one league off, or twenty, and he could not hope to happen upon them by chance.

In any case, the meadow grass was plentiful and tasty, the fruit still thick on the wild apple tree. Valadan was content.

The man did not graze. For the first day—after he woke from his faint—he scarcely stirred at all. Toward evening he gathered a few sticks together and made a fire, which he huddled close beside through the hours of darkness. The next day he was busier—searching out the stream that cascaded down a little ravine, ranging through the blackberry brambles that choked one bank. Valadan kept track of his movements with the help of the occasional curse that carried to his ears.

Scratched, bleeding, and still famished, Leith came out of the brambles. The first thing he saw was the horse, watching him intently. The breeze carried a scent of apples, which set his mouth to watering helplessly. The stallion had been eating windfalls under the trees, Leith realized, and he crossed the end of the meadow with what speed he could, hoping to claim his share. The stallion moved off as he approached, giving way but not afraid.

The deer had gotten most of the fallen apples before the horse, even the rotted ones, which tended to be sweetest. All Leith could discover in the long grass was the occasional cleft track. He gazed longingly up into the branches, whence small green globes swung. The tree's trunk was too thick to shake, there was no handy limb to climb, so he searched out a fallen branch and tried knocking some fruit down. Most of the apples were withered, and sour as his fortunes. Leith ate every one he dislodged, worms and all, and kept poking doggedly for more till one hard fruit landed smartly on the crown of his head. Tears sprang to his eyes, the black and the green equally.

When he had blinked his vision clear, he was already limping across the meadow, and this time Leith did not pause at the woodshore, but kept on into the forest, heading back more or less the way he had come. He might starve ere he reached the sea. Or perchance he'd find no fishing village there to shelter him—but certainly he'd starve if he lingered in the forest, lacking the means to hunt or trap. Island raised, Leith was a better fisherman than a hunter, and he knew it.

Valadan saw the man go, walking with a stride that suggested a purpose, and a longer journey than the trip to the swift-running stream. Splashes and an oath reported he'd crossed the chill water.

Thirsty, Valadan trotted to the stream and put his muzzle to the swift flow. On the far bank, broken brush marked the man's recent passage. The wind carried the scent of foot-crushed grass. So Valadan crossed the stream, grazed the grass, and at twilight the scent of woodsmoke led him to the man's camp.

The sound of a large body moving in the dark forest alarmed Leith. It seemed unlikely to him that any wild creature would challenge the protection of his fire, but he arose nonetheless with a cudgel of firewood in his hand, ready to defend himself. A dragon would have no cause to fear a man's fire. Of course, it would have little cause to fear a stick of firewood, either.

The ruddy firelight penetrated the woodland for only a couple of yards and made the rest of the night blacker by contrast. Leith waited, his heart hammering his bruised ribs. He whispered a plea to his Lady for Her protection, but She had long since retired from the sky.

After more cracklings, he heard a familiar snort.

The stallion? Had it followed him? Why?

He wanted to disbelieve it. He could get no sight of it, to reassure him. But wolves do not snort, nor do bears, so Leith was able—eventually—to relax sufficiently to snatch a few hours of sleep on the damp ground.

By sun-high the next day, Leith was positive he was being followed—and baffled that the horse should choose to do so. It had seemed most anxious to escape him when he rode it. He paid it no obvious heed, waiting to see what might happen. The stallion never came close, but it was evidently always nearby—he caught glimpses of black hide through the trees, or heard its movements.

Leith cherished no further hopes of taming the horse and riding off to seek his fortune. He had a very clear idea of what his fortune was likely to be—and it was all he could do to summon sufficient will to keep heading for the seashore. If indeed he was—he might easily have lost his sense of direction and be headed in quite the wrong way, into a still less hospitable wilderness. And the coast he had landed upon had been so bleak, it promised nothing but saltwater and seaweed for certain, so his destination held little promise even assuming he *was* making surely for it. Leith dined upon some mushrooms that, if not poisonous, were unluckily not quite wholesome, either, and left him retching for the better part of an hour's time. That the horse—which he could see whenever he lifted his head from the grass—could live so easily off a country that was not so slowly starving him to death seemed more unfair by the hour.

Scheming for ways by which he might trap something both unwary and edible, Leith was paying little heed to his surroundings, save when twigs caught on his ragged cloak and forced him to attend, or wet ground prompted a detour from the deer track he was following through the roadless forest. Therefore, the prince and the aurochs bull became aware of each other in the same breathless instant.

Leith froze in his tracks. The bull—all that beef, which he had not the smallest hope of butchering—lowered its head to peer at him from tiny eyes. It snuffled moistly, took in Leith's scent, and decided he was suspicious. Nervously the bull pawed at the forest duff, dipping its head to one side for variety and tearing the earth with the tips of its widespread horns.

Leith swallowed hard. The beast was bigger than any bull he'd seen in the Isles—it looked like a hairy mountain—but the signs of irritation and challenge it displayed were familiar to him. The smallish bull that had serviced the Lady's herd of white milch cows had behaved just so and been dangerous enough at a third this monster's height and bulk. Leith took a careful, retreating step, noting as he did the other brown bodies just visible through the screen of trees—the cows of the bull's harem, which it would certainly defend from blundering intruders. *A very wide detour this time*, Leith thought, stepping back and striving to look harmless.

His left boot cracked an unseen fallen branch. The sound was loud as a thunderclap. With a bellow and no further warning the bull drove at him, fleet of foot as any great lord's courser.

Leith turned and ran, knowing even as he began that flight was not escape. Not a chance of it. There was no nearby tree for him to duck behind—none large enough to stop such a monster's charge. Nothing large enough to hide him, either, so Leith had no choice but to keep running, and on the trail because the bushy woodland that wouldn't hide him *would* slow him down if he stepped foot off the pathway.

He got a good start and kept the measure, but his escape was going to succeed for only a moment or two more. If Leith ran till his heart burst, he was no wise as swift as a ton of wild bull. But something else just might be . . .

The black stallion had halted, staring at Leith as he pounded down the track straight at it, trying to decide if what had alarmed him was dangerous to it as well. It made up its mind and spun about to flee the unseen peril that had set the human in motion, but Leith was just close enough to fling himself at its back when the maneuver presented the stallion's side to him. He didn't get the whole way aboard, but he tangled his fingers in its mane and hung on desperately, scrambling till he got a leg on either side of the horse. The stallion, busy running, spared him no attention.

They pelted down the path at insane speed, dodging around and between tree trunks. Surely the bull could not match their pace. The very air was a blur of green. Leith looked back over his shoulder, expecting the relief of seeing the monster falling behind, winded and discouraged.

He beheld the glint of sun on one of the ivory-white horns, each of the pair singly as long as either of his arms. The right horn caught a low branch and sheared it off as he stared. The aurochs was not even slightly inconvenienced by the collision. And it was close, almost at the stallion's streaming tail.

What if they *couldn't* outrun it?

Leith peered ahead, through the onrushing greenery. He

couldn't see for any distance. The stallion had its ears pinned back tight, its head stretched out, nostrils flared to drink every possible wisp of air. A forest trail did not allow for anything like full speed—merely swinging wide of an inconvenient tree could slow them enough to be overtaken. The bull was enraged to the point of madness. Running full tilt into a tree might not much distress it—but they'd not fare so well, neither he nor the horse. In open country they'd have had better odds, but they'd been in the forest for days, and some parts were even worse choked than this.

Leith remembered the struggle he'd had not an hour gone, ere he came on the deer track—which he now suspected had actually been made by the wild cattle. After scrambling up a dry ravine that had looked promising to his eye, he'd wound up clambering awkwardly over a great tangle of fallen trees, jammed there in a season when the ravine was likely not so dry, blocking what he had hoped would be an easy path with a maze of branches.

That had been where? If it was close enough . . .

All at once he spotted it—marked by a torn-loose bit of his once-blue cloak, left fluttering behind when he finally won free. The salt-bleached scrap waved like a beacon. In a dozen strides they would pass it.

What they needed was to get *over* the snag of trees, to go where the bull couldn't follow. Leith leaned hard to his left—without reins he had no other way to steer—and kicked with his right leg. The stallion swung left with a snort. So did the bull, a bare instant behind them.

The snag loomed, dead ahead of them, and Leith saw now that it rose to nearly the height of the black ears pricked before him. No horse would attempt such a jump—but what other choice had they, save to die on the bull's horns?

Leith could feel that the stallion was about to shorten stride, to try at the last instant to either stop or veer off. Forestalling the mutiny, he clamped both legs to its sweating sides, squeezed hard, and further encouraged the horse with a shout. Too late now to turn, and probably to stop safely. If it wouldn't jump . . .

The stallion's forelegs left the ground. Its hindquarters thrust powerfully as it leapt upward.

They seemed to hang in the air for an age. Leith saw the crisscross of logs below, heard the bull crash against them. A cloud of dust rose into the air. He felt the stallion's back

rounding beneath him, and then it was stretching out its forelegs to land—quite lightly considering the height and breadth
of the jump—cantering two strides before coming to a plunging halt.

Leith's hammering heart was still tumbling somewhere in
midair.

I imagined that, he thought, reeling in his place. *It's not surprising, really, after everything that's happened. No horse
jumps like that . . .*

The stallion snorted and tossed his head. His mane slapped
Leith's cheek, stinging like icy water.

"Your pardon. I didn't mean to insult you." Leith put a hand
onto the shoulder just ahead of his knee and found himself bal-
ancing with the contact rather than merely congratulating.
"Could you let me down, before I fall again? I don't really feel
very well—"

As he spoke, Leith was gathering his nerve to slide to the
ground. He suspected his legs—trembling now with reaction—
wouldn't hold him up, and if he went tumbling he might break
one. If the stallion chose this moment to rid itself of him
once more, he might do worse. Hoping the ground was softer
than it looked, he twisted a hank of mane in both hands for a
surety . . .

And realized that the horse was calmly standing still, as if in
polite answer to his request.

Hardly able to trust such unaccustomed good fortune, Leith
dropped down, stepping back to keep his feet out of the way
of hooves, then staggering a further step. The jar of landing
made the forest spin around him, a pinwheel of green leaves
and bright sky, and he lost his balance entirely.

Warm breath brushed his face, too light for a breeze, smell-
ing of grass and apples. Unthinking, Leith put both arms
around the stallion's neck and held himself upright, trusting because for the moment he could do nothing else. He fully expected the horse to bolt on the instant, trampling him—but
when his head cleared the stallion was still there, not seeming
inclined to resent his clutching at it.

Leith pressed his cheek gratefully against the warm, glossy
neck. He felt the horse draw in an easy breath. How was *that*
possible, after such a desperate race? Frowning, he drew back
a little, examined the situation. Unless he had fainted unawares, very little time had passed—the bull was only just giving up its assault upon the fallen trees and moving noisily

away, snorting and snuffing and bellowing its disappointment at being thwarted in murder. And yet here was this horse, after a run that would have foundered any courser Leith had ever seen, barely damp with sweat and breathing lightly as if he had only just left off a day's grazing. Its nostrils were not even distended. It was too much to contemplate. Leith buried his face again in the long mane and let the horse nibble his hair.

"What shall I call you?" he asked, his voice muffled. Such a magnificent horse surely had a name, and a fame attached to it, but he had no way to learn it, which was a great pity.

I am called Valadan.

Of course he imagined the voice, inside his head but not admitted by his ears—yet Leith liked the ring of the name, even if it did come from his own crack-brained fancy. It had a proud, noble sound. And so he kept it, as he and the horse made their way toward the coast.

Valadan.

The Hill of Glass

ONCE THEY HAD come out onto the moors, they seldom saw a tree that was not sheltered along a streambed. Where trees might otherwise have broken the monotony of the sweeping expanse of heather and seeding grasses, there was generally found an outcropping of the land's rocky bones, fringed by wildflowers able to root and thrive in the shallow soil.

Cloud shadows chased one another to the horizon, untroubled by the often dangerous bogs that were most reliably revealed by being a more grasslike green than the actual grass at that season. Leith saw no signs of farming or any sort of husbandry, and was not much surprised—the country was windswept and soggy, marginally useful for pasture and better suited to being left quite alone.

There were goodly numbers of waterfowl, for the moorland contained many reed-fringed pools, besides the slightly drier bogs. The first nest Leith assayed robbing chanced to be a swan's, and an unlucky blow from the cob's wing bloodied his nose as he retreated in disarray from the furious bird's defense of its mate and offspring. Next time he chose more wisely, and got a pair of new-laid duck eggs for his trouble.

Crafting a sling from the last part of his belt that wasn't being pressed into service as a bridle, Leith eventually managed to add fresh meat to his diet—with a whole flock landing at once upon the pool he hid beside, even worse luck than his would have allowed him to hit one goose. His ill luck discharged itself cheerfully after the kill, when Leith had to flounder through neck-deep icy water to retrieve his dinner ere it sank, and discovered on the way that the pool held leeches of quite remarkable size and ferocity.

Once he had begun to eat with a semblance of regularity,

Leith's future seemed less bleak to him. There was still rain each day, refreshing the bogs, but generally wind would sweep the clouds away before sun-high, and the sunlight never failed to lift his spirits. It was possible to come upon long stretches of grassland unhazarded by bog or boulder, where a horse could be allowed to gallop, and that proved a joy beyond anything Leith had ever hoped to experience. He and Valadan went like a sailing ship, before the wind and nearly as fast.

There being no large features in the landscape, Leith had no gauge for the stallion's speed, but he suspected it was considerable. If he closed his eyes as they skimmed over the moor, he could imagine that they never touched the earth at all, after that first great bound that launched them into a run. So smooth were the stallion's paces, it seemed to Leith that Valadan never wearied, but ran farther than any horse could have run, unflagging as the very wind itself.

He had never, after their race together away from death at the aurochs' horns, given an instant's thought to the danger of falling. It was not only that he was a good horseman—Leith had a sense that the stallion had no desire to be rid of him now. A bond had grown between them, an understanding. Secure, trusting, Leith went with the horse as if its legs were his own, adapting without conscious effort to Valadan's every motion. Leaping to clear an unsuspected stream was never unsettling. Veering to avoid a boulder in the heather quite unremarkable. Valadan might pretend fright when a rabbit bounded up from the long grass under his feet, might leap sideways a good distance—Leith only laughed and slapped his neck, sharing the jest, and they raced off together, swift as a swallow on the wing.

Gradually Leith began teaching the stallion to adapt to him, as well. He taught Valadan to yield to the slightest shift of his rider's weight, to turn at a finger's touch on his side or his neck, to halt as if by his rider's unvoiced wish. The stallion needed little help to carry himself efficiently, but Leith taught him to use his hindquarters and round his back, to tuck his head and step as lightly as if he trod upon eggshells. He did all that without recourse to the bit, which was a horseman's crude control. Eventually the bridle served no purpose at all—save that the stallion would be expected to wear one, when he was sold.

It was an end to their partnership that Leith could scarcely bear to consider. But what choice had he? There might be a way of keeping this wonder of a horse for himself, but more likely there would not be, and Leith needed to accept that unpleasant reality from the outset, or have his heart ripped out through his own folly.

Heavy, salt-scented fog told Leith they were close to the coast—though not so near as he at first thought. The fog burned off by sun-high to let them travel with less caution and more speed, but still 'twas sun-fall ere the mewing of gulls could be heard high above and the crashing of waves felt through his worn boot soles when Leith dismounted.

Morning revealed that they had camped atop a lofty cliff, and just as well—the beach far below was white sand in pockets, but mostly a gritty mix of sand and shale that Leith's folk called *culm*, and there was no least fringe of it left dry when the tide's white horses came roaring in from their sea pastures to paw at the land. That the sea was generally rough was plain—the water in front of the cliffs was choked with rocks and stacks that had been part of the cliff once—before wind and wave had battered them loose and toppled them. There was no hope of passage along the shoreline itself. Leith turned Valadan to his left and rode along the cliff top, ever wary of the holes his experience told him to expect of such country. Once or twice he saw wave spray thrust up through such a hole, many yards back from what he would have taken for the sea's reach.

Surprisingly, they came upon a tree or two—pointing all branches straight inland as an indication of the direction and strength of the prevailing wind. None of the ground looked promising for husbandry yet, and such a hazardous coast would be fished by only the most foolhardy of folk—they had a journey ahead of them yet, Leith thought, and except for being always hungry, he did not much regret his fate. The country was as lovely as it was wild, and he felt no lack of company so long as he had Valadan's.

The first village they chanced upon lay nestled beside an inlet that offered a harbor's shelter—compared to the rest of the coast, at least. There was a passable trail down the cliff to it, and signs—the charred remains of a signal fire on the headland—that the village folk made a regular way up and down the cliff. Yet Leith hesitated and bit his lip. He was not put off by the steep descent—but did he want to go down at all? There were no more than a dozen small cottages below—from above the whole village lay under his inspection, nothing hidden. It would be a poor place, barely surviving, unlikely to grant hospitality to a penniless stranger and certainly unable to buy a horse from him.

Valadan looked seaward and tossed his head, pricked his ears. Leith followed the stallion's gaze with his own and thought he saw the dark shape of a sail against the dazzle. The morning's catch, on its way in to harbor? As he watched, the sail was lowered, and the boat came in under oars.

Leith touched his calf to Valadan's side, and they began to pick their way down the twisty trail to the beach far below. The track had not been made for horses, but Valadan, sure-footed as the wild deer, made naught of the treacherous downslope. Leith sat well back, to help him balance, and kept an eye on the boat. They arrived at the beach just as the little craft was being dragged up onto the shingle and every hand in the village was absorbed in bringing a fish-laden net likewise safe to shore.

Leith dismounted and lent his own hands to the task. At first the press of work was so great, as was the need to get the catch ashore ere it could escape the net, that no one took any note of him at all. Only once the fish were safe-landed was there leisure to notice the stranger in their midst, and by then Leith had been working shoulder to shoulder with one burly fellow for some moments, demonstrating himself useful. When he was called upon to introduce and explain himself, he had a friend ready to vouch for his goodwill. He was welcomed.

For his help, Leith was rewarded with his supper, and further with a night's lodging beneath a roof. For Valadan, there was an armful of salt-grass hay and the shelter of a boat shed's roof against the evening rain. The children gathered round to stare shyly at him—a horse had never been seen on their beach before, though in time past there had been a shaggy pony, used to drag the biggest boats ashore.

Over heavy mugs of thick barley beer, Leith garnered knowledge of his whereabouts. He had never heard the name of Esdragon spoken, and the fisherfolk seldom ranged much beyond the other side of some feature they named the Promontory, but Leith did learn the names and locations of the nearest few fishing villages and those of the market towns where the village's surplus fish—salted or smoked—were sold. The hearty beer went straight to his long-deprived head, and he slept like a stone, not worrying about ill luck for once.

No one seemed to mind if Leith tarried in the village the

next day. The boats had put out ere dawn, but the women and the old men were bustling about on the shore, laying fires of driftwood to smoke the previous day's catch for winter keeping. Leith joined them till the task was done, and later set to mending a ripped net. The women traded tales back and forth excitedly—the pilchard run was just commencing, and the first catch promised them a good year, with surplus to sell, the gods willing. There was a scent of prosperity in the air, over the tang of sea salt. The stranger could stay, since he was so handy, be welcome to bed and board.

Yet, though the boats stayed out on the waves long enough to worry the wives, the men returned with empty nets and tales of barren gray water. Leith bit his lip and told himself that fishing was like that, and pilchard runs known for their inconsistency early in the season. A day without a catch was vexing, but not unexpected.

Next day was worse—one of the boats holed itself upon a rock that normally lay safely to one side of their harbor place. It was never a true hazard, but the waves were wayward and the fishermen fell foul of it. And still not a sign of the great silver shoals of fish . . . on the horizon, a dark smear of cloud promised weather to keep the little fleet beached for a week.

At what would have been sunup, while the sky poured sheets of rain, Leith left the village without a word. The fisherfolk had been so kind to him, he could not endure to watch his luck pummel their fortunes as well as his own. He slipped away—they'd likely have forced provisions on him for his trip, and Leith felt he'd cost them too much already. He had worked for the food he'd eaten but earned nothing more, so best he be on his way.

The wind howled, and there was salt spray mixed with the rain. Leith tasted it on his lips, felt it run down his cheeks as Valadan scrambled back up the muddy track to the cliff top, to resume their journey.

They worked their way down the coast, which grew gentler by and by. Presently they were able to ride along the shore itself—the cliffs had dwindled away and retreated, leaving a broad skirt of white beach sand. Recalling what the fisherfolk had told him, Leith knew he must be nearing one of the larger ports—he couldn't quite recollect the name, but experience told him there'd be a sizable town wherever there was a decent harbor—likely an estuary, where river met sea and there was transport for goods inland as well as by saltwater.

When he reached that town—whatever its name—it would be time to see about selling the stallion.

Leith stroked Valadan's neck, consumed by regret. He'd never find—certainly not *literally* find—another horse of such quality, but neither could he see any way to support himself if he kept the stallion. With a bit of silver to start, he might be able to find himself a livelihood—Leith could read, and wrote a fair hand—but an apprentice scribe or a merchant's clerk would be hard-pressed to keep a horse fed and housed. He might cherish a wish of finding work as a horse trainer, but more than likely the best he could hope for—given his luck— was to be taken on as a groom, and again the stallion would have to go. The most good Leith could do for Valadan was to refuse to sell him to an obviously cruel master, or into a trade he'd be unsuited for. At worst—he had to hope it would not come to that, while knowing it likely would.

At moonrise, Leith knelt down and recited the chant of greeting to his Lady. He could not honor her as was most proper—with the distinctive song for the month, the day, and the precise hour of Her Rising. In the course of his misfortunes Leith had lost track of the days and was still struggling to orient himself, though of course he could effortlessly determine the *phase* of any given moon. He had greeted her only irregularly of late, and begged his Lady to forgive his unintended neglect of her in a land where She seldom showed Her face. He pleaded for her help with his decision. She might not want him for Her priest, but he asked that She not abandon him and leave him utterly alone.

Fog veiled Her pale face long before Leith was done with his devotions, but he closed his fingers around the shimmery gray moonstone he wore pendant on a cord about his neck, closed his eyes, as well, and thought of Her face as he sought an answer to his dilemma. Behind his eyelids, all was white moonlight, whatever the sky overhead might show.

Leith could not—try as he might—convince himself that his Lady had sent the horse to him. That was a pity, for nothing would have made him part with Her gift, not even starvation. But one fact was inescapable—Her horses, all Her animals, were white as Her face, and there was no confusion about that, ever. He'd get silver for the horse, and silver was Her metal, and that was an end of it.

* * *

Leith's heart was heavy as stone while they galloped along the sand. He should have been blissful. The tide was recently out, the sand firm and fine for running, but he was only covering distance, without joy, incapable of delight. The sun was shining, the silver gulls wheeled across a sky of blazing blue above a sea the color of an emeraude—none of that touched his dismal mood, far less altered it.

Leith scarcely could bear to think that he might never ride Valadan again after that day, but he could not escape the knowledge by wishing it so. It tormented him, an ache too deep for any balm. No use to argue with himself, to remind his heart that a horse is only a horse, not a human soul. No use to insist that he would one day ride so fine a horse again. Leith knew he lied, and each stride Valadan took forward only reminded him of the bleakness that was to come, when he traded his companion for a handful of silver and a joyless new life. Finally he slowed the stallion, as much to delay the inevitable moment as to avoid bringing him winded and sweat-soaked and unsalable into the town.

A headland thrust out into the glittering of the sea, and on its far side lay the harbor Leith had expected, likewise the river and the town. There was a castle, also, though he had not imagined one, crowning the farther height and protecting both town and harbor with its presence. That might be a likelier place to sell a very good horse than the town itself, Leith thought, but as he'd need to pass through the town on his way to the fortress, he could judge how the markets were, set a price.

In the midst of his calculations, he took note of the activity on the beach.

No fishermen here, dragging at nets. No beached boats. Great ships plied the deep harbor, many other craft of varying sizes rode at quaysides, discharging cargoes. What Leith beheld on the beach were . . . horsemen.

Twoscore of them or more, brightly dressed, their mounts caparisoned in dyed leather, trapped with silk in colors even the bravest rainbow did not boast. They milled about to no purpose Leith could discern—certainly they were not hunting the waterfowl that ran along the tideline, and were too small and common for gentlemen's sport. The riders might have been racing one another, Leith supposed, and he urged Valadan closer to have a better look. Racing, now—he had a very fast horse, and—it suddenly struck him—a means of earning silver that would *not* force him to give up that horse. Leith's heart gave a bound. Perchance his Lady had lent an ear to his pleas, after all, and shown him a solution he had been too dull-witted to imagine.

Closer to, Leith realized with keen disappointment that the riders were not in fact racing one another—but they were doing something odd indeed, whose purpose he could not make out. A hill rose with unnatural abruptness from the beach, glittering under the bright sun like glass, and the horsemen were attempting to guide their mounts up its steep sloping sides.

Surely the hill *was* glass—Leith could see the sky reflected in it, and the wheeling gulls. He could see through its edges, a little, where the sea waves lapped the beach. It *must* be glass—he watched a brown horse carry its rider halfway up the near slope, then helplessly slide back to the bottom once more, hooves unable to grip the slick surface.

But a hill all of glass? How had such a thing come to be? Leith had never heard of such a wonder. And if it existed, why ride up it—or attempt to—when it could easily be gone around? The hill stood alone, open sand all around it. It barred no passage.

Another rider, mounted well on a leggy blue roan, made a spectacularly unsuccessful attempt, and arrived back at the sand separately from his horse. He tumbled, the horse kept its feet but bucked and plunged. Both seemed distressed, overwhelmed. Valadan snorted, as perplexed as Leith.

A horse answered him, inquiring loudly as to his identity and purpose on the beach. Leith took his eyes from the unnatural hill and noticed a little group, men both mounted and afoot, taking in the proceedings as he did, without participating. He rode closer.

"What game is this?" he asked politely, when he was close enough not to shout.

No game at all, Leith learned, but a sort of a contest. Atop the Hill of Glass—unlikely as it seemed, he *had* been right as to its makeup—lay a golden ring, free for the taking to the horseman who could ride up and fetch it.

Leith's thoughts soared like the gulls. *A golden ring*—and he only had to ride to the top of a hill? Valadan caught his excitement and pranced under him.

At first he was in agony, nervous that one of the other riders would beat him to the prize before his turn came. Then Leith calmed, realizing that no horse had yet made way more than half the distance up the slick slope. Plainly, there was more to this contest than a quick gallop—he should spare a moment to learn from the mistakes the other riders were making. No one had said a rider would have only one chance at the prize, but why fail and risk injury? As Leith looked on, one man parted company with his steed rather spectacularly—the beast, frustrated by the hill, unable to go forward, reared and all but fell atop him.

Valadan was jigging, eager to compete as if he understood that his fortunes and future were staked on the outcome. Leith calmed him with a gentle word and strove to do as much for himself. Out on the hillside, another horse lost its footing and fell, shedding both rider and saddle, which gave Leith some respect for the risk of the task. Rider and tack had to be dragged clear, though the horse ran off unhurt, and the saddle was undamaged save for a burst girth.

The slope was steep, even had it been common dirt. A man might scale it, Leith thought—*he* could climb it, bad leg or no—he had climbed a worse cliff once, bent on capturing the chick of a snow-white gyrefalcon for his Lady's menagerie. But a man ahorse? That was something else again.

Leith was amazed that the thickset young men—some in weighty armor—got their gaily trapped steeds so far up the incline as many of them did. They returned dusty, scraped, dripping sweat and foam, trembling with exhaustion after tremendous efforts that had nonetheless failed. Some turned to give the hill a second glance, with plans evidently in mind—others rode away cursing and disinclined to risk necks and legs a second time in futility.

Some riders chose speed, others tried careful progress. Always the end result was the same—so high, and then the horses could force themselves upward no more. Their steelshod hooves slipped and slid, and even the proudest head could be thrust no higher. Some slid back a dozen yards, dug in and surged valiantly upward again, but inevitably they would end up upon the beach once more, having fallen far short of their goal if they did not actually tumble to the sand.

Leith reflected upon Valadan's round hooves, deep as bells and so tough that the worst country they had ridden through had never once made him regret having no means of putting shoes upon them. He thought of the stallion's short back, his powerful hindquarters, the willing heart that ordered both. He remembered the impossible leap that had saved them from the aurochs. Was it possible his stallion could climb where the others could not? Why, he did not carry the double load of man and armor—Valadan did not even bear a saddle's weight upon his back.

Valadan was looking at the mountain as if he owned it. His nostrils flared wide, scarlet as poppies. His eyes were alight with colored sparks, indomitable.

Still, he would need every advantage. Leith schemed furiously to give them to him. Most riders tried the same face of the hill, despite the obvious lack of success there. Had any of them troubled to scout the hill's other sides? Probably they had, but Leith decided to make his own inspection, just to be sure.

The fresh wind whipped sand across his face. Leith cursed and blinked, but not in time—a single grain flew straight into his right eye, as others stung his cheeks. A big grain, by the feel of it—actually it *felt* like a red-hot cinder the size, possibly, of a small cow. Or a large sheep, at the least.

Leith resisted the impulse to rub his eye, not easily. Better to let ready tears wash the sand away, while he bit his lip at the pain and knotted his fingers in Valadan's mane to keep them busy. But, even when Leith felt sure the grain was gone, the eye still pained him in the bright sun. As well to keep it closed a moment more, inconvenient as that might be. Leith looked at the hill again, squinting one-eyed, his nose running.

At first he couldn't locate it. He wiped his nose on his sleeve and blinked his good eye, too. He only saw a dune, like to any of dozens such along the beach, piled up by storm winds and waves. He must, Leith thought, have somehow turned about while he was blinded. Maybe he hadn't noticed Valadan moving. He'd been ducking, trying to avoid the wind-blown sand, and . . .

Then he saw the horse struggling up the shifting face of the dune, hock-deep in the sliding sand, its rider shouting and urging it on with a whip. Leith forced his still-weeping right eye open, and saw—through tears—the dazzle of sun on greenish glass. Saw the horse slipping and slithering on the bright surface till it arrived tail-first at the bottom, sweating, spent. Grains of sand powdered its wet flanks.

Leith felt dizzy. He shut *both* eyes.

"I wish you could tell me what *you* see," he whispered, leaning close to Valadan's neck.

Glass, came a prompt whisper into his head.

Leith opened his eyes and turned his head, first to one side, then the other. None of the watchers or waiting riders was close enough to have heard him, nor to have answered. Not a one of them was even looking in his direction. Every eye was fixed upon a heavy-boned gray then assaulting the slope, bearing a rider cloaked in scarlet vivid as fresh-spilled blood.

Leith looked forward and saw Valadan's right ear cocked back to catch his words. His next question.

My lord?

It was startling to be so addressed—where Leith had been owed the title, no one had ever used it. But it was still more disconcerting to be granted one's title by one's horse.

Leith closed his right eye once again and assessed the slope of the dune he saw. It appeared to be no steeper than any of the others, and not so high as to be impossible for a willing mount. Assuming, of course, that such a horse's rider wasn't quite mad . . .

It was surely madness to expect a horse to answer his questions, but Leith had another to ask. "If I were to cover your eyes, would you still trust me? Go where I tell you?"

The stallion snorted, startled, and sidled—then dipped his ebony head, yielding. *Where do we go?*

"Just up a sand hill," Leith said offhandedly.

No different, Leith told himself—the logical part of himself that was affronted by these conflicts between his senses and what he knew to be reality—from many another time he'd asked a horse if it would do a thing for him. Run faster, pass an object that frightened it, jump a log—only then he'd taken his answer from the tension in the horse's body, or the lack of it. But always he asked, and always he was answered. *This* sort of answer was truly unsettling, but hardly more so than the discovery that both his eyes did not see the same world.

Leith dismounted and shucked off his linen shirt. The offshore breeze raised bumps on his skin, and the rags left of his cloak were hardly much shelter from the chill. He shivered as he tied the shirt carefully over Valadan's eyes, being sure it did not impede ears or nostrils, both of which the stallion would need full use of.

There seemed to be no order of precedence set for the attempts on the hill. It was no great matter to stay out of another rider's way, and no one was all that impatient after witnessing a long string of failures. Leith remounted and watched for his moment. The big gray finally yielded, sliding back to the beach and stumbling away. No one else seemed to want to take his place—at least not at once.

Leith touched his left heel lightly to Valadan's side. The stallion bounded forward into a gallop, with never the slightest hesitation despite being asked to use his speed blindly. Shouts went up as the onlookers caught sight of them.

As they neared the foot of the hill, Leith took back on the reins, while his legs continued to urge Valadan onward. He felt the stallion tuck his hindquarters as they had practiced, never dreaming they'd need the skill for such a task.

They were but a stride away from the glassy slope when Leith remembered to close his right eye, so that what they attacked was only a simple dune of sand. The distinction did not matter a jot to Valadan, who ran in blind trust, but it mattered a great deal to Leith, who needed to believe their task was possible if he was thereupon to convince the stallion.

Momentum carried them a quarter of the way up the slope effortlessly. Any horse could get that far—the test was yet before them. Leith leaned forward, taking hold of Valadan's mane just behind the stallion's ears so that he would not slide backward—it was hard to stay in place without a saddle to help him, on such an incline. Valadan kept driving upward, fairly leaping up the slope, not allowing this pace to slacken.

With one eye tightly shut, Leith could see only half the landscape, and he had no desire to turn his head to take in the rest. He wanted to lift his head, to see how near they were to the top—but he feared such an action would affect his balance, and therefore Valadan's. Their margin for success was very slender, thinner than the narrowest crescent his Lady signed the night sky with.

Gulls were screaming about them, as if the air itself cried out. It might have been encouragement, or outrage. Sand flew to each side, thrown up by Valadan's hooves. Leith's right eye popped open for an instant—he saw a sparkle of glass chips against the sky and winked the eye shut once more, refusing to be distracted and lured to disaster.

Something still sparkled, in the sand just ahead of them. Leith knew what it had to be. With his right hand he grabbed a handful of mane and leaned down to his left, his left arm at its fullest stretch and only the toe of his right boot still on the off side of the horse to anchor him.

There was no time to think of falling. If he began to slip, he'd be on the ground before he had time to notice. Leith's outstretching fingers brushed sand and closed into a fist over the ring.

He tried so hard to haul himself back onto Valadan's back that he nearly shot off over the *right* side as the stallion plunged for an instant before beginning his descent. Unlike all the others, who had slid down tail-first, Valadan managed to twist about on the dune crest and now went down splay-legged in a mighty shower of sand, while Leith laid back to help anchor his hindquarters and prevent the stallion's tumbling forward onto his nose.

They reached the beach. Valadan reared as his hind hooves arrived upon the flat and tossed his head till he had shaken Leith's shirt from his head. The white cloth pinwheeled through the air, startling the gulls.

He had shaken Leith from his back, as well. The prince rolled over in a tangle of cloak tatters and a cloud of sand, winding up under Valadan's belly. The stallion turned its head back and sniffed him carefully.

Leith spat out a mouthful of sand. He opened his fist. There, clutched so tightly that it had left its copy pressed into his palm, was a finger-sized circle of carved yellow gold.

The Lady Kessallia

"I DON'T CARE if he *did* ride up the Hill of Glass and fetch back my ring! I don't care if he rode through the Gates of Death to get there! I will *not* wed some starveling, crippled peasant!" the Lady Kessallia declared fiercely, not troubling to school her voice to proper, mincing, ladylike tones.

"I don't know that he's all that crippled," her nurse mused, while she kept the subject of the discussion under observation. "He looks rather well made, actually."

"*What?*" Kess pulled the plump woman away from the peephole in the thick stone wall and snatched at the arras meant to hide it from uninitiated view. "Betsan, what are you doing? What's *he* doing?"

"He's getting ready to bathe," her nurse answered. "And by that, my lady, I'll make bold to doubt he's a peasant—not that they *like* to be dirty, and I'm sure they do *not*—but a fellow who generally bathes himself in a pond might not recognize a bathing tub right off. He might take it for a fountain and never think he was meant to dip himself in it."

Kess put one dark eye to the spyhole—but all she saw of the stranger was the back of his head, resting against the tub's high rim. Betsan had peeped earlier, whilst he was climbing in, and had an unobstructed view. Kess made an exasperated sound, flaring her nostrils. Behind her, Betsan chuckled.

Candlelight winkled on the polished copper rim of the tub, caressed the silky surface of the water. As if it filled the room before her, Kess could see the windswept beach, the steep-sided mountain of green glass she had crafted unbeknownst to any of Keverne's folk, who gullibly thought the magic some natural marvel sprung up overnight. She watched a black stallion plunging up it, with a thin young man clinging ever so

46

precariously to its bare back, then leaning down to scoop up
her cursed ring for proof that he had done the deed she had required. She should have thought to use a ring of smoke; that
could never have been shown as evidence . . .

"Don't be so disappointed, my lamb," her nurse interrupted,
resting a hand on Kess's pale gold hair. "You'll see plenty of
him in the altogether once you're wed—not fit you should see
more while you're yet a maid."

Kess flushed. The vision had fled at Betsan's first word, the
window of farseeing was tightly shuttered, and there was no
way she could open it again. Her visions came as they would.
"I wasn't looking for *that*!" she protested hotly, letting the tapestry fall back into place as she cast about for a plausible explanation to throw at Betsan. "As for having seen or not seen,
how's a man so different from a horse or a hound? And I've
seen plenty of *them*." She raised her head defiantly. "I was
merely curious whether 'twas a battle wound made him limp
so frightfully, when they brought him in."

"Oh, aye," Betsan agreed blandly. "Well, it didn't look so to
me. There's something a little the matter with that right leg,
but I couldn't see a scar—save the little one on his face. His
shoulders are quite nice. I like a good shoulder," she added,
flicking her tongue over her lips. "Wide shoulder, narrow
hips."

"I don't care," the Lady Kessallia muttered, her face flaming, her eyes fixed unseeing on the tapestry's threadbare glo-
ries.

"Oh, aye," Betsan said again pleasantly.

Leith could not recall with anything close to precision when
he had last soaked himself in a tub of hot water. In his father's
palace, certainly, but he felt as if more than a lifetime had
passed since that unappreciated day. Now he was clean, dry,
warmed by a fire that crackled cheerfully on the hearth—and
even comforted by food and wine. He had consumed every last
crumb of the bread and left only the bones of the roasted
chicken that had awaited him when he emerged from the won-
derful tub. The plate had been garnished with grapes, which he
had eaten with especial relish.

For all those comforts and refreshments, Leith was but
slightly less dazed than he had been when first he picked himself up on the beach. As he had arisen, shedding sand, a trio
of men in costly raiment ill-suited to a windswept seashore had

arrived at his side and tumbled over one another informing him that he had just won the hand—in marriage, all legal and proper—of the only daughter of Esdragon's duke.

Such, it seemed, was the purpose of the striving at the Hill of Glass, a task set by the Lady Kessallia to find herself a brave and noble and suitable husband, her father being long absent and her father's councillors being anxious on that account and pressing the lady for a suitable solution to the lack of a man's hand in the government. The gold ring was but a symbol, a proof of the task achieved. Leith—the ring on his finger—had been swept up by an excited throng and conducted with noisy rejoicing to Keverne—the castle he had spied earlier, perched on the sea-girt cliff top.

Leith had yet to lay an eye—green or black either one—on the bride he had earned. There had been far too many folk fussing and bustling about him for his taste—servants and courtiers who wanted to bathe him, barber him, feed him, clothe him, advise him, question him. After being so long solitary, the surfeit of attention was unnerving, if not actually frightening. Leith resisted politely but stubbornly. He insisted upon seeing Valadan stabled and accepted the tub of hot water, then sent all the folk away, and bathed and shaved himself with his own hands, and tried to use the respite to collect his scattered wits.

He was glad of the food in the end, and the clean clothing that was left in the stead of the rags he had stripped off before entering his bath. Eating, dressing occupied his fingers and his mind, forestalling the need to think—but finally the meal was disposed of, every last morsel, and Leith could put off the activity no longer.

Having won a bride—and evidently a dukedom along with her—was so far above his expectations for his future that Leith could not yet manage to take its meaning in. True, his royal father had arranged a high-born marriage for him, but Leith had never been so naive as to believe the ceremony would actually take place. If not the shipwreck, then some other disaster would have befallen him—or been arranged if it had not occurred naturally, courtesy of his ill luck and his father's desire to be rid of him.

He fingered the moonstone pendant and recalled afresh the night of his ordination as he stared into the greenish, translucent stone. The moonlight streaming through the center hole of the temple's dome, blessing him in a shower of silver as he bound himself to his Lady. The moon chimes, singing softly in the night breeze. Leith looked up from the stone, out the narrow slit that gave light and air to the chamber where he now stood, but the space was too slight, he could see nothing of the sky save that it was dark. Whether by cloud or because all of the castle's bulk lay between him and his Lady's face, Leith could not tell. She would just be lifting Her visage over the land, nowhere near the sea yet.

Instead of calling to mind his Lady's pure face, Leith found he was remembering how the moon chimes had clashed and clattered. How the tiled floor had moved like a carpet being shaken clean during the earthshake. How the solid temple walls had swayed and toppled and finally crumbled till not one stone of them stood upon another. He had covered his foster father with his own body when he realized they could not reach safety—Leith remembered less about that, though he had been told of it. There had been confusion and dust, and darkness after the moon-round lamps fell and went out. He had hidden his face from the disaster. He had shut his eyes, but refusal to see had not lent protection. A heavy weight had come down upon him then, sending him into a greater darkness than his own eyelids could provide.

The lesson in the world's unreliability was well learned. Even had his foster father lived—and the old man did not— Leith had from that moment believed in no future save the curse he had been born with. A golden ring on his finger made no difference—none at all.

Brychan the seneschal's resemblance to Esdragon's duke was not remarkable—the two men were blood kin, sharing a sire. Kess felt her father, the legitimate son, was the better favored of the two—Brychan had inherited his protruding eyes from his mother, along with a length of face that had been a standard of beauty in that lady's day. Such features mingled uneasily with those parts of Brychan's face that reminded her of her own father—the high-bridged nose, the thick dark hair. The distance between brow and chin made her father's squareness of jaw impossible for Brychan to achieve, and the somewhat unkempt beard he wore accentuated rather than masked the flaw.

"So, my lady, your task has been accomplished."

Brychan stated the obvious, which he often did—'twas he who had brought Kess the unwelcome news, hours ago, that a rider had managed to conquer her Hill of Glass and thereby claim her hand. Kess would be a long time forgiving her uncle his eagerness.

"It changes nothing," Kess said, mincing no words.

"But Lady Kessallia—" Brychan's eyes were well a-pop.

"Brychan, are we not agreed that my father must come home? The Hill of Glass was a task set to divert the people's attention while a search was made. True, neither of us supposed it would be climbed on the first day—but my mind is set upon this purpose. I am going to find my father. He planned to be absent a month—it has been nearer to three. He must be found, and I can do it. I alone."

"And what of the young man we brought in today?" Brychan asked, flustered. Probably he had already begun to make the marriage arrangements and could not decide how to set them aside.

"I will deal with him," Kess answered firmly. "He appears to be quite penniless and utterly without resources—it won't take much silver to buy him off."

Brychan stroked his beard, a gesture Kess had always found unpleasant. She swallowed back her irritation, watching as he worked out his next action, his brow furrowing with the effort involved. "Then I shall continue to ready your escort, if you are so determined."

Kess pressed her full lips together. She detested fighting for the same ground, over and over. "As I told you before, I will go more swiftly alone. Therefore, I shall *go* alone."

Brychan looked aghast and wrung his beard afresh. "Even were such a journey proper, it cannot be safe. My lady, let me insist! A pair of my soldiers will not impede you. They will assist you, protect you—"

And leave signs in your wake, that I may track you, till you come to some lonely place, Kess' uncle thought, behind the privacy of his own long face.

The Lady Kessallia had garbed herself with care and ceremony, in a gown of milk-white silk 'broidered with tiny, glowing pearls like droppets of moonlight. The raiment had been her mother's, worn but seldom. Her silver hair Kess left unbound as befitted a royal maiden. The tresses had been washed and crimped into a multitude of waves, and still their ends lapped the floor beside her delicate chair. Betsan had arranged them to good effect, so that the hair caught the light the candles shed, and Kess sat very still, both to avoid disturbing her coiffure and to foster the daunting dignity she had elected to project.

She was receiving, for the first time, the man who—by the conditions she herself had foolishly set—was to become her husband and lord, and her artful face paint could only slightly conceal her rage.

Kess had the whole of Keverne at her disposal, but she had chosen to receive the stranger in her father's great audience chamber, with its forest of thick stone pillars running down both sides. It boasted a dais that would raise her sufficiently to look down upon even so tall a person as the stranger appeared to be—also, its unglazed windows faced the sea below, and at this season could be guaranteed to admit drafts that would have the man shivering at her feet. Kess could have ordered the shutters fitted into place—it needed to be done in any case ere winter's storms arrived, and there had been ample time— but she had not done so. She liked the sound of the sea sighing, a sound regular as the breath of the earth. She took comfort from hearing it. It was calm, patient—everything her own breathing was not.

Doors at the chamber's far end unclosed, and a formally garbed Brychan ushered the stranger in. Others of her father's officials flanked him, happy witnesses to the brewing disaster. Some of them had the effrontery to look pleased. Kess made herself a promise—to curdle that pleasure the instant her father should be safely returned home.

Brychan drew back, but the stranger continued walking toward her, through the crisscrossing shadows the pillars threw. Kess looked at his face, alternately revealed and obscured, and felt terror brush her soul, like moth's wings.

She had accepted that marriage would one day be her lot. It would be arranged for her—it was the duty owed her rank and station. But *knowing* had in no wise prepared her for the reality—that one day a stranger would be bound to her for the rest of her days, to do with her as he would. Lips that she had never before beheld would be permitted to touch her, to breathe upon her. This man's lips looked to be quite ordinary lips, neither cruel nor fearsome, but they were strange to her— they, and he, brimmed Kess over with unexpected dread. And since she did not know what to do with fear, Kess gave her fury leave to smother it.

No one had been supposed to win her game. Certainly not

so eye-blink *soon*. A single day the Hill of Glass had stood siege, and now was sand once more. It had taken her longer than that to choose which illusion she would craft. Kess reined her anger, lest it swell beyond any control, and watched the man's face to distract herself. If she ordered him slain on the spot, her lapse of self-control would be inconvenient.

Too much chin, Kess judged. He'd do better with a beard to cloak the defect, but the stranger was fresh-shaven, so evidently that was his habit. Too much nose, for her taste, but nothing to be done about that. Nothing hid a nose, particularly if 'twas big enough to need hiding.

Kess looked straight into the man's eyes, as he took the last few steps—he still limped, a sort of hitch in his stride, like a horse going just a bit off. His eyes did not match, though in the shifting light of the torches the pupil of the left eye had spread to swallow most of the green and obscure the difference. He bore an old scar on his cheek, a sickle shape curling just under that mostly green eye, paler than the skin around it.

The man halted—and he did not thereupon kneel. Betsan might be right. No easily awed peasant this. But what was he, then? She knew the nobles of her father's dukedom, even the most obscure younger sons. He was none of them.

The torch flames behind her were so bright against the chamber's general darkness, it was all Leith could do to see the woman seated on the dais save as a pale glow—white dress, near-white hair. She dazzled, like a rising full moon. Her face—what he could make out of it—was still and remote. It was not the long oval court painters cast every noble maiden's features into—this woman's jaw was square, her nose slightly arched. Her full lips were blood red with paint—Leith guessed the rest of her face was painted as well. Her eyes, narrow as a cat's and black as Valadan's hide, suggested that not much got by the lady . . .

Kess held her father's rod of office in her right hand. She thumped its bronze-shod base sharply on the dais and was gratified to see the stranger startle at the sound. Satisfied that she had scored first blood in their duel, Kess smiled regally as she announced to him her name and titles.

"I am Leith, Prince of the Isles," he responded, very polite, and said no more.

That suited Kess, who had her own agenda and was not overly interested in any other's contribution to it, however prettily phrased or schooled to flatter her.

"I am told you have found my ring," she declared.

The stranger—Leith, claiming to be a prince—drew the golden circle from his smallest finger. He had rather large knuckles, and the ring stuck fast for a moment, making him struggle while Kess contemplated the expediency of having his finger struck off with the first handy blade. Finally he held the circle up for her inspection.

Kess did not deign to lean forward to receive the jewel. Movement would have spoiled her poise. "Yes, that is my ring."

The witnesses sighed happily. Well they might—for them, it was a hero tale sprung to wondrous life. Kess reminded herself that only *she* saw the tableau as a disaster.

"The Isles," she quoted. "Where are those?"

"Seven islands, most of them small, lying off the Strait of Carhasta." Leith tried to decide on a direction, a point of reference, and discovered that he could not. His cheeks went hot. "I'm sorry, my lady, not to be more precise. I'm not sure where I am *now*, you see."

"This is Keverne, the ducal palace. *In Esdragon*," Kess continued, when Leith looked not a whit enlightened by her gracious reply. She wondered impatiently whether the fellow's being a fool would make him easier to rid herself of—or more difficult.

"I was shipwrecked on your coast," Leith explained, shrugging as if he guessed her dismissal of him. "I've been following the shore—"

The councillors murmured together. Along a coast such as Esdragon possessed, shipwrecks were a commonplace occurrence. So were disoriented survivors. It was, of course, nonetheless a great wonder for one of those to stand revealed as a foreign prince, to have won a lady's hand in an impossible contest before he had even learned where he was.

Kess decided the proprieties had been as fully satisfied as need be and sent the old men away, dismissing Brychan, also. Betsan remained, appearing to chaperone—actually not too displeased to be sent away to doze beside a fire with a flagon of good wine and a tray of dainties. That left Kess alone with her prospective bridegroom after a dozen minutes, able to proceed with her agenda without sundry hindrances.

She had earlier ordered that his horse be brought from the stables. Now Kess tugged at a cord and let fall the curtain that had concealed a small alcove from sight. Within, Valadan lifted his head from the flake of hay spread to keep him occupied and nickered a greeting.

Leith went to him at once—much to Kess' displeasure, for when he did not return she was obliged to abandon the advantage of the dais and trail after him, unless she wished to address the back of his discourteous head.

"I know this horse," she announced, while Leith was busy rubbing Valadan's neck and whispering his pleasure at having a familiar sight in this strange place into the stallion's nearer ear. "My father bred him. He was stolen from us—but not, I think, by you," she added with a touch of reluctance.

"I found him in the forest, running with the deer," Leith volunteered, his fingers shifting to scratch the crest of the stallion's neck, while Valadan leaned into his fingers blissfully. "I thought he must have strayed, if he was not wild-born."

"He was reived away when he was a young colt," Kess insisted, as Valadan extended his nose to inspect her pearl-crusted sleeve. "Yet I would know him among a thousand horses, even were they all unmarked blacks as he is. His dam was my father's favorite mare, and it took a wizard charming down the wind to put her in foal. When he was born, the mare died and left him orphan. He was raised here, I saw him often. There is no other like Valadan, not in all the world."

Leith's heart gave a start. His fingers ceased their scratching. He had thought his choice of the name only an idle fantasy—very plainly, it was not. Valadan rubbed against him, agreeing, amused at his confusion but wanting the scratching to continue.

"My father was furious when he was stolen," Kess said, not noticing Leith's startlement. "He would sooner have lost half Esdragon than this horse. He pledged dire punishments for the thief, if the man were caught."

"I suspect that thief is beyond your punishment," Leith mused, frowning as he worked it out. "The first time I sat on his back, this horse gave me such a fall, I could scarcely walk for days." Of course anyone could fall off a horse—but it was the skill the stallion had shown that had puzzled him. "He relieved himself of me very surely—as if he had practiced it."

"You think he threw the thief, also?" Kess asked, more interested in the stranger's obvious affection for the stallion. He had not once looked at her since he went to the horse's side. Perchance he was afraid to. That quite intrigued her. She had hoped to frighten him off as a suspected horse thief, but if that was no longer possible, why should not other weapons come into her hands? Fear was easiest to wield, but not her only option. Her wits began to make quick shifts, readying fresh plans.

"I suspect he did, then escaped," Leith said. "Surely if a man went to the trouble of stealing such a horse, he would never let it go so easily—unless it hurt him so that he could not follow it."

Valadan merely snorted, preserving his secrets.

"I didn't know I was bringing him home." Regret colored Leith's voice. "I suppose he belongs to you." That being so, he'd lose the horse after all, because of the ring that had been meant to keep them together. His ill luck in full force, no question. Leith's throat ached with grief.

"You can keep him, if you'll take him away again."

Kess almost forgot herself and grinned at the bewildered expression on the prince's face—if prince he truly was.

"Come and sit down," she suggested sweetly.

Kess conducted Leith to a side chamber, where a cheerful fire was laid and lit and wine and food were handily set out. Having been forced to abandon her plan to overawe him with a regality he took less-than-little note of, she hoped that the food—which the fellow ate with a good appetite—would keep him off his guard as she got down to her business.

"My father was a hero in his youth," Kess began, more abruptly than she had intended. But then, she had never been good at starting a fencing match with little testing, irritating tap-taps. She much preferred simple, direct attacks.

Leith put down the tart apple he had been nibbling and gave the Lady Kessallia his full attention. It was hard to guess the meaning of her expression beneath all the face paint, but he strongly suspected she was displeased by his arrival, though she had been courteous while they dined. While *he* ate—*she* had not touched a bite, to the best of Leith's recollection. He hoped belatedly that his deprivation had not robbed him of all his manners. Had he been gobbling like a hog at a trough?

She had mentioned her father. Leith had at first supposed that the lady was much his elder, but while they sat by the hearth he tended to see her best with his left eye, which was farther from the fire's glare on his right hand, and he was forming an impression that the lady might in fact be younger than she had appeared.

"A very great hero," Kess went on. "He fought in many a

war, his feats of arms were widely sung of, not only in Esdragon. He crossed the Great Sea in search of adventure, and when he returned he brought a foreign witch queen he had won away from her people and taken to wife. She bore me to him, and then she died."

She's very young, Leith was thinking, marveling how the firelight negated the paint's deceit. Sixteen years, no more.

"At least, I was always *told* she had died," Kess continued unawares. "I never questioned it. Yet, half a year ago a rumor came to us that a fiery chimera had been sighted by hunters in the Beriana Mountains. At once my father called for his horse and his weapons. He told me he was going to seek my mother, never explaining how this could be done. He promised to return in a month's time."

"But he didn't come back?" Leith guessed, rather obviously.

Keiss shook her moon-pale head, no longer much concerned for her hair's array. "Messengers sent after him found no trace. He left me as his regent here, but I cannot much longer put off those who desire to see him—or forestall those who would seize his duchy should they learn he is absent and overdue, seeing a woman dead fifteen years." Disengage, to deceive about her line of attack.

"But you believe she didn't die?" Leith hoped he was following the discourse accurately. He had bent to pick up a ring and laid hands on a hornet's nest, he thought. Just his luck.

"I know now that she did not!" Kess said. "I was told lies from the moment I could understand them, and therefore never questioned, but my father knew the truth. My mother left Esdragon alive. The report of the chimera gave my father a clue—I know not what—some hint that told him where to seek her." Kess stared into the flames a moment, then turned her black eyes to Leith's face once more. "But the duke has been gone too long, and those who know this despair, count him lost, fear what will happen when all the folk know, and press me to take a husband, gain a man's hand to rule the duchy. To quiet them, I agreed, but upon a condition—I would wed only the man who could conquer the task I set for him." A beat of the blade now, to open a way for a thrust.

"The Hill of Glass," Leith supplied. The lady nodded.

"I intend to find my father. The hill was a stratagem, meant to keep the dangerous and the ambitious safely busied here while I went to seek him. No one would have guessed I was gone—I intended they'd all be too occupied with trying to ride to the top of a sand dune wrapped in a pretty illusion."

"And then I actually got to the top."

Kess glared at him, fencing no longer but thrusting for the kill. "I am not minded to wed some nobody from nowhere, Leith of the Isles, no matter what high birth he claims to have! I did not set this task with the intent that only a king's son on a magic horse could achieve it. *No one* was supposed to succeed! All I wanted was a month or so of time, when my suitors would be busy with something other than subjecting me to love poems and trying to elbow one another from my side."

"And I've spoiled your plans," Leith agreed, somehow evading being spitted on her blade. "Without intending to, or even knowing about them." He hesitated, then riposted. "Suppose I don't want to wed you, either?"

The paint hid the flush of anger on Kess' cheeks, but not the way her eyes widened with astonishment.

"Do I repell you?" She had been prepared to tell him graciously that she would allow him to keep the stallion if he left with it at once; she had not expected him to refuse her hand. She felt as if she'd been slapped with the flat of a blade.

Leith colored, observably since his skin was innocent of paint. "No. Much the reverse." He heard himself, blushed again. "It's only . . . I didn't understand what was involved." He spread his hands to express his helplessness, pleading for mercy. "A shipwreck brought me here, destitute. No friends, no money, no trade. I happened on the stallion, and it broke my heart to know I'd have to sell him to feed myself. You've seen him—to give up a horse like that? The contest looked like a way of keeping him—I thought if I could get the ring, I could sell it instead of the horse. If I'd known what the truth was, I'd have ridden away from your Hill of Glass instead of up it."

"You don't want to be duke?" Kess' amazement was so genuine, she dropped her guard. She couldn't think when she'd last seen a man who would not scheme to take her father's place, if the chance offered.

Leith shrugged. "I have other plans," he stalled.

"You're surely the only man in the duchy who'd refuse the coronet," Kess observed suspiciously, refusing to believe something so like a feint could be truth. It couldn't be *this* easy to rid herself of this inconvenient intruder.

"I imagine so." Leith lifted his shoulders again. "I'm also

the only man who rode to the top of your glass hill. Be that as it may, you don't need to slide a dagger between my ribs to get clear of this bargain, my lady."

Kess leapt to her feet, careless of dignity. Had their duel been with steel rather than words . . . "You *dare* to suggest I'd stoop to murder?"

Leith considered telling her just how often his own royal father had tried to murder him. Or at least those times he knew about. Instead he said: "I think you need to know your options, my lady. That's all. I meant no insult."

"Then you had better say what you *do* mean." Kess found herself wishing that she had a dagger after all. Her ample sleeves would have hidden a dozen weapons well and effortlessly.

"I wouldn't hold you to the marriage if we could strike another bargain," the stranger said thoughtfully.

"What do you want?" Kess' mind raced over possibilities. "The treasure you expected to get? Gold? Silver? Land—"

"None of those." Leith smiled wanly at her choices.

"*What*, then?" Kess sat once more, since he had never risen to match her posture and she was weary of waiting for him to observe the courtesy. As if during a sword bout, she seized the chance to catch her breath.

Leith fingered the scar on his cheek, which had stayed flushed after the rest of his face lost the high color his embarrassment and excitement had alternately lent it. An idea was shaping itself, a hope he would not let himself look at too closely yet, lest it vanish like mist under the sun's hot eye. He kept it just at the tail of his sight, for the moment. "I was born under a curse of ill luck," Leith began, and told the Lady Kessallia briefly of his ill-omened birth and the other disasters that had befallen him as he grew, mischances beyond any norm.

"After the priests sent me back to him, my father kept waiting for me to show some sign of witchery, to prove he'd been right to want to kill me for a demon. When I never did, I suppose I made him feel guilty, and that was in a way much worse. If he'd been wrong, the king wanted me out of his sight, so as not to be reminded of it, shamed by it. And there was the curse—best some other land should have it inflicted on them. Why make the Isles suffer it? So, he made arrangements for a political marriage and shipped me off. There was an unseasonable storm, and the ship sank."

"That's very unfortunate," Kess said sweetly. "Are you coming to a point about something?"

Leith swallowed the discourtesy and looked his hope square in the eye. It seemed very tiny, hardly able to stand on its own legs. It looked lonely. "You said your mother was a witch. Are you certain?"

Kess nodded impatiently.

"How do you know? If you were a child when she ... left—"

"You mean, apart from all the proper court ladies being only too happy to tell me—outside of my father's hearing—just what my mother was?" Kess set her red mouth into a tight, hard line. "She was a stranger, set over them. They'd say any lie. But they didn't have to lie about her being a witch, because she *was* one. I know, because I share my mother's blood, and I have powers as she did. I didn't hire a wizard to make a sand hill look like sharp glass. I did it myself. I can see things that are hidden and hide things that are seen. My mother was a witch—as am I."

Her look dared him to despise her for what she confessed, but Leith only looked relieved. His plan turned full circle and swallowed its own tail. It looked just a little better able to survive, out in the cold world.

"Do you believe your mother lives and that if you find your father you will find her, as well?" She must believe it, having taken such trouble to be free to seek her parents, Leith thought, but he wanted it from her lips.

"I do," Kess answered warily. "Why?"

"Witches can cast curses," Leith reasoned. "Surely a witch could lift the one that lies on me. Let me go with you to find out, and we'll call it quits."

Kess' immediate impulse was to refuse him, but as she opened her lips, the firelight touched the pendant that swung about the stranger's neck, and something came upon her, half scheme, half vision. She saw, in that compressed flash, a pair of horsemen leaving Keverne. Kess had no desire to accept Brychan's escort of soldiers, who would only slow her and spy upon her. Alone, she would be noticed, even if she disguised herself with the utmost of her cleverness. But pairs of post riders left Keverne on a regular message-carrying schedule, so regularly that no one noticed them at all ...

The Bargain

THE LADY KESSALLIA had told Leith the way to the stables, ordered him to lead the stallion there and pick out gear for it. Leith tried a dozen saddles before settling upon one. It was old, and its design was plain, without a single brass nailhead to decorate the front pommel or the high cantle at the back. The unfashionable tack seemed almost unworthy of such a magnificent horse as Valadan—but it fit. The last thing Leith desired was to gall a back that had offered itself to the novelty of a saddle so willingly.

A bridle he scarcely required, but the remnants of his belt were apt to give way ere long, so Leith chose a headstall of red leather that matched the saddle and fitted it with the mildest copper bit he could locate. Valadan mouthed the implement curiously, the taste of its metal unfamiliar to him but liking the way the fittings jingled, while Leith combed his mane and told him of the mad errand he had involved them both in.

There was no one about to overhear—the constable was long a-bed, and the grooms slept in a dormitory across the stableyard. The horses most apt to need constant attention—the duke's breeding stock—were not kept at Keverne. The saddle horses could easily get through a night's rest without human help, and the constable felt the stable stayed cleaner when the grooms lived elsewhere.

Leith loosened the saddle's girth, having assured himself that it was of a proper length and strong enough to stand the hard use of travel, sufficiently wide not to rub Valadan's hair on the way. He turned down the lantern the Lady Kessallia had lent him for his work, hung it from a peg, and sat down in the straw, resting his head against the wall. He dozed off at once. It had been a longish day. The hours since he'd ridden onto the beach were a blur, but not once had they included a bed. No telling how long he'd need to wait, and Leith saw no reason not to be comfortable while he did so. Beside him, Valadan rested a leg and dropped his own head.

Boot heels clicking against the stableyard's cobbles woke the stallion, who snorted a challenge and thereby roused Leith. The prince got to his feet, scrambling, as a cloaked figure slipped through the stable door, from the darkness outside to the dimness within, and unshuttered the lantern it held.

The Lady Kessallia dropped a clumsy bundle at his feet, without ceremony. The bundle came undone as it hit the straw—Leith thought it was clothing. He was still blinking at the sudden increase of light. "Put those on," Kess ordered, confirming his guess.

Leith repaired to an empty stall and did as she requested. The tangle of cloth gradually resolved itself into heavy trews, a soft linen shirt and a doublet of carded wool, all dyed various shades of sea blue. There were knitted half hose, stuffed for safekeeping into stout riding boots. The outer wrapping—which had captured a fair amount of straw as it tumbled through the stable—was a long cloak of dark gray wool, undyed and still bearing much of the grease of the black sheep's fleece it was spun from, which would help it to shed rain as easily as Esdragon's sheep did.

When he had dressed, Leith saw that he was the Lady Kessallia's twin, albeit that *her* cloak was not bestrewn with dirty straw. He brushed at the gray wool while Kess finished saddling a big bay gelding she had taken from one of the stalls. Her amazing hair was plaited into a single long braid that hung down her back and tapped the tops of her boots. The face paint was gone.

"My father uses post riders to carry messages through the duchy," Kess explained, tightening her girth. The gelding gave a grunt as she expertly applied her knee to his belly, then pulled the girth up another notch. "Two of them on the outer route are having a few days' rest."

Leith nodded, pretending he understood. Likely he would, given time enough—if the Lady Kessallia chose to extend that courtesy.

She was dragging forward two sets of leather panniers, one of which she slung in Leith's direction. He peeked inside the bags as he lashed them into place behind the cantle—one held about a peck of oats mixed with spelt, a winter grain his own folk grew for horse feed. The other bag contained a waterskin that would hang from the front of the saddle when it was filled, some packets of dried meat and fruits, a little sack of beans. He further discovered a hatchet, fishhooks and lines, a coil of light rope. There was a blanket, as well, which Leith rolled and tied neatly above the bags.

Kess produced another bundle, which gave off a muffled clanking as she set it down. She unrolled it to reveal a pair of longswords, a brace of daggers, sheaths and belts for all. "The outer route is rough country," she explained blandly. "The riders on it go armed."

Leith took the set of weapons she left him and belted them on. He wiggled his toes inside his new boots—which thankfully were new only to him—and therefore were well broken in and unlikely to pinch. Not that he thought his luck would allow him to escape blisters. Probably there was a nail working its way through the boot sole somewhere. He'd know in a day or so. He snugged the clasp that held his cloak at the neck.

Kess inspected him. "Not bad. It'll be cold at first light, put your hood up." Leith obeyed.

Kess frowned. "Not enough. We must be so ordinary that no one can say after we went or no." She put a finger to her lips, considering, then bent down and lifted a handful of stable dirt. She weighed it in her palm, whispering over it.

And tossed the ensorcelled dust into the air, so that it settled disguisingly over both of them. Leith sneezed. Kess wiped the last of the dirt from her fingers, smearing it down his chest. "Let's go," she said, pleased.

The reversed glamor worked to Kess' complete satisfaction. The two of them exited Keverne's gate without incident or outcry, just a team of dispatch riders off on their rounds, due back in a month's time.

For once, Esdragon's day did not begin with a shower of rain. Overhead, Leith's Lady rode the paling sky in waning magnificence till the sun vanquished Her and won the right to light their way through the farmland that made up this most hospitable quarter of the duchy. The roads were fair and seemed well tended to Leith's eye, the inevitable ruts and holes having been filled with gravel lest carts mire on their way to market during the frequent rains. Fords were well marked, with flat stones placed for wagon wheels to roll upon through the water.

At midmorning they halted in an orchard. The horses cropped grass and eagerly sought out windfallen fruit. Leith settled, sat up, shifted a half-rotted apple that had been both poking his back and staining his cloak. He lay back again in the long grass, relaxing in the sun's warmth. The grass was dry and soft. His lids grew heavy, but he knew they were merely resting the horses for half an hour, so he strove to stay wakeful lest the Lady Kessallia have reason at once to complain of him. He didn't need that, not so soon. Clouds dimmed the sun's face briefly. There were more such on the horizon, promising the rain postponed from the morning, and the lady might dislike getting wet. To forestall sleep, Leith sat up and looked about for a distraction.

Idly he drew forth the leather pouch that hung from a thong about his neck, alongside the moonstone. Leith loosened the drawstring, emptied the contents into his hand.

The worn pouch held an assortment of unlikely oddments: a rusty horseshoe nail, a moldy rabbit's forefoot, a blue glass bead, a round white pebble, a wrinkled chestnut, and some bits of dry green leaf. There had been a four-leaved clover when Leith had last examined them—now he discarded the faded bits, brushing crumbs carefully from the rabbit's furry paw. His misadventures had affected his meager possessions rather adversely.

Kess, reclining against a tree, took a slight interest. "What are those?"

"Charms," Leith answered, closing the pouch with a tug of the thong. "Things that my people reckon bring luck."

"Enough to offset your curse?" Kess found she was more interested.

Leith smiled wistfully. "I have no idea. They don't *seem* to work, but then again it might be worse without them. Or they might all be quite useless." His curse had never brought him fatal harm yet, but Leith had his own theories about why that was so. Whatever he could do to thwart the curse, he was willing to try, however strange-seeming. Lots of folk carried charms—though perchance not in the quantity and variety that Leith did.

The Lady Kessallia plucked a tiny flower from the turf and offered it. "Here. Speedwell. I don't suppose it can hurt. Vervain's a protective herb, too, maybe we'll see some today. And it's the horse*shoe* that's lucky, not the nail."

Leith gravely retrieved the nail from his pouch and buried it carefully lest one of the horses tread upon it. The sprig of speedwell he tucked under the clasp of his cloak, so it would not end as the clover had, useless bits.

"You could have hammered the nail into one of the trees," Kess said critically. "Or is that for wishes? Bad for the tree, too. There's a holy well near here," she recalled suddenly, ingenuously. "We could ride by it. Its waters bring luck."

Leith's face brightened at her helpfulness. "Lucky to drink from? Or to bathe in?"

"Bathe," Kess chose without hesitation, jumping to her feet. She pulled the bay's big head away from his grazing and began to snug the girth. He tried to hold his breath—she applied her knee once again. She turned from the activity to face Leith suddenly, her eyes more narrow than he had seen them yet.

"This curse of yours—just how *much* of it slops over onto the people around you? Do disasters only befall *you*, or am I going to have to hang myself about with smelly rabbit parts, as well?"

Leith dropped his gaze. He felt a hot flush spread across his cheeks. "My lady, I wouldn't have asked to come if I thought I'd put you at risk." He wanted to be truthful, but he sensed that if the lady thought he'd even remotely endanger her quest, he'd find himself abandoned in short order. He cast about for reassurances to offer. People around him didn't generally come to *immediate* harm—but earthquakes, fire, and storms *did* create harm and havoc in a raggedy circle around him. What could he tell her that wouldn't be half a lie? Her hard stare didn't make his selection easy.

One truth came to mind, finally, and was served up at once. "My father sent me away to forestall the curse, but the fact is no ill luck ever befell him *personally*, lady. His land was at peace, his shipping prospered, he had three sons other than me to choose his heir among. The king sent me away to prove he was *right* to have tried to kill me."

The lady was still regarding him with unallayed suspicion. Did she guess—or could she see—what a very narrow edge of truth he was treading? Not lying, but by no means disclosing quite all? She had *said* she could see things that were hidden . . .

The bay gelding took a restless step and planted a big hoof squarely on Leith's boot. Leith's eyes went wide, though he merely put a hand on the horse's shoulder and shoved till it shifted its weight off the leg. Then he stooped and lifted the hoof off his toe. Freed, Leith hobbled back a pace to safety and looked the Lady Kessallia full in the face, his mind made up.

"That's nearly as bad as it gets," he lied, and launched into an equally false confession. "Sometimes I think ill luck's as good as being immortal. When the ship sank, there were times when I *wished* I could drown—but I couldn't. If I fell over a cliff, I might break my neck—but then I'd be *dead*, and there'd be an end to the curse. It doesn't work that way. I'd just break an arm, or a leg. I may catch every ague that goes around, but I doubt I could catch plague with a net."

"That sounds perfectly miserable," Kess said, looking at him over her horse's rump, trying to ensure it didn't trample him a second time.

"It is, my lady," Leith agreed, hoping he'd succeeded and that she'd task him no further.

Kess scowled. "Stop that."

Leith, tightening Valadan's girth, looked over his shoulder at her. "Stop what?" he asked, quite baffled. Did she expect him to ride with a slipping saddle?

"Don't call me 'my lady.' Not even when we're alone— you'll do it when you shouldn't, sure as sure, if you get into the habit. I'm not a *lady*, I'm the duke's post rider."

Leith digested the censure and nodded. "What shall I call you?" Possibly she preferred that he address her as seldom as possible.

"*Kess.* Think you can remember?"

Leith put his foot into the stirrup and mounted, biting off a curse at the pain that shot through his bruised foot.

"You can soak it in the well," Kess suggested sweetly. "Cold water will take the swelling down, even if it doesn't prove out lucky."

The holy well was as cold as snowmelt, and Kess insisted it was reckoned unlucky to towel the precious fluid off the skin after bathing, so Leith rode on again in soggy discomfort. He had removed most of his clothing before climbing into the pool, but donning dry clothes over wet skin had the effect of soaking them from the inside out, and his hair dripped down his back unrelentingly.

Then the gray clouds began to release their freight of rain, soaking them from the outside in. The unwashed wool of their cloaks shed a good deal of water, but the wind tended to catch the cloth, letting the rain get underneath. Kess made no complaint, but Leith's lips were turning blue, and his nose was running. Every low spot in the road became a puddle to splash them, and if there had been a dry spot on him, it would not have remained so long, assaulted from above *and* below.

Near what should have been sun-fall, they came to a muddy crossroads and a sizable inn, where Kess announced they would stop. Arrangements were made for the regular lodging of the post riders and their mounts, she explained, at the inns along their routes. The horses got sweet hay and a measure of grain, the riders their supper and a bed, the innkeeps a lower tax rate when the duke's collectors arrived at year's end. A fair exchange.

The common room was dark and low-ceilinged, its air moist and pungent with the smell of wet wool. The inconvenience of the weather was not remarked upon. Supper was pork and cabbage, cooked to colorlessness and almost to tastelessness. Kess looked askance at her bowl when it was put before her, and inquired of Leith whether his curse ran to food as well as weather. Leith lifted a spoon to his chilled lips, decided he had dined upon far worse in the course of his wanderings, and finished every bite, wiping the bowl twice with a heel of stale bread.

It had been a long day's ride, though both of them were used to long hours on horseback. The day's-end rain had proved draining. They sat for an hour or so while their clothing dried and stiffened on them listening to the local men discuss the coming harvest—then Kess jerked her disheveled head in the direction of the stairs to the second storey, where the sleeping rooms were. Leith picked up the saddlebags—which were supposed to contain the messages they were assumed to be carrying—and followed her, squishing with every step and limping with half of them. His bad leg was always at its worst in wet weather.

Messages and dispatches on bits of parchment would have weighed far less than sacks of grain and dried food, which the bags actually held. Leith had quite a struggle to get up the steep, railless stair without taking a tumble back into the common room. He maneuvered the double load of bags down a dim corridor and through a narrow doorway, and nearly collided with Kess, who had halted just inside, cursing.

Leith peered over her shoulder, into the gloom her smoking taper scarcely lit, trying to discover what had so displeased her and to guess whether he might set his burden safely down ere he was obliged to drop it. His grip was weakening under the prolonged strain, his fingers cramping.

One window, with a sagging shutter, ventilated the slant-ceilinged space. Rain had puddled on the floor beneath it. There was a wide, low bed, shoved against the far wall under the eaves as if to make the room seem larger, an iron brazier that would have held charcoal had they purchased the fuel against the chill, a stand holding a pitcher of stale water and a slop jar—and nothing more, so far as Leith could see. Not a palace, and probably not even overclean, but a place to rest weary heads and bodies aching from being in a saddle all day . . .

Yet Kess was quite obviously upset. As Leith tried to sidle around her and set the bags down, he got a faceful of her hair, which she shook loose from its damp braid with an angry head toss. Leith, half blinded, managed to stagger clear, shed the baggage at last, and stay on his feet, but it was a struggle. The main thing that had kept him on his feet was a timely collision with the wall.

"Don't think we're sharing that bed."

Leith blinked, then finally understood what the trouble was. Travelers shared beds as a matter of course, packed in like cattle in a byre, as many to a room or a bed as the innkeep could contrive. He and Kess rated a room to themselves only because they were supposedly post riders, who'd be on their way early and might disturb any other guests put in with them. Kess' masquerade was too effective and had come round to nip her—the innkeep had no reason to think the young gentleman would object to sharing a bed with his fellow officer—and there was therefore no way she might demand other accommodations.

Before Kess could suggest he retire to the stable, Leith made himself useful by fixing the shutter so that it let in less of a gale. The night air was cold, as well as wet. Rain-laden gusts lashed the roof overhead, angry to be denied the room. With the air still, Leith could see his breath.

Kess prodded the straw tick on the bedstead, possibly hoping to discover fleas and a further excuse for anger. She beat a fair quantity of dust out of the mattress and routed a stem of straw or two, but no vermin. The blankets were threadbare, but reasonably clean—at least as could be seen by the most inadequate candlelight.

When she turned from assaulting the bed, Leith was curled

up under his soggy cloak, on the floor in the far corner behind the door, which he had closed and latched. Both sets of saddlebags were piled against the panel, to bolster the security arrangements.

As with the room, Kess could not *quite* find fault. If Leith chose to lie on the floor and yield the bed up to her without the briefest argument, she could not very well insist that he vacate the room, as well. That irritated her, so Kess took her temper out on the mattress once again. If Leith heard, he gave no sign of it. In fact, he kept his face to the wall, according her that much privacy.

Kess was tempted to strip and hope she'd catch him sneaking a look at her, but she considered the state of the sheets and in the end removed only her boots. She crawled under the scratchy blanket, whose wool seemed to have traveled straight from sheep to loom without benefit of soap or water, and turned her back, trying ostentatiously to rustle the straw.

If Leith noticed, he still gave no sign—unless regular breathing could be so interpreted.

Kess slept soundly—till the voice wakened her.

At first she mistook it for a new, annoying manifestation of her visions, inconveniently breaking in upon her repose. Gradually she became aware that the voice was *not* just in her head but actually in the room itself.

Someone was kneeling at the shuttered window, which was now admitting a narrow bar of moonlight. The voice was coming from the indistinct figure—a sort of chanting, words that Kess could not quite make out or that were in a language she did not know. She propped herself up on one elbow.

"What are you doing?" she asked loudly.

Leith leapt to his feet, banging his head into the forgotten slant of the ceiling, which had been safely above him when he knelt.

"It's moonrise," he explained, rubbing his scalp and feeling a bruise spreading under the hair. "I am—I was—bidding my Lady welcome."

"I thought you said the moon priests sent you away?" Kess queried suspiciously.

Leith rubbed his head again. Massage didn't seem to help. "They did. But my Lady didn't cast me out—She just has other uses for me, which She will reveal in Her own time. So I welcome Her each Rising, and listen to see whether She has some word of instruction for me." And he had needed, most especially, to know whether he had done right to attach himself to Kess' quest. It was the first chance he'd had to ask. He had no idea how to interpret the unexpected whack on the head. It might not be his Lady's doing, of course. He hoped not.

"You do this every night?"

Leith nodded eagerly, careful of the ceiling. "Whenever She rises. Or at the hour when She would rise, if there's a storm and clouds hide Her face." He had missed a Rising or two in his life, slept through some indeed, but Kess would not need to know of his frailties so long as they did not affect her, so he saw no need to mention them.

"Well, do it more quietly," Kess ordered. "You woke me up."

"I'm sorry." Leith felt his face go hot at his thoughtlessness, concerned only with his own needs. "I didn't intend to."

"How *do* you manage to wake up at a different hour every night? Or were you just shamming sleep?" she asked, her tone hardening.

Next she'd be accusing him of leering at her while she slept and staying wakeful just for that purpose. Leith tried to head that fancy off. "It's training. I know when the Rising will be, I wake just before, and sleep again after. Sometimes I hardly know I've waked at all."

"Nice for you," Kess said acidly. "Those of us not priest-trained don't fall back to sleep so easily."

Leith dropped his gaze miserably to the splintery floor. "My lady, I'm truly sorry. I was thoughtless—"

"Oh, leave off whining about it!" The room was chill, Kess wanted to crawl back under her blanket—it overrode her desire to punish transgressions. "Are you done saying good night to your mistress?"

Leith nodded. He could not perform further devotions now, his mind was much too disordered. Besides, Kess' skeptical gaze would make his tongue cleave to his mouth, if not choke him outright. He'd only commit mockery, if he tried to continue.

"Then shut up. And if you happen to wake up when the *sun* rises, and I've somehow managed to get back to sleep, wake me—I want to start early."

Breakfast was porridge of uncertain origin and a grayish hue best not closely investigated whilst it was being consumed.

Leith finished his meal quickly with his eyes half shut, and departed to fetch the horses before Kess could order him to do so. It might not be possible to work his way into her good graces, but he could escape her tongue.

Valadan was arching his neck and paying close attention to a chestnut mare at the stable's far end. The coy looks she flashed back at him suggested a reason—she was in season. She belonged to the hostler, who cast an admiring eye on the black stallion as Leith bid him good morning.

"Real quality, there," the man remarked conversationally, wiping a nose that had begun to drip just that morning. The cook was already sick, and the hostler feared he had a touch of whatever ailed her.

Leith agreed pleasantly to the compliment while he saddled Kess' envious-looking gelding. He remarked favorably in return on the mare's fine conformation, her obvious good breeding.

"She'd throw a nice foal," the hostler suggested, applying sleeve to nose once more.

Leith allowed as that was so, and they set in to dickering, while Valadan courted the mare with low nickers and soft snort. After a moment, Leith put his hand to the latch on the stall door.

Leith came away from the transaction with two pieces of hacksilver and a new charm to dangle about his neck—a well-worn horseshoe. The shoe must have come from a plowhorse, for Valadan could have fitted almost two of his hooves neatly inside its near circle, and it weighed heavy enough to bruise when it swung into Leith's chest. It did that as he mounted, and Leith winced at the impact, thinking he'd have done far better to pocket the charm instead of dangling it about his neck on a cord.

He had hung it crookedly also, as Kess was only too pleased to point out—Valadan had been quick in his business with the mare, and there had been no delay she could complain of, but Kess knew something had been going on, and wanted to punish Leith for his initiative on any account other than her own.

"You've let all the luck run out," she said, pretending to be helpful. "If it ever had any." She had let Leith wear the thing all morning before speaking up, reckoning slyly how the weight would make his neck ache. Sleep-lack always made Kess cross, and revenge always cheered her.

Leith could have guessed that there was no luck left in the shoe. They had been given a packet of food at the inn for a midday meal and had opened it when they halted to rest the horses. The bread inside was pale green with mold, and an egg, boiled in its shell, gave off a dreadful stench when Leith began to peel the shell away. One whiff had been sufficient to slaughter his appetite, and the stench seemed to cling to his fingers as they rode onward. He thought he might not be able to swallow their evening meal, either. No, his new charm had not affected his curse, not in the slightest. He sighed and threw the horseshoe into the roadside grass.

Kess poked him. "See those stones in the field yonder?"

The stones she indicated poked up like gray fingers amid the ripening barley. Leith wondered aloud why the farmers left them there, obviously in the way come harvesttime. They'd give the reapers extra trouble, possibly damage a sickle or two, he said.

"Because they're counted lucky." Kess dismounted and strode toward the ring of stones, with Leith and the horses trailing after. One stone shaft had long ago fallen onto its side, but the rest still stood on end, their tops a little above Leith's head, rather farther above Kess'.

"Spit on one," she bade him.

Leith did so. The rain had ceased during the night, so the stone was dry—his spittle left a dark gray splotch against a lighter gray.

"Feel any change?"

Leith had to admit that he did not—save that he preferred spitting on a stone to dunking himself into ice-cold water. He knew oaths were often sworn while the parties laid hands to a stone—the stone supposedly lending its stability to the oath. He had no idea what spitting was meant to accomplish.

"Picket the horses over there," Kess said. "There's another stone around here, if I've heard aright. We'll stretch our legs a bit before we go on."

By the time Leith had finished tethering the horses so they might graze without straying into the grainfield, Kess was across that field, nearly out of his sight. Leith caught up to her just as she was climbing a low rise, but he had to scramble to do it, and he turned an ankle stepping into a hidden rabbit hole. They went together down the far side, coming at last to a spot too wet for crop tillage just as Leith got his breath back. The place was green and full of rushes and sweet flag—in short, a bog. Possibly a true pond after a good rain or two. Leith saw a spotted frog jump away from their invading boots, heard it land in the water.

Kess picked a way across, avoiding the center and any spots of suspiciously vivid green, which would surely have water under them. The ground rose once more. One hill crested, and when they climbed one behind it, they halted at the summit, beside another stone set up by long-dead hands.

This stone was short and broad, more yellow-red than gray, and had a roundish hole cut clear through it—whether by water or man's hand Leith could not tell.

"Do I spit on this one, too?" Leith asked. "Or through it?" Spitting *through* openings ought to have virtue, he supposed. He had no notion what the rules were.

Kess was inspecting the stone with deepest concentration. "You could spit," she assented. "Or just touch it. But it's reckoned luckiest to crawl through."

"*Crawl through?*" Leith eyed the irregular hole askance. The fit looked tight. Probably the stone had originally been meant to be looked through—it was in line with the standing stones in the barley field a quarter league off, as he saw when he glanced back the way they'd come.

"Nine times. Sunward," Kess added, as if that were a given. Leith made a quick calculation of the direction and moved to the proper side of the stone. "Why not moonward?" he asked. Must the great hot sun take precedence in *every* land? Why was his Lady so little regarded? She who never smote with sunstroke, nor parched crops up with drought—

Kess shrugged. "It's a sun-stone. I've never heard of a moon-link to it. But please yourself." She sounded quite indifferent as to whether or not he took her advice.

Leith considered, then slowly unfastened his cloak, let it fall to lie on the wind-bent grass. The passage looked so tight—a sheep would have difficulty scrambling through twice. Nine times? He unbuckled his sword belt, laid his weapons aside on the cloak. "Will you count for me? So I don't lose track?"

Kess nodded solemnly, hiding a smile.

Of course he'd need no help to count. A man who could read and write could certainly count to nine without difficulty. Why, he could tick the numbers off without even using all his fingers . . .

By his fifth time through the stone, going from right to left, Leith had already discovered most of the rough spots likely to catch hold of him—leaving skin on several of the worst. He'd also located a patch of stinging nettles, growing where he could not avoid sprawling on each awkward exit. His right cheek was bleeding—he'd stumbled the fourth time he ducked to begin the passage and had hit his face on the granite. One of his knees was scraped raw, though the cloth over it had sustained no visible damage. His doublet was less fortunate—it had torn on a bramble as he tumbled out of the hole on his second pass.

The passage was brief—an arm span or less—but never easy. Each pass through was fully as difficult as the first, though always in a different way. He had to duck to fit his shoulders through, trying not to bump his head on the passage. Once he was halfway through, his feet were no longer on the ground, and he must wriggle and squirm till he reached the far side, trying not to fall out headfirst into the nettles when he arrived. Leith tried to keep his own tally along with the numbers Kess called out to him, but he was so busy with his task that he eventually lost count, exactly as he'd feared he might. He exited, caught his balance, lost it again, and sat down in the nettles. He looked dizzily at Kess, who shook her head.

"That's just eight."

Leith was sure she'd already called off eight, and he'd gone once after, but he was too disoriented to contest the point. He dragged himself through the hole a final time. Straightening as he backed out of the nettles, he staggered over to his gear. He put sword and cloak back on, then walked toward Kess, not giving the hole stone another glance. He'd seen it quite enough times, from every possible angle. He wiped the blood from his cheek, tried to nurse the crick from his back without letting Kess see. The nettle welts burned fiercely. They started back toward the horses.

At the bottom of the second hill, Leith's left boot caught on a grass tussock, and he went facedown into an especially wet bit of bog.

"So much for *that* wives' tale," Kess said as he picked himself up, dripping. "Or maybe you were supposed to strip first," she added, as if the further requirement had just occurred to her. "My mind's always such a muddle when I haven't slept well."

That night Leith was *very* careful at moonrise. The dusty little room they'd been sent to boasted no window at all whereby his Lady might enter should She wish to speak to him, so he crept barefoot all the way down to the stable. Better by far to

wake Valadan, who did not resent his company in the middle
of the night, than to risk disturbing Kess two nights running.

When he returned to the room—proud that he had evaded
every creaking board if not a splinter or three—Leith could
gauge his success by Kess' unchanged position. The bedding
at this inn was more questionable than the last—she had dis-
dained the blankets altogether and covered herself with her
own cloak, which if no longer clean was at least known. Lest
his luck betray him and cause Kess to wake while he was gazing at her—an activity she'd be certain to misinterpret—Leith
curled up in the corner he'd selected as being the least drafty
and dropped easily back to sleep. He'd had practice—when his
Lady rose late, the moon priests had always slept both before
and after their offices, and it was a skill their apprentices
learned well. Moonlight filled his dreams, of which he remembered no more than washes of silver.

He woke himself, coughing. The spasm refused to subside,
though Leith strove desperately to stifle it—fearful he'd wake
Kess if it went on long. He clamped his jaws, turned his head
into the crook of his arm. The measures seemed to help. He
held his breath to thoroughly break the cycle, then cautiously
drew air in through his nose.

And realized that he smelled smoke.

The cracks between the floorboards were wide as his fingers—earlier, cooking odors had drifted up from the taproom
below, mingled with the merry sounds of local folk downing
mugs of ale, drunken snatches of song, calls for more this or
another that—but all had been quiet below long ere moonrise.
Now there came a faint crackling, and when Leith put an eye
to the space nearest his nose, he saw a dull reddish light—till
his eye began to tear from the smoke.

"*Kess!* Get up!" He crossed the room in a scramble and
shook her shoulder. She swatted at him for his presumption,
only half awake. "The inn's on fire!"

Leith grabbed the saddlebags and his boots. Then the two of
them tumbled down the steep stairs, pounding the walls and
shouting to wake other sleepers. Leith unbarred a shutter and
helped Kess climb through the low window, for there were yellow flames licking at the front door already and no escape that
way. He threw the saddlebags after her. In the stable, horses
whinnied in fright.

The innkeep hastily organized a line of buckets passing between the well and the front of the building, and all the guests

lent their hands, but it was no use. Flames got into the roof thatch, which was damp enough on top but dry as old bones beneath. After that, they could only hope to save the stable while the horses were led out and far enough off that they'd stand tied without panicking. A couple of pigs were similarly rescued.

By first light there was nothing to be seen of the former inn save a heap of blackened timbers, piled up like a child's abandoned game. Leith wiped one smudge from his nose, leaving three others in its place, and looked dejectedly at the smoking mess. His fault, surely. His ill luck, close at heel as any dog.

Kess disagreed as they rode away into the dawn. "If the innkeep was careless about his chimneys, how is that *your* fault? The whole place was filthy. That miser could grip a copper till it squealed like a suckling pig—odds are the chimneys never saw a sweep the whole time he's owned it. Or else some kitchen slut was too drunk to bank the hearth so coals wouldn't tumble out. It's not *your* bad luck."

"It happened while I was there. Not before. It wouldn't have happened if I hadn't been there." Leith was recalling the innkeep's face, slack with shock at the loss of his livelihood between one dawn and the next. It seemed to Leith that all he ever left in his wake was misery.

"If you hadn't waked, *no one* might have gotten out! And they all did—no one burned. I don't call that ill luck," Kess insisted.

But Leith wouldn't answer.

Kess decided that Leith might sulk all he chose, and she spurred her horse ahead so she wouldn't need to look at his dour face. She kept that position till well after sun-high, whereupon she chose to resume her efforts to ease Leith's curse-suffering while they rested the horses.

They were sitting under an apple tree. Much of the red fruit still bobbed overhead, but some had been shaken loose by weather, and no one had gathered it in. The horses sought the windfalls eagerly, and Leith, not immune to the lure of sweets, had found a few, also. They had carried no midday meal away from the inn—well cooked though the food would have been.

"Eating windfalls makes you stumble," Kess said disapprovingly. "As the fruit fell, so will you."

Leith stared at her, his mouth full of apple. Now he was presented with a quandary—if he spat it was ill-mannered; if he swallowed it was unlucky. He plainly could not decide what to do, but after a long moment he swallowed heavily. "Truly?"

"There are lucky and unlucky actions," Kess said. "Luck isn't just what you carry in your pockets." She arose and snugged the bay's girth, put her foot in the stirrup.

Leith fed the rest of his apple to Valadan, who feared no curse. "What else is lucky to do?" he asked. Her people might have lore his did not.

"Picking up pins. Seeing a white horse. Threes are always for luck."

Leith digested the information. None of it applied presently.

"Turn your coat," Kess suggested brightly, as if an idea struck her. "In fact, turn every stitch you've got on! Then the curse can't find you. It won't recognize you," she said patiently, when Leith seemed not to understand.

Leith had not the skill to dispute her logic, so he dismounted again and obeyed her direction—behind a bush, which offered a modicum of privacy in return for a good score of thorn scratches.

"What about the boots?" he called, seeing no way of turning his sturdy footwear inside for out.

"Switch them left for right."

Leith felt more doubtful with each garment that he turned out and replaced—all the dirt and cockleburrs were next to his skin then, and that didn't seem especially lucky to him—certainly it wasn't comfortable. At last he remounted, ill at ease and thankful the few folk they'd passed on the road earlier were long gone. "How long do I have to stay this way?"

"Just till sun-fall." Kess smiled encouragingly. "You can turn them back when it's time to sleep. Don't worry, we don't come to another inn this stretch."

So at least no one was likely to see him in this disheveled state. Small comfort, Leith thought, supposing there would be worse yet in store for him. He was proved correct soon enough.

As they rode on, a bird flew over, low and fast. Leith gazed disgustedly at the white splotch spreading down his left shoulder.

"I don't think it worked," he called.

Kess was doubled over her saddlebow, holding her sides, helpless against a fit of mirth.

A Delicate Stomach

FOLLOWING THAT INCIDENT, Leith was receptive to no more of Kess' suggestions for improving his luck. He ignored her when she told him how a daisy picked precisely at sun-high, pressed and dried and carried, was accounted to bring good fortune—the flower representing the life-giving sun. He refused to carry the protective herbs she touted: rosemary, vervain, carline thistle. When he arose, he neglected to smooth away the impression his body had made in the grass while he slept, and seemed not to care that such neglect could give an ill-wisher power over him. Kess chided him for sewing a rip in his trews while he still wore them—such mending known to be bad luck—and Leith never lifted his head, even when he stuck the needle into his leg by mischance.

He had spoken no word of blame, but 'twas plain enough he'd finally seen through her lies. Kess regretted the premature end to her sport. A pity she could not have deceived him longer—Leith had been so delightfully accepting of the most outrageous cures. Then again, she had no more leisure for sport. They would be parting company soon, having left the post riders' route behind them with the last inn and passed two nights sleeping in the open.

Kess heard Leith chanting softly as the moon came up, but she gave no sign that she was awake, and had been for hours. She was wishing that she might call her visions to heel and have one sometimes when she desired it, not always suffer its being chance-thrust upon her. Kess struggled with the matter daily—had done so for the past year, when her mother's blood had first called her attention to its presence—and had no more success than Leith had in forestalling his curse. She had tried and tried to see where her father currently was—but she woke and lived and slept, quite untroubled by any sight other than the ordinary one of her eyes.

Weary of lying wakeful, Kess arose as quietly as if she sleep-walked and paced a few steps through the dewy grass. The damp would chill her when she bedded down again—if she did ere dawn. Leith had completed his devotions and now slept once more, under his Lady's white eye. The horses grazed, taking no notice of her.

The moon was dwindling, and there were clouds, but its late light guided Kess as she sought plants in the little wood they had camped beside. The half-light prevented her from tripping over Leith when she returned from her quest, with fragrant hands. Undisturbed, he slept unaware, while Kess stared narrow-eyed down at him.

She never felt safe looking very long at him when he could look back. It was not the mismatch of his eyes that troubled her—Kess knew he was no demon—but the notion he would know she took even the most fleeting account of him. Leith was lying curled on his right side, so it would be the green eye that caught her—she could just make out the hook shape of the scar on the tanned skin at the top of his cheekbone.

Had he been awake, she never could have let her gaze linger on his eyelashes—which were far too long—or his eyebrows, which slanted as they reached the bridge of his nose. Either of those features lay too close to his perilous eyes. So did his mouth, relaxed in sleep. Kess was irritated that Leith was not sucking air in noisily, or snoring it out again—if he had been doing anything to disturb her she would have felt free to nudge him awake, and probably would have forced him to break camp so they could begin the day's ride before dawn. She was awake anyway! And she was cold, and wanted to move about. How dared the lout sleep so peacefully?

Her thoughts seemed to have the power to intrude—a skill Kess had never claimed for herself and found rather disconcerting. As she glowered at him, Leith made a little whimper deep in his throat, and his eyelids began to twitch. A line formed between his slanting brows. His breathing quickened.

Good, Kess though savagely. *Wake up!*

But as they had inexplicably flowered, so did her powers likewise swiftly fade. Leith did not wake, though he looked as if he wished to. He turned his head restlessly, frowning more fiercely. His lips compressed, holding back an outcry.

All at once he rolled right over, and Kess sat back with a

startled squeak, caught spying and trying desperately to pretend otherwise.

"What's the matter?" Leith asked, his voice thick with sleep.

"I heard a noise," Kess lied. "Go check the horses." She quickly hid what she held in her hands, put it behind her back.

Leith disentangled himself—with some difficulty—from his cloak, and went shivering through the dew-soaked grass, till he could see Valadan grazing. His hip felt stiff, and he limped on the uneven ground as he went to the stallion. Kess' horse was nearby. Neither looked disturbed by anything other than Leith's unexpected appearance, which was merely a curiosity.

"They're fine," he reported presently to Kess. "Nothing's amiss."

She was poking the fire to life, feeding it wood, and had a pot of water standing ready. "Now we're awake, we may as well get started. You tack the horses, I'll cook."

Leith rubbed at his eyes and yawned, still barely awake despite his exercise. "The sun won't be up for another—" He slanted a look at the rim of the moon, laced with the trees his Lady was dipping behind. "Three hours, at the least."

"It'll be light enough by the time we're on our way," Kess insisted. "This isn't an inn—the food doesn't set itself cooked before us, and the horses won't curry themselves! Get to work."

Leith limped off again, and if he had more protests to make he swallowed them. He did apologize profusely to the horses for cutting short the grazing time they all knew well should have been their portion. His impulse was sincere, but in practice it was so broken by yawns as to be unintelligible. The horses stamped and fretted, unhappy to be bothered, difficult to work with.

Currying the horses and loading the gear took him a fair while. By the time Leith had finished, Kess was laying out hunks of journeybread, having dished up bowls from the cookpot. Leith sat down, wiped his hands more or less clean on his cloak, and started in on breakfast.

As he was expecting some sort of porridge, the strong odor of garlic startled Leith wide awake. The bowl before him was full of scraps of meat, a few grayish lumps of vegetables, and a lot of dark green leaves. He looked up from it and saw Kess watching him across the fire, daring criticism.

"We're putting in a long day," she said. "We're off the post route now, there won't be another inn, and I don't want to stop again before nightfall."

"The horses will want to," Leith observed, wondering what had Kess in such a prickly mood. Had the hard ground prevented her from sleeping her fill?

"It doesn't take as long to graze as it does for us to cook. This is the last hot food you're going to get till sun-fall, so eat up."

Leith dipped his horn spoon into the bowl, raised it to his lips. Not bad, the surfeit of garlic aside. He didn't understand yet what the fuss was about—they had never halted to cook at the midpoint of the day, inns or not. Nor was meal-making all that time-consuming. Kess had used the short bow she carried to acquire a fat rabbit the night before, and they had roasted it in mere minutes. The last scraps of that meat now graced the stew.

Porridge would have been quicker, surely. There was no need for hot food of any sort—they had bread and salty cheese, and could have broken their fast with those. However, at least nothing had burned down over their heads during the night. Leith ate his stew, discovering that he had appetite enough once he came fully awake. At least he could manage to swallow.

He supposed he could guess a reason for Kess' haste—the cold of the morning was a reminder that summer was ending, that the time they'd have to locate her father before winter set in was short. Kess was anxious, and short of sleep, as well. Small wonder she was less than congenial.

"Where's the last place your father was seen?" Leith asked conversationally as he cleaned his wooden bowl with a bit of very stale bread.

As if to make amends for her earlier sharpness, Kess seized the empty bowl and ladled up a generous second helping. Leith was inclined to refuse the fresh portion—the stew really was too heavily seasoned, once the edge was off his appetite, which it well and truly was by then—but he feared to offend Kess when she seemed to be attempting a kindness. He decided to swallow the stew quickly, so as not to taste it overlong. He could manage that.

"I had no word of him after he crossed into the mountains," Kess admitted. "I know he was bound farther, into the Berianas. I will start to ask when I reach Radak—he surely went that way. He had hunted in that country. There's not much else up there, from what I hear."

Leith declined to comment that her plan struck him as imprecise if not impractical. He was noticing a trace of discomfort—the stew was not lying lightly in his stomach. He felt almost too stuffed to breathe, and wished belatedly that he had found some way to decline the second bowl, risking Kess' feelings or not. He was thirsty from all the seasonings, but water would likely distress his stomach further after it had eased his mouth, so he held back. He wished for some tea, but Kess had made none—best he not suggest it. Leith struggled to focus on Kess, to keep his thoughts away from himself till the indigestion passed off. Riding was likely to be unpleasant—and to commence soon. He tried not to think about it.

"Anyway, I shall find him easily enough," Kess was saying confidently. "We're both looking for the same thing—my mother. I'm following the same rumors he did. I'm bound to run across him. What's the matter?"

"I don't feel very well," Leith admitted reluctantly. He had become queasy, and his face felt flushed, though the air was still cool against his cheeks. He shivered. His ears had begun to ring.

"You must have a delicate stomach," Kess observed, staring at him with interest.

"Not generally." Leith was starting to sweat. He got to his feet, pretending nothing was amiss, set the bowl down, wiped his forehead on his sleeve. His hands shook.

"Maybe you ate too fast. Or too much." Kess began to gather up the cooking things. Leith lent a hand, carrying the pot and the bowls to the stream. While Kess scrubbed them clean with sand, he busied himself with quenching the fire, telling himself that he should *expect* an upset stomach, after sleeping barely half the night, then insulting his insides with so much garlic, first thing. If Kess suffered no ill effects from the early meal, it was a wonder, but she'd probably admit to no flaw in her cooking.

The indisposition *would* pass, Leith told himself. He looked around for mint, while they were by the stream, but saw none, which was a pity. Chewing a few stems of the herb eased bellyaches, though it was even better brewed into a hot tisane.

An unprecedented wave of dizziness forced him to sit down and rest his spinning head against his knee. Whatever the problem was, it was *not* passing, Leith decided reluctantly. And that it was not did not seem to bother Kess. She continued to load her horse and scarcely spared him a glance. Surely she'd noticed he was no longer working at striking camp? Why was she silent?

Leith remembered—with a flash of apprehension—the care with which Kess had heaped his bowl. Her insistence that he get the "best" bits. Could he truly remember seeing her take a single bite of her stew? She had *held* a bowl, but had she eaten from it? He could still taste the cursed garlic in his mouth, with each breath. He'd scarcely been able to swallow a mouthful of the stew without recourse to the water bottle. What exactly had the herb been covering up?

He looked up and saw Kess looking back at him. The manner in which she regarded him—detached, with no trace of concern, and more than a hint of anticipation—told Leith the truth.

She'd poisoned him. A trifling bellyache wouldn't blur his vision, wouldn't make sweat start out all over his skin, from his forehead to his bruised toes. Plague might have—but Kess would have been worried about that. She didn't look distressed.

Indigestion could have given him chills, but never the violent shivers that now assailed him. Leith wanted to dash into the meadow and rid himself of the tainted food, even if it meant he had to eat grass first, like a dog. But his legs refused to cooperate. He couldn't even stand up, and all he could hope was that Kess didn't intend the poisoning to be permanent.

"I am going to seek my mother," Kess said, standing over him. The sun had risen over her left shoulder. Leith, in his confusion, mistook its misty disc for the moon, and the welcome-chant skittered through his mind, but his lips couldn't shape the words of greeting.

"I need to know what my mother is, what *I* am. I am not like my father's folk, for all they raised me to be so. I told you, I can see things that are hidden, but there are other things happening to me, too, and I don't understand them. My mother will. She will help me."

Leith could see two moons now and two Kesses bending down to touch his shoulder. "Don't be afraid. You aren't dying. But you aren't going with me any farther, either. Thank you for your help—I'm sure our disguise threw off anyone who thought they'd follow me."

She looked over her shoulder at Valadan. Leith saw she had

unsaddled the stallion. "I said you could keep him, if you'd take him away. In a day or so you'll probably feel well enough to ride. Crogen will be on your left hand, when you face the sunrise. They breed good horses there, by all I hear. That stallion can make your fortune—I'd just keep quiet about the curse, if I were you." Her twin mouths twitched. "Good luck."

Leith heard harness fittings jangle as she mounted the bay gelding. By the time he had managed to heave himself to his knees, Kess was riding away. He could see the white gleam of her braid, hanging straight down her back.

Through cracking lips, Leith whistled for Valadan. He didn't need a saddle. If he could get onto the stallion's back, Valadan's legs would carry him while his own could not. All he had to do was get up.

He lurched to his feet, staggered for balance, and did not even know he was falling. His head struck against something—the brief, sharp pain was the last sensation to trouble Leith for some while.

Seeing Things That Are Hidden, Hiding Things That Are Seen

IF THERE WERE days sandwiched between the nights when he lay ill, Leith could not distinguish them. He drifted out of one darkness into another scarcely less intense, and did not trouble himself over whether that darkness was internal or external. His best gauge of time's passage was as always his Lady's face, and when next he could focus on her clearly, She was turning that face away, very much on the wane.

He had made no attempt to rekindle the fire, though he huddled just beside its cold gray ashes. He could not gather wood to sustain a blaze, even assuming he could light it without setting himself alight. His cloak kept him warm after the fever's heat ebbed out of his flesh, and if there should be wild animals about . . .

Valadan snorted, reminding his master that he stood sentry. No harm would come upon him unchallenged. Comforted, Leith drifted back to uneasy sleep.

He woke at sun-high, with a fierce headache, a great thirst, and a stiff neck. All eased after he managed to crawl to the stream for a drink and a bath—the water was cold as Kess' heart, but it restored him, and for a wonder the sky stayed free of clouds till the sun had mostly dried him. Leith gathered a few twigs, made a tiny fire, and heated water in a cup he discovered in his saddlebags. He tended the scrape he had gotten on his forehead when he fell and brushed the worst mess from his clothing.

The notion of food was repellent, but Leith made a cup of thin gruel by boiling a handful of the horse grain—he did not suppose Valadan would begrudge him—and forced it down. He felt better than he had expected, once he had eaten. He still wobbled as he slowly gathered his gear, but his senses stayed

84

steady enough while he lashed it into place on Valadan, and as he carefully hauled himself into the saddle he was not troubled by faintness.

Valadan pawed the ground restlessly, arching his neck and dragging the reins through Leith's weak grip.

"I don't doubt you can catch her," Leith agreed, struggling to keep his balance. His legs felt limp as unbaked dough, his seat was unsure. "But which way did she go? It would help to start in the right direction."

He faced the horse away from the sun, which had climbed halfway past its zenith by then, and considered. At his back lay Esdragon—Kess had certainly not returned to Keverne. Somewhere on his left hand must lie Crogen, where she had suggested he go when he recovered. So he could rule out that direction, as well.

They had not been on a road, the last day they had ridden together—they had parted company with it a dozen leagues beyond the burned inn. The country was then and had remained fairly open, rolling hills that sported trees only along the river courses. Less need for roads there, and few folk about to make use of them. Kess could have taken any route that pleased her.

And, it soon appeared, conceal her passage by means of those powers she had inherited. Leith thought he should have been able to make out a hoofprint or two, even after several days, but he could not—'twas as if he were the first horseman ever to venture that way. The turf was unmarked, the distant hills gave him no hint of a likely direction, for he had no idea what lay beyond any of them.

Kess had been deliberately imprecise about her destination. She'd cleverly left him without hope of guessing where to start his search. Leith had no map, had not even a notion of how the land about him lay. The Berianas? Only a name, to him. Leith could see no mountains, even when he risked standing in his stirrups to gain extra height. They weren't close, and he'd stumble across a dragon's treasure by chance more likely than find the Berianas by design. His only hope was actually to follow Kess, and he couldn't do that, if he couldn't detect a single track where he *knew* she had ridden.

Illusion, Leith guessed. What was it Kess had said? That she saw hidden things, could hide things that should be seen? Like hiding a sand dune under a hill of sharp green glass? She'd claimed that for her work.

But that illusion had deceived him only till he got sand into his right eye and by chance looked at the hill while squinting through his green left eye . . . Following the thread of the notion, Leith closed his right eye, shutting out part of the afternoon, and peered again at the grass, leaning over Valadan's shoulder. The action made his gut twist and his head buzz, but he ignored the discomforts and watched the ground. Valadan jigged under him.

Now he saw the moon shapes that shod hooves had cut into the soft turf. They'd have been less obvious—and he might have missed them—if Kess had ridden away from him at a walk, but plainly she had sent the bay off at a hasty gallop. The tracks were not making for Crogen.

Leith loosened his reins, and Valadan bounded joyfully forward.

Kess reined in at the top of the hill, allowing her horse a moment to catch its breath before starting the long descent. She looked about her—cloud shadows slipped over the grass-covered hills, and the grass danced in the wind—ripples of green, brown, purple, looking like a sea on the land. Her spirits soared, high as the white-tail hawk that circled above her. She answered its thin cry with one of her own and urged the horse down the green slope.

She did not fear to be alone, that night beside her flickering fire. To be alone was to be free—free of whispers, of insults unspoken but plain, of rules and chaperones and duties. No Betsan to guard her behavior. No Brychan to set another's order to her days. The only checks on her now were of her own choosing.

Now, if only she could be free of the visions, as well . . .

The campfire flared as a drop of fat—she had shot a duck while passing a bit of marsh—dripped onto the coals. In the brief brightness, Kess saw the white waves that crashed against Keverne's lower walls whenever there was a storm and a flooding tide. She saw gulls flying, desperately seeking a course of safety between waves and sheer stone walls. Within those walls—which were no barrier to her magical sight—a small woman roved as desperately as the gulls, seeking a way out of her gray cage . . .

She could not see the woman's face, but it might have been her own. The image faded. Kess was gazing at the spitted duck, black and nearly inedible.

* * *

It was difficult to ride holding one eye tightly closed. Leith's left eye kept wanting to close too, out of sympathy or weariness. His right eye kept trying to pop open, and Leith found the resulting change in vision disorienting. He tried pressing his hand over his right eye, but that made for awkward riding, put him off his balance when he could least afford such a handicap.

And watching the ground closely while Valadan hurtled over it was proving less than practical. Leith grew dizzy and, after he twice nearly tumbled out of the saddle, decided he would be best off if he checked the trail only at intervals—with special attention to those places where a hill or a stream might have been used to further confuse Kess' trail. In the main, Kess seemed not to have availed herself of such local opportunities. She had set a more or less straight course, likely assuming Leith would never stumble across it out of the myriad possibilities, that the simplest concealments would suffice. Valadan's tireless stride ate up the leagues in steady pursuit.

Leith paused a time or two to rest him—but the stallion was never winded, or damp other than about his saddle girth. Always he was eager to be off again, pawing and tugging at the reins, bowing his neck and dragging Leith forward in the saddle until he let him continue. Kess had said that a wizard had charmed down the wind to sire him—perchance that one statement of hers was wholly true.

Valadan would have been willing to run the night out, but Leith was fearful of missing Kess' trail after dark. The country was higher and drier, traces of her passage were therefore fewer and slighter, even to his undeceived left eye. Such traces were generally where Leith would have expected to find them, but when night settled in his sight would be nearly useless, and he could go far wrong and never know till 'twas too late.

Anyway, Kess had at least two days' start on them. Probably three. There was no way they'd catch her after mere hours, no matter how willing or fleet Valadan was. Leith decided to bed down, get a night's rest, and be back in the saddle at first light. They'd overtake Kess in the long run.

Just as he was starting to swing down out of the saddle, his nose caught a whiff of woodsmoke.

It couldn't be—Valadan nudged his shoulder sharply as his boots reached the ground, and Leith staggered. He reexamined his doubt. They had made good speed, but even so could never have gone so far as Kess had, unless she had for some unknown reason sat still for a whole day—or more. And would Kess, who had hidden her trail past any hope of his pursuit, forget that smoke can be both seen and scented?

She might, Leith supposed. If it was impossible for him to have caught up with her, surely Kess would think that, too. She wouldn't have to worry about him for days. If it *was* Kess.

A horse snorted a question. Leith startled—the beast had been just the other side of a bush not ten yards away, invisible till it flung its head up into view. A dark horse, brown or bay, with a wide splash of white on its big face. It had a familiar look about it.

It should—he'd been grooming it, saddling it, following it for several days, bar these last few.

Impossible, Leith told himself, afraid to trust his legs while he made a closer inspection. It *couldn't* be Kess' bay gelding. Valadan was a swift horse, but *no* horse could make up two days' start, no horse could run that fast—

Valadan dipped his head modestly and begged Leith to scratch the spots where the bridle leather had made his skin itch, behind his ears, along his cheeks. He seemed amused by Leith's confusion.

Leith observed to himself that Kess might have traded her horse for a fresher mount. Or he might have, in his distracted state, lost track of how long he'd been riding—or overestimated how long he'd lain ill. Such comforting lies let him gather his wits, try to settle on a prudent course of action.

First, he'd reconnoiter. Make certain he'd found Kess and not merely her horse, separated from her by design or some mischance. Horses *did* stray, *were* sometimes stolen! Leith used the bushes for cover, and followed the tang of woodsmoke in the evening air.

The fire was of modest size, laid on a bare spot of ground handy to a willow-fringed stream but enough distant to escape the inevitable water-bred insects. Through a thin screen of brush, Leith watched Kess gathering up her cooking gear. There was no doubt that it was she—the twilight held good long enough to show him her face, when her silver braid alone would have been sufficient evidence for him.

The bay gelding whinnied. Valadan silenced it with a commanding snort. Leith watched as Kess looked up with some alarm at the exchange—then relaxed when there was no further noise. She should, he thought disapprovingly, have been warier of some harm befalling her only transportation—then Leith decided he should be grateful for her lapse. If she'd been more watchful, she might easily have ambushed him.

Well, he'd found her, whether sooner than he expected or not. Now he faced choices—he could either make himself known at once, or shadow Kess in secret for a few days. Either course presented risks, chiefly because Kess had that bow—a weapon she could use at a distance. Leith had no doubt that a woman capable of feeding him poison for breakfast would as readily shoot an arrow into him. And that Kess would likely shoot to maim, not kill, was hardly a comfort.

She was making for the stream, metal plate in hand. Certainly she'd wash it—possibly she'd want to wash herself, as well, get the dust out of her hair. She was loosening her braid as she walked . . . and she had left her bow behind, he could see it atop her piled blankets. Likewise her sword and her dagger—close enough to the stream, if needed, or so Kess would suppose.

Leith made his decision. When Kess returned, wringing her hair, he was sitting at her fireside, brewing himself a pot of mint tea. Her bow still lay where Kess had left it—but the bowstring was coiled up safe in Leith's pocket.

"How did you find me?" Kess shrilled.

"More to the point, *why* did I?" Leith asked wearily. He stirred a spoonful of honey into his tea and breathed into the mug, cooling the brew till he could sip comfortably.

Kess flung down her cleaned plate, which made a dull ringing sound before it rolled into the fringe of the fire. "I fed you enough wild lettuce and colic root to bellyache an ox! You *can't* have shaken it off this fast! You shouldn't have been able to ride for days—"

"I wasn't," Leith conceded. "It seems your father bred fast horses." He sipped his tea and sighed. He'd just chanced across the mint, but it was most soothing to his still-unsettled stomach. On occasion, accident outperformed design. He wasn't sure he'd have trusted a brew from any of the packets he'd discovered in Kess' gear, though each was labeled and most seemed innocent.

Kess' slender form seemed scarcely able to contain her anger. Her wet hair all but crackled as she flung it back out of her way, a curtain of white fire, shedding diamonds. Leith saw her eyeing the bow, taking note of where her other weapons should have lain. He'd tied her sword to Valadan's saddle for safekeeping and put her dagger through his own belt. He intended to unsaddle the stallion, of course, but for the moment he didn't care to allow Kess access to anything more lethal than the teakettle.

"We had a bargain," Leith pointed out mildly.

"We had no such thing, you ill-wished peasant!"

"You pledged you'd marry the man who brought back your ring," Leith said, as if she might have forgotten.

"Dead men don't plight troths," Kess hissed.

"Kess, I don't want to trap you." Leith set his cup down and looked at her earnestly, green eye and black. "I just want my curse lifted, if such a thing is possible. I can't live on the run, watching people's lives fall to ruin just because I stayed near them too long! I'm going with you to find your mother—I have to."

"I don't want you with me!"

Leith touched a hand to his stomach and almost smiled. "You made that clear. I'll do my own cooking from here on. But I'm going with you."

"You'll have to sleep," Kess said sweetly, her eyes deadly. "You might find you sleep *very* soundly."

Valadan strolled into the circle of the firelight, nosing for tidbits. Leith poured a dollop of honey onto his palm, let the stallion lick the sticky sweet before he arose to begin unsaddling him. He turned his back casually on Kess as he stood but kept watch on Valadan's ears, and knew when she got to her feet. Leith bent over the buckles of the girth as he spoke.

"If you wanted to kill me, I'd be feeding the carrion crows by now. You could have put a death-angel mushroom into that stew—"

He caught motion out of the tail of his left eye and stepped back as Valadan's haunch came toward him. Leith looked over the stallion's back at Kess, still brandishing the stick of firewood she'd intended to brain him with. Valadan, ears pinned, swung his head at her, his threat implicit.

After a few heartbeats, Kess flung the brand away, into the darkness. It thudded on the ground. "Call him off."

"I don't have to," Leith said, setting the saddle down. "He won't hurt you. And you won't hurt me." He smiled. "You know, it's a funny thing—horses hardly sleep at all, and not nearly so sound as people."

Behind a Fall of Water

THEREAFTER, LEITH COOKED his own meals. He supposed Kess had accepted his stubborn refusal to be driven off—but why take chances? Particularly as her acceptance had been forced. Mostly the fare was fish, because if Leith was unlucky he was still skilled in the fisherman's art, island-bred as he was. He caught enough most days to make up for not allowing Kess her bowstring back for hunting small game. It was still too soon for that much trust. Meals were monotonous, but neither of them went hungry.

Fish were easy to come by—they were working their way upstream along the bank of a river Kess named the Est, and they stayed by it for nearly a fortnight. Kess said they would cross it eventually, but it was deep, wide, and unfordable until one came close to its mountain source. Its tributary streams would have been reckoned major rivers elsewhere—luckily most of those drained lands on the farther bank.

Leith guessed Kess was telling the truth about the Est's impassibility—he could never have flung a pebble from one bank to the other, and he heartily agreed about not attempting crossing till conditions improved. His luck would certainly ensure him a thorough soaking—catching dinner did, two times out of three.

Kess' back—which was all Leith lately saw of her—was straight as the quiver of useless arrows she carried strapped to it. Leith had no notion what signs she followed to guide her quest, but he was coming to suspect she might not be altogether sure of them. Kess would not deign to answer his questions, so Leith read what he could from the tension in her shoulders. Her braid of hair switched slowly from side to side, like a cat's tail—that only indicated her horse's motion, not Kess' mood, but her moods were never long secret.

When they halted for an hour's rest and grazing at sun-high, Leith knew better than to intrude upon Kess' ill temper. While she stared gloomily into space, he put the finishing touches on a flute he had begun to carve some days past, after happening upon a likely alder branch while fishing. He had burned carefully through it from one end to the other, using a twig heated in the fire, put holes in the correct places on the tube thus made—and in the end he could play a tune to honor his Lady each moonrise. Possibly Kess would prefer a sweet air to his quiet chanting. Possibly she would not. Leith blew a few notes, testing, made a run of melody like a ripple of birdsong.

Kess stirred. "What's that for?"

Leith made a finicky adjustment to one of the holes, then put his knife away. "My Lady is almost at the end of Her cycle. This tune tells how I lament Her passing, how glad I will be when She is reborn."

"Is this besides the chanting?" Kess narrowed her eyes.

"It replaces it," Leith assured her, with haste.

Disarmed, but not happy about it, Kess stirred pebbles with her booted toe. "Did anyone follow you? Or weren't you noticing?"

While he'd been on his own, he supposed she must mean. "I wasn't feeling very well," Leith pointed out reasonably. "I didn't see anyone." Actually, he hadn't thought to look.

"Because I hid *my* trail. Not much point to it, with you blundering along after me, leaving sign a blind man could read."

"I never saw anyone," Leith protested again.

"They're back there," Kess insisted, turning her knife hilt so that it flashed the sun. "Nonetheless."

"Who?" Against sense, Leith found he was searching the landscape, expecting folk to appear out of it.

"Probably the escort Brychan wanted to send with me. The one I took you in place of. Or one of my cousins—my aunt wants to be sure I don't escape before she can marry me to him."

Leith decided it would be unwise of him to point out that no one could have followed him had Kess not left him behind as she had. At least she was consenting to speak to him once more, however unpleasant the track of the conversation.

* * *

Gradually the broad river valley became a canyon—the walls rose on their left hand as they rode, forested in places with thick stands of larches and conifers. The river lay just below them on their other side, but Leith was certain that it came right over the trail they rode in times of heavy rainfall—he could see where the water had carved the base of the slope, where not a tree was to be found, but only quick-growing small plants, scrubby bushes, annual herbs.

Leith scanned the sky, wanting to find it cloudless. There was nowhere for them to go but back the way they'd come, should the river rise over its banks. Pointing this out to Kess seemed risky—he held his peace and kept his worries about what would happen if his luck came into play in the safe privacy of his own skull.

They were picking their way through rocks—small ones underfoot, lying between larger boulders so close-set that the horses could not always find a way between, but were forced to scramble over, hooves ringing and scraping. There was little dirt to anchor vegetation—the river regularly swept all that away, Leith was sure—just the jumble of rocks, tending steeply uphill. Kess' mount proceeded cautiously, and Valadan followed in a like manner, sure of foot. Again Leith fretted over what would happen should a hard rain fall upstream. He did not like to think of retracing such a difficult route in haste. He liked even less the realization that the rain he dreaded might already be falling, ahead and unseen.

"This is worse than your Hill of Glass," he observed. "At least that was only sand underneath."

"And still none of those fools made it to the top," Kess said scornfully. She seemed to have forgotten that she'd chosen the task with the intent that it be unachievable.

"You should have brought your suitors along, to test them," Leith suggested. "You'd have been rid of them soon enough."

Kess drew rein and held a hand up for Leith to halt, as well.

Hooves ceased to clatter upon the rocks, the echoes died away, and the loudest sound was the rush of the river just below them. A few birdcalls cut the air, sweet and sharp. "What?" Leith asked.

"Listen." Kess ordered sharply.

There *was* another sound, very faint, somewhere ahead. *Thunder.*

Leith's heart misgave him. He wondered whether he had somehow attracted the rain by dreading it so steadily. A new facet of his curse, or had it always worked so, unbeknownst to him?

He looked back, calculating the distance they had covered on the narrow, twisty way. Two nights they had camped right by the water, almost in it, having no choice. That meant at least a day to ride back to safety—on such a trail they dared hope for no greater speed. Rain would not raise the river level *instantly*; they might surely hope for the hours they'd need . . .

"We're nearly there," Kess announced, unperturbed. "Come on."

Leith stared. It was no use—strain his eyes as he might, he saw no sign of a crossing. The far bank was just that—far. Even had there been room to make a running start, Valadan could not have overleapt it, and Leith would never have thought to ask him to. The channel was deep, running fast, and full of rocks as the trail. How was Kess sure they were near the place she sought?

She was already some yards ahead. He'd have to catch up first, if he intended to convince her to turn about. She wouldn't heed arguments shouted at her back. Leith put heels to Valadan's sides and set off in Kess's wake.

The matter began to seem urgent—the thunder was louder, the storm was closing in, probably sweeping down the valley. Soon it would be right over the top of them, and rain would make the trail treacherous ere it flooded it. Or lightning could strike them. Leith urged Valadan to a greater effort, up the winding trail at reckless speed, which the stallion willingly obliged.

A dozen bounds later, they nearly collided with Kess. She was dismounted, standing on a boulder that was taller than her horse and gave her a superior vantage point.

"There!" she declared, pleased, handing her reins over to Leith as if he were a laggard groom.

Leith stood in his stirrups to see where she pointed. The bay sidestepped just as he did, its suddenly tight reins pulling him off balance. Leith lurched forward and bruised his ribs on the pommel as he fell back into his saddle, but he thought he'd seen something uptrail before he was distracted. A whiteness, like the crest of a breaking wave.

"What is it?" He shouted the question. The thunder was very loud.

Kess made no answer but climbed back into her saddle, retrieved her reins with a jerk, and led on. Soon they were close enough to see the answer she had not offered, close enough to be soaked by spray—but they could not discuss it. There was little chance they'd hear one another over the roar of the waterfall pounding before them. Kess retreated a few dozen paces, and they picketed the horses in a ferny spot, where the spray of river water made a constant dew.

"The headwaters of the Est," Kess shouted, because the noise of the water was still great.

Leith nodded, looking with interest at the source of the mighty river. It was a long and narrow fall, like a white horse's tail swishing down the lofty cliff. He was relieved beyond measure that they didn't seem to be in immediate danger of being drowned by an unlucky cloudburst. What he had heard as thunder was merely the ever-present voice of the waterfall.

"This is where we cross," Kess informed him.

Startled, Leith looked from the waterfall to her face, then back again. She *had* said "cross." He was certain of that. The fall's white tail hung over the top of a sheer cliff. Assuming 'twas narrow enough above to be jumped over, he still did not see any way of getting their horses to the top, and he thought he would not have relished the climb himself.

"Exactly how?" he inquired, loudly, so she'd hear him.

"We go behind the water."

Leith was sure that was what she'd said, improbable as it sounded. Else his ears were deafened by the rush of the water and his brain was making up nonsensical translations of words it could not distinguish.

Kess beckoned and led him close to the base of the falls, where spray nurtured ferns and slippery mosses, which rendered the footing treacherous. Leith placed his boots with greatest care and managed not to tumble into the river, though he did bang a knee against a boulder when an unreliable rock rolled under his foot and threw him sideways. He twisted one hand into the ferns, grasping stems for a safety grip. Small use, he thought—with his luck he'd probably just uproot them.

The water fell in a solid-seeming column. Leith knew that it was *not* solid, and guessed it might be more of a curtain of water, which they could pass through if not see through. But when he held a stick out into it, the branch was torn from his grasp and whirled away, lost to sight into the roiling white water of the pool at the fall's base.

"I don't think so!" he shouted to Kess.

Her eyes narrowed, and Leith flinched. "What do you know

about it? Cook yourself supper, and get some sleep—this will take some time."

Leith kept one eye on Kess as he cooked himself a pottage of grain and dried beef. She had left him to untack and feed the horses, pausing only to snatch up one of her packs before retiring to the top of a tallish boulder broad as a cottage, some dozen yards from the falls. Twilight deepened, the last glow faded from the sky, and night fell, but Kess did not withdraw from her perch. She had a fire up there—not, Leith thought, for supper-cooking. He could smell herbs being burned, when the wind was right. He thought he heard chanting, as well, a patter of high-pitched words above the deep voice of the falls.

His own office was hours away—it would be some while ere his Lady raised Her face high enough to peer over the high canyon walls. And She was far on the wane now, an ancient sickle of silver among the stars. Leith regretted that, as he gazed at the first points of light in the sweep of periwinkle overhead—the waterfall's pall of mist, ever-present, seemed likely to produce the rare moonbow, the sign that his Lady of the Night was in no wise inferior to the sun when it came to crafting beauty.

But a waning moon would not shed sufficient light to produce the bow—and if they were yet encamped by the waterfall when the moon came full again, Leith thought his Lady's power would be more than offset by Kess' fury.

High atop her rock, Kess bent to her work. She drew lines on the mossy stone with handfuls of dust, pointing upstream, curving them to mimic the river's course. At farthest end, she had laid her fire, which now blazed merrily and stank bitterly. Leith had supposed correctly—she was not cooking.

She spared a thought for her father, to wonder how *he* had crossed the Est, if he had used this same route. She knew of no other—but her father would have worked no spell such as she attempted. Perhaps he had not needed witchcraft. Rainfall had been heavier earlier in the season. Natural conditions could have favored a crossing.

Kess smiled. More than likely, Leith assumed she was attempting to dry up the flow of the river, so they might scramble across its muddy bed. He'd never suspect she was bent on doing the very opposite—*increasing* the flow over the falls.

Imagining the expression on his long face distracted her a moment, quite pleasantly.

Work still awaited her. Kess drew out a branch of fern and dipped its feathery tip into a bowl of river water. Weather charms were common among her people, though seldom in Esdragon did anyone choose to make rain, which came most days whether one willed it or no. Still, Kess knew a rite for producing it. Betsan's educational offerings had been thorough, though the old lady never suspected just how apt a pupil she possessed. Kess would not require a wind, loosed by undoing knots tied into a kerchief to contain its blustery power after it had been whistled up. She needed no lightning, no thunder, no hailstones. Simple rain would serve her need, and she knew how to get it.

She used the fern branch to sprinkle water onto the dry rock, over the dust, into the fire. She said words of control and binding, very rapidly so that the syllables fell quick and sudden as fat raindrops. She spattered her miniature of the river, to indicate where she wished the rain to fall. When she reached the fire, she let drop after drop fall into it, till the flames were finally quenched, and the clouds over the river were served notice of what she desired—a hard, drenching rain, dropped on the country immediately above the Est's falls.

Leith was playing a slow air on his flute when he realized that Kess was descending from her rock—cursing the difficulty of doing so in full darkness. He arose and made haste to assist her, only to have Kess stomp on his upreaching hand. He got her safely to the ground and nursed his pinched fingers in secret so as to escape her mirth over his clumsiness.

"We need to be ready at first light," Kess informed him, stepping toward the fire and spreading her hands to it, to warm her wet fingers. "It will take awhile for the rainfall to affect the falls, but we don't want to miss the best moment—"

"Rain?" Leith asked, forgetting his fingers. His expression was every bit as delightful as Kess had anticipated. His slanty eyebrows rose nearly to his hairline, and his long jaw dropped.

"Upstream. To swell the falls," Kess said smugly, not explaining further.

Leith couldn't see what use a greater volume of water would be. Surely a stream—any stream—was easier crossed in time of drought? Why had Kess been using charms to provoke rain instead? It made no sense, but when he pressed for an explanation, Kess only laughed—and pointed out pleasantly that his Lady had risen unacknowledged, behind his back.

Dawn showed the falls unchanged visibly from the previous evening. Leith held another stick out and soon lost it to the force of the dropping water. Kess stood by the horses, the patient one for once—though she snapped at Leith for playing obviously futile games.

Come sun-high, the volume of water was rapidly increasing. Nor was it so pure as it had been. Where the pool at the base of the falls had been a deep green like summer woodland, it was now a frothy brown, resembling ale from an inept brewmaster.

Kess spared no attention on color changes in the pool. Instead, she kept her eyes fixed on the cliff the fall sprang out over. Leith shivered in the dampness and watched her watching, wondering what she was expecting to see. The horses stamped and shifted restlessly, hooves scraping the rocks, harness jangling. Time crawled by.

"That should do." Kess took hold of her reins and led the bay gelding straight for the falls.

Leith scrambled to his feet. He was about to call a question, but Kess was already disappearing into the spray, dragging the horse after her. There was no time for hesitation—Leith followed as swiftly as he dared, lest he miss the way. Nerved for the worst, he stepped into what proved to be only a thin curtain of spray.

He realized—at last—the purpose of the rainfall. As the volume of water increased, the falls were pushed out farther and farther over the top of the cliff. A light flow of water trickled down the face of the stone, but a heavy flow arched out *over* it, leaving a space between rock and water. They were indeed crossing the river—crossing *under* rather than over or through.

It was far from an easy passage, and not one a sane man would choose, Leith thought, stumbling through slippery dimness. Small wonder Kess had chosen it so happily. The way was narrow, damp, and chill. He could see his breath in the water-filtered light. There were pools remaining underfoot—some of them hip-deep as Leith inevitably discovered. None of the rocks was dry, and most of them were slick. The loud roar of the water falling just beside them precluded conversation or warnings of troublesome spots. Its pounding filled the air, vibrated the rocks underfoot. There was so much moisture in the air, an incautiously deep breath set Leith coughing till he could barely keep his feet. At his shoulder, Valadan snorted to clear his own nostrils. They were breathing as much water as air.

As they neared the far side, a bulge in the rock forced them into the actual edge of the falls. There was coarse sand underfoot, worse by far than the slippery rocks, for it flowed back and forth with the water and seemed bottomless in unexpected spots.

Kess lost her balance and was unable to keep a firm grip on the bay's reins as she struggled. The gelding seized the opportunity to give way to panic and tried to charge back the way he had come. Kess clung to the ends of the reins until she was dragged back into the sand, where she fell with a splash as the horse tore free.

Leith found himself caught between Valadan and the frightened gelding, his only choices to be slammed into the cliffside by a horse or to be shoved out under the falls. He elected the falls, and dodged that way to avoid the onrushing gelding. Valadan went past him, lunging at the bay, teeth bared—and the bay did turn, more terrified of facing the stallion than of braving the loud water.

Doubling back, plunging hastily through a space no wider than it had been an instant before, Kess' horse crowded Leith again. In fact, its barrel brushed him solidly, while its near hip spun him around. He flailed back, trying not to fall, stepped backward into the bottomless sand, and lost his sense of direction entirely. He struggled to get out from under the waterfall, unable to stand because he could find no firm ground, swallowing water in great unwelcome gulps, unsure whether he was moving toward safety or toward the greater peril of the main part of the falls. Would he know only when the current snatched him? He could hear the pounding water with his whole body, not only his ears alone, but could not give a direction to it.

His clutching fingers tangled in some sort of underwater weed. Leith took a firm grip, hoping to pull himself out of the water, hold himself in place till he got his bearings. At least he wouldn't be swept to his death, if he could hold on.

Horrified, he felt the weed pulling away from him, and he knew the current must have him after all, despite his care. He gripped harder, more desperately—and realized that the weeds he had caught hold of were really the hairs of Valadan's long tail.

Leith located solid rock by banging his knees into it, and managed to get his boots wholly onto it. He coughed, and spat out water and sand, wiped both his eyes, and coughed again, thinking his ribs would snap under the strain, but helpless to stop or even control the spasm.

Through water-bleared eyes, he saw Valadan, head turned back to regard him with bemusement. Leith hastily let go of the stallion's tail. Just ahead of Valadan stood the dripping gelding. Beside her horse, Kess was no less bedraggled—there was no inch of her that was not streaming water or nearly liquid sand.

"They do say witches have trouble crossing running water," she observed, and coughed on the last word.

But Leith had an uneasy suspicion that his ill luck had commenced to spread once more—like ripples on a still pond.

A Crystal to See By

On the far side of the waterfall, their first priority was to find a sheltered spot where a fire could dry wet clothing. Alas, all was rock and mud, inhospitable and exposed, though overhung with trees and shrubs. The wind picked up. The only flat spot to be seen lay directly in the spray zone from the falls, and from the look of things, Kess' rainfall was still lashing the watershed beyond. There was nothing for it; they must climb out of the Est's gorge to seek shelter.

The first two ways they assayed proved impassible. Leith suspected recent landslips, and feared they'd be caught in another, before Valadan shoved through a screen of fern and put them on a sheep track that took them up the cliff in a few terrifying scrambles. Rain pelted them, the wet wind lashed them. Kess looked distressed, unable to discover a means of calling off her spell.

After a miserable hour, a copse of pines promised shelter and fuel for a fire. They dismounted, unsaddled, made a fire and a camp of sorts. Leith, worn out from the trek and his earlier struggle to avoid drowning, fell asleep the instant he was more warm than cold—not caring whether his luck insisted on the fire's setting his clothing alight once it had done drying it.

He awoke with a start, uncertain what might have disturbed him, a crick in his neck and both his eyes burning from too brief a sleep. For a moment he had no idea where he was.

On the far side of the fire's glowing embers sat Kess, staring down at her cupped hands.

Leith strove to blink sleep from his sore eyes. Lest he startle Kess into an angry rebuke, he sat up cautiously, wincing as a score of new bruises introduced themselves to him.

He need not have been so careful—Kess paid him no attention. She never once lifted her eyes from the object that lay in her palm.

Leith cleared his throat tentatively. That got him no response either, so he leaned closer, craning his neck to see what she cupped that held her so rapt. The fire's dimming glow twinkled upon it—a palmful of common sand, with some bigger bits lying at its center. Leith knit his brows. He could have gathered such treasure from any fold of his clothing. Why did she stare at sand? Why would anyone?

All at once Kess came back to herself—and whether truly startled or merely irritated, threw up her hands and leapt to her feet. The sand, flung, went mostly into Leith's face, probably not by accident or even ill luck.

"How dare you—"

Leith tried blindly to get to his feet, his eyes tearing so that he couldn't tell whether Kess truly intended the violence her tone promised. He staggered back, tripped over his saddle, and measured his length backward on the soggy ground.

"I only wanted to see what you were looking at," he protested, rolling to be safer from her boot toes—which the experience of the past few mornings told him bruised his ribs most effectively. Thus Kess woke him, if by mischance he overslept her.

"It's none of your business!"

"It was certainly uninteresting." Leith, having rolled right to his feet, began ejecting the sand from his clothing. There was a lot under his collar, sure to be a misery every time he turned his head. Barely dry, he found he was longing for a bath. It had been the same way after the shipwreck, he recalled.

"The moon's come up," Kess informed him nastily. "Isn't there some nonsense you have to babble? You're getting awfully careless about it."

Leith, having given the sky an involuntary, guilty glance, turned his still-running eyes back to Kess. His Lady was worn away to the merest slice of Herself, and She had not quite cleared the hill on the horizon. "It's not nonsense," he said in a hurt tone. "It is a courtesy. My Lady does not forget me, and it would be rude of me to fail to greet Her in the proper manner."

"You know, she rises every night whether you're here to say hello or not." Kess settled herself by the fire once more, happy to take the edge off her mood with a philosophical discussion she was certain to win.

"I perform my duty wherever I am. I am not required to concern myself with what happens in places where I'm not."

"She doesn't pay you any heed!" Kess snapped.

"Neither do you," Leith pointed out.

Kess' face took on a dangerous aspect. "Why should I?" she asked, with deadly grace.

"You *don't* have to," Leith fed a few sticks to the fire and wondered whether he had gathered wood enough to last out the night. If he hadn't, he'd hear about it, without doubt. And be sent out in the blackness to rectify the error, with Kess doubtless hoping he'd miss his way and fall into the river. "It's certainly none of *my* business if you doze off staring at a handful of sand. Or if you really don't know where we're going, or have the least idea where your mother is. *I* insisted on coming with you. You tried hard enough to send me back—most folk would have stopped short of poison—so you don't bear any responsibility."

"I *do* know where my mother is!" Kess insisted hotly. "Or I will—"

"These mountains we've crossed into—the Berianas?" Leith waved a hand at the great dark that surrounded the yellow circle of firelight. "This is where your father was headed, isn't it? And that's as far as the trail goes—that's all you know." It was all she'd told him—for reasons he guessed at.

"I *will* know more!" Kess shoved a stick into the fire. Leith suspected she'd have been delighted to do the same with him. Sparks rose into the dark, winked out.

"How?" he asked, figuring that at least he'd be ready for her. He was at a disadvantage every time she caught him by surprise. Next time, her weapon might be more devious than poisoned stew.

"If you listened, you'd know. I told you, I can see things, hidden things. Not only when I'm close to them, not like just seeing through a third-rate glamor, knowing glass is only sand."

Leith shrugged away her disparagement. He waited patiently, forcing Kess to continue.

"I see things in windows, in mirrors, in jewels, in water—in crystals. There are crystals in sand, you know," she added, as if to an idiot child.

Leith blinked. "You weren't asleep? You were having some

kind of vision?" Suddenly he wasn't sure that he wouldn't prefer that she'd been lying. If she *could* see the things she
claimed, who knew where such sight stopped? For all he was
seeking a witch, he was nervous of arcane powers close at
hand.

"The crystals in sand are too small to use," Kess admitted
reluctantly. "I can see only tiny flashes. A face, a hand—I
can't tell whose, or where, or when. But if I had something
bigger to look into, something that didn't shift and flicker like
a flame does, I *know* I could use it to find my mother—"

"Kess—" Leith discovered he was more frightened *for* Kess
than *of* her. He realized just how deeply he had believed that
she *did* know what she was about, even if she schemed to exclude him from it. He'd trusted her, however foolishly. The
middle of an uninhabited wilderness was not the spot he'd
have chosen to lose his illusions.

"*Listen to me!* There are bits of crystal in the sand. They
wash downstream, like any other rock. So, if we go upstream,
above the falls, we'll find the place they come from. And we'll
find whole crystals, big enough to look into."

Perhaps she wasn't mad after all. Leith supposed he could
hope for that, having so few other options at his command.
None, in fact.

The rugged Berianas might be uninhabited, but they were in
no wise free of human influence. As they proceeded along the
course of one of the Est's tributary streams, Leith saw indi-
cations that groups of men had camped in some of the
meadows—there were weathered remains of fires, bigger than
a hunter would have laid for a single night's rest. There were
trails, overgrown but obviously cleared at one time, too broad
to have been made by the hooves of mountain sheep, still bearing the hoof scars of iron-shod pack beasts.

Such signs pointed the way to their goal—a narrow opening,
timber-shored, hard by great heaps of loose rock. Leith poked
his nose cautiously into the dark doorway, wary of spiderwebs,
whilst Kess examined the mounds of shattered debris outside it.

"What did they mine here?" Leith asked, abandoning his ex-
ploring to join hers. He tripped over the half-rotted remains of
a carrying basket, a web of spokes and straps and splinters.

"Gold, probably." Kess sifted a handful of gravel from the
base of a rock heap. "Maybe silver. There are certainly crystals
here, but that wasn't what the miners were after. This isn't—

wasn't—a gem mine. They wouldn't have smashed the rock so. You don't find rubies and sapphires in company with silver except at a jewelers, and you don't risk destroying them. The rock was just trash to them, to be crushed and hauled out." She let the sand fall. One day rain and the nearby stream would send it to the Est. "I'm not going to find what I need here—I'll have to go inside for whole crystals."

"Inside?" Leith looked apprehensively at the narrow slot that was the mine's mouth. The yellow sunlight penetrated no more than a dozen feet—and that was therefore as far as he'd ventured. Beyond lay absolute, uninviting darkness.

"Certainly. Of course, you can stay out here if you like," Kess offered generously.

And be left again, Leith guessed. Depend on it, she'd find a way, if he let her out of his sight. "I'll come with you," he said cheerfully, and set about making Valadan and the gelding comfortable.

He could hope they wouldn't be long inside. Leith eased the girths but left the horses saddled—they'd be less likely to stray if they were not completely at their ease, he thought. Though he supposed Valdan would keep the bay close by in any case. He had found, days past, that there was no need to hobble either horse. Valadan stayed within call and saw to it that the bay did likewise.

There was the stream to give them water, with a small patch of grass or two along its banks, and hardy plants scattered all through the rocky place. The horses would be safe and comfortable for the hour or so he and Kess would be underground. Surely it would be no longer than that. There was no reason it should be.

Kess had discovered a few dry sticks of wood leaning just within the opening, and was putting one to its intended purpose—with a bit of rag and some of their cooking oil, she was fashioning it into a torch. Leith followed suit, though he would have been happier to find lanterns, or candles. While Kess made a second brand, he filled the waterskin and shouldered one of his packs.

Kess looked up from her fire-steel as he rejoined her, but did not leave off striking sparks from a chunk flint to kindle her torch. "Sure you don't want to drag a horse along, too, to carry that load?"

"The water inside might not be good," he said. A trickle issued from the mine mouth, but it dwindled away ere it reached the stream. Probably just seepage, maybe tainted. "And there's no telling what we might want inside. Why have to come back after it?"

Kess evidently could not refute the speculation. Rising, she plunged at once into the mine mouth, not pausing to allow Leith to light his torch from hers till he protested twice.

He might just as well not have troubled over making or lighting the brand. Kess strode boldly ahead, well able to see where she was placing her booted feet—and all the while her torch was right in Leith's face as he followed, dazzling him at best, often outright blinding him. If he stayed close he risked being seared and singed, if he fell back he risked missteps on ground he could scarcely see.

Happily, the passage seemed to have been used to haul ore to the surface, and so had been well cleared to make the work easier. Possibly the miners had used carts and ponies—there was room enough to the sides if not so much overhead.

Save for a chance-fallen cobble or two, the shaft was as smooth as the best-kept road in Esdragon. The wooden props at the sides were carefully hewn and did not project out into the way. Leith ran his fingers lightly along the right-hand wall, feeling chisel cuts made by miners likely long dead.

There were not so many as he expected. In places there were none at all, and he realized that parts of the shaft were natural, a fissure through the rock. So the miners would have first found the mine, and as they worked it enhanced the underground path they found, then extended it in quest of ore.

Had they found all of it? Leith scanned the walls, the low ceiling, seeking a glitter in the rock. He could not expect to find gold nuggets for the plucking—the mine would hardly have been abandoned if it still produced treasure. Still, there might be riches within the walls, a king's ransom only inches away. Couldn't one buy a cure with gold? If only there were some way to get at it . . .

Despite that interesting avenue of dream, Leith was less and less happy about venturing where his Lady could not look upon him. He had never been deeper under the earth than the cellar where the priests put root vegetables for winter keeping, and the knowledge of the weight of the soil and rock over him was unexpectedly distressing. Each step downward increased his discomfort. Suppose his Lady forgot him, as he willfully removed himself from Her sphere of influence? Suppose She misunderstood his desertion of Her and became angry? It was only by Her grace that he, cursed and demon-marked, even drew breath . . . Leith shook his head helplessly, but the bleak worries had found a home, like bats in the darkness, and refused to be chased away by such simple means.

The air was still good, when they reached the first branching. In fact, a cool draft of it moved past them, seeking the mine mouth, making the torches stream. Kess hesitated a moment, then chose the right-hand way, which descended the more steeply. Leith could hear the drip of water somewhere to one side, though the rock underfoot was dry and the walls felt likewise to his fingers. Still he told himself he heard water, lest his imagination give a worse identity to the sound. He wished, too, that he had not thought of bats. The torches might disturb them, and as the ceiling was low they were not so very far overhead.

The way twisted, following the vein of the ore. The shaft dwindled to little more than shoulder-width for half a dozen feet, then broadened once more where it cut through softer rock. Leith was in awe of the work the mining must have required—he could hardly guess how long it would have taken him to hammer a basket of rock free, much less carve out a passage basket by basket, with pauses between to carry it away.

The vein of metal had split, or been thought to split—they were presented with another branching. Leith took careful note of it, for this time Kess chose the left-hand way—by what means she made that choice he could not guess—and he did not want to lose track of the turns they must repeat returning. A right. A left. So far, simple. But how far did Kess intend to venture? And was she choosing at random, or by some means he simply didn't understand?

Kess ducked beneath one of the lintels that propped the shaft's ceiling at intervals dictated by the rock above. Leith, blinded by her torch and not warned by his own, did not.

The unexpected impact on his forehead knocked him straight onto his back, and he banged his head a second time, on the tunnel floor. Bright sparks shot through the darkness arching over him. For an instant Leith had no notion what had happened, or where he was. He would have been hard put to state his own name.

Smoking torch held high, Kess turned to see what the noise had been and glared back at him. "Are you coming?"

Leith, lying very still so as not to invite further misfortune—

such as the roof's falling in on top of him—said nothing. In truth, he was thoroughly dazed, and had heard her question but dimly.

Kess sighed as she retraced another two steps. "Are you hurt?"

Leith turned his head to look at her as she jabbed a boot into his ribs. She was blurred at the edges—there were tears of pain in his eyes. His first sensation had been of surprise, and he was only just aware of how his head hurt. Kess' question seemed unnecessary. Leith lay back again, dizzy and disinclined to answer the obvious.

Kess poked him harder. "Are you intending to lie there all day?"

Leith shook his head resignedly, feeling grit against his scalp. He climbed to his feet with great care, leaning against the shaft's wall whilst Kess held the torch uncomfortably close and inspected him.

"Anything hurt besides that lump on your head?" she asked, frowning and poking.

Leith began to shake his head, then flinched as a spark jumped from the torch and stung his left cheek.

"Try watching where you're going," Kess ordered. She fumbled in one of her pockets. "What were you doing, anyway? Looking for gold?"

"You might have mentioned that the ceiling dropped," Leith complained, wondering whether she'd led him into the prop on purpose. He rubbed gingerly at the swelling on his forehead, which was coming up rapidly. Touching it hurt, but he persisted, wondering whether he was bleeding, and if the wood had left splinters.

Kess had found what she sought—a packet of herbs, by the pungent scent released as she first crushed it in her hand, then moistened it with water from the skin Leith had brought.

"You know, I don't think you're ill-wished at all." Kess pressed the damp packet against Leith's forehead and used his fingers to keep it in place whilst she tore a strip of cloth—from the tail of his shirt—to fashion a more permanent binding. "It's just plain, simple carelessness. You don't—"

"One word, that's all it would have needed," Leith said wearily. "'Duck.' 'Careful.' Or, if you were feeling uncommonly generous: 'Low spot.' That's only *two* words. You could have spared them—that's lots less than you're beating me with now." She'd almost tied his fingers into the bandage and seemed not to have noticed.

"I assume it's headache makes you so cross." Kess was already walking on, certainly not caring whether he followed or not. "So I'll make allowances."

By her tone, not many. Leith went after her while he could still see her torchlight, leaving his own smashed-out brand lying behind unnoticed. He just managed to avoid the next lintel, when he saw Kess' torch dip slightly to pass under it. She said no word at all of warning.

His bashed head throbbing and the wet herbs dripping water into his eyes, Leith took no special note of the next few moments of their journey into the mine. He strove to bear in mind that he was a good deal taller than Kess—it was possible he might need to duck even when she did not. The roof drew ever nearer to the floor—Leith learned to keep one hand on it as he went, so as to have some warning of changes beforetime, since Kess would plainly give him none. He avoided cracking his head a second time, though he tripped over debris unnoticed on the floor—a lintel had slipped and allowed a loose bit of roof to do likewise, and Leith had to scramble to keep his feet when he blundered into it.

There was just room to climb through between the roof still above and the roof now lying on the floor. Kess did, and Leith managed the passage in time to keep her torchglow in close sight. She never once looked back, though Leith supposed she could hear him well enough, as he slipped and cursed and sent rocks scattering.

The glow was faint, but it was nearer than Leith had supposed—he bumped against Kess as she knelt peering at something he could not make out. She shoved him and his apologies away irritably.

"Is it another roof fall?" Leith asked. That seemed likely, given the state of the rest of the shaft. Maybe they'd have to turn back.

Kess pulled the torch out of a slit in the wall. Its full light, though not so intense as it had been when fresh, still effectively blinded Leith—a point Kess seemed disinclined to note, though he yipped and put a hand to his face. "There's a whole wall of crystals inside," she announced.

Leith gave the opening his half-blinded attention at once. Kess held the torch behind him, for a wonder, and as his sight cleared he could see flashes of color from the walls within—which did indeed seem to be made entirely of crystals.

But the fissure he was looking through was less than two of his hand-spans wide.

"We can't fit through here," he pointed out, wondering if there might be crystals on the floor as well as the wall—he might be able to reach those, if he put his arm in up to his shoulder. He had long arms. If the floor wasn't too far away . . .

"*I* can get through," Kess replied imperiously. She was prepared to demonstrate, having already doffed cloak and belt, to stand as slim as she might. She looked like a blue reed, tipped with white gold.

Leith did not at all like the idea of Kess' venturing alone into that unknown space—not to mention taking their only light with her when she did it. He flexed his empty fingers—which should still have been gripping his torch if he hadn't been so careless with it. That he still had a sore head was no fit excuse.

"Be sure there's a floor," he urged Kess, as she began sliding through the fissure. She threw him an exasperated look and shoved the torch into the slit.

"*I'm* not the one with the supposed ill luck," she said, and followed the torch, sliding easily between the lips of stone.

He should have known—there was no way of stopping Kess, once she'd set her mind. And best he not think of how the stone hole had reminded him of a mouth, just then . . . "Find a good one," Leith suggested, and settled himself to wait in whatever slight comfort he could, in the narrow dark the torch left behind. He was yet somewhat troubled by dizziness, and his head hurt with each step he took, little flares of pain. Rest was very welcome.

Kess looked slowly over the wall of crystals, wanting to choose the best before she set to work with her dagger hilt, to knock her selection free. The largest were in a band roughly as high as her waist while she stood—toward roof and floor the quartz points were smaller, throwing back handfuls of torch-light. There were pictures only she could see in every sharp facet of every crystal, movement and bright colors that owed naught to the light she carried with her.

Over a running sea, a small ship made swift way. Her father stood braced in the prow, younger than she had ever known him, a sword at his belt, a shield on his back, his arm about a woman whose face Kess knew from her own mirror—the hair was black where her own was nearly white, but the narrow eyes, the arched nose—those were the same, and now Kess knew from whence she had inherited them: from Raichim, her mother. The vision faded as she was marveling at how young her mother was—no more than a girl, and tiny as a doll.

Another edge of clear crystal beckoned, showing Kess the wet towers of Keverne rising above the harbor. It was a night of wind and storm, when the sea spray was flung as high as the glazed windows of the duke's chamber and mingled with the rain to soak the heaps of wood laid ready for lighting on the headland—bonfires to celebrate the birth of the duke's heir. No hand put torch to those piles—it was not the custom to do so for a daughter, but only for the son her mother had not borne to her lord. Kess whimpered.

She turned her gaze swiftly to another facet—and saw a dark bay mare proudly refusing every earthly stallion but surrendering to the wind itself, and bearing that wind a foal black as the night sky, while a wizard stood watch in the darkness.

The tip of a crystal glowed, showing her the moonlight shining on a domed building, which slowly, silently, crumbled to the ground.

She turned her head an inch, feeling her spine creak with the effort. Kess saw her father's face, older now, stern. His lips opened, but it was not Kess' name he said. She turned again, now saw her formidable aunt, giving advice to the duke on what sort of wife he would be well advised to choose, now that he was in his right mind and not the thrall of some foreign witch.

A flash of green, and she beheld the sea breaking upon the shore and an exhausted man dragging himself out of it, onto the gray sand. He fell to his knees, then onto his face. Doggedly he lifted his head once more. He opened his eyes for an instant—one was black, the other green as the sea.

Betsan, sitting before a sea-coal fire, telling a tiny girl tales of marvels and magics, assuring her that she, too, could work such wonders. In her blood, 'twas.

A new crystal, but her aunt once again, dictating a letter to her son Challoner, wherein she urged him to hasten back to Keverne—there to wed with his cousin the Lady Kessallia, and claim her mad vanished father's vacant place . . .

* * *

Leith came awake with a start and scrambled to his knees, peering frantically into the opening of the crystal chamber. He had a bad moment, wondering whether the whole thing had been a dream, induced by the knock on his head—he wasn't certain there'd be a room beyond the opening at all, or that Kess would be inside the chamber if it *was* there.

But he saw her almost at once—crouched against the far wall, unstirring.

Another stone, this one full of fire. The red color gave way slowly to deep blue—Kess beheld a lake, nestled in forests of pine. An island within the lake, a plume of smoke rising from its central cone.

Fire again. A lone horseman, riding up a rocky slope. She could not see his face.

Fire. An animal made all of fire, the sort one sees in the flames of a winter night's fire—but living, powerful, terrifying. Kess forgot she had come to choose a single crystal to give her sight where she sought it. She looked from one side of the chamber to the other, and there was no tiniest plane of rock that did not assail her with visions, assault her with sight and sound and scent, batter her with memory and prescience.

Kess tried to close her eyes, recognizing her peril, but it was already too late. She was captured, overcome. She could not even faint. In her extremity, she tried to call to Leith, but could not remember his name. She wailed for her mother—it availed her no more than it ever had. She curled herself into a ball on the floor, screaming to drown out the voices, turning her head to avoid the sights, but even there the crystals pressed into her flesh, and there was no escape. It was as if her eyelids were glass, no barrier to the visions.

When Kess screamed and fell to the floor, Leith redoubled his efforts to reach her. He had discovered that he could get his arm, his shoulder, his head and neck into the chamber, but at that point he stuck fast, and Kess had fallen just out of his reach.

Pulling back, he hastily snatched up his sword and battered at the edges of the rock slit with its heavy pommel, heedless that he was cutting his hands on both the sword and the crystals. Chips of stone flew like startled bats. Leith tried the opening again, too soon, withdrew at the cost of some skin, and hammered yet more frenziedly. Kess' screams had become moans, fainter and fainter.

A good-size chunk of stone broke free, landing on Leith's foot. Heedless, he stormed the breach once more. Cloth tore, and so did flesh, but Leith tumbled inside, gasping, and landed on the rough floor. Crystals stabbed at him, bruising where they could not pierce heavy woolen cloth. Kess had dropped her torch, and it shifted as he knocked against it, making the crystals on the walls above glitter like so many watching eyes. The flashing drew Leith's attention, and he put aside the pain of his landing.

There were pictures in the crystals. Leith blinked hard, but still he saw them before him—swords and castles and running horses, beasts made of fire, ships on the seas. The profusion nearly drew him in—he had no notion he was witnessing those same visions that had finally overwhelmed Kess, making her scream with terror first. There was Valadan, surely. What other horse looked so, ran so? And there *he* was, Leith himself, riding up the Hill of Glass on Valadan's back.

He could not stop watching, could not tear his eyes away, though Leith knew he should. He had to help Kess. Something was wrong, she was in trouble, she needed him—but there was so much to see, so much the crystals could show him. Maybe even the origin of his curse—or its cure. All he had to do was keep watching.

Kess moaned, and Leith tried to turn his head, to see what troubled her, and whether it could wait till he had found what he sought. His neck was stiff as old leather, wet and left to dry without oiling. At best he could turn his eyes, and that not even enough to see Kess. He saw instead a man in a moon-white cloak, bent over a squalling babe that lay in a patch of blood-dappled moonlight—himself!

If he could shift his gaze, fix his sight on another crystal, might he not get another vision? Leith wondered. An earlier one, perhaps? He had been told the tale of his birth and rescue. Leith watched as the man who would become his foster father carried him away, past the sun priests making their signs against evil, beginning to cleanse the birthing room. The vision had told him nothing he had not already known. If only he could look elsewhere . . .

Some faint recollection of the day he had come upon the Hill of Glass prompted Leith to shut his right eye. On the instant, he was simply inside a tiny rock-walled room, too deep underground for his comfort—how *long* he had been there, idling where his Lady could not see him, Leith had no idea. The disorientation terrified him. He looked around, one-eyed.

Kess lay on the floor beside the flaring torch, moaning, her hands pressed over her face, so tightly that the fingers were bloodless. Leith, keeping his right eye carefully shut, took hold of her. The first thing to do was to get her away from the crystals—

Kess shrieked at his touch and flailed out, striking with both her hands and her feet, arching her back. Leith lost his hold and his balance, fell onto the sharp crystals, felt one slash his leg, another his face. The visions tumbling around him were tinged with bright scarlet until he remembered to close his right eye once again. It shut the visions out and halved the confusion in the chamber, if he could keep the eye from reporting what it saw.

In a moment Kess made that easier for him—she landed a blow to his face with such accuracy that his right eye swelled closed almost instantly. Leith got hold of her again, nonetheless, and pinned her hands safely to her sides. She kicked at his legs, but he dragged her steadily toward the opening in the wall, inch by inch.

Arrived at that goal, he tried to shove her through. Resisting, Kess stuck tight as a cork. Leith pulled her to him again, keeping careful hold of her hands. She still struck out at him, but the force of her blows was less if she could not draw her hands back, so he hung on grimly and endured her battering.

Leith worked his way out of the too-narrow space, scraping his ribs badly, then pulled Kess through after him. She bloodied his nose with the top of her head, and he was helpless to prevent it. One of her boots slammed into his knee, and he fell as the leg gave way under him. After that, Leith simply sat on her and waited for Kess to cease kicking. Finally she lay more or less still, panting.

He couldn't see her very well—the torch still lay within the crystal chamber. Leith rose, reached in carefully, took hold of the splintery end of the pine branch, and drew it forth, relieved. He intended to take very good care of the brand. It was, after all, the only light they had.

The torch went out.

Lost In The Dark

THE FULL CALAMITY of the moment took an instant to settle in. Leith held the torch with one hand, and with the other he fingered gingerly about his left eye—thinking that Kess might have blacked it as she had his right, only perhaps not so swiftly. Except that the eye reacted normally to having a finger poked into it, he learned nothing. So far as he could determine, he had it open.

Next, Leith felt the far end of the torch. He got his fingers blistered, but he could tell that was by residual heat—no matter how determinedly he blew on the wood, it refused to rekindle. After a dozen increasingly desperate attempts, he was forced to admit that the wood was cooling, that he could not see because the torch had burned out, leaving total darkness behind it. When the sun came up, it would still be dark, and there was no moonrise under the earth.

He groped about for Kess and found her after an awful moment when he could not. She was curled back into a tight ball and did not answer to his calling her name, though he tried as doggedly as he had tried rekindling the torch. He was afraid he might have hurt her in subduing her—or for that matter that she might have hurt herself, thrashing heedlessly about on the bed of crystals. His fingers, so bruised and burned, were the only tools he had for investigating her condition, and they reported no lumps on her head, no wetness that could not as easily have been blood from one of his own cuts. Kess was breathing, very deeply and with a reassuring regularity, but she was unresponsive to him.

The thing to do was to get her back to the open air, Leith decided. He found his pack and the waterskin, though he did not remember shedding either during his frantic entrance into the cave. He reclaimed his sword, which rang against the rock when he bumped it and told him its location. He discovered Kess' cloak by similar means, stumbling over it. The near fall in the pitch blackness was most unsettling, and he had to sit down a moment to recover, lest panic take hold and cause him worse trouble. Though how anything could be *much* worse, he did not know.

Finally, Leith sought the edges of the slit that led into the pocket of crystals, thought the directions out carefully, and lifted Kess. He began to work his way up the shaft, in the impenetrable darkness. He told himself it would be a simple enough trek—they had only followed one or two branchings, and he had been careful to note where those were. He was glad of that now. He had not anticipated retracing the way blind, but he knew the distances they'd walked between landmarks. He would be slower, carrying Kess instead of following after her, but he could easily allow for that in his calculations.

Leith kept in mind that the ceiling was low and managed not to bump his head again—it already ached quite sufficiently from the earlier encounter. He remembered that the floor was rough and did not stumble overmuch. He shifted Kess till he could carry her more or less with ease. At least she wasn't fighting him any longer—with luck, she wouldn't wake till they were safe outside. He came to a branching and went the opposite from the way they had taken coming in—because he was returning, and all directions had to be reversed. He was pleased he could think of that. He was calm, had his wits about him, despite all.

The ceiling had been all right on this stretch, Leith remembered. He hadn't had to duck. He straightened, used one hand to balance Kess, and walked with more confidence. True, Kess was heavier than he had imagined, and he was a touch winded, but there wasn't so very far to go. Just a few more hundred feet, and he should be seeing daylight.

Just then he ran straight into a wall.

Leith didn't know whether he actually knocked himself out, or only sat down very hard on the rock floor. His ears rang like a brass bell. His heart hammered his chest, as if it wanted to escape him, to find some greater safety elsewhere. Something hot and wet ran down his cheek, tasting of salt. He didn't know whether it was tears or blood. The wall should not have been there, Leith thought, but it incontrovertably *was*. When he stretched his hands out he found it right away.

Kess, though dropped, seemed unhurt. Leith picked her up again and retraced his steps. *The turning*, he thought, chagrined. *I remembered wrongly.* But there had been only the two ways, so the other would be correct by default. All he needed to do was retrace his path. Not a problem. Just go back, and choose the right way this time.

He found the turning—he hadn't gone so far as he'd thought. In the dark, distances confused. Now he couldn't imagine how he'd picked the wrong fork, for the proper one tended uphill, just as it should. Back to the surface, the sweet open air. Leith didn't remember the way having been so twisty, but he kept a hand on the wall—the hand he wasn't using to steady Kess on his shoulder—and made good time.

He had been making good time for quite a *long* while before it occurred to Leith that something was wrong. Very wrong. He should not have been able to walk for so long without coming to the surface. Unless his time-sense was disturbed—but his years with the moon priests had honed it keenly. Despite the darkness, despite the befuddling encounter with the wall, he knew how much time had passed. Too much.

He sat down to rest, Kess in his arms, then rose up again because there was something on the floor, something that was not comfortable to sit upon. Sticks scattered all around, and a biggish boulder—he cleared the floor with his hands and picked up the boulder, which was too light to be a rock after all. It had holes in it, two with another below them. And it had teeth . . .

It took Leith a moment more to realize that he was holding a skull, and that the sticks on the floor had been the dead man's ribs.

Leith rested a hand on Kess' cheek. Her skin was warm, so she still breathed and her heart still beat. She had not waked while he had slept, by any sign his fingers could read.

In the unrelieved darkness, he had no way to judge whether his sleep had lasted for a moment or an entire day. Leith supposed a brief doze was likeliest—he still felt quite weary, certainly neither rested nor so stiff as he'd have been if he'd sat for hours on the cold rock. He thought he must have made every wrong turn available for his choosing, and he no longer had the slightest idea—or even thought he had—of where he was.

He was getting better about not running into walls, sensing them before he stunned himself against them. And he had brought them safely through one stretch where the roof was so low he'd been forced to crawl backward on his belly, pulling Kess along by her wrists after him, and he'd never once banged his head on anything. But his new skills had been learned in the wrong places, and too late. Leith was lost, and not unwilling to admit the fact—to himself, since Kess remained unaware of his presence or anything else.

He leaned against the wall, fingering the moonstone hanging on the cord about his neck. Without light, the gray moonbeams that chased each other through the stone were invisible—Leith could feel only the thin silver wire that caged the water-smooth stone.

It had been the dark of the moon when they entered the mine. His Lady was weak then—perchance She had no notion where Her servant had gone, far less any awareness of his distress. That was what he had feared from the outset. He had knowingly removed himself from Her sphere of influence and could not therefore expect Her help now, in his extremity.

Leith whispered a chant of supplication, all the same, to the one constant in his wretched life. He recited first the numberless mercies She had shown him, from the instant of his birth and ever afterward. He confessed his faults and failings, his weakness and his unworthiness of Her notice. Hardly daring, he then asked one further boon of his Lady—deliverance. He wanted, above all, to see Her face just once more. He couldn't bear to think of dying in the dark—of crossing over into the greater dark unaware. It would be the worst of his curse, without doubt.

Could he offer nothing in return? It seemed despicable, to only take and take, and then whine for more. Slowly, his mind recalling the knots and thongs and telling his clumsy fingers what to do, Leith withdrew his wooden flute from the safety of his pack. He put the end to his lips and began haltingly to play airs and graces, praising his Lady where Her face had never shed its gentle, magic light. Each note was surer than the preceding one. His dry lips delivered air steadily to the instrument, his fingers became nimble in coaxing out whole ripples of sound. Notes became music, became prayer.

Leith played on and on in the darkness, beyond the formal tunes the priests had taught him, beyond praise and invocation, playing his own memories of Her light upon the rolling sea, upon the opal mist rising over the salt-grass meadows of the Isles. He played moonshadows and moonbeams, the moonbow he had not seen. He played the stars that attended his Lady as

She walked through the night, wrapped about in Her gown of twilight blue, tangled in Her silver hair. He played crescents and discs, perfect coins and sickles so slender that they could scarce contain the stars they framed, sharp enough to reap the wind. He played tales of waxing and waning, of apricot-yellow harvest moons and the cruel cold light that washed the land with pale blue at the mid of winter. He played of how She sometimes watched over the day, more powerful than Her brother the sun, who never ventured into Her domain and shone at night. He played of Her surpassing gentleness, Her light that neither burned the skin nor baked the crops in the fields.

He played till his fingers cramped, and never noticed. He played on and on, till he was faint from spending all his breath on music—and still Leith played, for while he did, his Lady was with him, though he sat upon cold stone that would never see Her light till the end of the world plowed up the land and tore open the deeps of the earth.

Leith's mismatched eyes played him tricks in the dark. All his senses had done similar misdeeds—he had heard many a sound in the unrelenting night, where dripping water counterfeited rescuing footsteps. He had felt many a draft of air that promised an exit to the outer world—an exit he could never quite locate. His eyes were made to see in light—deprived of it, they nonetheless made reports to his brain, and Leith could no longer distinguish truth from wishes.

The moonstone was faintly glowing at the end of its tether, lying upon his chest. The charm was so familiar, his mind had produced an exact copy of it, one he could see despite the utter darkness. Leith sighed and closed his fingers about the stone.

The light vanished.

Leith's breath caught in his throat. His fingers could not obscure an *imaginary* light. He opened his hand, let the stone swing free, and stared down his nose at the dim silver glow.

Never had he known the stone to glow with its own light—not even at night, under his Lady's influence. Whatever light fell upon the gem merely played within it, dancing through its translucency in imitation of moonbeams. It did not produce its own light. It never *had*—could this be his Lady's doing, a guide sent to lead him back to Her side?

Leith knew he should test the theory, walk one way or another, see whether the glow increased or dwindled. Yet he could not bring himself to leave Kess lying alone—suppose he lost his way again and could not find her? He dared not risk that. So, he shouldered her once again and set off burdened, trying to decide if the glow of the stone waxed or waned, or stayed just as it was.

False steps taught him as surely as true ones—when Leith turned back and the stone's glow faded, he understood that he was meant to follow the glow. When he went forward, the glow brightened encouragingly. It never increased past a certain intensity—which could never be called other than faint—but he could follow it. There was no other light to mislead him, in the underground blackness. The light remained too dim to warn him of obstructions and low spots in the roof, but Leith had been dealing with those for some while without benefit of sight. A fresh bruise or two served for a reminder.

Still, the falls, the unexpected contacts with walls of solid stone, took a toll. Leith had food, he had water, he could rest when he chose—but Kess' weight on his shoulder was all the time harder to balance. Weariness settled on him like a poorly crafted mail shirt. Leith's knees were apt to buckle, and he discovered himself more than once lying on the cold stone, lacking the strength to rise, not remembering having fallen. He could not judge how long such intervals lasted—conceivably he lay so for hours—and woke faint with hunger, his throat parched. The glow of the moonstone urged him onward, and if Leith could not walk he could still crawl, but his progress was achingly slow, and he had no idea how far he still had to go. Too many times he did not go at all, but came back to himself stiff with cold and sleep, unsure whether he had dreamed most of his progress, wishing he had dreamed all of his predicament.

The shoring timber he sat slumped against was pine, the stumps where its branches had once been projecting slightly to either side. Leith used those handy stumps for a ladder and climbed to his feet once more. He kept a hand on the timber, retaining its support while he waited for his legs to acknowledge his return.

Dimly he realized that he had thought to climb back to his feet because he could see to do so. He had *seen* the handholds on the wood, not groped for them. Leith turned his head slowly, certain he was dreaming, unwilling to wake in darkness again.

Beyond the framing edge of the timber was a sky spangled with stars, each of them brighter than the glow of the moonstone about his neck—and riding among the handful of stars, a newborn fingernail moon.

A Guide

LEITH STUMBLED OUT into the cool blue night, weeping with relief at being aboveground once more. He dropped to his bruised knees, but not for the pain's assurance that he dreamed no more. He stammered a hymn of welcome to the newborn moon ere his Lady's crescent set behind the upreaching mountains and She thought him ungrateful, unworthy after all of Her careful salvation . . .

The cold breeze dried tears and sweat alike on his upraised face, refreshed his body like the sweetest springwater. Leith had swallowed a dozen gulps of it before he tore his eyes from his Lady's thin bow and looked about. What he saw and did not see bewildered him. There was something amiss with the scene before his unblacked eye—or rather several somethings missing from the scenery. There were no horses. There was no untidy heap of mine debris, oreless rock and broken carts. There was no stream of water, no tiny meadow. Scarcely any flat ground at all. There was a sort of a ledge, and just beyond it the ground fell away in a steepish slope, which he had nearly tumbled down, bare shattered rock and coarse sand, like culm at the shoreline of an island.

The truth made Leith's heart sink and his head spin. He and Kess were at last free of the mine—and utterly lost. They had gone in one way and emerged at another point entirely. Their ordeal had left them afoot, foodless, without most of their gear, without the least idea how to proceed.

Leith refused to tamely accept the disaster. He wet his cracked lips as best he could and whistled for Valadan. The horses had merely grazed themselves out of sight, he told himself, and he had spent far more time wandering about in the dark than he ever had looking around before he went into the mine. He was remembering wrongly a landscape he had taken little note of, and that was all.

The whistled notes echoed from the rocks, then faded away. Leith's bottom lip began to bleed. Otherwise, nothing happened. No horses appeared.

Leith sank to the ground, beyond despair. With his luck, could he have expected any other outcome? He might quite easily have wandered all the way through the mountain's heart ere his Lady led him back to the air. How else could it be? Valadan wouldn't come in answer to his summons. Even a magic-begotten horse couldn't hear his summons over such a distance. No, Valadan was leagues away, and likely to stay there, patiently awaiting his return.

He closed his fist over the moonstone and watched with burning eye as his Lady withdrew behind the next ridge of the Berianas. It wasn't Her fault—a mere newborn sliver, She lacked power to do better by him, but She'd tried, all the same. Leith was not ungrateful and wished Her to know it, with all his heart.

His unbruised eye was so accustomed to the dark, he found he could see well enough even once She had set. There was not much about anyway, just sand and rock in varying arrangements. The sand would be more comfortable for Kess to lie upon than the rocks—Leith retrieved her from the mine and bore her carefully to a sheltered spot. He laid her down, with one of the packs for a pillow, and tucked her cloak tight about her, to fend off the chill of the mountain air. Kess did not stir, no more than she had within the tunnels. She was insensible to his touch, deaf to his whispering of her name.

Leith took off his own cloak and laid it over her, then reached for one of Kess' hands and rubbed it between his own. Her fingers were cold—but then so were his, besides being bruised and smashed and torn by rocks. Leith put his ear to her chest and heard the muffled thumping of a heartbeat, felt breath stirring his hair. He raised his head again and peered anxiously at her in the starlight.

"Kess? Can you hear me?" If she could, she saw no reason to make a response. "Kess, we're out. We're safe now."

Leith glanced around the empty landscape and shuddered. "Safe" might not be the best description of what they were, after all.

"Kess? You can wake up now." He squeezed her hand, then shook her shoulder gently. "Really."

But she did not. Leith coaxed the last few drops out of the waterskin, onto a rag he'd torn from the tail of his shirt, and carefully wiped Kess' face. He could hear a rushing sound, and he thought there was some sort of water nearby, but he didn't like to leave Kess to seek it out. Between the terrain and the darkness, he might come to grief, and the water wasn't worth the risk of not being able to get back to her. He plied the rag again, dabbing its coolness on Kess' temples.

If he could reckon time at all—and Leith was by no means sure he could do that—then Kess had been insensible for two days, perhaps as long as three. He hadn't been in a position to do anything about it, or worry over it, and in fact it had made travel a bit easier—Kess was indisputably easier to transport when she wasn't able to flail at him continually. He had hoped Kess was only suffering the ill effects of her exposure to a surfeit of vision-inducing crystals. Leith remembered how the insistent visions had beaten at even *his* dull senses, and knew it had surely been worse for Kess, if she'd been able to see those "hidden things" half so readily as she'd claimed. She had certainly been overwhelmed. He still remembered her screams.

But . . . he had fallen so many times in the mine's darkness—and most often had dropped Kess when he did it. Had she taken some harm from that? It seemed reasonable to suspect that she had. He had found a bruise on her temple, left behind when smudges of dirt came away on the wet rag. She had a red scrape on one cheek. He had battered himself against numberless walls—suppose he had knocked Kess against one and not realized it? He might have hurt her worse than the visions had.

Leith touched the bruise gingerly. There was no swelling under the discoloration—the lump on his own forehead was still much in evidence, and yet he was wide awake . . . He slid his fingers through Kess' hair, feeling the rest of her scalp. Not a trace of a hurt, but she remained oblivious to his presumption in touching her.

She had herbs in her pack. He ought to search for them, put them to use. But what herbs, and how to use them? Leith had lost his own bandage long since, and did not trust himself to choose a remedy based on dim memories of what the herbs Kess had used on him had smelled like. Probably by day he could find something to soothe her—but would she then wake? She didn't appear to be in any pain.

Well, he seemed not to have smashed her skull against a

rocky wall or floor. Pulling the cloaks away, Leith did his best to check her limbs. Certainly no major bones were broken, and though he found ripped cloth there wasn't blood, dried or fresh. So it was the visions, then—and he had not the least idea what the remedy for that would be. He put the warm cloaks back over Kess and let his hand lie a moment where her neck curved into her shoulder.

"Kess, wake up now." He joggled her slightly. He thought for a hopeful instant that she had begun to turn her head—then he realized that the motion came from his touch, as her head rolled limply from one side to the other. He fussed with the pack, so that it would better cushion her head, would not leave her with a stiff neck when she finally arose. "Kess, please. I swear to you, we're out. No more visions. Open your eyes—"

Kess looked slim as the new moon lying there beside him, as insubstantial within her torn and dusty cloak as the glow that chased through his moonstone. Incapable of mocking him, of kicking his ribs to awaken him when she decided morning had come and it was time to strike camp—whatever the sun showed, whether or not it had risen. Kess was always so brimful of life and energy, her physical body hardly able to contain it all, her spirit always seething like a kettle at the boil. To see her lying so still was unnatural, heartrending. Leith had never seen her full mouth immobile, seldom seen her lashes lying quiet on her cheeks . . .

"Kess," Leith whispered brokenly. She didn't answer. He wasn't even sure he saw her breathe. In the dark, he had been able to think she merely slept, but now that he could see her, the pretense ended. She wasn't sleeping, and he couldn't help her. Leith put his face into his hands and felt tears leaking hotly between his laced fingers. The salt burned in his cuts.

"Kess, please come back!" The words burst from his bleeding lips. He seized her by the shoulders, lifted her till her face was close to his own. Her hair spilled over his fingers like moonlight. "Please don't leave me here alone! I can't stand it!" Leith clutched her tight to him, put his lips right against her ear. "Talk to me—even if it's only to laugh at me, even if you have to frown. Hit me! Curse me! *Only open your eyes—*"

It was his second supplication of an almost unending night, and quite as desperately uttered as the first.

Kess didn't recognize the face the starlight showed bending over her. She could see at best only half of it—there was blood dried black all over one side of it, and only a single eye glinted. Then Leith shifted, and she saw that his right eye was swollen shut, surrounded by a bruise almost as dark as the one gracing his forehead.

She had gasped in a breath to scream before she recognized him, and now it set her coughing. Kess struggled to sit up ere she choked, and Leith helped her, got her upright and steadied her till the spasm had passed.

Kess leaned gratefully against his chest—then realized what she was doing. She shoved Leith away with surprising force, so that he went sprawling onto the sand as she leapt to her feet.

"What else did you walk into?" she demanded to know, jabbing a finger in the direction of his face.

Leith picked himself up, feeling a small measure of relief, mixed generously with irritation. He brushed sand off of his trews. "A wall or two," he mumbled, not meeting her eyes. "I tried not to be so . . . careless . . . but it was dark in there after the torch went out."

His words bordered on the insolent, even if their tone was matter of fact. She still couldn't catch his eye, so Kess looked about, and doing so noticed what was missing from the landscape far sooner than Leith had. "Where are the horses?"

"I would guess where we left them."

Something in his tone alarmed Kess. He did not hesitate, but he had wanted to. "Where are we?" she asked accusingly.

Leith spread his battered hands, as if to ward off blows. He was looking at her now, with apprehension.

"Don't you *dare* tell me you don't know!"

Leith obediently swallowed his explanation.

"Are we *lost?*" His expression made the answer plain to Kess, even in the faint starlight. "How did *that* happen?"

"Just my luck," Leith answered miserably, looking away again. "The torch went out, when I dragged you away from the crystals. I couldn't see. I thought I'd kept track of the turnings—I *know* I did—but there are so many tunnels in there. I suppose there were some I didn't see, when we passed them by . . ." He trailed off uncertainly. Kess could guess the rest. She likely already had. Leith decided not to speak of his Lady's part in their escape—he did not think he could bear hearing Kess mock their deliverer.

"Just your luck," Kess repeated acidly. "Well, *that* about says it all!"

* * *

At least they had food, for Leith had somehow contrived not to lose their packs. They broke their fast with strips of dried beef and hunks of stale bread, both of which went down more easily when first light helped Leith locate the spring he had heard bubbling nearby. The water was so cold as to make his teeth ache, and it was a great misery to bathe his battered face in it, but Leith kept at the task, knowing time would only make the cleansing more uncomfortable. He had to soak crusted blood away, which caused the shallow cut at his hairline to bleed afresh, but Kess bound the scrape for him—a kindness Leith had in no wise anticipated from her.

It might be that Kess was belatedly grateful that he had insisted on taking his pack into the mine. She might not have taken hers without his example, in which case they'd be starving as well as lost, afoot, and in trouble.

"I've had dreams as long as I can remember," Kess volunteered, turning over a heel of bread in her hands, looking at it rather than Leith. "Most nights. Realer than real. Then, when I was twelve, they started to come while I was awake. I would look at a spot of sunlight on the floor, catch a glint of a candle's flame in a glass goblet—and suddenly I was seeing things no one else could."

Leith supposed that had been interesting.

"I told no one," Kess went on. "How could I? I knew what they thought of my mother, what they would say of me. I have tried to learn to control what I see, to use it—"

"But it hasn't worked?" Leith guessed, not a great stretch.

"The chance-come visions are too unreliable! One day I might look into a mirror and see the coast of the Promontory, as if I'm looking out a window instead of into a bit of silvered glass hung on a solid wall. The next day—and the next, and the next—all I see is my own face. Sometimes when we'd feast in the Hall, I couldn't eat for watching things that weren't there, seeing them in every torch's flame, trying not to let on. But when I *need* to see—to know what hand my aunt really had in my mother's leaving, what harm she's plotting now—I only see a bit here, another bit there, and just when it gets interesting the torch flickers, or the sun goes behind a cloud, and the vision's gone. But if I had a crystal—"

"Because a crystal doesn't change?" Leith hazarded, knowing he risked a rebuke if he was wrong.

"I could look into it, learn to look past the surface—I did

that a little with the sand. I *know* I can learn to harness the visions—"

Leith agreed that she could. He didn't *know* that Kess could do as she vowed, but it seemed likely. Nothing stood in her way for long. Why should this be different?

"We're just going to have to go back in," Kess said, picking a thread of meat from between her teeth and not caring whether Leith thought her indelicate.

In fact, her words had kept him from noticing her actions. *"What?"*

"Oh, *you* don't actually need to." Kess waved a hand dismissively. "You just help me make a few more torches, so I can see my way. We know the crystals are in there. I'll try to come back this way—"

Probably she would do no such thing, but Leith was not concerned about desertion. "Those crystals almost killed you! Even if you could find your way back—Kess, we were in there for *days*! Those tunnels—" He had no words to describe the black labyrinth he remembered, and gave it up.

Kess regarded him with what was possibly patience. "It's the only way I know to find my mother, Leith. There's no trail from here on unless the crystal shows it to me. I said you don't have to go back with me." She arose.

"You're not going, either!" Leith struggled to his feet, as if Kess might try to dash past him on the instant.

Kess was, however, searching for torch-makings. There was a tuft of dry grass by her feet, a small stick or two—Kess snarled at the sparseness of the vegetation and ranged farther.

Leith limped after her, still protesting. His hip hurt as it always did come a morning, and he was bruised or scraped or cut over the greater part of his body—to compound his misery, he had a stone—more likely half a dozen—in his right boot, and when he stood it had shifted. Lodged against his instep, it had been only an annoyance, but when it slipped farther under his foot it dug into him with every step he took. Pursuing Kess was torture.

"You might never find the crystals again, much less your way back!" he insisted.

"If I find crystals I'll have a guide, won't I?" Kess pounced upon a bit of wind-scoured wood, possibly once a tree branch.

"You *tried* that—" Leith wanted to curse her obstinacy, which was as natural to her as her breath. "All those crystals were too much for you. I know—even *I* could see things in them."

Kess looked startled by that revelation, then forced her face into a frown. Anger was an emotion she was familiar with, could deal with. "Do you have a better idea?"

"You wouldn't listen to me if I did." Leith took another step, inadvertently put his full weight on his right foot, and cried out.

"What's the matter?" Kess asked sharply. "Don't think I'll stay here with you if you pretend you're hurt, because I won't—"

"I *know* you won't." Leith sat down and began to drag at his boot. He had no idea what was in there—besides his foot, of which he was suddenly keenly aware—but one more step like the last and he'd be crippled for true. "You'd be delighted to leave me."

Blisters he anticipated, and was not disappointed. Quite a few of them were torn and broken, but the pain went well beyond that. Something had stabbed his foot. Leith upended the boot and shook it, while Kess began to exclaim over another branch she'd discovered, which should make a torch or even two. She took the fortune for a sign of the rightness of her plan.

Sand and gravel spilled out of the boot. Something large fell out on the ground, bounced once. Leith picked up the offending stone, expecting to see his blood on it.

The rock was half the length of his long thumb, and about as thick. One end was naturally pointed, the other jagged where something—maybe his sword pommel—had cloven it loose from the rock. It was a crystal of quartz with half a dozen irregular sides, clear as springwater at its tip, white as a new snowfall at the base, misty between the two extremes. It lay in his palm, its weight all out of proportion to its size, promising visions.

Leith knew he hadn't trodden upon it beyond that final, bruising step. Likely it had fallen into the loose top of his boot as he fought his way to Kess, had been stuck against his calf until just lately slipping down to make itself felt under his sore foot. He stared at the crystal, slack-jawed. He could see straight through one face—but if he turned the stone about, the way was veiled, mysterious. He'd come out of the mine not only alive but in possession of what Kess sought, all unawares.

That his remarkable luck had for once worked for good dazed him. It wasn't an outcome he had much experience with.

"Kess—" he managed to say.

"I'm not going to argue any more about it, Leith! I can do without a horse if I must, but I am *not* going home, and I am *not* going to—" Her eyes lit on the object in Leith's upraised hand.

"I had to use my sword to make the opening wider when I brought you out," he explained, round-eyed with the wonder of his discovery. "There were chips of rock flying all over—I suppose this one fell into the top of my boot—"

He got no further before Kess flung herself upon him. She snatched the crystal, clasped her hands about it, and sank down, heedless that she leaned against Leith's leg while she sought the heart of the stone with her eyes.

"Be careful—" Leith warned, knowing that he was a fool for expecting Kess to show caution in any matter.

But a solitary crystal seemed incapable of showing Kess more visions than she could handle, even supposing she threw herself at it unprepared. She hadn't started screaming yet, which Leith found reassuring. Her lips were parted, her eyes had softened focus, and the line between them had smoothed away.

She seemed likely to be busy awhile. Leith contemplated removing his other boot, as well—not supposing he'd find more wonders, but his left foot was surely as blistered as the right, and exposure to air would start it healing. Since they'd now be depending on their own feet, they must have the same care as the horses' hooves—or better, being less durably made.

Something rang against a rock, and Leith leapt to his feet, blistered or not. Kess squawked a protest over the balance she lost as he removed his support, but Leith paid her no heed. He wrenched his sword free of its scabbard. He had seen no sign of any wildlife, no sort of creatures at all, and a wolf or a big cat would move silently, would not likely have given itself away—but there were other perils, even if he could not guess their identities at once. He took up a guard position, while Kess copied him and looked to her own weapons.

There came several more ringing sounds, then a scrape or two, followed by a mighty snort. Valadan's up-pricked ears rose into sight over the top of a ridge, followed instantly by the rest of the stallion's head and neck. In another moment he had scrambled into full view, and Leith went stumbling over to him, shouting and making the stallion startle.

"You *did* hear me! I thought I'd never see you again—" Leith buried his face in the black mane, flung his arms about the stallion's arched neck. His nostrils filled with the tang of horse sweat, sweeter than any perfume, to him. He felt a gust of warm breath down his back.

I had to go around the side of the mountain, Valadan said— offhandedly, as if the matter were merely a trifling inconvenience. *The way you took was much shorter, but a horse cannot use it.*

Leith thumped the horse's neck, then hugged it round again with both his arms. Valadan's coat felt like sun-warmed silk beneath his cheek. Losing him had been a disaster Leith had walled away, refused to contemplate. Now he wiped his eye and struggled with a wash of emotions, loss and relief swirling together.

"Is my horse coming, too?" Kess asked, behind him.

Valadan shook his head so that his bit jangled and his knotted-up reins danced. *He has gone back to his stable, if he has found another way over the river.*

"I don't think so," Leith translated, wondering what the gelding would do about the waterfall. "It's all right. I can walk."

"Better put your boots on first," Kess suggested sweetly.

Retrieving his footgear, Leith managed—with some small difficulty—to force his swollen feet back into them. Kess frowned as she watched him struggling and listened to the rather frequent and unmuffled curses.

"Walk on those blisters today and you won't be fit to travel for a week after," she pronounced with annoyance. "They'll break, they'll fester, and your so-called luck will have had nothing to do with it."

Valadan snorted, either punctuating Kess' statement or offering a solution of his own. Leith finished checking the girth, refolded the blanket strapped behind the cantle, and eyed him critically. The stallion's back was short and strong, solidly muscled, very well coupled.

"He could carry us both," Leith decided. "Except on steep spots," he amended, recalling the country they traversed.

They wrangled elaborately over which of them should ride behind—Kess preferred to steer her own horse, and had never in her life ridden upon a led horse, as timid ladies did. Leith

made to give in, but Valadan settled the matter finally—
refusing to stand still while Kess put a dainty foot into his stirrup. Leith could not reason with him. Kess was thereupon constrained to ride behind Leith, holding onto his belt, giving him
direction rather than simply forging ahead and leaving him to
follow her if he dared. She had perforce to swallow the anger
this caused, though it choked her.

That reversal struck Leith as unnatural and unnerving—but
he managed to bear it with equanimity.

The Chimera

"I KEEP SEEING horsemen behind us," Kess fretted, as she lowered the crystal to her lap.

Leith shook his head and went back to currying Valadan. "Even if they managed to get across the Est, there's no way they'd have tracked us through the mine." He couldn't have retraced his steps himself, and said so.

"They're back there," Kess insisted, and pressed her lips tightly together.

"But you can't tell how *far* back," Leith suggested, wielding a brush to lift dust clear of the black silk coat. "They can't be close enough to worry us, that's all I'm saying."

Kess slowly undid her braid, finding him obstinate and not answering him on that account. She selected a few silver-gilt strands, wrapped them twice about her hand, and sharply yanked them out by the roots. Leith's eyes watered at the thought of the pain—his right eye had just opened that morning—but Kess paid heed to neither discomfort nor sympathy. Plaiting the silver strands, she bound them about the base of the crystal till she had made a cord from which it hung securely. She slipped the cord over her head and put the crystal inside the blue linen shirt, next to her skin. Closeness should intensify the visions, help her to focus—she thought, and wished she *knew*, instead.

They had made little progress in distance that day—they were both of them so bruised and battered, the first grassy spot they spied had tempted them to halt and rest, lest no similar suitable spot should offer itself later in the day and they should be without the least comfort. Leith had dropped almost at once into an exhausted sleep, and Kess must have done likewise.

She was furious when she arose and saw the sun sinking in rosy glory, but she cast no blame about, for once.

Leith did not regret the time lost. They had each been in desperate need of a restorative. An evening and a night of the same would repay them with a longer journey on the morrow. He felt as if he could sleep for a year and a day, and not find it tedious.

"Besides horsemen, what did you see in the crystal?" Leith asked. Finishing with Valadan, he had produced a needle and a hank of thread from his pack, and was making shift to deal with the worst damage to his clothing. Where modesty permitted, he removed the articles first, to thwart the bad luck that came with mending what one still wore. Still, Kess noticed that the needle found his fingers often and unexpectedly, though Leith seemed to have some skill at the task, and probably plenty of practice.

"Rocks," Kess answered shortly.

Leith managed to miss his fingers two stitches in a row. He bit off the thread, reknotted one end, and began upon another rent, this one in the thigh of his trews, where crystal had sliced cloth clean as any knife.

"Like before?" he asked, stitching at the awkward spot. "What sorts of things did you see, then?"

"It varied," Kess said, consenting to a serious exchange. "Usually it was things past, if I could tell at all, that is. Sometimes I couldn't. Things that happened before I was born might as well have been in the far future, if I couldn't see someone I could recognize." She frowned, following the reasoning through. "Except visions of what's to come tend to be very shifty—they show things that haven't happened yet, and what *may* be changes constantly."

"Could you direct the crystal, make it show you what you wanted?"

"If I couldn't, what use would it be?" Kess snapped viciously, startling Leith so that he jabbed first his finger and then his leg. He dropped his uneven gaze and tended to his sewing, giving his attention to keeping his skin safe.

"I'm sorry," Kess said unexpectedly, surprised by the guilt she felt in the absence of any rebuke. "Yes, I could change what it showed me. I didn't *have* to watch those damned horsemen the whole while. I could . . . it's a little like watching something out the tail of your eye, while you're facing the other way. A little. It's very difficult, but I can do it, and I'll get better at it."

Leith said nothing and did not look up—except Kess realized that he *was* looking at her, through the cover of his lashes so she wouldn't be aware of it. His green eye gave him away, its lighter color showing even in the uncertain firelight.

"What?" Kess asked rudely.

Leith inspected a strip torn almost free from the hem of his doublet. Better to finish cutting it away, he thought, and used his dagger to sever those few threads that had not already been parted. "I just wondered . . . maybe if I knew *how* this curse was laid on me, it would help me to find a cure . . ." His voice trailed off—he was afraid to hope at all, and regretted being forced to mention it.

Kess could think of no polite way of explaining that she seldom saw anyone else's past or fate in any of her visions—only her own. Self-absorbed, she had never before seen the omission as a lack, or in the least way unusual.

"Oh. I thought you might be wondering whether I could tell yet where we should go next, or if we were still wandering," she dodged.

"That, too." Leith nearly smiled. "There's not much to eat up here, and winter's not far off."

"I wish I had left my bow tied to *your* saddle," Kess said, regretting once more that *she* did not ride a magic-bred horse. Any useful things she had left behind in her saddlebags were on their way back to Esdragon, out of her reach and no help for it because an ordinary horse could not go where Valadan did.

"I've still got the bowstring." Leith produced it from a pocket, with a conjuror's flourish.

Kess flushed, reminded that Leith had the essential part of her hunting weapon because he had rightly presumed that she might put an arrow into him, to discourage his participation in her quest. *His* quest had meant nothing to her then, and it still meant very little—she had forgotten it entirely until he mentioned learning how it was cast upon him—except that it was just as well she had not managed to drive him away. He was proving useful from time to time, and his horse—bred by *her* father, Kess did not for an instant forget—spared her feet and speeded a long journey.

"Maybe I could make a bow," Leith offered softly. "If we came across some suitable wood."

Kess snorted. "And fletch me a quiverful of arrows, as well? By the time you straighten shafts and chip flint points to do for the heads, spring will be here."

Leith shrugged and was tempted to try for some sleep, wherein at least Kess' tongue would let him be. But he remembered there was one subject that vinegar tongue had not touched—the question he'd so tentatively put to her. She had avoided it rather neatly. He envied her the facility, but decided not to let her get away with it.

"I'm not asking you to try to *lift* my curse," he said, and saw Kess' eyes narrow, when he returned to the subject without her consent. "I know that isn't where your skills lie. But if you could just tell me whatever you've seen—"

Kess wondered whether she dared tell him she hadn't looked, and didn't intend to. She decided against such raw truth, for once, and put on her brightest smile for masquerade.

"Why, of course I will! And don't worry about us wandering—I know where we're going."

Her second statement was true. The crystal had given her, at the last, a clear sight of an island in a round blue lake, no place she had ever seen before in her life. The island looked like a mountain in miniature, with a plume of smoke rising from its peak. So distinctive a feature would be easy to locate in any landscape. Her father might not have been able to find her mother's hideaway—the vision showed no hint of him—but Kess had no doubt that *she* could.

The slopes they descended were on the lee side of the Berianas, and plainly those few clouds that succeeded in crossing over the crest had done so at the cost of letting fall their precious freight of rain on the way—the mountain slopes were dry and barren of trees.

There was some grass, enough to feed whistling marmots and Valadan, but firewood was in short supply. A vantage point—of which there were plenty—showed that the next night's camp should be better supplied. Leith could make out dark green smears of forests at the edges of the great plain lying below them.

Though he might be forced to cook it over an inadequate fire of quick-burning grass, Leith had hope of varying their diet with a fish. The stream they had camped alongside might just hold a few speckled trout, though its water had an unpleasant odor that Kess said was sulfur. The water came down over a lip of rock and spread out, wide and shallow—Leith suspected a deeper pool upstream, and climbed to seek it and the fish, leaving Kess settled comfortably on a patch of soft grass, her crystal cupped in her hands.

There wasn't moisture widespread enough to support a forest, but there was mint on the streambanks and a tangle of honeysuckle vines alongside the mint. Night-blue hummingbirds darted among the blossoms, or into Leith's face if he chanced to be in their path. He climbed a few hundred feet, with the stream.

Leith had been expecting a pool, but he came instead to the spot where the water welled up out of the earth and dared a broad fringe of smelly tan mud till he was close enough to inspect the highest pool of the stream, its source.

He found no fish, and for good reason. The turquoise-green pool was *hot*. Steam curled from its surface into the cool mountain air. Leith tested it cautiously, with first a finger, then his entire hand. He smiled till his bruised face ached. Too hot for fish, maybe, but not too hot for *him*. On the Isles there were springs hot enough to boil a chicken in, springs that spat scalding water onto the unwary—but there were others such as this, with water suitable for soaking a weary body till it was refreshed, not parboiled.

Leith retraced his steps, past the bubbling mud, to apprise Kess of their good fortune. She would welcome a hot soak quite as much as he would, Leith was certain.

The ground quivered, under his boots. Leith looked down at it, thinking he had blundered into mud once more. He had not. He was well past the mud, on dry ground. He stared. Small pebbles were dancing upon the sandy surface, bouncing into and off of one another. On the little flat they had chosen for their camp, Valadan was racing about, throwing his heels up as if he misliked to keep them in contact with the quaking earth. Trying to keep out of his way, Kess looked at the surrounding hills, her face white.

"*What is it?*" she called, to Leith.

Leith slid dramatically down the last few feet of the slope to land beside her. A loose rock turned under his weight, but he managed to keep his feet, feeling muscles strain and knowing he'd be feeling their complaints for quite some while. "It's an earthshake," he answered breathlessly. "I should have guessed—I found a hot spring." The earth often danced in spots where such waters sprang forth—at least it did in the Isles.

"Will it stop?" Kess looked alarmed, despite Leith's offhand explanation. Tides she understood—the sea was fluid, changeable as she was herself—but the land was solid unless the sea waves mined beneath it. The earth should not roll under one's feet. 'Twas unnatural.

The vibration underfoot was already subsiding. Valadan snorted once or twice, tossed his head, then returned his attention to the tasty grass. An unseen bird began to sing, in sweet defense of his territory.

"It has," Leith observed. "For now." He glanced at the stream—it ran muddy now, from silt jarred loose upstream. He suspected the warm pool was not so clear at the moment, either, and regretted the loss of the chance to bathe.

"Is it dangerous?" Kess wanted urgently to know.

"Likely not." Leith frowned, recalling the quake that had toppled his Lady's temple and dashed his hopes for a future in Her service, but he decided he was not lying to Kess. That ground had heaved like a bucking horse—he still remembered how helpless he had felt before its power. This shift now passing had been more like the stirring and stretching of a cat that dozes in the sun. And there was no roof over their heads, to fall upon them. Not so much as a tall tree. "No more so than a thunderstorm," he decided truthfully.

They were shaken out of sleep twice over the next several nights, and once Valadan halted upon a high ridge and would not budge no matter how earnestly he was entreated. Presently the earth had trembled again, and the dusty way before them twitched like a dying snake. Valadan had stepped off once the dust had settled—far sooner than Leith would have suggested or insisted upon.

Leith became most particular about their campsites, after a tumbling stone bounced down a steep slope and bruised his shoulder just as he was waking during a shake. To bed down at the foot of a hillside was to invite burial in a landslip, something he had never previously taken account of. Sometimes at night they spotted fitful glows on the horizon, like the campfires of a vast and distant army—if the bare mountainsides could support or conceal such a force of men.

First thing every dawn, Kess climbed to the highest spot she safely could reach and gazed first at the landscape, then into her crystal. On the third such day she came rushing back breathlessly, her pointed face alight.

"*I saw the lake!*" she panted.

Leith put down Valadan's near forehoof, which he had been inspecting for trapped stones or other signs of trouble. He gave thanks again that the stallion had flint-hard hooves that stood up well to the rocky trails—for certain there was no way to get him shod should he have required it. "How far?" he asked Kess.

"Tomorrow. Maybe next day!" Kess whooped. "There's a pass—a saddle. We need to climb up to that, and through. But it's there, just as the crystal showed—the lake, the island—"

"And your mother's there?" Leith pressed.

"Never *mind* your doubting questions! Let's go!" Kess gave the girth buckle a tug, sliding the tongue into its proper hole. Valadan switched his tail across her, irritated at her presumption.

Leith only smiled to himself, thinking that perchance the stallion could get them to the lake sooner than Kess anticipated. He gathered up their gear, careful to leave nothing behind. Kess was in no fit state to pay attention to such petty details.

The intervening slopes proved unsuited to any of Valadan's powers save endurance, however. There was no flat space where galloping was feasible, nor could they climb other than at a walk, not and stay mounted. They progressed steadily, but unremarkably, and had only just reached the saddle come sun-high.

The pass was bare brown rock and yellow-gray dirt. Sun-struck in the mid of the day, it was disconcertingly hot. The rock walls threw the sun's heat about from one side to the other without letting a single uncomfortable degree of it escape, and the very air shimmered, mocking the coolness of nonexistent water. There was not so much as a blade of grass to cast the relief of a shadow. Leith could not remember casting an eye—of either color—on such a barren place.

He suggested that they should pause for rest and food. There'd still be light aplenty left when the pass was no longer a furnace, at twilight. Kess argued that they could easily traverse a league of open ground, then camp in sight of the lake. There were trees to shade them on the far side of the pass, whereas the spot where they presently stood offered naught but hot rock on every side and baked grit underfoot. Seeking even marginal comfort would mean retracing their steps by more than half a league, something Kess was insistent they avoid. She could hardly bear even the brief pause they had taken in the unrefreshing shade of a huge rock, while they discussed the matter.

Leith rather wished that Valadan would prove unwilling to go on—he would not have forced the issue. The heat had throughly sapped his ambition, and he saw no purpose in pressing on under the sun's hammer. But the stallion moved out at a light touch of Leith's heel to his side, and they stepped into the sun's full glare. Leith felt sweat trickling down his back, which was heated by the sun, by his woolen cloak—and by Kess, pressed tightly against him, craning over his shoulder.

"Can't we go faster here?" she wheedled into his ear. "It isn't like the slopes. This is flat—"

Leith shook his head, and Kess hissed as he bumped her jaw.

"Look at those rockfalls," he said stubbornly, reeling from the box Kess had given his ear in repayment. "There's no telling what we might stumble into. Anyway, don't you want to keep an eye out for some sign your father came this way?"

A roar sliced across Leith's question. With it came a hot wind, tearing down the hillside just ahead like a landslip, visible by the dust it whipped up and dragged along. Valadan halted, prancing, and Leith reached a hand out to pat the stallion's sweat-soaked neck, which was arched like a drawn bow before him. Valadan's ears tried to train in all directions at once.

"Just wind," Leith said reassuringly—then realized that there was something *in* the wind, a something so bright that looking at it was like staring into the sun—something coming full at them.

Fire was Leith's early guess, wondering how there was anything left to burn in that bare desiccated place. Only he had seen grass fires, when the Islanders burned off the old heather so that the new green growth would find the spring sun more readily, and he knew that fire traveled *up* a slope, never cascaded down it.

The thing that rushed upon them roared and crackled, and as it came head-on, none of them truly appreciated the speed with which it traveled. Leith stared at it almost without alarm. It had a beast's shape—a lion's head with a flaming mane wreathing about it, he thought, a writhing dragon's tail trailing fire and sparks behind it. It roared again, and white flame spouted from its gaping jaws. A quarter league off, they felt the blistering heat of it, added to the sun's . . .

Kess screamed, right in Leith's ear. It was information, not panic, he realized. He had forgotten that her father had gone hunting a chimera.

No Way Around

THOUGH HE KNEW what he watched, Leith still stared dreamily at the chimera as it rushed at them, mesmerized as if he merely regarded the familiar flicker of a campfire, saw therein those bright wonders that do not walk in the real world. He had no sense of danger in those few interminable seconds. It was Valadan who saved them, snatching the reins free of Leith's inattentive fingers, ignoring the bit as he whirled and ran for all their lives. His wind-sired speed was barely sufficient to carry them safely ahead of the flame-beast. Few winds can outpace fire, and a chimera's prey seldom escapes it.

They reached a powdery upslope bare ells in advance of the chimera's breath—a small pine that had found a pocket of fertile soil and a few drops of precious moisture went up like a torch as they passed it, victim to a blast meant to sear them. They shot over the top of the rise, sailed into the air, and landed scrambling, far down the opposite slope, where Valadan strove to continue galloping, refusing to sacrifice the slightest crumb of the momentum he'd attained. His tail was singed at its tip, for it flew back behind him as he ran, a yard closer to peril.

Leith let the stallion gallop till a low branch nearly removed his head from his shoulders. He heard no more roaring behind them, and reasoned that if there were unburned trees about to put his head at risk with their boughs, then the chimera did not normally pass that way. Taking a tight hold on the reins, Leith sat back. Valadan fought him for a moment before consenting to slow his pace, yielding only by reluctant degrees. After a dozen more strides he halted at last and stood still, his wet flanks heaving.

Leith looked back and could discover nothing more ominous

than green branches interlacing, which were no peril if one didn't ride through them at breakneck pace. He lowered Kess to the ground and joined her swiftly, shooting another glance back to be sure dismounting was truly safe. Still no sign of any fiery pursuit. Birds, put to flight by their precipitous arrival, settled back among the branches. Squirrels chattered and scolded. Evidently the chase was over.

Leith's own breath came as hard as the stallion's. He dropped to his knees in the pine litter, most unexpectedly, and since he could not rise stayed there, panting. Kess was doing likewise.

"So that's a chimera?" Leith inquired conversationally, as he climbed to his feet somewhat later. "And your father went hunting one? On purpose?"

Kess inspected the tip of her braid, which was as blackened as the end of Valadan's tail—except that on her pale hair the singed bits showed plainly, a reminder of too close a call. "I've never seen one before," she said in a tiny voice.

"Nor I," Leith seconded. Valadan snorted, agreeing, as Leith stumbled along beside him, endeavoring to walk him cool, unable to allow a hot horse to stop running and simply *stand*—a very good way to kill a horse—but he suspected he was in worse shape than the stallion was, for Valadan had long since recovered his breath. His coat was already dry, his step sure, whereas Leith's own legs were yet rubber-jointed and he was still sweat-soaked, skin and hair and woolen clothing. As they paced to and fro, Leith leaned for support on the horse's strong shoulder and wondered just who was tending whom.

Kess dropped her braid and attempted to scry an alternate route for them with her crystal, but she cried out and dropped the stone after only an instant's peek, as if the crystal had burned her. Try as she might after that, she could not compose herself to look past the fire. Leith paused in his walking, looking a question at her over Valadan's shoulder.

"We . . . we have to get past it," Kess stammered, her voice quaking to match her hands, which had let the stone fall again. She had just witnessed the chimera's snarl at close range in her crystal, seen its breath blossom forth toward her, and she was not wholly convinced that it might not escape the stone and crisp her. "There's no other way to the lake."

"Are you certain?" Leith finally allowed Valadan to halt. By rights the stallion should still be furnace-hot and half foundered, but the same magic that bequeathed Valadan his speed evidently enabled him to endure the rigors of that speed as no ordinary horse ever could have. No use pretending he needed to be walked cool, whatever *should* have been the case. "We could go around, you know."

"You saw the slopes this morning." Kess sounded distraught. "They're too steep. Most of them are cliffs, or heaps of loose rock. That pass is the only way through."

"Did we actually look for another way?" They hadn't needed one so desperately as they now did, that was certain. They'd looked for a best way, no more.

"The earth dances all the time here. The hills rearrange themselves. It's a wonder there's even this one way through."

Leith swore, knowing Kess was right. He stroked Valadan's nose, the skin soft as a maiden's cheek. A warm breath puffed over his fingers. "No offense to you, my friend, but I don't think you can outrun it the whole length of the pass. Therefore, we don't go *past* it."

"Maybe we could sneak past while it sleeps," Kess proposed eagerly.

Leith could not convince himself that such a creature *would* sleep—he knew fire did not unless carefully banked—but he was willing eventually to creep back to a point from which they could spy out the pass. Valadan could not hide so readily as they, but he followed along, as much for his keener senses as for his speed—which Leith hoped they would not require a second time that day.

Leith was astonished to discover what a distance their flight had covered—they walked for better than half an hour ere they came out of the trees and stood at the base of the slope they had leapt down. "How fast *are* you?" he whispered to the stallion, who merely played with his bit and made no other answer.

Dry brush offered slight concealment along the top of the rise. There hadn't been much to begin with, and it was blackened and crisp. A red butterfly sailed past, seeking a landing place and finding only charred twigs.

"Not much doubt about this being the place," Leith whispered. "Though I can't say I paid it close attention the first time we passed by."

The brush offered nothing by way of protection, and in its present state not all that much of concealment, either. Leith crept upslope in the lee of a granite boulder, a stone he hoped would deflect flame. He could hear Kess following, close as his shadow. He edged a few inches to his left to make room for her, then peered over the top of the boulder.

The chimera was crossing from one side of the pass to the other in a whirlwind of dust thrown up by its lashing tail. It shone so brightly that it illuminated the dust rather than being veiled by it. Frequently it roared thunderously, and puffs of white fire issued from the bright cloud. As they watched, such a flame caught a panicked ring dove trying foolishly to overfly the pass. The bird fell to earth, charred feathers fluttering slowly after it.

"It seems upset," Leith whispered.

We escaped it, Valadan observed coolly from below.

And it might be unaccustomed to losing its prey, Leith thought. He wondered why it had given up its pursuit. He had not been looking back at the thing, and had no idea *where* it had actually abandoned the chase, but he thought only the hot breath had come upslope after them. There'd been no snatch of claws, no clash of jaws. Not that he regretted any of that. Their escape had been entirely satisfactory, beyond question.

It comes down a slope like thunder, but it climbs poorly.

Leith took another look, to see what Valadan meant. The horse was right—and he thought he saw why.

"It doesn't have any legs," he pointed out to Kess.

"*Should* it?"

"It moves like a snake." She regarded him blankly. "*Watch.*"

Side by side they huddled behind the boulder, ready to dive for deeper cover if they were noticed. The rock was sun-heated—Leith could feel his skin breaking out in a sweat once again. The chimera's every breath seemed to increase the temperature of the air. A hawk, riding updrafts far overhead, suddenly veered away, as if even it did not feel entirely safe.

The chimera continued its relentless patrol of the pass—side to side, end to end. It did not miss one inch of ground that Leith could see. Back it went, and forth, seeking furiously for three intruders who had eluded its grasp.

"You think it's trapped in there?" Kess asked.

Leith shook his head, and black dots swirled across his field of vision. He slid down to sit beside Valadan, where the sun was less intense. The chimera might strike more swiftly, but the sun could smite them as surely if they let it. He wiped sweat from his brow. "No. It could climb out. Snakes climb trees, after all. I think it just couldn't climb *fast* enough to catch us."

"Then we *did* outrun it?" Kess frowned, considering the implications.

"Don't even think about it, Kess!" Leith wanted to shake her, lest the dangerous idea take root. "We didn't outrun it on the flat, and we're lucky it came at us so close to the slope. It must pick off anything that goes into the pass."

They each spared a doleful thought for Kess' father. But at least, Leith thought, the duke had been expecting to encounter the beast. He wouldn't have blundered upon it as they fecklessly had. He might well have avoided it altogether.

"If it doesn't climb well, why can't we go around it, up the slopes?" Kess asked, squinting.

"Because its breath reaches farther than its jaws," Leith explained patiently. "Because we couldn't possibly get high enough or go fast enough on those slopes. We'd likely start a rockslide and wind up right in the the thing's lap."

Valadan nosed Leith's hair, blowing gently.

Kess, however, was furious. "Won't you even *try*? What's *your* plan—sit here till winter?"

Leith cast a wary eye back at the slope and hoped Kess' outburst wouldn't attract the chimera's notice. In case it had, he got back aboard Valadan and helped Kess up behind.

"I have no objection to going around if we can do it at a safe distance," he said. "Let's go see whether that pass is really the only way through."

After two days, Leith had to admit that Kess had been right—if they could not use the pass the chimera guarded, then they could not reach the lake her crystal showed. The Berianas were a wild jumble of rock and forest, and every likely route proved impossible in the end, or else led them in entirely the opposite direction from what its beginning had given hope of.

They tried toward the sunrise first, but sheer slopes pushed them back continually, and if there was any end to the range, any spot where they might slip through, it did not seem likely they would discover it ere winter set in. They found a pass, rejoiced and ventured through—then found their way blocked by cliffs in every direction that might have been useful. They retraced their way, fighting disappointment.

Toward sun-fall was no better—stinking mud and mists of steam warned of hot springs more extensive than those they had already seen. Some spouted like whales, to Valadan's great startlement. They braved scalding and pressed on, finding little alive save the restless rock. The earth quaked beneath Valadan's cautious hooves, and finally they topped a rise to find a river of molten rock just on the other side, flowing sluggishly and throwing off a sullen heat much like the chimera's.

Leith wiped his brow and sighed.

"What is it?" Kess asked, craning over his shoulder. "Can't we get by?" That she could not lead in their present situation was a torment. She wished her own horse a miserable trek back to Esdragon.

"It's earth-fire," Leith said wearily. On some of the Isles such thick fire burst through the soil's skin betimes. If it reached the sea it threw up clouds of steam, and it blackened all that it touched. There was no fighting it—even the cold sea scarcely quenched it. He had seen villages abandoned if they lay in the path of such a flow. There was nothing else to be done.

"Earth-fire dies after a while and turns to rock," Kess said, plainly with some mad notion of crossing on that fresh-made stone.

"And sometimes more and more comes," Leith answered, forestalling her. "Or it cools in waves, like ice on a pond when the wind's blowing. It's safe one minute and impossible the next." She would not talk him into trying a crossing.

They waited for nightfall, to see by the glow how extensive the outflow was, and beheld in the darkness an awesome golden river spilling down the mountain flank without cease, its edges winking like rubies, rafts of dark stone afloat on it. Even Kess admitted there was no hope of further passage, and at dawn Leith headed them back the way they had come.

Leith cherished a brief hope that the chimera, like the earth-fire, might have only a brief life. Both were fire creatures, born on the trembling slopes. Such a hope did not seem quite beyond reason. But from the edges of the forest they could already hear the chimera roaring. They made camp, seeing no point in going closer with night drawing on, and decided to stand watches in case the monster had begun to venture out from its steep-walled lair. It might even be aware that they had returned, and they therefore kept their campfire small, lest it draw the chimera out by some tiny kinship.

Leith had the dawn watch, and by the early light—whilst

Kess still slept—he quietly curried Valadan and trimmed the burned tips of the stallion's tail hairs away.

Inspecting the horse's legs, Leith found a deep slice on Valadan's off heel. The discovery grieved him, for the cut had plainly happened days earlier and should have been tended to long ere that morning. He should have checked Valadan at once, after their race away from the chimera—and because the stallion had never limped a step, he had been foolishly neglectful.

"How did you do this?" Valadan might pay the injury no heed, but a hair deeper and the cut would have lamed him.

A sharp stone. Valadan turned his head back to regard Leith with one dark eye unconcernedly.

"Must have been *very* sharp." Leith pressed gently on the edges of the wound. It had not closed tight, but he wanted to be certain there was no dirt trapped inside, to fester. Another reason the wound should have been tended earlier. He might need to open the cut and cleanse it. His fingers felt no heat, found no discharge, and Leith thought he might be able to leave well enough alone. "A sword couldn't have done this better," he observed. There seemed to have been no bruising, either—just a deep, clean cut.

Valadan, unruffled, gathered in a mouthful of tender grass. The cut did not pain him, nor had it bled overmuch. He had forgotten it, and would do so again if Leith allowed it.

Leith's curiosity about the sharp rock did not ebb. He frowned as he stowed the grooming tools away, trying to recall the sorts of rock that could hold such a fierce edge. Kess, a glance assured him, still slept. Finally, he made his way to a point from which he might overlook that final slope they had fled over—the slope that had dissuaded the chimera from further pursuit.

He was too far away to see much. But the chimera was nowhere in sight. Leith thought he could hear it, but only faintly. Far away, he hoped. If it was close and merely quiet, he'd be in a great deal of trouble—for one bright instant.

He left his vantage and approached the slope, climbing up to the charred bushes. Still no sign of the chimera, and its noise still seemed to place it a good distance away, so Leith clambered cautiously through the brush, ventured a few steps downslope into the pass. He watched the ground carefully, lest the loose stone betray him, and strove always to be silent as a mouse or a vole—whatever was too small, too insignificant to be chimera prey. He was not heartened to recall that even a bird as small as a dove had not been overlooked.

Leith had thought he might find flints on the slope, but the rocks he encountered looked more like black glass. Shards caught the early light, flashing here and there, half buried but with wicked edges exposed. Small wonder such a stone had cut Valadan's heel—one did likewise to Leith's fingers as he dug it out of the loose debris. He put the fingers into his mouth and studied the stone with respect.

Here was the reason the chimera had not pursued them up the slope—they owed their lives to it. Probably the monster knew of the stones, might have learned they were painful. Wood it could burn, iron it could melt—but it took earth-fire itself to melt stone. The chimera could not burn the stone out of its path—and a thing that crawled on its belly would not likely care to slice itself to ribbons as it went.

A roar sounded, rather closer than the last, quite distinct, and the breeze felt hot, unless that was his ready imagination having at him. Leith made haste up the slope, snatching a stone or three as he went, for use in the plan his mind was so reluctantly shaping.

Chimera Hunting

"I *KNOW* I said you couldn't outrun it," Leith explained to Valadan as he bound the stallion's tail into a war club. He had just finished braiding the stallion's mane—the small, tight plaits were less ready to take fire than free-flowing hair, especially when wet. "But you can run rings around that monster while I stick a spear or two into it. That's all the speed we need to have."

Valadan snorted and tossed his braid-bedecked head. It might have been pride—or consternation.

No need to guess which Kess was trying to express.

"Did you ride headfirst into a tree branch or something?" she inquired acidly, watching Leith's preparations. She had her back to a tree, her fists clenched. "Scramble your brains worse than usual?"

Leith did not spare her a glance. Instead he inspected his spears—poles cut from the straightest oak saplings he had been able to locate. Two were short, for throwing. The longest one was intended to be used as a lance. The weapon heads were palm-length blades of carefully chipped black obsidian, their edges knapped sharp as razors, so thin they were transparent, almost colorless.

"Are you ready?" he asked Kess, ignoring her question.

"No." She remained leaning against her tree. "Tell me again what I'm supposed to be doing while the chimera's cooking you."

Leith lifted his shield—solid planks of oak sword-chopped from a lightning-blasted stump, pegged to a crossbrace and secured with a grip of leather straps. It seemed heavy. He couldn't decide if its weight would be a comfort or a trial. "I'd ask you to chant a farewell to my Lady, but there's no time to

149

teach it to you. What you're going to *do* is get as high up on that far slope as you can and cross through the pass. You claim you can hide things that should be seen, and from what *I've* seen and not seen, you didn't lie. So the chimera shouldn't know you're there if it's busy with me. And please don't look back, no matter what you hear, because if you don't get through there's not much point to this." He fussed at the straps, not convinced they'd hold—though likely the shield would do him little service once the chimera's breath had caught it a time or two. Wood took light easily, even if wet.

"Why are you doing this?"

Leith led Valadan into the deepest part of the small stream and began splashing water over both of them. The spears and the shield had soaked all night. "Because wet things burn more slowly than dry things," he explained patiently, and poured water over his head. He knew exactly what Kess meant, but he didn't feel capable of explaining his motives to her. They didn't hold up even under his own scrutiny.

Leith thought his plan was sound—even after hearing Kess attack it constantly for the past day and a half. It was their best chance. He was also aware that his scheme was highly dangerous and likely to get him killed if his luck permitted such a finality. He was willing to risk that fiery fate, so that Kess might get across the pass, but he could not rationalize it to her. He didn't even want to try.

The gray wool cloak was black with water when Leith lifted it out of the stream and struggled to drape it over his shoulders. He and Valadan were both soaked to their skins, as wet as they might contrive to become. The sodden folds of his cloak hung heavy as mail when Leith tried to adjust them, and everything he wore clung to him. Riding promised to be a miserable experience, but the trade offered some protection.

Leith fitted a sloshing boot into the near stirrup and mounted awkwardly, settled into the wet saddle. Kess handed him his shield, then the three spears. Leith put the lance shaft and one of the throwing spears under his right knee, keeping the final spear ready in his hand. He'd soon need it.

"Remember," he said, his teeth knocking from the chill of the water, increased by the fresh breeze. "Don't look back."

Kess looked down at the crystal, cupped in her pale hands. She shook her head but would not look at his face.

"Are you ready?" Leith asked again. He would have insisted that Kess soak herself, too, but he wanted her free to run as fast as she was able, and wet clothing would slow her without gaining her any real safety. He legged Valadan out of the chill water and headed for the pass. He wanted to call "good luck" to Kess, but dared not. The irony aside, his voice would have given away his trembling.

Leith rode the entire way down the obsidian-flecked slope and out onto the floor of the pass, unchallenged. There was neither sound nor sight of the chimera, bar a freshly charred bird or two. They passed the sun-bleached bones of what might have been a deer. Leith hoped he did not likewise find the bones of Kess' father.

They had allowed Kess a little start, to make her way to the farther slope—she had a good distance to cover and only her own legs to carry her—but Leith did not want to let her go too much in advance of them. It was no part of his plan that the chimera should ever know Kess was trespassing upon its territory. It had to see him first and be safely occupied. That way she'd cross unmolested.

Leith put up the hood of his cloak and knotted the wet strings tight at his throat. The soaked wool would protect his face from searing, at least in the beginning. He began, very softly, to chant an office to his Lady. It was not his intention to become a suicide, and he wished that She might know this, but the chimera could have other ideas—it was a sun beast, he was sure, and the sun held full sway over the high, baked pass from dawn to dusk. He might not be able, after, to thank his Lady for those mercies She had so consistently shown him.

Valadan's hoofbeats echoed from the hot rocks to either side. It sounded as if an army were on the move, but there was no response, no challenge. Leith felt a touch of unease, a foreboding. Where *was* the chimera? Was the monster ignoring him, and stalking Kess? He couldn't see her—and he *should* not be able to if her spellcraft was working—but nevertheless he fretted, unable to dismiss his fear. Kess wouldn't be able to go so fast as he did, even with the start he'd given her. If she'd fallen behind, the chimera might somehow see her first, pursue her in place of the more obvious target. He had warned her of that very thing—but had she heeded?

He and Valadan had reached the midpoint of the pass, heat-shimmery sand and rock surrounding them on all sides, no escape now within their reach. The great heat was pulling water out of cloth and hair—already Leith's face felt dry and tight, though it would soon begin to sweat, and his bound hair no longer dripped down his back.

Where was the chimera? They hadn't gotten nearly so far the last time.

Though they were each anticipating it, the chimera's roar startled both horse and rider mightily. Valadan shied hard and whirled about to face the sound, while Leith fought to keep his seat—feeling he'd been left astride empty air, a dozen yards away. Fortunately his soaked trews were practically glued to the saddle, and he could not be parted from his mount. He took a firmer grip on his shield, raising it a little. It weighed considerably more than most shields, and his arm was unused to it and would soon weary—but only stout oak stood a chance of resisting flame for even the briefest while, and there had been no time to refine his design.

The chimera came shrieking down the near slope like fire out of the heavens—the drop gave it momentum as well as the advantage of surprise, Leith thought, huddling behind a shield that seemed useless for all its solidity. Tried to think. Mostly he was terrified, and standing to face the monster's rush was the hardest thing he had done in the whole of his life.

Kess picked her way through the loose rock and gravel-laced sand of the slope, thinking: *Leith was right. We could never have outrun it up here.* It was hard even to walk, with one foot ever uphill of the other and the footing so uncertain. Her instinct was to run, but if she did that she might lose hold of the illusion she had drawn about herself, the illusion that kept the chimera from seeking her out.

As yet, there was no sign of the creature. Kess did not think it was likely to spring from ambush—it seemed to stun its prey with a dramatic attack—but she kept alert for movement, all the same. When Valadan came out onto the floor of the pass, she noticed him at once and turned her head to look, in defiance of Leith's urgent pleas. But that one look was all she'd spare him—Kess had no intention of going back to help when the chimera struck.

From a little distance, Leith's overbold features contrived to look heroic. Distance whittled away the length of his jaw, sculpted his nose to a sort of grace. And she could see only one of his eyes—she knew it was the green one, but his brow threw a deep midday shadow into the socket, masking the odd color.

He and the stallion made a noble picture, pacing so slowly

over the hot ground, weapons at the ready. Kess hurried along, trying not to fall behind. She looked at Leith again, out the tail of her eye. He looked sick with dread, scared to death—and just then the chimera roared.

Leith's instinct was to hurl a spear straight into the oncoming whirlwind. He held back—though his right hand shook as if it had a will all its own—because he knew he could never throw the spear over such a distance and hope to hit anything with it. His heart insisted, demanded instant response to the danger, but Leith knew á distance that felt safe to throw from was *not* one he could hit from. His head won the argument, at last, barely, and stayed his hand.

The chimera's high-pitched howling was unnerving—it made Leith think the monster was even closer than it was. So hard to measure the distance with his eyes, while it came at him head on, confusing him as to its progress. The beast's pelt was as bright as the sun, hard to look at. Tears sprang to Leith's eyes when he tried, yet he had to keep it in sight.

Valadan was wanting to maneuver, but Leith held the stallion steady with seat and voice, feigning a calm he did not feel, letting the chimera close with them. He couldn't tell one moving target from another, Leith felt certain of that. And the distance still seemed too great. He waited. Fire rushed upon him. Each of his heartbeats spanned an age. *One more,* Leith promised himself, and when it came, he made his throw.

He aimed straight into the gaping maw—head on, the chimera offered no better target. A harder throw might have entered the throat and hit something vital, but the monster's breath charred the oaken shaft despite its long soaking, and the obsidian blade fell useless to earth, to be trampled like any common cobble.

Leith snatched up his second spear and hurled it after the first, with more desperate force. It fared no better—the chimera's tail scythed over its back and struck the weapon aside before the tip could bite monster flesh. The shaft burst into blue flames as it fell away.

Leith took a grip on his last spear. The chimera was now so near, he could see that it *did* have legs—a pair of tiny limbs just below its neck. Claws were opening and closing, brighter than lightning, like separate little mouths.

Above the claws, great eyes glowed like earth-fire, shifting, boiling, all but smoking. Bright gold, orange, dull red—the colors swirled and flowed, ever-changing against the intolerable white-gold coat. They were rimmed with jet black, to direct the prey's gaze into the snare. Watching, Leith forgot to be afraid. He stared without apprehension, while the monster came closer and ever closer . . .

When Valadan flung up his head and slammed him solidly in the chest with the crest of his neck, Leith's first emotion was anger, for the blow bruised. Then outrage—what had he done to deserve such action? Panic superseded, as his returning wits showed him just how *close* the monster was. Ice-cold fear thrust back the enthralling heat of the chimera's eyes.

Leith swung Valadan sharply to the left, to have him moving, to veer the stallion clear of the fiery breath. He would not have thought it a novel tactic—any but the most basic of strategies were beyond him—but the chimera did not seem to expect it. Perchance chimera prey customarily stood amazed longer than Leith had, till the thing fell upon them. At any rate, it whistled past without attempting to alter its course, and Leith charged at it as it went by, urging Valadan into a gallop, to put speed behind his spear thrust.

This time, he dared not cast from any distance, safe or otherwise. Such folly would leave him only one chance—and not a likely one—at killing the thing, and if he failed he'd have to get into even closer range, in order to use his sword on it. Therefore the lance, to thrust and stab and a mere ten feet of no longer wet oaken shaft to set the distance.

Leith's aim was high. The obsidian blade sliced the chimera just behind the white-gold mane—sliced, but did not bite, the supple dragon's body. Flames writhed upward. Valadan, too close to stop or even turn away, leapt clear over the chimera's back while Leith strove to recover and readied himself to renew the attack.

But they had hurt it, if not fatally. The chimera shrieked and whirled, and they barely avoided its breath as it snapped in the direction of its back, trying to attack the pain. Suddenly there was no hope of getting sufficient distance for another charge—Leith stabbed down with the lance shortened, trying not to overbalance and fall atop the monster. Its back was a writhing mass of flames, fluttering like golden feathers. He hit something again, still not solidly. Fiery breath curled around his shield and scorched his cheek, dried and singed the hood of his cloak in an instant, adding the stink of burned wool to the hot wind.

Valadan darted from one side to the other, as if he read Leith's thoughts before Leith shaped them. He reared, leapt, feinted and spun, dancing a deadly measure. They were never still the barest instant, lest claws or teeth or flames should in that moment outguess them. The stallion's eyes were bright with their own sparks, his ears flat back out of harm's way. His teeth were bared in challenge.

Leith wanted to get behind the beast, but as he managed that he discovered the whipping tail was fully as dangerous as the flame-breath and more solid. It lashed up and caught his shield such a blow that the wood split and his left arm went numb from wrist to shoulder. The rough planks were sizzling with steam as Leith regained his seat, and his shield arm was well-nigh useless. He fumbled for his stirrup, lost in the encounter, found its security at last. It felt hot under his boot.

Still, the fiery tail was but a single peril. The claws could not reach them, the breath could not sear them. Valadan leapt and dodged and made whatever shift was necessary to keep them behind the chimera, which maybe could not see them so well, either, if they could just stay in the right spot.

Leith leaned over the right side of Valadan's neck. The braided mane pressed against his burned cheek. He held the lance shaft tight to his side and chose his target. The wide spot just back of the mane—either the thing's heart or its lungs ought to be under there somewhere, if it had either, and maybe he might even pin the beast to the ground, then cut its head off, like a snake's. Only the tail to watch out for, and it would come up like a scorpion's, once the chimera realized what he was about.

Valadan dodged the tail, danced past it, let the chimera just catch sight of him—then feinted back the other direction. Leith leaned out, aiming the lance as the chimera's body curved nearer to him. As if he jousted, he locked the shaft firm to his side, clamped between elbow and ribs.

The obsidian point hit, solidly at last, with Valadan's speed providing the thrusting power. The impact drove Leith's breath from his lungs, rocked him back against the cantle. It also shattered the oaken shaft, with a snap like a whip crack.

Leith flung the half-yard of wood he still clutched away and with numbed fingers tore his sword clumsily from its scabbard. Every blow struck now would carry a new risk—the chimera's heat would course up the metal blade and sear his hand, and the harder he struck the worse 'twould be. Thus he'd chosen spears for his primary weapon, but all were gone now. The thing's heat might actually *melt* his sword, but Leith had no choice. Metal would last longer than his bare hands.

The chimera writhed and bent into a ring, snapping its jaws at the bit of spear still embedded in its back, while Leith stabbed and slashed at anything he could reach, determined, unflinching—and not bothering the monster to any serious degree. The chimera knew how to deal with man's weapons. In an instant its fierce internal fire could liquefy steel, and the weapon that now pained it would cease to exist. In a moment . . .

Volcanic glass was not so quick to melt as bronze or steel. It was born of earth-fire, and only earth-fire could unmake it. The chimera rolled over onto its back, hissing like a giant's kettle come to the boil, and flames shot from its jaws and nostrils. It rolled upon the spear shaft, and even as the splintered oak took fire, the obsidian blade was pushed deeper than ever Leith had managed, shoved home by the chimera's own weight. The tip pierced its furnace heart. The monster's own flames began to blacken it.

Leith, noticing that between desperate blows, hauled Valadan hastily back. Something was happening—the chimera had been immune to its flame, as a snake to its poison. He might somehow have hit something vital.

The heat increased, and it seemed only prudent to retreat yet more, though Leith held his sword ready to strike if need be. All the air seemed to have gone—Leith gasped and felt as if he smothered. The chimera curled in upon itself, pumping out one gout of white flame after another. Its mane snapped and crackled. The tail went gray-white with ash and crumbled away, from the tip in toward the body. Valadan retreated another dozen steps from the unpredictable flames, but none pursued him, though the hot wind they gave off whipped about him.

Finally all that remained was a great cinder on the ground, in the middle of the pass. A breeze blew, suddenly and unexpectedly cool. Far away, a hawk cried sharply.

Leith pulled his hood back and let the welcome air wash over his skin. The woolen cloth was so hot, it nearly blistered his fingers. He fumbled at the lacings, gasping, his charred shield getting in his way. He needed to breathe . . .

Under him, Valadan's sweat-soaked sides heaved, and the stallion trembled as he endeavored to stand steady. Leith came back to himself with a piercing stab of remorse—exhausted as he was, he had his own two legs to stand upon, and for his part in the combat they had just survived, Valadan deserved the consideration of having his rider's weight removed from his back at the earliest moment 'twas safe.

Leith kicked out of his right stirrup, staring all the while at the ashen heap that had lately been his enemy. How silent the day suddenly was! He thought he'd hear the chimera's furnace-roaring all the rest of his life, in his nightmares. He swung his right leg high, dismounting. It was more of a struggle than he expected—he was exhausted, and his legs trembled like Valadan's. He wondered if they'd support him on the ground. Grimly Leith forced himself to stand straighter in the left iron, so he'd clear Valadan's rump rather than clumsily—and unforgivably—kicking it.

As his right leg came over and the left stirrup took his full weight, charred leather parted abruptly. His support so unexpectedly deserting him, Leith pitched backward toward the ground. He was too astounded to fall properly, to tuck his shoulder and roll safely out of it—never having fallen from a horse while freighted with battle gear, he lacked a handy reflex to overcome his surprise. He snatched at the stallion's neck, but Valadan's braided mane offered his stiff fingers no hope of a saving grip. Leith fell, helpless as a meal sack.

But for the unfamiliar burden of his makeshift shield, he might only have jarred down bruisingly hard on his backside in the sun-baked dirt, at worst sprawled awkwardly and scraped an elbow as he tumbled under Valadan. Instead, Leith landed smack on his rump, and the shield's cumbersome weight sent him straight over backward. His head met the ground with a jolt. His breath left him. Lights, bright as the chimera's pelt, exploded behind his eyelids.

Half a heartbeat later, the treacherous shield's long edge, charred and split but still solid oak, came up out of nowhere to fetch him a nasty blow on chin and jaw.

Leith's teeth knocked together. Another burst of light, tinged with scarlet. His ears filled with a great rushing sound, like a storm-tide crashing in upon a hapless shore.

He still gripped his sword. It clattered against a rock as the strength went out of his arm, but Leith did not hear. A wave of darkness swept him away, even as an increasingly remote corner of his mind registered outrage at the anticlimactic injustice of the accident—just his luck, to defeat a monster and instantly be undone by a bad harness strap!

Rescued?

VALADAN NOSED LEITH'S shoulder gently. Kess, when she breathlessly arrived, was none so considerate. She lifted the shield clear of him, undid the straps from his unresponsive arm, flung the bits of blackened wood away.

"There's no time for this foolery!" she hissed at him. *"Get up!"*

She gave Leith a hard shake to bolster her message, but he did not hasten to obey her—did not even moan a protest at her rough treatment. His still face was waxy pale, save where the chimera's breath had left it pink and blistered. He had lost half his left eyebrow, the hairs singed clean away. His right cheek was scraped where the shield had hit it. The wood had cut his chin, as well—blood and soot trickled along the line of his jaw, toward the blisters.

His nose was bleeding, his lip, too, but Leith didn't appear to be bothered by pain from any of his hurts. He seemed really quite peaceful, with both his eyes gently closed and exactly alike for once. Kess—disobeying orders, of course—had witnessed the outcome of the combat, then watched Leith tumble out of his saddle just afterward. She would not have been much surprised to discover that he'd broken his neck—his landing had been graceless even by *his* standards—but the first thing she'd sought and found upon reaching Leith's side was confirmation that his chest rose and fell, more or less normally.

He drew breath, but that was the only sign of life Leith gave. He responded to neither her touch nor her words. Which meant, Kess thought, that he'd either fainted from his burns while still a-horse, or else hit his head when he fell. Possibly he'd contrived to do both. That sort of disaster was not beyond his capacity. She looked about for water to dash into his face, but of course there was not a drop to be seen. Even Leith's clothing, so recently dripping, was dry as old bones, and useless to her.

A glint of sunlight caught her attention. It proved to be the pendant Leith wore around his neck, next to the bag of patently useless luck charms. Its greenish pale hue was nearly a match for Leith's complexion at that moment.

Kess had striven all morning—ere they set out to cross the pass—to discover something of use in her hard-won crystal. Save for those horsemen—which even *she* could not believe were anywhere near—Kess had seen nothing. Possibly she had been afraid to look too deeply, flinching from the thought of seeing the chimera's snarl again, even safely trapped in crystal, defeating her visions. Now the moonstone offered her a sudden, unbidden view.

She beheld again the familiar, perfect lake, the island set within it like a jewel. Then she saw a single figure crossing the rude causeway that linked island to shore. A gray-cloaked figure and distant, but by the near-white hair she knew it was herself.

Herself, all alone . . .

Well, Leith had said not to turn back, whatever she might hear. And upon the thought Kess *did* hear something, a noise among the rocks, as if one stone slid upon another in the blasting heat. She got to her feet, so rapidly that her head swam, and turned to face the peril while the vision went to rags behind her eyes.

A puff of wind swirled around the cindery remains of the chimera. Thrice it circled—Kess counted carefully—then made off for the far side of the pass.

Kess didn't know whether to take the wind for a sign or not. She had seen no wind like it, but the furnace of the pass produced odd updrafts, which the rocks bent this way and that. It *might* be a guide, coming as it did on the heels of the vision . . . She stepped over Leith and moved a few paces, following the moving dust, drawn after it. She made a decision: Leith could catch up later. She was amazed she'd ever considered waiting for him. She wouldn't have turned back to rescue him, had the chimera been victorious.

Faster to take the horse. Kess reached for the trailing reins.

Valadan laid his ears back, giving her an ugly look from under his singed foretop. Nothing moved but his ears, yet the stallion's threat was implicit. He understood her intention.

Best not, Kess reconsidered. She set off on foot for the far end of the pass. The wind was gone, but she had seen the path it took.

Leith wondered whether he might be dead—caught after all by the chimera's flame, his unlikely victory only imagined, a desperate fantasy . . .

No. He hurt far too much. He'd seen dead men—they didn't look as if they still suffered. Whereas he did. His neck felt as if someone had attempted to tear his head loose from his body and had almost managed the feat. His teeth ached, all the way along his jaw. And when Leith unwisely tried to lift his head, there was worse in store—waves of pain of such intensity that he perceived them mainly as colors, blood red and lightning-white. That such pain did not allow him to escape back into unconsciousness was particularly cruel in his dizzy estimation.

Like any tide, the agony eventually crested and at length began to ebb. Finally Leith accepted that his imminent death was unlikely—accepted with no little regret, since he was fairly sure such an event would have put a welcome end to his pain.

"What happened?" he asked faintly, his lips scarcely parting. His mouth was stiff, and his jaw hurt, from the tiniest motion.

The stirrup leather was burned, and broke, Valadan reported miserably, somewhere nearby. *You fell. I could not help you.*

But it was not Valadan who was supporting his aching head, pouring water between his parched lips. No horse had hands to do either. Leith opened his eyes, braving the bright sunlight and the pain-stabs it created.

The figure leaning over him swam in and out of clarity, never quite sharp enough for him to recognize, but Leith determined at least who was *not* trying to assist him.

"Where's Kess?" he whispered, surprised.

"Where indeed?" a strange voice asked. "Lucky for you I happened along."

A chill washed over Leith, from his chest to his toes—a presentiment of danger that almost succeeded in clearing his battered head. He decided not to answer, to be guarded in his questions as well. At least until he had some idea of how matters stood.

"Were you with my cousin, then?" the voice probed. "But of course you must have been. I saw no other tracks. And what were you fighting here? Is this some of Kessallia's doing, or did bandits burn your camp?"

Leith would not answer. He tried to deny he even recognized Kess' name—he thought he might manage such a deception, given his obviously distressed state.

His actually distressed state betrayed him in very short order. The stranger thoughtfully helped him to sit up—only he wasn't especially careful about it, and a sudden jolt made the dry landscape swirl like the center of a whirlpool. Leith's gorge rose. He struggled desperately against the nausea, but pain whiplashed through his head all the same, causing his stomach to heave and empty itself, and instantly the pain inside his skull redoubled. The world broke up into a thousand fragments of shadow and sunlight, and shutting his eyes did not shut out the swirling, which went on and on.

After that episode, Leith had no idea what he was saying—or not saying. The earth rocked and twisted under him—he thought for a confused few moments that he must be out upon the sea again, about to be cast overboard for ill-wishing the ship. He could feel his cracked lips moving, could hear a voice he thought was his own speaking—but he had no idea what betrayals it was engaged upon.

The edges of the world continued dancing. After an especially intense interval of the unusual motion, Leith realized that he had been lifted, set atop Valadan's back once more. The roaring in his ears came and went. He tried to ignore it. His hands and feet tingled, cramped.

"Don't want you falling off again, do we?" the strange voice said brightly, into his left ear. Leith trained his jumpy vision upon his own hands, which were bound to each other with a twist of rope and thence tied to the pommel of his saddle. He next realized that his feet were likewise linked together, by rope, under Valadan's belly. He was tied onto his own horse!

Leith began at once to struggle, trying frantically to kick loose of his bonds. The attempt cost him his precarious balance, but as he was beginning to topple out of the saddle a large hand clapped onto his shoulder and steadied him.

"None of that, now! I can as easy tie you belly-down on the horse—and I will if I need to—but I wouldn't like to ride with my head hanging down, if I were you. Your brains might just run out."

Valadan turned his head back, nosing the toe of Leith's right boot gently, surreptitiously. *Sit still,* he cautioned.

Leith forced his instincts into check. True, he seemed to be a captive, but that was no reason to panic and finish off killing himself. Whoever this stranger might be, he could not know that Valadan was far from an ordinary horse. If Leith waited patiently, he could be certain of rescue at the first opportune moment—no rope could long withstand an assault from Valadan's teeth. Anyway, Leith had realized—had been forced to recognize—a most unpleasant fact: He was too dizzy to escape if he *did* manage to get loose. He'd only fall again, a disaster he was unwilling to repeat. A snatch of memory came back like a hammer-blow—a brief flash of falling when he had expected to dismount. A startling fall, followed by a very hard landing on his head. He didn't want to experience either again anytime soon, Leith thought, still tasting sickness in his mouth.

The constant pain in his head damped down gradually to a throbbing that kept ragged counterpoint to his heartbeat. His vision would not clear—moving his eyes or his head made the images jump and his stomach twist uneasily. Leith squeezed his eyelids tight together and waited for the pain to ebb again. It did, barely, till he could tolerate it.

"That's better," the voice said approvingly, mistaking his weakness for obedience. "Now let's just see where my cousin has gone."

Kess was hot, dusty, and pushing herself onward to escape her thoughts—which, carried with her, picked and pecked at her whenever she relaxed her vigilance to the slightest degree.

The mountainside beyond the pass was vile country, hardly improved by the cool of the early evening. Every hollow was brimful of berryless brambles that tore clothes and flesh while offering no bounty of food by way of recompense. Most of the better places to walk sported snakes and serpents, soaking up the remainder of the day's heat from the stones, disinclined to yield their places and apt to hiss startlingly. The trails were rocky—easy enough for a horse to handle, but bruising to feet and legs more delicate than Valadan's. Kess cursed her stupidity with every sharp point she trod upon.

She should not have allowed the stallion's challenge to cow her. She should have mastered him. She should have thrown herself onto his back—he would have had to obey the bit, the reins . . .

And of course left Leith stranded, hurt and afoot, too.

Better him than me, Kess thought, but her heart wasn't in it. She wondered why; she was fairly certain Leith had expected to come out of the chimera fight *dead*, not merely blistered and fainting. He'd *ordered* her to desert him, in advance, expecting disaster.

An order she'd been only too happy to obey.

She struggled along until the sky was a deep violet and the ground before her a featureless gray murk. All the while, Kess continually worked her charms to keep herself unseen. The deceits might make it hard for Leith to find her, had he recovered enough to follow—but there could well be another chimera about. Nor was Leith the only person who might be trying to track her.

The stranger had a well-developed nose, a high forehead, and russet-colored hair with a beard to match, which managed to be wispy and wavy all at the same time. The firelight made it impossible to determine whether his light eyes were blue or gray. And the edges of things still shivered, as if Leith watched them through the chimera's flame, compounding the difficulty.

Not much resemblance to Kess, Leith thought, though the man had styled her "cousin" more than once. Getting a sight of the solid-boned dun the man rode, and the armor and other warlike gear tied behind his saddle, Leith had cherished a faint hope that he might have found—or rather been found by—Kess' father, but he saw now that was only a desperate fancy. This man was plainly too young, all else aside.

Just as plainly, he had been following them for some while. Leith had refused to answer any more of the questions put to him, an intransigence the stranger seemed to take in good part. When he halted at dusk to make camp, he had heated water and washed Leith's face clean of the chimera's soot, even shaved those bits of Leith's chin that were neither bruised nor blistered.

However, he had first bound Leith's ankles together, and only left his hands loose whilst Leith ate the small bit of food he thought his belly would tolerate. It was in fact all Leith could do to chew—his jaw ached and was much swollen. His neck was stiff, wrenched when his shield hit his face at an awkward angle, he thought. He could manage nothing more solid than soaked bread, and only a very little of that, quite slowly. Leith kept patiently at it only because he knew he needed to regain whatever strength he could, and food would speed recovery, could he swallow it down.

The stranger, who was a tall man and well muscled, ate rather more, and then bound Leith's wrists securely to one another.

"It doesn't matter to me if you don't talk," he said companionably, finishing a last knot. "It would likely be quicker if you told me where she's bound, but Kessallia's afoot and we're not, so we'll catch her up soon anyway. I'm a good tracker," he added confidently.

Not once Kess starts hiding the trail, Leith thought, but held his peace. He was bewildered, a condition that did not ease even as the rest of his thinking slowly cleared. The puzzle took what little attention he could muster. Valadan had reported that Kess had seen him fall, had departed when she was unable to rouse him.

That made sense of a sort—at least it was completely, utterly like Kess, to abandon him when she had the chance. But why her haste, such that she denied herself Valadan? The chimera was slain, no threat, and Kess didn't know this stranger was following them. Even Valadan had not known until the dun gelding had nickered, upon catching his scent. And by the time that had happened, Leith had been lying insensible for a good two hours, by the stallion's reckoning. Kess had been likewise two hours gone.

Kess *had* known they were not alone in the Berianas, however. She'd seen it in the crystal, Leith remembered. *He* was the one who'd been so certain none could have followed them through the abandoned mine, or stumbled upon them afterward by unlucky chance. He had let logic blind him, when he knew his ill luck had naught to do with logic, and had never seriously considered that they might not be alone on their quest, or that some other party might prefer that they fail at it.

Kess dreamed of a chimera.

It crouched beside her mother, and her mother's right hand rested without harm upon its flickering flaming head, smoothed and restrained the waving mane of fire.

With her left hand, her mother was beckoning Kess nearer, but Kess could stir neither of her dream-feet. The chimera was snarling at her, and its touch would consume her, she was certain. All her life, folk had jeered at her witch blood, and often she had wished she did not bear its taint.

Now she feared she did not carry enough.

Leith was greatly heartened to discover no sign of Kess' passage as they moved on, next day. He was rather more alert—his head still ached fiercely, but the worst of the dizziness had been slept away. He sat relaxed upon Valadan's back, kept there by his own improved balance rather than depending on clever roping and Valadan's care of him. He was, of course, still bound hand and foot, unable to so much as wipe the sweat from his brow, shade his eyes from the glare of the sun above. Or to investigate the lump on the back of his skull.

Leith knew it was there, where the worst of the throbbing had heavily settled itself. He thought the wound had bled— when the stranger had drawn his hood away from his face, the cloth had been stuck to something, and his hair seemed matted when he turned his head. There were interested flies buzzing about. Leith supposed poking fingers at the lump would only have made it hurt worse, and he ought to have been grateful to be so absolutely relieved of the temptation to meddle. He was not minded to be grateful to his captor, however. Not for any reason.

Leith was careful to feign greater weakness than he felt, now and again, to mask whatever recovery he managed. No sense letting the stranger discover that he felt well enough to contemplate escape, and it was simple enough to ride with his head drooping, as if he were still in a daze, his wits knocked loose and not yet quite returned.

The position also proved useful for a close watching of the ground they rode over. Leith heartily hoped they had strayed off of Kess' trail entirely, but from time to time he squinted his right eye closed and peered through the left, trying to see whether they had by mischance stumbled across the path she had concealed. By sun-high he noticed that their passage was in some instances not so difficult as it appeared it should have been—a sure sign to him that Kess had gone before them, sowing charms of confusion in her wake.

Leith gave no sign that he was aware of the discrepancies. The stranger seemed genuinely heedless. He turned back from an illusionary rockfall to choose an easier way, and they rode for the remainder of the day in a direction Leith felt certain was contrary to Kess' before halting to make camp.

Continuing his sham, Leith stumbled to his knees when he was untied and permitted to dismount. The stranger helped him up, then sat him down with his back propped against a tall rock and gave him a few sips of stale water. Leith kept his eyes shut while the water soothed his parched throat, since weakness would surely put his captor at least a little off his guard.

"Too much sun," the stranger decided worriedly. "I shouldn't make you ride so long." He steadied the waterskin against Leith's lips, which Leith had allowed to go slack. No harm in the man's thinking he was too faint to stir.

He very much hoped that the stranger would on that account neglect to tie him securely—but Leith found himself being trussed up once more after their supper. He flinched away from the rope, which had already chafed his wrists while he rode.

"Why are you tying me?" he asked plaintively. "Are you a bandit?"

As Leith had guessed he might, the man with the rope took the query for an insult. He flushed, and the next knot he put into Leith's bonds seemed looser than it should have been.

"I have a piece or two of hacksilver," Leith volunteered. "In the pouch. You're welcome to it—"

"Keep your money. I'm no thief." The man stepped back from him.

"Then could you please untie me? I—"

"If I untie you, I won't dare turn my back on you, will I?" A few twigs were fed into the fire, which had dimmed. "Count yourself lucky I'm doing this—if I left you loose you'd just wander into trouble out there. It wouldn't have to be another chimera, you know. A panther could do for you—or a bad step in the dark. There are plenty of mountainsides to fall down, and you're not steady enough to climb onto your own horse."

Leith gave up his appeal to chivalry. He fixed his hopes on that less than perfect knot, wondering where his advantage lay. If he made no further fuss, but seemed to slide into a doze, he might not be watched too closely. Then a few knots in a rope wouldn't hinder Valadan. Just as soon as this fellow bedded down, was safely asleep . . .

"Feeling better?" the stranger asked from across the fire.

Leith, startled, jolted out of his plans for escape. Evidently he wasn't adept at deception. "My head hurts," he said, as if grudgingly—but it was no lie, and would not be for some while.

"It probably does. And riding all day in that blasted sun's not likely to cure it in a hurry—but I think we both know we can't risk delay. Kessallia—"

Leith gave the stranger what he hoped was a blank stare.

"Don't pretend you don't know anything about it!" A branch snapped between big hands. "You asked for her by name when I found you, first thing when you started to come back to yourself."

Leith tried to look mournful. He would have clutched his head for effect, except his hands were tied. So, he merely whispered that he remembered falling off his horse—and not a great deal else. It was, he thought, a wonder the useful excuse wasn't perfectly true.

The stranger pressed his lips together disgustedly and fed bits of branch to the hungry fire. "Nice try. You talked your fool head off when I found you, you know that? I know perfectly well that you were with my cousin, and I have a fair idea where she's bound. Some lake, with an island. I know you're worried about her. If you care for her at all, stop playing stupid games and help me find her before she runs across another chimera."

Leith's heart misgave him, though he tried to keep his expression unconcerned, as if a stranger was spoken of. The peril was quite real. If not a chimera, there could be mountain cats, snow leopards, or cave lions. Possibly bears. Wolves. Kess was alone, and afoot. If this person could help him find her before some danger crept up upon her . . .

But had he been rescued by the man, himself, or taken prisoner? Tying him to his saddle—well, he *was* hurt, and the bonds had certainly prevented his falling again and doing himself more damage. It might even have seemed perfectly reasonable to bind him that first night, lest he stray away in a daze and suffer some harm while his rescuer slept. But beyond that first night, the ropes began to seem more sinister confinement than rough benevolence. For himself, Leith could have chosen to risk trusting despite that—but not for Kess. He dared not. And yet he risked her if he did not, for she might be in grave need of help.

"What will you do, when you find this cousin of yours?" he asked softly.

The stranger's head came up, as if he had not anticipated the capitulation. Leith stared back, convinced he could ask without giving away more than whatever he already had. Anyone, after all, could be allowed a certain amount of curiosity about a situation he'd fallen into the center of. Surely he could avoid betraying Kess outright yet still gain a crumb of information.

The man across the fire tensed his jaw while he thought. "I shall take her back to Esdragon," he declared—as if he had convinced himself the objective could be gained as simply as that. "The government's in a shambles, and they don't even know she's gone. Brychan's not up to overseeing it. I'll take her back, and I'll wed her, and I'll set the duchy to rights."

"Just like that?" Leith asked, trying to imagine such a wonder as Kess tamely riding back to Esdragon in her cousin's company, much less all the rest. He decided he couldn't—he hadn't hit his head *that* hard.

"It didn't have to be like this, you know," the big man said. "Her father should have given her to me before he decided to seek his own death. You don't set a ship adrift before the wind with no hand at the tiller—Symond was mad, and that's doubly proved. He abandoned his duchy, and he left Kess unwed when he went."

"She's searching for him," Leith said, figuring he wasn't admitting anything the stranger didn't already know.

"Then she's mad as her father was," the man replied, then added flatly: "Symond's dead."

"So you just drag her back, and never mind what she wants—what she needs?" Leith suspected he was going to stay tied up awhile longer.

The stranger snorted. "It's for her own good. No sense Kessallia ending up in a chimera's belly, too. So tell me— where is she?"

Leith regarded him in puzzlement. "Where's who?"

A spate of furious curses. "Are we back to that? I thought you'd come to your senses."

"It comes and goes," Leith told him sadly. "Like the headache." He raised his bound hands a trifle, tried to shrug.

The cursing redoubled.

Kess watched the moon rising, unheralded by chant or flute song. She had thought she would welcome the relief from darkness, but she suffered a strong desire to hide herself from that ever-calm white face. She wondered where Leith was at that moment, if he too watched the moon rise—or if his eyes were fixed on it sightlessly, vultures having removed the flesh from around them . . .

Kess shook herself angrily. Leith had been alive when she left him, there was no reason to suppose that had altered. Probably he was cheerfully greeting his mistress a league or so away. She got her crystal out and clasped it gently.

The stone was easy to see in the silver moonlight. Clear at the irregular point, then misty, then pure unsullied white at the base, where Leith's sword had riven it free of its sister crystals and the rock they had all sprung from. There were striations on some of the flat sides and a few infant crystals the size of sand grains, clinging. Inside, in the misty part, there were mountains, and deep chasms, and planes that caught the light and delivered it back in shattered rainbows. One could imagine many shapes, depending upon which face one chose to examine . . .

One could do in fact anything, because the crystal remained all the while just a finger of cool, dead stone. Kess stared till her eyes burned fiercely with the strain and her jaw ached, but she was granted no vision. The crystal refused absolutely to open its mystic heart to her. She turned the stone this way and that, so that one facet after another became a perfect mirror for the moonlight. Here a triangle, now a kite shape, like a shield. Now a straight-sided shape she knew no name for, irregularly five-sided. Now one triangle set over another. Tiny, or large, surfaces smooth as glass or faintly dimpled, chipped or scored.

It was to no avail.

Study as she might, no vision came to guide, to console or comfort. Kess sat alone beneath the cold uncomforting moon, with a dead piece of stone in her sore hands.

She wanted her mother. Her mother would heal her, instruct her, make a thousand slights and insults fall away at a touch. She would have visions she could use, power she could bend to her will, not bow helplessly before.

Kess looked into the crystal again—that empty tip of ice-clear stone—and knew a touch of dread, that her hopes should be likewise empty, her mother dead after all and as far beyond her reach as the moon overhead.

The stranger besieged Leith a trifle longer, tried his stubborn defenses with blunt words and sharp logic. Leith resisted, still pretending ignorance and memory damaged by his fall, and was finally punished by being left to sleep where he sat, his back to the cold rock, tied so he was unable to so much as wrap his cloak tight against the night chill. The moon rose. Leith began to whisper the welcome chant, then decided that he might as well speak aloud—Kess was not there to be annoyed, and he did not much care if he displeased her cousin in one more particular.

Signs of Passage

HIS FEET HAD been left unbound, so when they halted and the stranger dismounted, Leith unthinkingly copied him.

Doing so, he forgot he'd no stirrup on the near side, and after a heart-stopping slip, he wound up clinging to Valadan's neck as best he could with his bound hands, till he touched solid ground with his dangling toes and could stand.

The near disaster took the last of Leith's forbearance. "Will you let me have the use of my hands for half an hour tonight?" he inquired savagely. "Let me rig a new stirrup before I kill myself!"

The stranger chuckled. "Should have taken better care of the last one. If you'd waited till I told you you could get down, this wouldn't have happened." He prised Leith's fingers loose from Valadan's unraveling braids and spun him around. "You're lucky you didn't go on your head again. And I have no intention of cutting you loose. You don't deserve the consideration. You're not in the least cooperative." He wiped sweat from his sun-reddened brow and waved a fly away.

Leith, bound, could do neither. "Being tied up like a prize pig has a lot to do with that!" He was wishing with all his heart that just *once* he could make his curse yield to his will—what he wouldn't give to inflict some unchancy disaster on this man, upon the instant! Nothing elaborate as curses went, but even a couple of fat juicy boils on his bottom . . .

You're upset because you got a scare, a cool dusty corner of his mind pointed out. *It has nothing to do with being tied and everything to do with almost falling again. You'd feel just the same if your hands had been loose when it happened.*

It was true. Leith's stomach still churned uneasily, and he'd thought he was about to be sick again, just from the fright.

And had the stranger not been there, he'd have lashed out at anything handy, even Valadan. Leith chastized himself for the folly. He couldn't afford to panic. He had to *think*, if he hoped to get free.

The stranger had shifted his attention to his original purpose. for dismounting—making a close examination of the ground. He bent down, peering, and Leith entertained a brief foolish notion of trying to overpower him, possibly choking the man with the rope that prisoned his hands. Common sense and an assessment of the man's breadth of shoulder dissuaded him.

"What have you found?" he asked casually.

"Boot tracks," came a muffled reply. "Here. And here again." He pointed, to emphasize.

The man was as competent a tracker as he'd claimed. Leith would never have noticed the scrapes in the dust, the faint scars upon the rocks. He supposed they *were* tracks, but at the same time he doubted they were Kess'. Squinting produced no sign of her, not the slightest hint. Leith kept the notion to himself. Let this man think what he liked, and go wrong as often as possible—that suited him very well indeed.

"Now let's just see where they take us." The stranger caught hold of his horse's bridle and reached out for Valadan's.

Valadan reared back in alarm, then bolted. Brushing past the big man, ignoring Leith's startled pleas that he halt, he pounded down the dusty track for half a furlong, till he was nearly out of sight. Leith whistled frantically, alarmed at the desertion, and after an anxious moment the stallion came dancing back, snorting and arching his neck, plunging and trampling the ground, stepping as if each footfall were upon burning coals.

Leith ran up to him and seized the bridle with both hands, heedless of being dragged if the horse moved suddenly again. "What's got into you?" The stallion nuzzled his chest and snorted at him. Leith thought he was glad he hadn't been aboard during the precipitous flight. He wouldn't have stayed in the saddle long enough to escape, if such had been Valadan's design. So what . . .

Let him try to track now. The stud rolled an eye at Leith, merrily. Rubies and emeralds flashed. Sapphires glittered like sunlight on lakewater.

Understanding dawned. Leith grinned, though it hurt his face. He let loose of the bridle, lowered his hands, stepped back. The stranger was cursing steadily as he walked ahead of them, obviously in some sort of difficulty. On the dusty ground, Valadan's hoofprints were plain, his fresh trail obvious.

The other, fainter signs were quite obliterated.

Searching for tracks under the fullest glare of the sun's hot eye was a miserable pastime. The rocky defiles were as ovenlike as the pass had been, and nigh as devoid of shade. Betimes a ledge of rock would cast a bit of darkness, but the rock gave back full measure of the heat it received, and there was no relief in shadows save to the eyes. Nor was there water other than that which they carried, and Leith could not reach the waterskin behind his saddle, far less unstopper it to drink. His mouth was as dry as dust, while the rest of him was sweat-soaked, the heat and moisture held close to his skin by heavy wool cloth that scratched and chafed till he wanted to weep.

He did not suppose Kess would have come this way. It didn't lead to her goal. There was no sign at all that she had gone ahead of them and precious little evidence that anyone else had done so, either. A faint few tracks proved all at once—at a flat spot that might once have held a rare rain puddle and briefly thereafter mud—to be those of a wild sheep.

The morning sky had been pale blue. Now it had gone white, with the sun blazing brighter white at its zenith. Leith closed both his eyes for a moment's relief, then opened the left the barest trifle and scanned the ground through lash-shade and unidentified but useful magic. He saw no tracks. Kess had not been this way, and was more than likely several leagues away, close to achieving her quest.

Ahead, her cousin cast imprecations on women in general and stupid girls in particular, and drained the last drops of water from the flask he carried.

How long before the man gave up his search? Hardship didn't appear to offer a clue—he had food, and didn't seem concerned about it, so probably he had ample supply for a few days' searching. There'd be water about somewhere, even if it wasn't in the man's flask at the moment. And the fellow *knew* Kess was in the Berianas, close—that part was Leith's fault, however unintentional. He'd been ever so much larger and more obvious than a smudged footprint, lying along Kess' trail, pointing this man straight to her.

There might be an amend he could make for that, Leith thought, blinking sweat out of his eyes with little success. If he set aside his schemes of escaping and rejoining Kess, if he stayed with this fellow, could he not see to it that no chance of missing her trail went unexploited? What Valadan had done already, he could copy, expand. He could ensure that this "cousin" of hers never ran across Kess. He'd only need to keep at it for a day or so—surely by then Kess would have reached the lake, the island—and if her crystal told true, her witch mother.

And *he* would at the same time have lost his hard-won chance for a cure. It would suit his curse just fine, to permit him to get close and then deny him, turn him away, goal in sight yet utterly unattainable.

Leith was fairly certain that he could find the lake, even without Kess at his elbow. But what use to find it tardily, after she'd been there for days? Why should her mother consent to help him, unless he was seen to have helped her daughter? Supposing he helped Kess by staying away from her: What did that gain him? Kess would call it no help at all, certainly, and there would be no way he could disprove that dismissal. Thinking of what she'd have to say to him made his head buzz.

No, that was flies again. Leith tried to raise his hands to shoo them away, was thwarted by the rope that lashed him to his saddle once more. A fat fly, its eyes pale green and its body blue as sword steel, gave him a nasty bite on the back of his right hand. Valadan, hearing him hiss with pain, gave a vigorous sweep of his tail, which would have rid them both of insect pests—save that his tail was yet mostly braided into the war club that had saved it from chimera flame. It thumped uselessly against his haunch, and the stallion blew a great snort of exasperation.

Tomorrow, Leith silently promised them both. They'd escape, and he'd rejoin Kess, neither too early nor too late. He tried not to think about the role luck must play in such a scheme—and what that would inevitably mean to any hope of success.

Kess had dreamed of chimeras, hunting her through the mountains. The sun was well up when she woke, curled into a cramped, uncomfortable ball, presumably trying even while she slept to make herself tiny enough to escape the monsters' notice. She disentangled herself and crept out from her rocky lair. She was loath to expose herself by climbing high enough to get her bearings, but she knew no other way of checking her course toward the lake save by sight. She was not making anything like the time she had anticipated—either the distance was greater than it had looked, or she was making mistakes. There were unexpected features to the terrain, this side of the pass. She got confused, and afoot she was far shorter than atop a horse—her arc of vision was much reduced. She could miss her way by a yard and never know what she could not see.

No use attempting the crystal—she had a headache, and grit in every seam of her clothing, and no inclination for yet another disappointment. The lake was close, only a ridge or two away. She'd find it, no matter how the terrain conspired against her. Had she come so far, to balk at a few blisters on her dainty feet?

Was that a noise, behind the rocks? Something big, moving? And was the air too warm for the sun, alone?

It was far too much like her dreams. Kess ducked back into a crevice and wielded all her arts to conceal herself.

Something passed by. She heard the tick of claws upon rock, the rattle and hiss of sand and pebbles shifting. With all her attention fixed on being unseen, Kess could not see what disturbed the earth near her. When the sounds of passage faded, she arose and peered with one eye round the nearest edge of rock. Something glittered, then vanished. There was a faint smell of burning hanging in the air, like incense.

She could see which way the chimera had gone. The sensible thing to do was to go another way herself. But Kess remembered her dream and decided 'twas wiser to be the hunter than the hunted—and certainly more true to her nature. She gave the monster a dozen heartbeats' start, for prudence—then slipped along after it, set on the course it had shown her.

Travel would have been bearable once the sun's heat waned, but of course they could not track properly after the light went, and it unfortunately went before the heat. The sky held bright a long while, but they had been forced to camp when shadows clotted the ground between the hillsides. The big man was displeased—he had certainly expected to have Kess in his clutches by then, Leith thought. Indeed, he'd hoped for it on the previous day and been thwarted, though he might not guess how.

For his own part, Leith didn't know whether to continue rejoicing that they'd found no trace of Kess or to fret on that selfsame account. Surely it was all to the good that she'd escaped. She was free, and was he not doing his utmost to see that she stayed so? Anything he could contrive to lead her stalker astray . . .

But alone, Kess *might* come to harm. He tortured himself with that a while. The Berianas were not a pleasure garth. There were hungry beasts. Poisonous snakes. There were rock-falls, earthshakes—sunstroke, for that matter. Leith didn't know whether Kess even had food or water with her, or means to make fire . . .

Kess would, Leith suspected with a clear head and sinking heart, be perfectly fine without him, despite all the perils that might lie in her path. There was not a thing he could think of that she could not handily face down. He stared into the yellow tongues of the cookfire's flames, trying not to be reminded of the chimera. He might never be able to enjoy a winter fire again. Truly, he would do better to fear for himself than for Kess—because if he lost her, he lost his chance of having his curse lifted. The conclusion was inescapable. If Kess reached her mother without him, there was no use his finding her at all, ever. She had not wanted him along on her quest. Even when he'd been useful, it had meant nothing to her. She did not need his help, not in the slightest particular, and she would certainly not speak his part to the witch. His only hope had always been to arrive at the island with Kess, right by her side, refusing to be dismissed.

Well, he had come far, too far, had risked too much, to let it all fall to pieces at the last instant. He dared not wait longer, hoping still to mislead—the tactic had served out its purpose, and he discarded it. He and the stranger would part company that very night. Leith found it hard to keep his nerves in check—he itched as if every inch of his skin had been attacked by flies and fleas, and sitting still was a torment.

Since 'twas vital that he betray nothing of his intention, do nothing that might get him trussed up more firmly than he currently was, Leith forced himself to feign sleep once they had taken their evening meal. He calmed his mind, envisioning all of his Lady's phases, recalling each and every variation of the welcome chant in finicky order, adjusted for the season of the years and the shifting times of Her risings.

"Not going to fuss at me about untying you?"

Leith opened his eyes, blinking. Moon-shapes faded, a central one resolving into the stranger's high-domed forehead, lit by yellow firelight. "Is it likely to do me any good?" he asked disinterestedly.

"If you tell me where the lake is, it might," came the sly reply.

"The lake?" Leith did not need to feign puzzlement. He thought he must have fallen asleep—perchance his Lady had rewarded his devotion with a few moment's release from fretting. If so, his curse had curdled Her intent, and now he was thick-headed and confused just when he might need whatever wits he still possessed. He seized the first explanation to hand for the question. "There's still a little water in my waterskin," he volunteered. "Not enough for the horses, too, but horses are very good at scenting water, they'll find—"

"I'm not concerned with getting a drink. There's a spring in those rocks yonder."

"Oh," Leith said stupidly, having forgotten. There *was* a spring, they'd watered the horses. And had a meal. A very little sleep was quite a befuddling thing.

"We've missed Kessallia, somehow," the big man explained. "Maybe she had more of a start on us than I expected—tracking her's a waste of time. You seem pretty sure she's headed for this lake, so instead of finding it by following her, we'll try intercepting her there."

"And you think—after dragging me around these mountains tied to my horse in the blazing sun for the past my-Lady-knows *how* many days—that *I* can tell you how to find the lake?" Leith stared in genuine amazement. "I didn't know where it was *before*. I was just following Kess."

"Just doing whatever she told you?" the stranger scoffed, seeing through the lie.

"You don't know your cousin very well, do you?" Leith asked sadly.

"I know she's a spoiled, petted child, with a knack for getting her own way no matter how dangerous it is. And if you'll help me protect her from the consequences of that, I'll see you get whatever it was she promised you."

"That's tempting," Leith admitted. "Which one were you intending to make good on?"

"Which one?"

"Well," Leith held up a finger. "She's promised to wed me, which rather interferes with *your* plans for her. She's also poisoned me—" He held up another finger. "Abandoned me,

threatened to bludgeon me, and left me to feed the ravens."
He'd run out of fingers, he discovered.

"All that?" The stranger's eyes were starting from his head.
"Are you sure you want to find her?"

"Not at all," Leith said agreeably. "That's why staying with
you seems like such a splendid idea. If I *knew* where the lake
was, I'd never tell you."

The profusion of curses that flew across the fire gave Leith
pause to consider the wisdom of closing his eyes again that
night. His Lady had done well to let him nap while 'twas safe.

Leith actually did doze a brief while, howbeit—and when he
woke, sat quietly listening to the stranger's breathing, which
steadied and deepened as the fire died down to ruddy coals.
When there had been no movement for upward of an hour—
his Lady's face assured him of the time's full passage, a surer
clock than his anxious instincts—Leith struggled to sit straight,
away from the rock behind him. He looked again—still no
movement across the fire. He wet his lips and whistled softly,
hardly louder than the bats squeaking overhead in quest of insect prey.

Valadan abandoned his grazing on the instant. Carefully casual, he drifted closer, taking the occasional mouthful of grass
as he came so as not to alarm the stranger's dun, or inspire it
to follow him. Leith watched the progress, which seemed to
him by inches. Finally he could turn his head no farther, and
Valadan was out of his range of sight.

My lord?

Leith felt breath, warm and moist on the side of his neck.
He smelled crushed grass. Silently, he lifted up his bound
hands. Some horses grew clever about untying knots with their
lips and teeth, he knew—and Valadan was far cleverer than
most. No word of instruction was needed between them.
Valadan's head came over his shoulder. The plate of his jaw
rested against Leith's cheek. His whiskers brushed Leith's
hands. Lips touched the rope.

Once his hands were free, Leith swiftly dealt with the cord
hobbling his legs. He did not, however, leap to his feet. Flight
had its attractions, but patience won out over panic. If the
stranger should unluckily wake, he would likely think his prisoner was still secured.

He still had a problem to solve. He could have stunned the
stranger as he slept—there were suitable rocks lying all about,

and any stick of firewood would have done the job yet more handily. But Leith's own head still ached, and he was not eager to deal a like pain to anyone else—even a man who'd been hauling him along like a live war trophy. Nor could he consider binding the fellow in his sleep—a nice enough idea, but the big man would surely wake at a touch—and if they struggled, Leith cherished no illusions as to the likelihood of his coming out victorious. The stranger had shoulders an ox would envy, and arms to complement them, wrists thicker than Leith's forearms.

There was a method he'd learned from his Lady's herbers, when he had assisted them at tending the injured folk who flocked to Her temple in search of aid. It was oftentimes advisable to render a patent briefly insensible before performing a healing likely to be painful or unpleasant—setting a broken bone, say, or stitching a wound closed. There were herbs that might be given, but such could be imprecise, no matter the herber's skill. The patient's age and general condition, the extent of the injury—even the very season in which the plants had been garnered must be taken into account, and mistakes were too easy to make. A concoction might work too well and kill the recipient—or it might not work at all and leave him victim to pain. Best have another method in reserve, and the priests did . . .

Leith took a moment—a space of two breaths—to make sure of his recollection, to locate in memory the spot where the nerve passed over the bone. Then he rose and crept quietly around the dying fire. He crouched down and laid one finger lightly on the spot, where the stranger's thick neck joined his admirable shoulder.

The man's pale eyes came wide open at the touch on his bare skin, and Leith realized warming his hands would have been prudent. Desperate, he pressed down hard, catching the nerve between his strong fingers and the man's own bone. Despite the less than ideal circumstances, he was precise—the stranger's eyes rolled back till only their whites showed, and his formidable body, tensed for struggle, went limp as his senses left him.

Leith was quick with the two lengths of rope he had to work with—having no notion at all of the amount of time his mercy allowed him for the accomplishing of his essential task. He put all the knots at the back, but he left a deal of slack between one and the next—he wanted the man out of his way, not trussed helpless so long that he starved to death. Folly, perchance, but preferable to cold-hearted murder. Assuming of course that his ill luck did not send some wild beast prowling before the fellow could work himself free. Leith secured the last knot, guiltily, and omitted several others that he might have tied, but he finished the job, guilt or no. If he tried to compensate for every possible mischance, he might as well tie himself again, as well—or crawl under the handiest rock.

Leith saddled Valadan swiftly, scrambling up with a tallish rock taking the place of his missing stirrup. He had already unhobbled the dun, looped a light rope about its head. Now he ponied the gelding behind him as he rode away. He thought he heard a moan at his back, transforming into a curse in midbreath, but it was hard to be sure whether he heard or only expected to hear, over two sets of clattering hoofbeats.

In the dark, it was especially difficult to pick apart Kess' hasty confusions, but Leith wished to send the stranger's horse *away* from her trail, and to do so he needed first to find her trail himself, so he searched diligently. After perhaps a league of combing dim goat tracks, he found what he sought, and sent the dun galloping away by flinging pebbles at its eel-striped rump until it took the hint and fled. Leith turned Valadan's head the opposite way and secured his seat.

"Let's go!" he said, and gave the stallion his head.

Uncertain Reunion

KESS HEARD THE drum of hoofbeats on the trail behind her and hid herself by every means at her disposal at that particular moment—she ducked behind a projecting rock, scooped up a handful of gravel, and flung it back the way she had come. Thereupon she spat out onto the gravel and let the illusion thrive until anyone riding down the track would have seen it cut across by a deep ravine, water a-sparkle in its distant bottom—and if sensible, such a someone would have turned back to seek a more plausible route for a gentle-born girl to have chosen to set her little feet upon.

Leith rode dry-shod straight up to the rock Kess huddled behind, squinted one-eyed around, and slid carefully down from Valadan's back.

"Care to ride for a while?" he asked politely.

Kess stood up, fighting an urge that utterly terrified her—to confess to Leith just how glad she was that he'd found her.

For the past days she'd been tormented by merciless recollections of exactly what she'd done—letting Leith risk his life to advance her toward her goal, then going on while he lay senseless, helpless on the ground, prey to any and every harm that happened along. Remorse was not an emotion Kess was overfamiliar with—therefore she had no least idea how to deal with it. She might have abandoned Leith without a qualm, might never once considered going back to look for him—but every thought of him had slashed her tough conscience like a shard of glass, and the pain was acute.

Leith leaned against the sandy rock, regarding her with those mismatched eyes of his. Not saying an accusing word—just looking and letting her own heart do all the blaming necessary to render Kess throughly miserable.

"Are you all right?" Leith asked, frowning a trifle. His face was not so mobile as it had been—the burns had begun to slough skin, and the bruise on his chin had ripened to a painful shade of purple, gone green at the edges—but he did his best. "Kess?"

"I'm sorry!" she blurted, and began to weep. Except that, instead of disarming tears being shed artfully as she'd intended, Kess followed her explosive apology with an incoherent collection of sobs and gulps for air that threatened to render her incapable of staying on her feet unassisted. She half lunged, half tumbled toward Leith, eyes streaming, throat aching.

"It's all right," Leith said hastily, putting his arms around her to keep from being shoved over backward himself. "Kess, it's all right." Her head bumped him hard on the jaw, and the edges of the day went gray. Leith staggered, but managed to hold onto her and stay on his own feet. He ran into the rock behind him, and suspected a crop of fresh bruises was being sown.

"No, it's not!" Kess raised her face, nearly bumping him again. "I knew you were hurt, and I *left* you there—"

"You probably thought I was dead," Leith offered charitably, tilting his head to escape another insult to his sore jaw. He didn't doubt that he'd *looked* dead. "Anyway, I *told* you not to look back—"

"I knew you weren't dead!" Kess sobbed, muffled against his chest. "You looked awful, but you were breathing. I checked. And then I just left you *lying* there—"

Leith decided that if the confession went on much longer, Kess would be very sorry she'd made it, when she came back to her normal senses. Her clutches reminded him that he'd bruised a rib or two, falling—but that pain was nothing compared to what he could expect later. He gave Kess a little shake and held her at arm's length, forcing her to look at him—assuming she could see through her tears and her hair.

"Listen to me!" She didn't, so he tightened his grip. "It was my own fault—I didn't check my gear as I should have, and that stirrup leather was old and cracked. It couldn't take that kind of use. It broke when I put my weight on it, and I fell off. That's all." He lied for all he was worth. "You've been right all along—it's not bad luck, it's not a curse, it's just carelessness."

Kess had drawn back to regard him with suspicion. "It's all

right that I left you, because you were careless and had a stupid accident?"

Leith nodded gravely—and rather carefully. "You've got troubles enough."

Kess wiped her nose on her sleeve. "If you really believe that, you must have knocked your head wide open back there!"

She sounded more like herself. Leith touched a hand to the back of his skull, winced at the contact, and set himself to ignore the dull pain. "Let's not talk about it," he suggested. "We should keep moving."

"I quite agree, but what changed *your* mind?"

Leith led Valadan to a handy stone and scrambled onto his back. Leaning down to help Kess, he reminded himself that he had strips of leather in his pack, and should rig some sort of stirrup next time they stopped. There might not always chance to be a suitable rock nearby, and leaning over made his head swim disconcertingly. Also, riding with one leg a-dangle was wearisome. He'd be better off with no stirrup for either foot.

Kess was eyeing Valadan askance. "The last time I got near him, he tried to bite me," she complained.

Leith frowned, recalling no such misbehavior. Valadan's manners were impeccable. He had never known a horse so considerate. All at once Kess went scarlet with shame, remembering the circumstances and what she had been attempting to do at the time. Saying no more, she gave Leith her hand and let him help her up. Valadan studiously ignored her efforts, neither hindering nor easing them.

"We've got company," Leith continued, and felt Kess stiffen against his back. "Of course you knew, didn't you? Why else confuse your trail? It wasn't to keep *me* from finding you?"

Kess focused her attention upon the weave of the threads on the back of Leith's doublet. The regular crisscross pattern made such sense—some threads running this way, some that, to create in the end a web of cloth. Kess felt her own threads had been twisted on the loom when she was begun, snarled past all hope of making a useful, coherent whole. Cursed, some would hold.

"I knew someone else was up here," she admitted, reluctantly. "I was afraid it was my father."

"Afraid?" For Kess, that word was merely an expression, Leith supposed. He frowned again. "But we're looking for your father. Aren't we?"

"I told Brychan that I'd find him. Why else would he let me

go, even with his picked escort? If I could bring his master home, there'd be order in the duchy again. Brychan *adores* order. He'd agree to anything for that. But I lied—it doesn't matter to me whether I find the duke. He can do as he pleases."

Kess tightened her grip on Leith's belt, as Valadan maneuvered them down a steep spot on the trail, close to a sheer drop. "I've lived sixteen years with my father, Leith. Quite long enough to know he can't tell me what I am—what I might be turning into. Only my mother can do that. My father would give me his life, but he can't give me what I *need*, so it doesn't matter whether I find him or not."

Leith fingered the burn on his cheek gingerly. It was tender, nearly raw still, round about the scar that was all but an hour as old as he was. "If I was the demon the priests expected, I could have killed that chimera just by staring at it," he said thoughtfully, while Valadan picked his dainty way between pale tan boulders. "Sometimes what people believe about you just isn't true."

"That's precisely why I have to find my mother—to find out the truth, about her and about me," Kess said fiercely. "Why should witch women only be granted the power to curse and wreak havoc, to raise storms and ruin crops? Male wizards heal, create. A wizard made Valadan! No one says *his* blood is tainted!"

Leith watched Valadan's little ears, magic-begotten as the rest of him. One listened for dangers ahead, while the other was cocked back to catch Leith's slightest spoken wish. The horse was not despised for his origin, that was true. He had never been able to think of himself as a demon, either, Leith realized, nor ever needed anyone to tell him he was cursed. Whereas Kess—well, plainly she'd been surrounded by folk only too ready to tell her just what her vanished mother had been, what she therefore must be. It made a difference.

And he had his Lady, Her presence always a comfort, a buffer against the world's ills. He wished he could hope that Kess would accept even a tiny measure of such protection.

"I thought at first that it might have been your father who found me," Leith said, explaining what had befallen him over the days they'd been separated. Kess had discovered some aloe plants nearby when they camped—the toothed leaves held a healing balm under their rough exterior, and she had stroked a palmful of the sap along Leith's jaw already, to soothe burns and bruise alike. She intended doing the same for the lump on the back of his head, but first she had decided to bathe the clot of dirt and dried blood away. Leith gritted his teeth—he knew Kess was *trying* to be gentle—and strove to fix his thoughts on something else to banish the discomfort. "But he kept calling you 'cousin.' And he's younger than your father would be, surely."

"What does he look like?" Kess poured more water, most of which went down Leith's back. "Hold still," she ordered, when he shivered.

"He's a big man," Leith said, his teeth chattering. "Not heavy, but tall." He tried to remember details. He could have described the man's back very well indeed, but he didn't suppose Kess would find that helpful. "Reddish hair, lots on his chin, less on his head than there used to be, by my guess. Light eyes. He had armor tied to the back of his saddle, mail and a helm. Looked well used. A big sword, too."

"That sounds like my cousin Challoner," Kess said thoughtfully. She deftly peeled another aloe leaf, squeezing the healing sap onto her fingers. "The one who expects to get the duchy by wedding me." She worked the aloe gel gently across the bit of Leith's scalp she'd managed to soak clean. The revealed lump was plum color and plum size, but there was no fresh bleeding, Kess was relieved to discover. She thought the swelling might be starting to subside. "His mother thinks she's arranged it. I know she sent word to him, to get himself back to Keverne—it's one reason I left when I did, to get out before he showed up. He was away, warring."

Leith blinked, almost choked. *"Excuse me?"*

Kess colored, realizing belatedly how one word might be taken for another. "Well, I'm sure he does that, *too*, but I should have said 'fighting.' " She wiped her hands clean of aloe juice. "Challoner sells that big sword you saw, wherever there's a war or a neighbor's quarrel. My father did the same before he settled down to rule. I'm surprised he didn't boast about it to you—it's a way to make a name, and a fortune."

"Only Challoner's mother thinks he should marry the fortune instead?" The aloe salve seemed to work—Leith's face felt much better. His burned cheek was soothed, and his headache was at least no worse. He wasn't sure about his teeth—one still felt loose. He wondered whether he could eat an aloe leaf—or suck the juice out of it, at least.

"She's planned it for years. She drove my mother away, but

my father refused to set me aside to please her. So as I was still there, smack in the way of her son's advancement, she had to try something else."

"Are you sure you didn't play into her hands?" Leith asked worriedly. "If she wanted you gone, and you obliged her by leaving—"

"If I find my mother, it won't matter," Kess said, narrowing her eyes—a warning Leith took due note of. "What did you do with my helpful cousin, anyway?"

Leith fished out a strip of leather and began fiddling with it, shaping a stirrup loop. He was tired of hunting for a rock every time he wanted to mount up. "I tied him up and chased his horse off. I couldn't figure out whether he was keeping me for a hostage to bargain with when he caught up to you, or just doing a poor job of rescuing me, so I decided to part company with him when the chance offered itself."

"You're learning," Kess said approvingly.

"He *did* seem concerned about you," Leith pointed out, in the interest of fairness. Which might only prove that Challoner didn't know his young cousin all that well.

"He wants to take good care of his claim to the dukedom, that's all," Kess said dismissively. "Challoner has *always* known where the butter-side was to his bread."

"Still," Leith persisted, turning his attention now to attaching the new stirrup to his saddle, "He helped me, even if he likely had selfish motives for doing it. I didn't want to leave him to starve, but tying him so he could get free means he's sure to be on our trail again when he does. I'm sorry."

"Don't be," Kess said magnanimously. "He won't catch up, even if he catches his horse, which he probably won't. We're close, Leith. I swung away from the lake to hide the trail, but now it ought to be safe to go straight there—and Valadan's fast." Kess clutched the crystal tightly in her left hand, though she did not have to hide its darkness from Leith—he saw no more in it than she now did, and would not question her. "We'll be there day after tomorrow," she promised, willing her words to be true.

Ambushed and Besieged

LONG-NEEDLED PINES AND short-needled larches clung to the steep slopes wherever they could, providing a welcome measure of relief from the combined heat of the sun and the sun-baked rocks. The trees did not have an easy lot—Leith saw many a place where the thin soil had proved insufficient to support their full weight and had given way beneath them. Earthshakes had likely helped to topple others, which lay piled up in vast tangles, too often in low spots where their trail would most reasonably have been. Valadan always found a way through or around, but the going became painfully slow.

Three hours past sun-high, they got their first glimpse of the lake. Kess leapt down from Valadan's back at once and went running ahead with frantic eagerness that Leith made no attempt to check. He knew the distance was likely greater than it appeared from that lofty spot, and thought Kess would pause when she tired, and probably wait for him rather than going on afoot in the heat. He had seen some signs of deer and either wild sheep or goats—there would be leopards to prey upon them, Leith supposed, but those big cats would hunt by night, and there were no signs of charring to indicate these forests harbored another chimera. He had fretted for no reason. Kess was safe.

Leith rode alone with his thoughts, drowsy from the sun's assault and the long day's ride after very little rest. He imagined his Lady's loveliness, coolly mirrored in the blue lake he had not yet had a clear sight of, and shaped in his mind the tune he would play for Her pleasure beside its sapphire waters.

Valadan's explosive snort roused Leith from a pleasant if unintended doze. He looked around, supposing that Kess had indeed been forced to halt, as he'd expected. The lake, so near to the eye from above, was in reality separated from them by a narrow valley and a steep ridge that they must yet climb over.

"Not with the light that's left today," Leith said reassuringly, leaning to pat Valadan's slightly damp neck. The sun's heat was considerable whenever they emerged from under the trees, even toward day's end. "We'd be in shadow trying to go down, and Kess would never agree to stop once we were that close. If there's water this side of the ridge, I'll make sure we camp now. You—"

Midword, Leith was flung hard against the pommel as Valadan whirled under him. He regained his seat, trying to see what had startled the stallion. "A deer," he suggested, when nothing hove into sight. He *might* have heard a sound, a footfall among the trees, but his ears were not so keen as Valadan's and he had not truly been listening.

Then it follows us.

A strange thing for a deer to do.

Leith guided them hastily into a patch of larch shade. "Why didn't you say so sooner?" He looked back, finding no sign of pursuit, certain it was nonetheless present. Challoner already? That seemed unlikely—or very unlucky, which of course made it all too possible.

Valadan dipped his head, and Leith felt a prick of remorse. At least the stallion had been *awake*. And what with the wind, and the rocks continually sliding here and there, it wasn't exactly a silent spot. Valadan had warned him at his earliest suspicion, and deserved no rebuke. Whatever was back there declined to show itself. Hiding, when they'd been seen, wasn't much of an option. Leith made a decision.

"We'd better find Kess." He put his heels to Valadan's sides, unnecessarily.

The twisty trail prevented speed unless 'twas taken in trade for the risk of a fall. They came down it fast all the same, Valadan's hooves spraying dust and pebbles, sliding around the sharp turns, leaving white scars on the rocks. A low-hanging branch slashed Leith hard across the face—doing no real damage, but the sting set both his eyes to watering, and he could see nothing clearly as Valadan stamped to a halt on the flat.

Leith spat out a pine needle and wiped his eyes on his sleeve. His surroundings cleared as if by magic—just as startling as an ensorcellment, too. Kess was sitting on a rock beside the trail, and she was not alone. Beside her stood a stocky man clad in travel-stained gear, his once-scarlet cloak faded and as gray with dust as his once-black hair and beard. The sword in his hand winked sunlight from the gold on its hilt and the wicked edge of its blade.

"About time you caught up," Kess said. She inclined her head in the older man's direction. "This is my father, Duke Symond of Esdragon."

The duke seized Valadan's bridle as Leith dismounted. "Do you always ride down a strange track like that?" he asked furiously. "It's a wonder he still has a whole leg under him."

Valadan danced away, till he saw he could not shake the duke's practiced hand on his reins. He steadied instantly as Leith reached to claim him.

"I do when I'm being followed!" Leith spared the man no further attention. "Kess, there's someone behind us, close. Staying out of sight—"

In the middle of his breathless explanation, something shot past the tip of Leith's nose, passed under Valadan's jaw by a quarter inch, and thudded home in the duke's chest. Except that the duke reeled back from the blow, none of them moved.

A second shaft sprouted miraculously from the dry ground at Leith's feet just as the duke staggered past the limit of his balance and fell. An instant later the snap of the bowstring reached Leith's ears. He jumped back from the arrow, snatching at Kess.

A dozen trees had but lately lost their precarious hold on the rocky hillside and toppled—their drying crowns on the ground, their exposed roots high in the air, propped upon the slope. Leith made for that small shelter with desperate haste, Kess going with him because he refused to release her. Something whistled past his left ear. He and Kess scrambled over the first fallen trunk, and as she dropped to the ground, Leith looked back for Valadan.

The stallion still stood by the fallen duke. Leith whistled urgently, his mouth gone so dry that little sound came out.

"Get over here!" He started to run back for the horse and caught his toe on a branch, tripped and fell hard against one of the trunks.

For once an unlucky fall was actually fortunate—two arrows sang through the air Leith had just emptied.

Valadan marched purposefully toward him, with the duke clinging to the stirrup loop Leith had rigged on the left side, dragged along through the hot dust. Leith pulled the older man to safety under one of the trunks while Valadan leapt gracefully over the next, and they both withdrew as far into cover as they could manage, twitching at the least sound or touch that might have been an arrow.

Dirty roots brushed his hair, and Leith realized they were sheltering under the next bit of earth likely to fall. He hoped it didn't intend doing so any time soon, as he backed yet farther under it. Those arrows were the more immediate peril.

Kess knelt by her father as Leith left off dragging him. "Is it bad?" she asked—then swung about on Leith, temper blazing. "You had to leave Challoner his bow?"

Leith, astonished, had no idea whether he had committed the stupidity or not. Had he ever seen a bow? He couldn't remember, but if he'd seen one, surely he wouldn't have left it behind . . .

One bowman cannot shoot two arrows at once, Valadan pointed out, but Leith had no leisure to consider the point or argue it to Kess. The duke was struggling to sit up. He had his right hand fisted over the arrow shaft and was tugging determinedly at it.

Sweat poured down the man's face, streaking the dust. His teeth ground together. Leith snatched at his hands, to stop the duke's worsening what was already a nasty wound.

"Good lad." Kess's father grunted approvingly. "Now, pull the barb out."

Leith stared, feeling sick. Blood welled around his fingers. The duke's gray eyes fixed on him encouragingly.

"It's deep," Leith protested. He had hunted deer often enough—the Isles teemed with them—and knew well the damage an arrowhead did to flesh. "It will tear you," he said, thinking the duke might not understand, probably did not know how solidly he had been hit.

"Less trouble if it had gone right through," the duke agreed, with a professional soldier's detachment. "But there's bone in the way, you can't push it through." He craned his neck to keep the wound in view, having failed to prop himself on an elbow. "It'll come out, though—but I can't get the angle right, to do it m'self. Give it a good pull, there's a lad."

Trapped, Leith thought, wishing himself elsewhere, and put both hands on the shaft. The arrow was fletched with common unmarked gray goose feathers, dappled with a single spot of red blood now. There was no help for it. The arrow had to come out, so the wound could be dressed, the flow of blood staunched. If the butchery were to be done, best it was done at once, and cleanly if he could manage it. Because if he had to start cutting, to get the barbed head out . . .

He nodded to Kess, who had gone moon-pale when she realized what her father wanted. "Hold his shoulders."

While both Kess and her father went white-lipped, Leith yanked on the shaft, taking care to pull straight back on the shaft, not twisting it. Just back, along the path it had made, entering. It wouldn't be easy, the flesh had swollen already, and if the tip had lodged in the bone . . .

The barb resisted till Leith despaired, then slid out, followed by a little gush of blood. The duke groaned once, as if he were giving up his ghost, and Kess slapped one hand over the wound to staunch the flow while she fumbled with the other for bandages.

"Always wear silk . . . next to your skin," her father was advising her faintly. "Even under mail. It wraps the barb, makes the arrows come out cleaner."

Valadan squealed a warning, and Leith recalled belatedly that their attackers would have had time to close upon them with something more than arrows. He scrambled up, snatching for his sword with hands already bloody, just as a man hurled himself headlong over the fallen trunks. The impact sent them both sprawling to the dirt.

Leith somehow fetched up on top and, having finally dragged his sword clear of its sheath, held it shortened at his assailant's throat.

"*Wait*—" Challoner gasped, his broad chest heaving under Leith's knee.

Challoner did indeed have a bow—a crossbow, which was demonstrably not the weapon used to attack them. It fired short iron bolts—utterly unlike the long shaft Leith had pulled from the duke's shoulder, the mates of which sprouted from the ground beyond the fallen trees thick as if they'd been sown for a martial crop. Kess took up a watch post, arming herself with the captured weapon, and made certain they were not surprised a second—or a third—time, while Leith finished binding Challoner's hands to one of the tree trunks.

"This isn't necessary," Kess' cousin was insisting, not for the first time. "I came to *warn* you—"

Leith ignored the protest, also not for the first time, finished the knots, and went to see how the duke fared. "Better safe than sorry," he said, indicating Challoner with a tilt of his head.

The duke chuckled, then winced. Leith carefully inspected the swathing of bandages Kess had hastily arranged. There was no bright stain of fresh blood on the torn blue cloth, he was relieved to note. The arrow hadn't—by some miracle—cut a blood vessel, but had buried itself in muscle thick enough to withstand the assault.

"All these months I've been up here and never saw a living soul till today," Kess' father said in wonderment. "Now half the population of Esdragon's here, shooting at one another. How many of them are there?" The duke's nod also was directed at Challoner.

"He says he thinks half a dozen," Leith relayed. He hadn't decided whether he believed the count.

"If they all have bows, that's very bad news."

Leith knew it. "They have to see us to hit us," he pointed out hopefully.

The duke shook his head. "If they've bolts enough, they can shoot blind and hope to get lucky. They know we're trapped. The difference of range doesn't favor them with us hidden in here, but if they should decide to come in after us . . ."

Leith knew that was truth, however unpalatable. Also there were less than a dozen bolts for the crossbow, after which their best weapon was useless to them. He didn't doubt that Kess was an excellent shot, but they were still at an immense disadvantage. Bad news indeed. "Think they'll come in after dark?"

"You'd be well advised to stand watches."

Leith nodded. He had actually been wondering whether their attackers would even wait until night fell. As he arose, a dangling root brushed his burned cheek. Dirt sifted down his back, dusted his hair. "I just hope the rest of this slope doesn't decide to shelter us permanently," he fretted.

The more he reviewed their situation, the worse it looked. With a surfeit of dead wood all about, they still dared not risk a fire's revealing light, and might therefore suffer from the cold of a mountain night—especially a wounded man. They had no water, save the little Leith had been carrying, and it had been long, hot hours since he had filled the waterskin. There was very little left. Valadan had no water and no food, either, but he was busily chewing the bark from one of the fallen trees when Leith glumly paused to check on him.

"You could have gotten a dozen arrows in you, you know that?" Leith leaned his head wearily against the stallion's warm shoulder. Valadan nuzzled his hair, breathed down his neck. "Of course you do. Mind, I'm not sorry you did it—I wouldn't have wanted to leave him out there, and I'd have liked going out after him even less! I just don't like pulling arrows out." He touched Valadan's flank, already somewhat singed by the chimera. Arrows in that, as well . . .

They were not shooting at me. The stallion used Leith's chest to soothe an itch somewhere over his left eye.

"That's no guarantee." Leith stood his ground against the scratching, with some difficulty. He didn't dare remove Valadan's gear—no telling when they might need to move quickly—but Leith eased the girth and slipped the bit so that it hung free under the stallion's chin, to make his browsing easier.

I will hear if they try to come close after it grows dark. Had they horses, I would have known they were behind us days ago. The stallion's eyes flashed fitfully, unhappy that he had not detected the pursuit anyway.

"Maybe they had to leave their horses when they crossed over the river," Leith said. He realized he was assuming their attackers were the horsemen Kess claimed to have seen in the crystal. They might just as easily be mountain bandits—or Challoner's men, unsuspected. Leith patted the stallion's neck, careful of a crisp patch of hair that perhaps had tender burned skin under it. "We've both had other things on our minds," he said, excusing them both, and went to see how Kess fared at her sentry post.

If their ambushers were thinking of closing in, they had given Kess no sign of such intent. She kept the crossbow trained on the likeliest approach and never shifted her narrowed gaze while she spoke with Leith, which reassured him as he made his way back to her cousin.

Challoner's bonds were pulled painfully tight—the man had evidently been struggling with them the entire time Leith had been off on his rounds, and the set of his jaw told the tale of his lack of success. Leith was careful to squat down well out of his possible reach.

"Untie me!" Challoner commanded.

Leith smiled wickedly. "Only to eat. Isn't that the proper

procedure? And I ought to warn you—we have *very* little food."

Dark color rose in Challoner's face, as he took Leith's meaning. "Fairly shot. I didn't have to keep you tied so long as I did—I wanted you to lead me to Kessallia, and I didn't want you slipping off. I suppose I should have just let you *think* you'd escaped and then followed you!" The tone shifted, became pleading again. "But remember, you were hurt. You'd have wandered off and into the gods know what, if you'd been able."

"Possibly even into your confederates," Leith agreed pleasantly.

"They're not *my* confederates!" Challoner gave his bonds a nasty, futile jerk. "I've been following *them* since yestermorn."

Leith raised his half burned eyebrow in polite disbelief.

"I was trying to find my horse," Challoner insisted. "It seems to have strayed."

"Very plausible," Leith said approvingly. "Looking for your horse." They both knew the horse in question was leagues off.

"When I saw Brychan sneaking along on your trail, I somehow didn't think it likely he'd mounted so heavily armed a rescue party for Kessallia, so I stayed out of his sight—"

"*Brychan?*" the duke joined in, in a shocked voice. "My seneschal? My father's bastard?"

"I think he's hoping to raise his status," Challoner said. "Were you and Kessallia both to disappear, he'd find himself in a very strong position. Vacant thrones seldom stay so for long. Someone fills them. Brychan can go home with a tragic tale of how you and your daughter met your ends, and claim himself a dukedom."

"So might you," Leith pointed out helpfully.

Challoner had begun to turn toward the duke, then been brought up short by his bonds and Leith's observation. He jerked back toward Leith, glaring. "*Untie me!* Have you any notion how humiliating this is?"

"Yes," Leith admitted. "Probably better than anyone. Put yourself in my position—what would *you* do? We can't keep watch on them and you, as well."

"I want to talk to my uncle!"

Leith shrugged. "I didn't gag you. You don't require your hands to talk, do you?"

"Would I have come in here, if I were in league with those men out there?" Challoner had left off struggling, probably realizing that looking dangerous would not much advance his case.

Leith considered the logic of it. "I think you might. The duke's wounded. Kess would probably trust you—at least a little, and that little might be enough. That just leaves me you've got to get past. So no, I will not untie you."

"Quite right," the duke said, grinning in his beard despite his pallor and obvious discomfort.

"*Uncle!—*" Challoner gasped, shocked.

"Did you trail my daughter all this way out of concern for her safety—or concern over the throne she's heir to? Challoner, your motives may be pure as the air, I've no way to judge, and trying makes my head ache. But the lad's right, we can't trust you. We haven't the resources to spare for such luxuries."

"Please yourself!" Challoner spat. "One favor—leave me here, when you try getting yourselves out of this bolt-hole."

Leith rubbed at his temples, which had begun to pound with a headache quite unrelated to his fall. Their situation, the present moment aside, was just as grave as Challoner's last jibe indicated. They daren't abandon their shelter, yet it could quite easily be transformed from security to trap. It was quite possible Brychan and his bowmen had already ringed them about, cutting off every means of escape. If it occurred to them, they could bring a largish chunk of hillside down with very little effort, burying all trace of the duke and his heir—Challoner, as well, assuming he was telling the truth and had no part in Brychan's scheme. If he was lying, then they were spared one peril out of many. Dirt pattered down constantly—Challoner shook a dusting of it from his head—the furious gesture suggesting a bull penned up long enough to be dangerous to release. Leith kneaded his forehead and thought fighting the chimera had been preferable—at least simpler, and not open to constant question.

He looked up, met the duke's eyes and smile.

"Kessallia did not finish introducing us."

"No." Leith slowly realized that was quite true. She'd been interrupted, but he thought she might not have troubled even if she'd had the time to spare. "No, she didn't. I'm Leith, Prince of the Isles." His title had never meant much to Leith—but he wasn't an unwashed peasant Kess had gathered up from the roadside, and out of some threadbare vestige of pride, he wished her father to know that.

"The Isles." The duke nodded. "I guested there some years gone. Probably with your father?"

"Quite likely." Leith hoped there wasn't some tender reminiscence to follow—in which he could not join. It could prove embarrassing for both of them.

"Well, Leith of the Isles, ere we become fast friends and boon companions, there's a matter I must touch upon."

Leith looked at him, puzzled. The duke was sitting straighter, no longer relying upon the log at his back for support. His color was no better, but his mien was serious—whatever this was, it mattered more to him than his wound.

"I most sincerely hope you won't take offense, but . . . your face. Did my daughter have anything to do with that?"

Leith flushed, where his battered skin was not already some less than usual color. "No! Sir, I trust *you* won't take offense, but if any man gave your daughter cause to do this much to him, I doubt she'd stop while he was still breathing!"

The duke chuckled. "Well said. Well said, and well deserved! You understand I had to ask? As her father?"

Leith nodded. "The truth is, sir, it was a stupid accident, and Kess wasn't even there. My stirrup leather broke, and when I fell my shield hit me. Or I hit it. I don't much remember. Does it look that bad?" He could only judge by the feel of it, having no mirror—and was trying not to, much of the time.

"Bad enough. Since you didn't get it trying to dishonor my daughter, I may hope that it feels better than it looks. What brings you up here, with Kess?"

"I'm under a curse—"

The duke's eyes widened, disbelieving. His hand went to his dagger—happily, Kess had borrowed it to cut bandages and had not returned the weapon. As his fingers groped, so did his tongue, but no words won forth save as sputters.

Leith made haste to explain what had sounded like an insult. "It's something I was born with, sir. Ill luck dogs me, smites every spot I linger overlong in." He mentioned his shipwreck, finding Valadan, solving Kess' task as a means of keeping the horse, discovering victory to be only another face of his bad luck.

"Kess wants to find her mother, same as you, sir. And I thought that if she did, if I helped her, just possibly the lady could lift this curse from me. That I could prevail on her to try, anyway. It seemed like a chance—to be free of it, that's all I want. I didn't think I'd be putting Kess at risk by it, not in such a short while. I'm sorry about that, sir—"

The snap of the crossbow being fired catapulted Leith to his feet, his recitation of guilt abandoned. He was two strides nearer to Kess when a scream split the twilight. It did not die away, but was repeated thrice ere it began to change to a heart-wrenching moaning.

"Where?" Leith asked, searching the night and seeing nothing. He had his sword out, ready for whatever might come over the bulwark of logs.

"Up there." Kess touched his left shoulder, so he'd have a start on following her gesture in the gloom.

"Trying to get behind us?"

"He didn't make it." The moaning went on. Kess coolly reloaded the bow, turning the crank with a steady clicking till the mechanism stopped, ready to shoot once more.

"Did you—Challoner says that's Brychan out there."

"I heard." Kess' voice gave away nothing, certainly not that she'd been betrayed by one of the few people at Keverne she'd even partly trusted. Her jaw was taut, her mouth set.

"You were right," Leith confessed. "About the horsemen behind us. And I led them right to us. I just don't see how they followed us—"

"They didn't. Behind the waterfall, maybe, but not through the mine. There's no way they could have managed *that*. No, you had the right of it." Kess said it grudgingly—but she said it, all the same.

Leith adjusted to the notion that there was one single trouble he wasn't being held to account for—though he probably should have been. He couldn't seem to get the knack of it. The moaning—fainter now—was most distracting. "Then how—"

"I didn't see, either, till Challoner said it was Brychan out there." Kess gestured at the darkness with her chin. "He and my father hunted in the Berianas when they were young men. There weren't chimeras here then, but the game was very plentiful, much better than in Esdragon. They know all the ways in, the crossings over the Est. The one I found—that's a secret way, a *hidden* way. Which is probably why *I* could find it."

Hiding things that should be seen, seeing things that are hidden . . . Her words came back to Leith, as if they had a life of their own.

"There are probably ways across farther upstream than we

went. My father knows them. So does Brychan," Kess added dismally.

"But you were hiding our trail—"

"Not all the time." Kess shook her head. "It's exhausting. I only did it when I thought I needed to. And my father wasn't trying to hide his at all. Once we'd caught up to him, it didn't matter *whose* track Brychan was really on. He has us all."

"Go rest your eyes awhile," Leith suggested gently. The moaning had ceased, finally. A cricket chirped. Otherwise the night was silent, and not a waiting silence, either. Just the sort of quiet when nothing was going to happen. "I'll stand a watch."

Kess looked dubious. "Can you shoot one of these?" She tightened her grip on the crossbow.

"I'm nowhere as good a shot as you, but I know how." Leith smiled wanly. "For instance, take your finger off the trigger if you're going to point that at me."

"Don't waste shots. We've no bolts to spare." Kess handed over the weapon, frowning.

"I'll call you if I see anything," Leith assured her. He pointed the bow at the outer darkness and kept it trained there. "The moon'll be up soon. My Lady will help me keep watch. And Valadan has sharp ears." The stallion snorted and stripped more bark from a fallen tree, munching with relish. "Anyway, there aren't enough of them to risk that stunt again."

"Assuming *they* don't know that, keep in mind you're the one they'll try it on first! Watch out for knives in the dark."

With that happy thought, Kess left him. Leith watched her walk to her father's side, settle beside him. Their conversation appeared strained at first, probably because it could not be private, but soon father and daughter seemed to relax.

After a time his Lady lifted Her face, to peer down serenely upon him. Leith whispered his respects to Her ears, lest Kess chastize him on grounds of giving his position away to the enemy by incautiously chanting. It might have been better had his Lady veiled Her face—Leith didn't know. He didn't like their besiegers to have light to move by, but moonlight would let him see them, if they moved carelessly. Probably his Lady knew what She was about, and he was simply too weary to see Her design as readily as he should . . .

Leith came awake with a start, just as he was dropping the crossbow. It discharged itself as it landed, the bolt skidding over the ground to bury itself to the flights in a fallen pine trunk.

There was no outcry. Leith's relief at this changed swiftly to alarm. Had Kess given in to Challoner's pleas to be released, and had her cousin betrayed her kindness? He should have warned her that all the dangers didn't come out of the darkness.

Valadan snorted as he rushed past, but Leith failed to heed the reassurance that he was the most startling thing in the area. The world was a confusion of moon-cast shadows of roots and logs, logs resting on the ground with tiny shadows under them, shadows that might hide any peril.

One of those shadows sent him sprawling. Leith lay suddenly facedown in the dirt, one arm twisted painfully behind his back, Kess' breath hot in his ear.

"What are you *doing*?"

Leith went limp with relief, then tensed again when Kess wrenched his arm higher. He risked confessing his lapse and his miserable failure at his sentry post. Kess abandoned him in favor of the crossbow before he was half done, muttering imprecations under her breath until she had made certain the weapon had taken no harm while in his charge.

"I suppose it could have been worse—if you'd shot yourself in the foot, everything in the mountains would be awake by now. I think the time's come to get out of here, don't you?"

Leith agreed in principle, if the specifics still eluded him. He was mostly just happy when Kess allowed him to regain his feet. His ribs felt bruised, his arm nearly dislocated.

"Maybe they don't keep any better watch than you do," she was saying. "We'll just have to hug the shadows along the cliffside and hope for the best."

"Trust to luck, you mean?" Leith asked, incredulous. "While they move along the ridge and cut us off? There's not a scrap of cover for us, and plenty for them once the sun rises."

"Got a better idea?" Kess rejoined tartly. "Your mistress whisper some splendid strategy in your ear while you were dreaming of her?"

Leith ignored the taunt. He deserved it for having fallen asleep at his post. "Maybe." He swallowed, but his throat was suddenly so dry and painful that tears sprang to his eyes. "Take your father, and go now. I'll stay behind and cover your retreat. If no one follows you, then I'll try to make it look as if we're all still here."

"And *then* what?" Kess' tone would have curdled milk. But he was letting her leave him. Surely that had some appeal, still.

"I'll come after you. It'll be a little darker between moonset and sunrise. Easier to slip out. I'll even bring Challoner, if you think that's a good idea," he added.

"I think it's a dreadful idea, but Father might object if we left him." Kess scowled. "Who gets the crossbow?"

"You do. Just don't shoot *me*, when I catch you up."

Leith strained his ears for some further clue to Kess' progress, though he knew he should not desire to hear any at all—any sounds *he* could hear after this while could only mean Kess and her father had met trouble. If all had gone well, they were well out of casual earshot. Valadan also pricked his mobile ears, monitoring their slow progress more surely and by his calm reporting nothing amiss.

Leith unsheathed his knife and cut the bonds on Challoner's ankles. Then he slid the tip of the blade carefully between the man's wrists. Challoner barely waited for the cords to part—as they began to yield to the knife-edge, he wrenched his hands apart and lurched to his feet.

"You're welcome, I'm sure," Leith said, putting his knife away. He fetched Challoner's short horseman's sword and handed it over.

The big man fumbled the blade, nearly dropping it. Probably his hands were numb yet, unreliable. Leith went to Valadan and adjusted the girth, lest he forget under pressure later and wind up under the stallion's belly in a slipped saddle. He felt safe enough—despite Challoner's obvious fury, the man couldn't swing a weapon he could scarcely grip. After he had full command of his limbs again—well, that was for future worrying. Leith slipped the bit back into Valadan's mouth. There wasn't a scrap of tasty bark left on the tree trunk anyway.

Challoner had his fists on the sword hilt when Leith looked up, and was leaning on the weapon, waiting for his legs to uncramp and steady. "Symond seems rather taken with you," he observed.

Leith made no reply. None appeared to be required.

"Not that it matters," Challoner pointed out. "He won't give Kessallia to you. Or his duchy."

"I don't want his duchy." Leith was weary of making the

same point, over and over. No one seemed to believe him anyway.

Challoner scoffed. "You've put yourself to a lot of risk, then, in an enterprise you stand to gain absolutely nothing from. Killing a chimera, by the gods! You don't mean to tell me you did that just as a kindness, so Kessallia wouldn't get her cloak scorched on this fool's errand of hers?"

Leith sighed and rested an arm across Valadan's neck. His hip was hurting him, the old ache so deep in the bone that no rest or salve or massage could ever quite reach it. It was always at its worst in the mornings, or when he'd been too long immobile, or was weary—each of those factors now came into play, all at once. He couldn't recall when he'd last slept intentionally, just for rest, not drowsing at his post or half swooning from some injury.

"If Kess reaches her mother, and I've helped her do it, then I can ask the lady to free me of this curse," he said, tired almost to death of confessing the shame that drove him. "That's all I want. No kingdom, no royal bride—just a normal life with normal luck."

Challoner grunted, disbelieving. "You shouldn't be so quick to throw away a rich bride, then. That normal life's not so comfortable if you're starving."

Not likely that so much as a day's fast had ever impeded the man's growth, Leith thought, glancing at him sidelong. His size didn't speak of past privation. "Kess says your mother intends for *you* to marry her." He didn't report what Kess thought of the scheme.

"I have the blood-right," Challoner said, a simple statement of fact. "And the strength of hand Esdragon needs. You—and Kess' harebrained notions—are not going to interfere with that."

"I'm not trying to," Leith whispered. And truly he was not, but the thought of Kess matched with her cousin filled him with dread. Kess would fight to her death rather than submit to any fate not of her own choosing—he had seen horses like that, not so fortunate as to have come to his Lady's folk for their training, broken to saddle only when their spirits were likewise broken by clumsy hands and cruel methods. They lived and bore riders and were useful, but never the half what they had been while wild and free, never the half what they might have been. Leith wanted with all his heart to prevent such a disaster in Kess' life, even if it meant that he had to stay where Kess specifically didn't want him—at her side—all the rest of his days.

Challoner massaged his hands irritably. "How far do you think they'll have to go, to find a place where they can climb out of this trap of a valley?" Once out of the narrow spot between ridges, Kess and her father would be less prey to ambush, though harder to track.

Leith shrugged. Kess would need to go slowly, to stay silent in forbidding terrain and confounding darkness. And though the duke was wounded in his shoulder and not his legs, the man did not have his full strength and must move with some care and slowly. "We'll follow them at moonset. That's about an hour from now," he added, not even needing to look at the sky to know.

"Sunrise isn't so much after."

Leith was well aware of that. They'd have only precious minutes of gloom to aid their escape. His plan, so hastily conceived, was crumbling away even more rapidly, and Leith was permitting the decay. He did not intend to tarry long pretending they were all of them still in hiding, deceiving Brychan. He didn't truly believe such strategy would work, and he suspected Kess had let his plan proceed unchallenged only because it had allowed her to move out of their prison when she wanted to—first. Maybe she hoped to desert him once again.

And if getting himself and Challoner out proved unworkable—well, that was Leith's problem. As was the matter of covering Kess' retreat when he'd let her take their only distance weapon. Leith supposed he could always throw rocks—but he'd be best off just to slip away. Before Kess got too far ahead of him.

Kess turned an ankle on a treacherous rock and cursed beneath her breath. Just behind her, she could hear her father's panting progress. She should not have been able to, but the rough climbing was taking a toll. The duke's wound might even have opened again—he said not, but Kess knew he would lie about it.

They were not making anything like the speed she had hoped for. The only clear ground lay under the moon's revealing light, and keeping to the edges and the shadows meant being forced onto the worst footing, sharp rocks loosely anchored, steep stretches made perilous by sheltering gloom.

Kess halted, rubbing at her ankle, and let her father recover his wind.

She fished out her crystal—a measure of desperation, since it had showed her nothing of use recently and she had no time to waste on it—but there was not sufficient light to set it working. Anyway, did she *want* to be ensnared by a vision, however briefly? Kess decided she dared not and put the pendant stone back inside her shirt.

"What are you up to?" her father asked.

"Nothing," Kess answered, but she knew she said it too quickly to be believed. "Nothing that works," she added bitterly.

"Some charm Betsan taught you," the duke suggested, then reconsidered. "Kess, I knew well what your mother was when I took her to wife. I will not despise you for having her blood as well as mine."

"The rest of Esdragon does!" Kess spat, surprising herself.

Symond sat down, on a tallish rock. "Only if you judge the whole land by a few fools at Keverne, most of which are unfortunately my kin. And they didn't hate Raichim for her witch blood—they hated her because I set her in a place they felt belonged to their own interests. I came to know that too late, but I came to know it very well." He paused and fumbled at his shoulder. Kess leaned close, concerned, but Symond waved her back. "You have my blood, as well, Kessallia. 'Tis a combination no one in Esdragon can stand against. Not even Brychan."

"What about Challoner?" Kess shivered, remembering that he was behind them as well as less-known dangers.

"What about him, daughter?"

"He seems to think I belong to him."

"Doesn't that answer your question?" Symond chuckled. "Would I give you to any man *that* much a fool?"

Kess scowled in the dark. "We need to go on. Or the point is going to be moot." She thought she'd heard a noise, a scrape of leather upon rock, but all was silent, and she might have sensed only some small animal, hastening for cover ere the sun showed it to its enemies. There was sand underfoot now, sifted down a sort of dry gully from above. Now the moon waned and the light was less contrasty, Kess could see that it was a likely place to ascend the ridge, easy enough that the duke could certainly manage it now that he'd rested. Certainly the best way they'd seen yet.

* * *

Already there were birds calling—the night was over, all save the last technicality of it. Both horizons glowed gently—moonset and sunrise would be close to coinciding. Leith supposed the birds were a good sign. They would have fallen silent if men moving about had disturbed their routine.

"We'll be in a very bad way, trying to sneak out of here in daylight," Challoner fussed.

"You can go now, if you want," Leith offered generously. "If you think Brychan will recognize you before he shoots."

"He's as likely to shoot at me as any of you!" Challoner thundered. "Is that the only way I can prove to you that I'm not in his pay?"

"He might be in yours," Leith said. "But that's too complicated to think about, so early—"

Valadan snorted and pawed the dust violently, showering pebbles. *We should not tarry,* he advised Leith, arching his neck and mouthing his bit.

Leith quickly went to him. Were Kess and her father in a place of safety? Had they gone out of even Valadan's hearing, or had they stopped sooner? Was there trouble? Leith badly wanted to know—but did he also want Challoner to know that he spoke to a horse as if he expected answers of it? He hesitated, his hand on the reins.

His questions must have been self-evident. Valadan pawed again, sending back another stinging rain of stones. *I can hear no sounds at all from the place where Brychan was. So it has been most of the night. If he still sleeps, we can put him far behind us. But if he is no longer there . . .*

Leith put a boot into the stirrup loop.

"What now?" Challoner asked, face a place half oval between his hair and beard.

Could Valadan travel at speed under a double load? Challoner was a big man and outweighed Kess by half.

We outrace men, not chimeras, the stallion observed negligently, dancing, hauling on the bit. *We need not leave him.*

Of course, Challoner *had* asked them to do just that. The sarcastic request delivered much earlier came back to Leith, temptingly.

All the same, he gave Challoner the opportunity to change his mind, and extended a hand to help the man up behind.

A Witch's Weapon

LEITH COULD NOT decide whether to be dismayed or relieved that no flight of arrows sang after them when they burst from their tumbledown shelter and galloped away. He could think—*now*, when the facility had become utterly useless—of several ways Brychan could have made shift to slip past them at the very outset of what they'd taken for a siege, leaving a man behind to convince them he had settled down to wait them out. The man Kess had shot, for instance. Now she and her father might be walking into whatever ambush Brychan had managed to lay, with no shelter in reach *this* time.

He urged Valadan to speed, careless of the perils underfoot. The valley floor was sand and rock, sparsely covered with grass. There might be a hole or two, but Valadan had the advantage of better night sight than any human's and could take care of himself. Certainly the horse did not object to their pace, and willingly increased it. Challoner might have had more words to say about it, but the rushing air carried his protests well away from Leith's ears.

I can climb here, Valadan announced—and did so on the instant. Leith grabbed a thick handful of mane and leaned forward to free the stallion's hindquarters, while Challoner hung onto his belt and cursed, being unable to do much else.

There was no trail, and Leith had no notion why Valadan had chosen one nearly sheer spot over another that looked no worse. He thought unhappily of the good target they would make for arrows, but none came winging to seek them. He knew the shifty, wracked earth could give way without warning, that they could tumble to their deaths—but they did not. Challoner's insecure and pretty nearly dead weight might have dragged Leith out of the saddle by accident or design, but

204

Leith kept his seat despite the odds, and they topped the ridge in a cloud of rose-colored dust just as the edge of the sun's bright disc rose above the sunward ridge.

Suddenly the morning's colors were intense. Below and ahead, fringed by a dark green pelt of pines, blue water sparkled like a sapphire, catching the day's first light. There was an island off-center in the lake, a cinnamon-colored pine-mantled cone whose tip sent up a faint thread of smoke, just as Kess had described it. Leith's heart lifted. Kess' visions were true! Then he shifted his gaze from the horizon to the immediate.

At Valadan's stamping feet lay a dead man. A crossbow bolt stuck jauntily in his throat, fletchings whispering in the morning breeze.

Two paces to the right of the first corpse lay a second, with one bolt gone into his shoulder and another buried deep in his right eye.

Three paces beyond the second body stood an archer, the arrow nocked to his bow a clothyard shaft easily capable of spitting Leith and Challoner behind him, as well, with a single shot.

Beyond the bowman, four figures faced one another in tense pairs—Kess and her father, another archer and a well-dressed man with an air of command about him. Kess had what was likely her last bolt trained at his chest. The bowman had drawn upon the duke, who had been trying to drag his sword out of its scabbard before being ordered not to.

Brychan turned his head toward Leith. "Off the horse," he suggested mildly.

The archer tracked them as they dismounted. One of the knots in the stirrup loop shifted, giving Leith a very bad moment. His earlier fall flashed before his senses, and his heart hammered even after he realized that he was safely on the ground after all—as safe as he might be with an arrow trained upon him.

"Over there," Brychan ordered, gesturing toward Kess.

Leith obeyed slowly, keeping his hands well away from his weapons. He was limping—there was no help for it, he had not been afoot long enough to work the stiffness out of his hip, and the morning was chill. He was not sorry to be forced to move so haltingly—it drew out the ordered action, gave him space to think, to plan.

Assuming that there was any plan to be made.

"Now that all in your party are safely accounted for, my lord," Brychan said politely, "I will have your ring."

"Certainly," Duke Symond replied, his equal in courtesy. "Come and take it, you misbegotten error in my lord father's judgment." His fingers tightened on his sword hilt.

Brychan frowned. "This is folly. You have no choice in the matter."

"Alive or dead, I have that choice. I believe I have made it."

Brychan stroked his beard. "I will not trifle with you and bargain to spare your daughter's life if you yield to me, Symond. She'd have my heart's blood, soon or late."

"Soon," Kess pledged, through her teeth.

"You see," Brychan said to the duke, ignoring the outburst otherwise. "I dare not spare her. But if you will yield me your seal, I will allow you quick deaths, cleanly dealt."

Challoner shifted next to Leith, but the archer's eye was hot on him, and he dared not so much as loosen his sword in its sheath. He glared at Brychan, the uncle who had been naively passed over in his mother's power games—as if a bastard could be safely reckoned without ambition or imagination.

"I will not, for example," Brychan explained, "give Kessallia to my soldiers to sport with, while requiring you to watch."

Leith thought such "sport" was likely to be refused, if the archers in question had any sense of self-preservation—or any sense of Kess' temperament. Her lips were as white as the fingers still gripping the crossbow. She looked perfectly capable of tearing out a man's throat with no other weapon save her gaze.

"I'll not hand you a dukedom you have no right to." The duke shrugged. "A pointless answer, I do not doubt. You seem to have the upper hand here. Yet a man must cling to honor—if he possesses it."

Brychan colored at the impugning of his own honor. His pale eyes fairly started from his head. "You handed me your dukedom when you made me your seneschal. A crust for the brother who could never be quite a brother, a crumb of pity. Yet now there is no corner of Esdragon where my hand does not reach. You left your land, deserted your people to go seeking after fire in the mountains—now the payment for your folly comes due."

"Was it folly to offer my brother a place where he could

serve his people honorably? But it was never enough for you, Brychan. You wanted it all."

"And now I have it." Brychan glared at Kess. "Lady Kessallia, lay down your weapon. I wear mail beneath this doublet, you cannot slay me. And 'twill do you no good to spit another of my bowmen, as the other will certainly shoot your father—and he will not aim to give him a painless death."

Kess spat curses at her base-born uncle, but her witch blood seemed to fail her—Brychan stood unscathed, sneering.

"I hold to my promise," he said coldly. "You cannot live, and your father cannot live—and alas, Challoner, the same mischance must claim you, who had hoped to rescue father and daughter. A most tragic day! But you may die as painlessly as possible, lady. Do yourself that mercy."

"Do yourself the mercy of cutting your own lying throat!"

Leith took the bow out of Kess' trembling hands. It was easy enough to do—she expected no treachery from him, had forgotten he was by her side. "Enough. Killing you will be the least of what he can do to you."

"Good lad," Brychan purred happily.

"This is probably all your fault," Kess said, glaring at Leith, furious that he had taken her by surprise. "I don't know how, but it is!" She knotted her hands into fists. "He didn't specifically say so, but he's going to kill you, too. You *do* know that?"

"I *said* I was cursed," Leith explained. "Frequently, if you recall."

"I should have believed you!"

The archer was grinning at their exchange. Leith smiled back, sharing the jest, shrugged—and pulled the crossbow's trigger.

His aim—since he couldn't be seen to take it—was a touch off. The bolt merely clipped the archer's shoulder, but the startled man loosed his own shaft wildly, sending it winging harmlessly between Kess and her father. He snatched swiftly for another arrow, and Leith hurled the empty crossbow at his head. The man ducked, dropping the arrow and scrambling after it.

There was an astonished yell, as Valadan seized the second archer's shoulder in his teeth, preventing the man's putting a shaft into Leith's back. The stallion lifted the man clean off his feet, shaking him like an oversized rat.

The airborne archer let his bow fall. Leith dove after it. Kess did likewise. They knocked heads, and as Leith desperately tried to blink his vision clear of a swirl of black sparks, Valadan's hooves came down on the bowstave, nearly crushing his fingers. Next instant the dangling bowman dropped on top of him, driving Leith's breath from his lungs.

Leith squirmed free—aided by the archer's sudden impulse to hie himself away from the unequal fight as hastily as possible. He looked around, at mayhem.

The duke had his sword out and was laying about him with a will, albeit one-handedly. Challoner was facing down the archer Leith had wounded, sword to drawn bow. Toe to toe, neither had an obvious advantage as to speed.

Kess had scooped up one of the fallen arrows and jabbed the steel barb savagely into Brychan's foot. Challoner, scuffling for advantage against his opponent, collided with the duke, and the mischance gave Brychan a moment's peace, which he used to seize Kess by her long braid, dragging her cruelly to her feet for service as his shield. The duke swore, a bowstring twanged, and Kess went at Brychan with her teeth.

Leith tackled the archer before he could nock another arrow. Challoner staggered, looking amazed. Brychan, his face a-bleeding, strove to shove Kess onto her father's sword. Valadan squealed and reared against the rising sun.

The earth began to dance.

Leith dug his hands into the stony soil, which crumbled away as rapidly as he snatched at it, refusing to be gripped. One of his fingers bent in a direction it had never been intended to accept—Leith never noticed the pain. Sharp edges of broken rock cut and stabbed at him. There was dust everywhere. He couldn't get his legs under him—the ground kept moving away, throwing him off his feet as fast as he gained them. The whole of the ridge was sliding hurriedly toward the lake below, and he was falling endlessly. Amazingly, he never did strike the solidity of the ground, though he was surrounded by earth and stone, breathing dirt and pelted by gravel. He was tossed helplessly in the midst of the landslip—Leith could not direct his course, nor intercept Kess as she tumbled shouting past him. He reached for her, missed by inches as his nonexistent footing betrayed him yet again. He saw Brychan and the duke higher up, struggling with one another as they slipped backward. Metal rang, the sound all but lost in the deeper rumbling of the earth. Someone cursed. More earth shifted. The mountain's bones creaked.

The dirt buried Leith, blinded him, choked him. Objects hit him, or he hit them—he couldn't distinguish. When he abruptly reached flat ground, the earth he sprawled upon was yet heaving like a carpet a-shaken, and he was flung down on it each time he contrived to gather his legs under him and rise. Leith won briefly to his feet again just as Valadan came bounding downslope. He dodged back to give the stallion room—and blundered straight into the path of a cartwheel-size boulder, which clipped his right leg smartly and sent him rolling once more, unable to tell where earth left off and dust-colored sky began—had he been able to look past the pain that threatened to fling him out of his senses.

The earth-shake faded away to shudders, such as a horse might use to shift a bothersome fly settling on its flank. Finally, the motion subsided utterly. All was still. Dust began to settle.

Brychan heaved himself to his knees in the unnatural quiet. Symond sprawled a pace away; it had come to this: the two of them alone in a bowl of earth, under a dome of sky. He seized his brother's slack arm.

"Now I will have that ring," he grated, coughing, and began tugging at the duke's signet.

Symond's left hand groped about for the sword he had lost, falling. His fingers closed on dust and pebbles. He flung them into Brychan's face and rolled to his feet hastily while his half-brother cursed and tried to clear his vision. Symond stumbled upon the loose ground, caught his balance and found the hilt of his dagger, still in its sheath.

"Were you *ever* loyal?" the duke asked his seneschal, as if to offer him some crumb of redemption before seeing him on his way into the afterlife.

Brychan laughed and dove for the knife.

He should not have bragged to his niece that he wore mail—Symond had heard, too, and stabbed his enemy's unprotected throat, quick and clean and emotionless as if he butchered a hog.

Leith arose unsteadily, cried out as he first put weight on his bruised leg—then recognized that it held him up, and so 'twas not broken and must serve him, no matter how stridently it complained. With one hand pressed to his thigh, as if to hold in the pain, he began to search for Kess.

A dirt-shrouded body lay half buried at the bottom of the hillside. Leith battered his hands trying to dig it out sufficiently to identify it—and when he saw 'twas one of the archers, he almost fainted, his relief mixing uneasily with nausea at the sight of a rock-smashed skull at very close range. He wiped his fingers in the dust, not wanting to think what was on them, bar his own blood.

Valadan sniffed at a boot, which was poking up between two dislodged boulders at a most unlikely angle—given that there was still a leg inside the boot. *The other archer,* he volunteered, and Leith was only too pleased not to have to investigate the matter further.

Challoner had fallen clear of the worst of the debris, but he was just as dead as either of the bowmen. Leith thought he might have perished the instant the arrow hit him, because the now-broken shaft looked to have gone straight into his heart. A trickle of blood ran through the dust beside his mouth. Probably he had known nothing of the terrifying wild ride on the crest of the landslip, or the luck that had kept him somehow atop it. Luck took many forms. Leith straightened and staggered onward, his leg threatening to give way beneath him with each step, repaying his obstinate abuse of it with alarming slashes of pain.

Where was Kess? *Buried?* Leith lurched dazedly about, prying at rocks, digging with his torn hands whenever he saw anything that looked like a scrap of blue cloth. His senses swam, his eyes deceived him. Every heap of rock held secrets. Kess could be under any of them.

Smothering? He couldn't find her. There was no sign, none at all. Leith called Kess' name till he lost his voice, and he kept digging till his strength failed him, as well, and all he could do was lie sobbing in the dirt, too spent to draw breath.

A sharp toe found his ribs. "What are you yelling about?" Kess asked crossly.

Leith shoved himself up, his face muddy, bleeding, his mouth dropping open. *"You're alive!"*

"Of course I'm alive." Kess stared at him. There was a smudge of dirt on her forehead, another on her chin, but she was obviously unhurt. "Did you think my own mother would kill me?"

Leith tried to get to his feet, but his bruised leg was far past its limit. He could not stand. "Your mother?" he asked, sitting there bewildered.

"She sent the earthshake to save us. I'm going over to the island." Kess inspected Leith with a critical eye. "Why don't you go down to the lake and wash some of that dirt off? My father's already there."

Leith finally succeeded in getting to his feet, but he could not hope to keep up with her. Already Kess was six paces away, and widening the gap.

"Kess, wait! Are you sure—"

Kess smiled back over her shoulder. "I'm sure."

While Leith hobbled slowly toward the lakeshore, Kess made for the end of the narrow causeway that linked the island to the steep-sided valley surrounding the lake. She harbored no least doubt that the landslip had been her mother's weapon to protect her—had she not felt herself lifted atop the sliding dirt, had she not been carried to the bottom almost tenderly? True, treacherous Brychan and his men were dead—probably that had been intended, just as it had been intended that her father and Leith and Challoner should not be buried under rocks, even if they had not been so carefully shielded as she had herself.

The causeway was difficult to cross, being made of rocks of a variety of sizes, laid down so that passage from one to another was just barely possible if close attention was paid and the crosser was nimble. Kess was pleased. Leith would be a long time getting across, and her father would surely stay with him—which guaranteed her a space of privacy. Neither of the men had any part in her quest, which was about to be achieved.

At the causeway's end, a figure stood waiting. Kess' heart beat fast. Her feet skipped over the boulders, and she flew like a bird into her mother's arms.

Raichim

LEITH FOUND THE duke kneeling at the water's edge, dipping a hand to fetch a drink. The sight reminded Leith that his own mouth was yet painfully clotted with grit he had not the moisture to rid himself of. He dropped down clumsily, trying not to further insult his bad leg—and to his brief dismay discovered he'd misjudged the irregularity of the grass-fringed shore. The edge was a lot closer than he'd suspected, actually a little *behind* him, as he tumbled headlong into the lake.

The clear water was chill as snow, and Leith's teeth were knocking even before he surfaced. The depth was a shade too great to allow him to stand—he got his legs under him, but could find no firm bottom beneath the cold mud. The duke caught hold of his doublet just as he started to flounder under again, and helped him climb out onto the grass.

"I know Kess likely told you to drown yourself, lad, but there's no need to obey her so straitly! She doesn't mean the edge she puts on her tongue," Symond added apologetically.

Leith shook water and dripping hair out of his eyes, probed his left ear with a finger till the fullness of water trapped inside left it in a warm spill down the side of his neck. "She just told me to wash. Did I shift the dirt, or will I have to go in again?" He shivered, as much at the thought of daring that wintry water deliberately as at the fresh breeze whipping across his wet skin. Valadan snorted, moving past to stretch his neck and have his own drink without undue incident.

The duke, filthy as if he'd just lately emerged from a pit mine, muddy at the edges, chuckled. "Wait till it dries, and we'll see what we can brush off. That's a hell of a curse."

Leith wondered why he should feel such instant shame at something that had been laid on him through no fault of his own—what sin could a baby commit, to deserve cursing? All the same, he did not raise his face. There was a twist of water weed about his calf. He put his attention to disentangling it.

"Mind, Kess holds it's naught but carelessness. That you imagine most of it."

Leith had wished to be convinced of that once. He thought upon Challoner, lying dead on a ruined hillside far from his home, his hopes and schemes and life all come to a summary end. The man ought to have been as safe as the rest of them. The landslip had spared him. A matter of inches, and the archer's hasty, lucky shot would have found no fatal target. "No," Leith said, wishing with all his heart that Kess could have been right.

"I didn't intend going. If I had, I'd have laid plans—I'd have taken you with me, my little Kessallia! I'd never have left you—but once I was gone, I couldn't get back. And later still, when I might have managed it, I couldn't force myself to return to Keverne. I was a coward, but I could not go back."

Kess, unwilling to be parted from her mother a second time by so much as an arm's length, followed Raichim about the rock-walled chamber step for step, as if she feared her mother might vanish a second inexplicable time, like one of her own unreliable visions.

"I needed you so much," she exclaimed, as if that could alter what had been. "I used to *see* things, things that weren't there! I didn't know what they were, so finally I decided I was mad. I thought your blood had made me so—everyone *said* I was tainted. I couldn't ask anyone about the things I saw in every mirror and candle flame, and they told me you were dead."

Raichim's eyes flashed, black fires that rivalled Kess' own. "Those awful women! Any skill they didn't possess for themselves was evil. Soul-dead crones! And of course so was I evil, for having what they did not and for taking a place they all craved—evil and better dead. If I had been a humble weaver of cloaks, they would have said I was demon-taught! I left before they could kill me with their slanders, so they attacked even the memory of me, to an innocent child." Raichim tossed her head, the long, still raven-black hair switching like an angry panther's tail. "I was a *queen* among my own people. They will not have told you *that*. I was a queen, but at Keverne I was a laughing-stock, because my customs were not those of Esdragon. Barbarian, they called me to my face and worse behind my back, because they never suspected I might know, or did not care if I did. Your father was shamed by me before a year had gone by, because I bore you instead of the son he desired."

Kess knew well that they'd all have been happier if she'd been a son—but her father had raised her as his heir. She had never felt lessened in his eyes, but only before all the rest of his court, which chose to belittle her because she wore skirts, which did not allow her to hold power, but only to pass on what she'd inherited to a husband.

"My father loves you," she protested, because it seemed to Kess that if the duke did not love the mother, then he would not love the daughter either.

"Love?" Raichim's voice broke on the word. "He did not love *me*! Symond loved a shadow-shape, the size of me, the form of me, that would be and do what he chose—a shadow that was tame and safe for what he named love!"

Kess was taken aback. She had dreamed all her life of her mother, told herself how her mother would cherish her if she lived, if she but knew her—this creature was a stranger, wild and dangerous as the chimera in her dreams. Kess did not know her at all, and the ground beneath her boots seemed insubstantial, as it had when the hills began their death-dealing dance.

"He came looking for you!" she cried, protesting her own doubts. "Why did he do that, if he doesn't love you? He left me, with hardly a word of farewell, because he heard a tale of a chimera being seen up here. Why did he do that?" She knew a sudden terror, that her father might love her mother more than he did Kess herself, and that neither of her parents might love their daughter all that much. Where, then, did that leave her?

Raichim's eyes had lost their focus, as she looked past Kess into some distant time, when she had been as young as Kess now was. "The chimera is the badge of my House. There have been one or two about this last year—when the liquid rock rises through the cracks in the mountainsides, then are chimeras whelped. Sometimes they are drawn to me. They cannot cross to the island, but I have seen them on the ridge tops."

Kess wondered nervously whether her mother would be grieved—or angered—to learn that Leith had slain one of her deadly pets so that her daughter might pass by it in safety. Would the chimera perchance have known her, recognized her, let her pass unhindered, if she had given it the chance? Should a witch's true daughter fear even a beast of fire? Had she failed a test she had never suspected?

"Mostly the blood of the mountain manifests itself here as hot water in the spring, not chimeras. I find that much more convenient. Will you have tea?"

Kess frowned. "Mother, I will have answers!"

Raichim looked at her appraisingly. "Had I known you had such an overflowing measure of my blood, I would have made sure to take you away with me! Patience, Kessallia."

Kess creased her brow still more. "All right. Tea. But—"

Her mother dipped a pot into the steaming pool that also gave pleasant heat to the chamber and measured a fragrant scoop of dried leaves into it. She set the tisane aside to steep, while Kess fidgeted from one foot to the other, though the floor underfoot was no more than comfortably warm.

"The moment I was able to rise from the bed where you were born," Raichim said, setting the jar of catmint back in its place with great care, "I ran away from my ladies—who were mine only in that they had been ordered to attend me—and went walking alone on the clifftops. It was foolish. There was a great storm blasting, a storm such as never struck my homeland. I had never seen anything like it—yet I did not fear it. It suited my heart. I had not been able to slip out of Keverne in months, and I was half smothered with coddling and slanders. I, who was not used to having folk about me at all—how I suffered, never being free of them for an instant! That storm was the first kindness Esdragon had shown me. I was in such distress, I could think of naught but the freedom I had lost the day I followed your father away from my homeland to his."

Raichim closed her eyes, threw her head back so that tears were prisoned under her lids, unable to run down her cheeks, therefore nonexistent. "I lifted up my arms to embrace that welcome stormwind, and I did not even know that I had willed myself to take a bird's shape until the wind lifted me, swept me up in its strong dark arms."

Kess' eyes went wide. Could *she* hope to do that? Take another shape? Be a bird? *Fly?*

"I was terribly frightened," her mother admitted, as if she guessed how Kess' avid thoughts must dangerously run. "I could not undo what I had done. I was too weak to escape the wind. I did not have the strength to fly, and I thought I would be dashed against the cliffs, or thrown into the sea. So I held my wings open with all my will and went wherever the wind chose to bear me. After many hours the gale foundered at last and left me here, too battered to take to the air again. In time I regained my strength, but I had lost the key to the spell—I could not take the bird-shape again. Here I was. Here I stayed."

Kess gazed out over the lake, the pine-cloaked slopes of the great bowl which cupped a pool of blue water that knew neither tide nor spray.

"This is so far from the sea. How do you bear it?" she asked plaintively.

Raichim laughed. "This is very like the land your father took me from, Kessallia. The sea's sounds are as foreign to me as these dancing mountains must be to you."

Kess realized that she did indeed long for the sea, whose breathy whisper had never been far from her ears, though taken for granted till she turned her back upon it to go seeking her mother. The daily tides sounded through Keverne like a heartbeat. When there was a storm its sound could not be escaped, but at any time one could find it, merely by placing a palm to any wall.

"Here *I* rule," her mother was saying. "Not a mouse squeaks in these mountains that I do not hear of it."

"Then you *knew* Father was here?" Kess raised her brows and her voice. "He left Keverne *months* ago, seeking you, chasing rumors. He told me he'd been wandering up here the whole time. He said a chimera ate his horse and very nearly him."

"Let the months be as years," Raichim muttered darkly, straining leaves out of the tea. Taken with the action, it sounded like an incantation.

"Would you have hidden from me, too?" Kess wailed.

Raichim set the teapot down in surprise. "I *could* not have hidden from you, Kessallia. You have the means to seek me out."

"But I *don't*," Kess confessed, in a terrified rush. "I saw such strange things when I didn't at all want to, and then after I got the crystal I could see a little when I chose to—but now the visions have stopped, and the crystal is empty no matter how I look." The vanishment of her powers had frightened Kess far more than their unexpected appearance, and even Leith had no idea how many days she had been forging ahead absolutely blindly, while pretending foreknowledge. Nor did anyone know that, during the terrible night after she was reunited with her father, the crystal had refused to show her anything at all, be it ever so trivial. Trembling, tearful, Kess waited for her mother to tell her that she was no witch after all, but only a small, frightened child of no account to anyone.

Raichim smiled gently and offered her daughter a cup of tea, with a spoon of honey to sweeten it. "Everything in nature has its cycle, Kessallia. Ebb and flow, like the tide or the wind. Even the earth-blood below the mountain roots. Now your powers come to you, as and when and *if* they will. When you have learned to call upon them, the cyclical effect will not be so pronounced. Drink your tea, and calm your heart. You will learn best when it is quiet within you."

"Months I've tramped about up here, lad, and never a sign of yonder lake. I would swear I've stood on this very spot and not seen it. Want to get across to that island now, before she remembers to make it vanish again?"

Leith, mostly dry after a span of hours spent drowsing in the sun, climbed carefully to his feet. His right leg ached yet, pain enough to cancel out the hitch in his hip, but it moved as it ought and showed no immediate threat of buckling under him. "Seems like a good idea," he agreed, having retreated far enough from the water's edge to be safe from another slip. The sun was on the far side of the midpoint of the sky, traveling steadily toward the toothy horizon.

They clambered easily enough onto the end of the causeway, up atop a tumble of boulders that more or less made a roadway, and began to pick a way over. There was water visible between the stones, reeds and cattails growing everywhere. A dragonfly whined by, hunting insect prey.

Suddenly the duke snatched at Leith's shoulder, holding him back. "Easy, lad! That misstep's like to drown you. The water's deeper here."

They were a good way out from the shore. Leith teetered, looking down into the deep gap he'd nearly stumbled into. It was reed-screened, visible only at the last instant, and he had not seen it at all. He would have plunged in had the duke not restrained him. The near escape made his heart pound, and there was a sea-sound in his ears once again. He started to lose his balance. The duke's grip on him tightened as he wavered.

"What is it?" came the voice in his ear. "Step back from there now. Easy does it."

Leith shook his head distractedly. Something about the dizziness was familiar. He shut his right eye, tight, as he had become accustomed to do whenever he trailed Kess. Though why she would choose to confuse a path she knew he had *seen* her take . . .

He saw dry stones ahead of his boots. Dry, and nowhere near so tumbled about as the rest of the causeway had appeared. The stones were laid close, with no deep gaps of dark water yawning between. Leith stepped forward, to the duke's consternation.

He neither sank nor fell, but stood dry-shod, safe. The duke muttered something to himself. "You get used to it," Leith explained, still squinting, looking ahead.

"I had forgotten—it's been so long a while—"

Leith could not easily believe Kess had ever dared play such tricks upon her father—but perchance the knack of crafting illusions was not exclusive to her. Perchance it came to her through her mother's blood. In which case, these illusions might not be Kess' doing. That made a certain sense.

"Expect worse," Leith counseled. Valadan, swimming alongside the causeway, snorted water from his nostrils—possibly a comment, possibly not.

Once they were over and off of the causeway, the illusions waxed more puissant. Even Leith had a hard time picking out the way—all he saw, though he concentrated until his left eye burned as if hot coals had been put into it, was a tangled wilderness of brambles and thorns, with pools of standing water the only relief between them. The reality—which seemed only shadows to him—was barely a degree more hospitable. A high-pitched whine promised blood-sucking insects by the swarm, and numberless jabs at unprotected skin proved the pests were no illusion. There was not a scrap of cloud overhead, nor any trees to ward off sunstrikes. Leith's head ached from the heat, his battered leg wanted to fold under him with each forward step, and what he desired beyond any goal was simply to turn back, to retreat from the shore.

Leith recognized with a stab of relief that his wish was the key, or at least a clue—if he forced himself to go the way he *least* would choose, he would certainly be aimed at the trail Kess' witch mother had hidden with such care and craft. He was right every time he tried it—face down something miserable, and it let him pass. Gritting his teeth, Leith kept moving onward, with Valadan following him nose to elbow and the duke bringing up the rear, holding the tip of the stallion's tail.

Leith's feet reported that he was climbing uphill. His eyes suddenly insisted he was about to smash into a wall of speckled granite. Leith flinched, shut both eyes, and pushed on, expecting to connect with stone, probably break his nose. Nothing like that happened. The step left him a little off balance, so he took another, still going forward.

Earth began to crumble beneath his right boot, so Leith bore instinctively to his left. He risked a look, beheld a trail leading over the edge of a precipice and no choice about it—but his feet somehow found him another way, when he closed his eyes to the disconcerting sight of the drop and pushed onward in a direction he'd have preferred to shun. Brambles tore clothes and skin, but he shoved through them, and heard the duke cursing a horse-length behind him. Gnats hummed, stinging wasps buzzed threateningly in his ears. He heard the whisper of a snake moving through dry brambles. Leith ignored it all, desperately. He felt weary to death, but still he set one foot ahead of the other.

Leith managed another pace forward. Then finally he halted, dizzy, his head spinning so that the earth seemed to shake and quiver once more—save that Valadan was not acting as if the ground were anything but solid under his four hooves. Leith raised a hand to his head, pushed wet hair away, and the aching in his temples let up at last. He opened both eyes.

Ahead of him lay a little flat space, thickly turfed, the grass starred with tiny white daisies, taller red hawkweed. Valadan shouldered past him, dropped his head, and fell to on the lush food.

Beyond the greensward, the rock bones of the island rose once again. There was a dark fissure facing them, a triangle handspan narrow at the top, two cubits wide at the base, and evidently quite deep. A little stream of water drained from it—warm, when Leith bent to put a testing finger into it.

The duke was at his side when he straightened. "Think they expect us?" There were footprints marking the grass, two sets.

Leith shrugged. He kept his eyes on the fissure, lest it vanish. After a moment Kess emerged from the cave, followed closely by a small woman. The stranger was garbed in deep scarlet woven all over with jagged flashes of lightning—which Leith supposed most appropriate. Kess herself should dress in such plain warnings—it would only be merciful, considerate to those she met.

Kess' black eyes were narrowed against the bright sun, evidently, rather than with anger. "Father!" she cried, and ran to him. The duke put his good arm about her.

Kess looked over his shoulder, took note of Leith finally, and recollected her manners enough to point a finger. "Mother, this is Leith, Prince of—" She frowned. "Where was that again?"

"The Isles," Leith supplied patiently, with a little inward shake of his head at her. He faced the witch, whom he had sought with a tenacity that was surely a match for Kess' own, and bowed to the fullest degree of courtesy his sore muscles and battered leg would permit. "My lady."

Kess' mother inclined her head to him. It was more notice than she gave to her husband—she had not acknowledged the duke with the briefest glance.

The duke took the initiative, setting Kess aside and striding forward with purpose. "Raichim, I have missed you."

The witch queen fixed her narrow dark gaze on him at last. "Our daughter speaks well of you, Symond," she said grudgingly. "I receive you for her sake. Is it true you have made her your heir?"

"It is true. Though—" He scowled at Kess, who met his baleful eye without a flinch. "—she witlessly abandoned Esdragon to come in search of me."

"I was looking for *both* of you," Kess protested hotly.

Neither parent paid any heed.

"Though she's not the son you wanted?" The queen was no taller than Kess, but she stood as straight as a spear, her head held high.

"My child and yours—who else should be my heir? I found no fault with Kess when she was born, and I find none now." The duke's forehead furrowed. "Though I might esteem her the more if she would show this young man a place where his horse might feed without imperiling your garden," he added.

Kess chuckled. Valadan had worked his way to the edge of the grass and was eyeing with interest the feathery tops of a row of carrots that bordered the plot of tended ground before the cave mouth. Leith hastily took hold of his bridle and coaxed the stallion away from the vegetables. Already one hoofprint marred the edge of a lettuce bed.

"Come on." Kess waved a hand at him. She took a dozen steps, then became ensnared in a skein of brambles. *"Mother—"* she began indignantly.

"Permit me," Leith said, closing his right eye and steering her safely around the tangle even as Kess' mother lifted a hand and caused her illusion to fall away.

Supplication

"This ought to be far enough," Kess pronounced briskly. "Grass. Water." They were by the lakeside once more, but the spot was less rocky, more fertile. Leith guessed it had always been so, the inhospitability all sham. "Come on."

"Kess."

She halted, so impatient that she turned only her head back to face him, and her feet seemed barely to touch the ground. "Take his saddle off, and come on. He's not hot, he'll be fine here."

"He wanted to talk to her." Leith pointed the obvious out to her gently. "Without us there. Let him have some time." He began to strip Valadan of saddle and bridle unhurriedly.

Kess rejoined him, stepping warily at the edge of his reach, as if she expected Leith to snatch at her, to be fool enough to think he could detain her by force. Leith sighed and sat down carefully on a smooth boulder, stretching his bruised leg out a bit to one side. It hurt, but that was because he was changing its position. Once he settled, most of the pain leaked rapidly away.

Kess tugged a tuft of grass that had managed to root upon one of the boulders. It came loose into her hands, to be toyed with. "It was you, wasn't it?" She began to shred the grass stems. "Who found the way up to the cave? She said the duke would never do it. She didn't let on, but she was amazed when the pair of you showed up. You should have seen her face."

"Her spells are very thorough," Leith said sincerely, paying a compliment. "I could barely see the cave, by the time I finally got to it."

"I know. I saw *your* face." Kess smiled at the memory, flattered by extension when her mother was praised. "You looked

221

terribly uncomfortable. How long do we have to wait out here?"

It was Leith's turn to smile, at Kess' utter lack of anything resembling either patience or tact. "If you will wait with me till moonrise, I will thank my Lady for our safe deliverance," he proposed.

Kess sniffed. "As if your Lady had aught to do with it! 'Twas my mother's spell saved us."

"She's full bright," Leith coaxed. "There's not a cloud to veil Her face. And it's a beautiful tune, the welcome melody. You haven't heard it before—I hadn't finished the flute yet, last Full." He fetched out the instrument as he spoke and put it to his lips. Sweet notes drifted into the evening air.

His Lady was bathing Her face in the lake's icy waters ere Leith finished his playing. His heart was so full, he thought the joy of the music might actually bring him some harm, that his heart might burst, or—Leith didn't know what he expected, or dreaded, only that some wonder seemed imminent. His lips and jaw had ached at the first few notes, then all pain was forgotten and there was nothing but moonshine and magic. It was over far too soon.

Kess broke the silver spell, slapping noisily at an insect and insisting that they go back at once. Leith climbed to his feet obediently, stowing the flute safely away—then stumbled so precipitously that Kess actually took note of his difficulty.

"Leg gone to sleep?"

"No." Leith pressed a hand tight to the weak leg. "A rock hit it this morning." He tried to shove the pain away with his fingers. It didn't help all that much, but he began to lose his fear of collapse. "It's all right—it's just gone stiff on me."

Kess poked his calf, ignoring Leith's flinch and smothered curse. "There's a hot spring inside the cave. You should soak this. And my mother will have herbs, for a poultice."

"I'd rather tend the source of the trouble and have her lift the curse," Leith said. "Did you ask her about it?"

"Imaginary curses weren't foremost in my thoughts," Kess said airily.

Leith swallowed his disappointment and picked up his saddle. Best, perhaps, that Kess had not troubled to inform her mother of a curse she did not believe in. At least he could put his case to the witch queen without the need to work around Kess' prejudice. Probably—did his leg not ache so cruelly, he would actually rejoice in the way things had worked out. Probably.

"Kessallia looks well," Raichim said. She had gone back into the cave, and Symond had followed her, though she had not invited him to dog her steps—no more than she had permitted him to find her, after so many months of fruitless search. She wished she might ignore him, as she had then.

"She's more like you each day."

"More than you may guess." Raichim picked up a hank of combed wool from the basket that lay beside her rowen-shafted spindle. She teased at the wool with her fingers, but though she gazed in its direction, it was not in her sight. "Esdragon will not much like the taint I left in her blood."

"Raichim—"

"You should not be here, Symond." She twisted the wool fibers tight, into a great lumpy knot.

"I'd have set out sooner, if I'd had any suspicion you were here. And arrived sooner this season, if the trails hadn't coiled back on themselves like snakes whenever I set my foot to them." He took an unsure step toward her, halted when she smote him at last with her gaze. "I came straight from greeting our newborn daughter to see how you fared, the night Kess was born. You were gone from your chamber, your women were in a dither, frighted to tell me, too stupid to look for you. I found your cloak lying on the wet cliffside, caught on a tuft of sea-pink. I thought you had thrown yourself into the sea, and had she not been my sister, Amalthea would have followed you, for telling you falsely that you disappointed me with a daughter—then leaving you unwatched, untended."

"The past is dead, and I am not, Symond. Distress yourself no more with it." She had shredded the wool to fluff, and let it fall away.

"And our love? Is that dead, as well?" he pleaded.

"Kess said you loved me still." Raichim smiled indulgently. "She is fond of pretty romances, as all young maids are. I explained to her that you loved a dream of me, but had found the reality less than pleasant to dwell with."

"Then you've lied to her. *I* never did."

"To deny truth—is that what you mean by not lying?"

"I love you, Raichim. I did so then, I do so now."

"As you did then, you pledge me your heart with words. But a man's words are naught but air," she accused.

"Will you have deeds?" Symond asked irritably. "What does it need to satisfy you, woman? Shall I slay you another chimera?"

Raichim's eyes were narrow. "You need not have killed the first beast, to lay as a trophy at my feet. I told you so then—the Beast of my House is kin to me, and I do not fear it alive. Killing it was pointless."

Symond smiled, hearing echoes of a long-ago rage, remembering what had come after. "Ah, but I was desperate to impress you," he said. "There were so few ways I could do it. And I hoped that my burns would inspire your pity, at least keep me lingering in your care long enough that you might learn to love me, also."

Raichim flung the spindle across the chamber. "Poor chimera, murdered so that you might cozen your way to my side!"

"And then I discovered there'd be no trophy, but only ashes," the duke said, chastened.

Raichim's eyes clouded, recalling a young warrior, singed and miserable and disappointed in what he felt was his best hope of attracting her notice. She *had* pitied him, and that had led her into a tangle of hurt far worse than any of her witchery-augmented thickets of thorns. She was not minded to be so torn again—ever.

"There *is* a deed you may do," she offered slyly. "Save that you never will. You would not be willing to turn about, Symond, now that our positions are reversed and you are powerless where *I* rule."

The duke stared at her, looking for the trap, the deceit. Then he began to chuckle, realizing what she thought.

Raichim glared at him. "I thought not! You might at least have pretended to think it over."

"No need, Raichim. It seems only fair, to me. Though perhaps too easy a way into your good graces. Look you, I have spent these long years ruling Esdragon, breeding good horses, raising our daughter. It is a humbling thing. The dukedom will endure when I am forgotten dust, Kessallia is unlikely ever to do my bidding—or any other man's—and my horses can be stolen away. Power, prestige, are naught but sham. I will leave it all behind, and gladly, without one regret, if it gains me the only thing that should ever have mattered to me—your regard. Or if not that, then at least your sufferance until I come to deserve better."

He stepped toward her again. Raichim was too astonished to retreat a step and keep the measure between them. His touch was delicate, so as to provoke no resistance, and she lifted her lips to meet his, hardly knowing she did so.

The way back to the cave, no longer guarded by sorcery, was easy to find even in the blue light of the evening. Leith set his saddle down where an overhanging rock would shelter it from most weather, and Kess for a wonder waited while he stowed it, so that they ventured into the cave together, as much side by side as the narrow way permitted.

Firelight washed the stone walls with warm tides of yellow and apricot. There were thick white pelts of the long-wooled mountain sheep laid about to offer seats, and a meal was set out. There were spotted lake trout, poached in the hot spring, lying on trenchers of obsidian. Black clay bowls, polished to a sheen bright as the volcanic glass, held fat raspberries—red and black and pale yellow. The duke's forearms were stitched with bramble scratches.

There was honey waiting to be spread upon the thick crusts of fresh bread, and more honey to be drunk with the meal—the sweet stuff distilled by arts close to magical into a potent mead.

There were small formalities of welcome exchanged as they sat down to the food. Leith noticed that the duke settled close by his wife and that a measure of the tension and anger seemed to have gone out of her. Something had been settled between them while they were alone—Leith was glad, for Kess' sake. What it boded for his goal, he dared not guess.

Nothing was said about tending his leg—the food took all their attention. In any case, after his third cup of the sweet mead, Leith was unaware of any pain—a state he found delightful for its very novelty. The spirit had stung his still-swollen lip a trifle at his first sip and had burned a startling bright path down his throat to his belly—felt like clean down to his toes, in truth—but after that all was warm peace, cozy as the firelit cave. Leith watched the ruddy light dancing over Kess' hair, which she had unbraided and left loose about her shoulders. One tendril, straying, had entangled itself on a burr stuck to his doublet, and Leith reached out carefully to free it, with an apology ready for Kess, but she only smiled and suffered the touch without rebuke. The honey-wine had brought a sparkle to her eyes, pleasant companion to the fire-roses in her cheeks. He wondered if he dared say so.

A small hand, laid upon his knee, brought Leith out of his reverie with a start. He looked into narrow dark eyes, so like— and so unlike—Kess'.

"You are a long way from your Isles, Prince."

Leith nodded. The statement was perfectly true, beyond dispute. It was also a prelude, he thought, not an empty courtesy, and he waited to hear what would come next.

"I know what drew Symond to this place, and Kessallia— but what has brought you hither, on a way that must have been easier to stray from than to keep to?" Kess' mother asked.

Leith swallowed hard, wishing belatedly that he had anticipated this questioning, or that it had come at some more fortunate time. His mouth was sticky at the corners, his head buzzed like the bees that had made the mead possible by distilling nectar to sweet honey. It would be, he thought, just his luck to lose his chance at having the curse lifted because he was too tipsy to explain about it properly. He was a fool—*one* cup of mead would have been quite sufficient. Whyever had he taken three?

Kess' mother was slightly more patient than Kess herself was wont to be, and neither poked him nor prodded him with a sharp comment. Leith, somewhat encouraged by the small courtesy, found his tongue at last.

"I am in need of having a curse lifted, lady," he said earnestly. "I came hither with Kess because I hope you will help me." Not wishing to sound boastful, he said nothing of whatever small help he had been to Kess, and did not mention how Kess had refused that help at most opportunities. He had no idea what she might have confided to her mother—it would be very like Kess never to have mentioned him at all, Leith supposed.

Raichim frowned at him. "Help you? How shall I help you? A curse is best lifted by the one who laid it," she instructed sternly. "*Who* cursed you? Why? Do you deserve a curse?"

Leith blinked at the attack. He heard Kess gasp beside him. Actually, he had often wondered if he *did* somehow deserve his curse and—just his luck—did not realize the fact. But he'd never had it put so, to his face.

"My lady, I can't answer you. So far as I've been told, I was born with it."

"Born with it?" Raichim's brows drew together till they

were nearly one. "Did you kill your mother, coming into the world?"

"No." Leith shook his head. "She lives still, and bore my father other children after me."

"Any of *them* cursed?"

"Not that I have heard." He had had very little contact with the rest of his technical family, having been isolated like a contagion from his birth. Still, had there been others like him, he thought he would have been given to know of it.

"What sort of curse is it?"

"Ill luck." Receiving a nod when he looked for it, Leith explained at some length, beginning with his royal father's first sight of him. When he reached the point where his ordination ceremony had been interrupted, the witch queen held up one slim hand, halting his narrative of woe.

"Enough. I can offer you my sympathy, Prince of the Isles, but nothing more. I cannot help you."

The sensation of disaster was so familiar, Leith hardly took note of it. Disappointment was a very old companion.

But his trials had taught him—if nothing else—the virtues of perseverance.

"A woman who can make the earth dance to her tune should be able to lift a curse," Leith insisted stubbornly.

Kess gasped again. The queen's nostrils flared wide, and she held very still. Leith took fresh note of the lightning pattern woven into her gown—she was all storm cloud and heaven-fire, and he had just spoken so as to provoke her. He might be about to learn what a *true* curse was like. Perchance she would show him the mercy of a quick death, assuming his luck would allow it.

Of course, a curse that could not be lifted might yet have a thing or two added to it.

Leith realized he had been holding his breath. He could not continue to do so forever, and when he let it out—carefully—it caught in his throat. He lifted his cup and took a too-hasty sip to stem the coughing fit ere it took a firm grip. The swallow of mead went down the wrong way—predictably—and he spent the next few moments choking helplessly, while Kess pounded him between his shoulder blades—nearly the only spot whereupon he had not previously been bruised. By the time the spasm subsided, Leith's eyes and nose were dripping, and he was heartily wishing the queen would curse him to his death and have it over with for good and all.

"*Why* should I help you?" Raichim asked into the relative silence, while Leith struggled to steady his breathing and Kess held ready to strike again.

Leith wiped his streaming eyes on his sleeve, then rested his face against his fist. "I could stand *this*," he whispered brokenly. "But the worst never happens to *me*. Crops fail. Cattle die. Ships sink. Inns burn to the ground if I stop there. Folk who *aren't* cursed suddenly *are* if I happen to be around. If you can't help me, lady, then I think I will have to find myself some lonely spot such as this, where at least there will be no one around to be hurt by me."

He started to get to his feet. The leg had gone stiff again, but Leith refused to coddle it, because it would only need to carry him a few steps, till he was out of sight, beyond the fire's light. After that, it could fall off if it liked.

"*Wait.*"

The order was very softly spoken, and Leith would have sworn he'd imagined it, conjured it out of air and need, only Kess had bounced to her feet and put herself in his path, so that there could be no mistake.

"Sit down, Prince of the Isles," Raichim continued reluctantly. "You shall have my hospitality, at the least. I do not fear to be cursed by your presence, and I will help you if it is possible—since you do not ask for your own sake alone."

Proposals

KESS CLOSED HER eyelids dutifully and began reciting the formulae her mother had commended. She rattled the arcane syllables like a hard rain, flawlessly and without sense, then opened her eyes expectantly.

"Kessallia, the exercise is meant to cleanse and focus your thoughts. Rushing through it like a runaway horse utterly defeats that purpose." Raichim wound fresh-spun thread about the spindle and set it whirling once more, not even glancing at her daughter.

Kess sighed and repeated the chant at a less rapid pace. "Nothing happens," she protested.

"I am not surprised." Raichim made more fine thread. "You complain that you cannot control your Sight, but I see no evidence that you can control any other part of yourself. And what you seek to master cannot be learned in a single morning. I doubt that you learned to walk on your first attempt, Kessallia. All skills are learned by practice, if they are learned at all."

"My other magics didn't take this long to learn!"

Raichim snorted. "*Magics!* Disguisings and weather charms! Kess, your 'magic' is all tricks, such as any person could learn if she chose. What I can teach you goes beyond, into the priestess-gift that troubles you so."

"The priestess-gift?"

"The legacy of my blood. I did not suspect you bore it in such hearty measure—even among my own folk it appears erratically. I am greatly at fault, that I left you to cope with it alone. Had I known, I would have remained with you no matter what the cost."

Silver flute notes drifted in through the cave mouth. Kess

cocked her head at the sound, which went on and on over the bubbling of the stream, sometimes in harmony, never quite in discord.

"Pleasant," Raichim agreed.

"Distracting."

"Not of necessity. Music can aid your task, provide a focus as you turn your eyes farther inward."

"It's better than the chanting whenever the moon comes up," Kess conceded. "He was right about that." She shut her eyes, fumbled over the words of her own calming chant, then looked at her mother once again. "What are you going to do about him?"

The spindle worked its way down the newborn thread to the floor, was reeled back once more. "He's fasting, for a day and a night. Tomorrow I will know more."

"*Can* you help him?"

"That depends a great deal upon the curse. It's a wonder he still lives to fight it, something so all-encompassing."

"I suppose he owes it all to Valadan, but how he ever made it to the top of the Hill of Glass—" Kess began, shaking her head.

She stopped and put her hand to her lips. It was too late—her mother's sharp eyes had left the thread and fastened onto her daughter's face. Or, quite possibly, onto her very soul. Kess, blithe and unwary, had stepped into the snare.

"What is this, Kessallia?"

Kess made a halting explanation, holding back anything she dared. "I needed to keep the young men busy, while I went to find Father. They were pests. It was a sham. No one was supposed to make it to the top of the hill—"

"But *this* prince did?"

Kess nodded reluctantly. She had never disputed what Leith had accomplished, only what she was obligated to do in return. "But it doesn't matter—"

"It *does* matter, Kessallia." Her mother laid the spindle down and looked alarmingly grave. "You gave your word, in a matter of magic. Even you should know there is a weight to that." She put her hands on Kess' tense shoulders. "You set a task, with your hand as the prize. I had better be able to help him, for you must keep your pledge and wed him."

"Never!" Kess leapt to her feet, throwing off her mother's touch. "You're supposed to be helping me, not selling me away!"

Leith stopped playing in midnote as Kess ran past him. He lowered the flute. All that remained to tell of Kess' hasty passage was a bit of dust she'd kicked up from the path, settling slowly like flakes of gold in the slant of a sunbeam.

Raichim exited the cave more slowly and paused by him. "I suppose there's no need to ask why you never mentioned this," she said, frowning. "Does her father know?"

"It's *not* why I came with her," Leith insisted, taking no offense at the suggestion that Symond might not care for him as a son by marriage. "Kess has no obligation to me, except for letting me come along, to find you, to ask about having the curse lifted. We agreed that at the very first."

"*You* agreed. She cannot," Raichim said sternly.

Leith shook his head. "I won't hold her to the pledge." His expression hinted at some sorrow held back with determination but not entire success.

"Very noble, and it matters not in the least what you do," Raichim explained carefully. "Kessallia comes of two royal houses, with mine being the more ancient, the more steeped in sorcery. She gave her word, and she worked a magic—there was a binding made, though Kessallia neither intended nor understood it. However pure your intent, you cannot absolve Kessallia of consequences and responsibilities. She pledged to wed you, and so she must."

Leith stared at the flute in his hands, not seeing it. "And if I went away?" he asked, almost inaudibly.

"Kessallia would be obliged to wait for you." Raichim tried once more to make the truth plain. "Whatever *you* do, she pledged what she pledged."

Leith looked stricken. "Then she's stuck with the curse, as well?"

"All the more reason to cure you," Raichim said, sighing. "Remember, take no food, and drink naught but water from the lake. When the sun rises tomorrow, we will begin to see what may be done."

Leith had had a very thick head when he had waked—eased somewhat by a dip in the chill lake waters when he bathed travel dirt and chimera soot away. He had thought the headache mostly cured, but it returned to strike with a vengeance as he fretted over what the queen had told him. Seeking distraction, he ventured off to see where Valadan might be, hoping he would not run headlong into Kess—or her father, who had taken a bow and gone hunting very early. Leith's heart was heavy, despite his ineffable hopes for his future. He didn't want to quarrel with Kess, or struggle to reassure her father that he had no designs upon her.

The instruction to fast was not especially troublesome. Leith had gone hungry often enough and long enough to know full well that he would not expire of starvation in a single night and a day. After the unaccustomed onslaught of the mead, his innards might even be the better for a brief respite. Reaching the spot where he had left Valadan, he found a track or two to show him where the stallion had wandered. The dew-sparkle had dried, but the morning was still fair, the air yet cool and refreshing. Leith walked on. With the forbidding illusions no longer in force, the island was a pleasant place, welcoming even.

The trail led him eventually to a little dell, surrounded by aspens going gold, carpeted thick with pink-blossoming clover. Valadan raised his head, jaws busily grinding the latest mouthful of fodder.

Leith went to him, hugged his sleek neck. "You must be the only living thing my luck *doesn't* affect! By rights you should have colicked on this rich stuff by now."

Valadan shook his head, slapping his mane gently against Leith's face. He nuzzled his master's shoulder, plainly content and in the best of fettle. His enthusiasm nearly lifted Leith from his feet, till he realized the stallion was using him to scratch an itch and was likely to dire need of a grooming.

Not having had the foresight to bring brushes along, Leith pulled handfuls of coarse dry grass from under the aspens, and rubbed and polished Valadan's coat until the hair took on the sheen of sable silk. He used his fingers to tease snarls out of the stallion's mane and long tail, till each hair fell straight and free, floating on the breeze.

The most plaguing aches melted from Leith's muscles as he worked under the warm sun, stretching and bending as the task demanded. He let the moment possess him, chose not to fret over anything beyond the next tangle. When he had finished he stretched out on the fragrant turf, yielded himself up to fatigue, and slept while Valadan grazed alongside him. The wind and the birds sang counterpoint to each other in the aspens, and drifted through Leith's dreams.

A touch on his shoulder disturbed him. Leith sat up, expecting Kess, wondering how she had resisted jabbing a toe into his unprotected ribs or his still-tender leg. He was startled to discover the duke kneeling beside him in her stead. Confused, scarcely awake, Leith carelessly put his left hand too close to a feeding bee, which stung him in fright.

He bit his lip as he scraped the stinger out, feeling pity for the innocent bee, dying for a curse it knew naught of. Leith wanted suddenly to weep—not for the trifling pain in his hand, but at the memory of all those others who had died or suffered loss just by being too near when his curse assailed him. Not wanting Kess' father to take him for a weak fool, he blinked his tears into check and sat still.

The duke shooed other bees out of his way and sat himself down in the clover. "No sweet without sting, eh?" he asked. He waved a hand at Valadan, grazing unbothered by the buzzing insects. "I could have wished him taller, but what a heart! Big enough for two of him."

Leith agreed, though the turn of the conversation perplexed him. He thought he must not have come fully awake, the bee-sting notwithstanding. Surely Kess' father had not waked him to talk of horses?

"Shook that archer of Brychan's like a rag. I have never seen the like. You teach him that trick?"

Leith laughed at the absurdity of teaching a stallion to pick up humans like windfallen apples. "No. It wasn't a skill I ever dreamed he'd need."

"'Tis of the blood, that courage. A thing's nature—sometimes it's obvious and sometimes it isn't, but it never changes." The duke rubbed at his shoulder, where the healing wound might be itching. He had taken no fever in it, which Leith thought was a great mercy and an even greater wonder, all circumstances considered.

"I loved Raichim for what she was, but I took her to Esdragon, and I never should have done such a cruelty," the duke said ruefully. "I should have known better. It was not her nature to be happy there—and certainly not now, with all that's changed. She will never go back with me." The duke played with the carved leather scabbard of his dagger. "So I am not going back, either."

Leith wondered why he was the recipient of the information. It was a private matter, none of his concern. The question must have shown on his face. The duke had raised an eyebrow, awaiting it.

"Someone must go back, howbeit, else Esdragon will be in a turmoil it deserves not to suffer. Kessallia is my declared heir, and Brychan surely had not time enough to undermine her position—else he'd not have tried to kill her." He fidgeted with the dagger again. "And whatever she may say as to her intent, I understand Kess gave her word, and that you met the task she set. Met it fairly."

He must, Leith realized, have been back to the cave. How long had he lain sleeping? What had chanced—or mischanced?

"Sir—" Leith tried desperately to head the topic off. It had been an *accident*. He hadn't intended to win himself a bride, willing or otherwise.

"Don't interrupt." Symond cut him off. "I don't want Kess going back alone, to face the trouble that whoreson of a seneschal surely left, atop the sort of thing her mother met with. I failed Raichim then, but I have learned a thing or two since those days, and I will not fail Kessallia. Swear to me you'll go back with her." The duke fixed him with a stern glare. "And don't pretend you don't want to—I saw your face, when you thought she might be under what was left of that hillside. Kess means something to you."

Leith's heart pounded in his throat, having evidently torn loose from its customary mooring in his chest. "I gave Kess *my* word," he said, trying not to remember how he'd felt when he'd thought he'd lost her to the landslip. "I gave up my claim on her, in exchange for the chance to have the curse lifted," he managed. "And I won't go back on my word. If the curse *can't* be lifted, I won't risk Kess by staying near her. But I'll see her safely back to Keverne, sir. I *can* promise you that," he added fervently.

The duke glowered at him. "Half-measures don't suit me, lad. And this isn't the last you'll hear of this." He found Leith's miserable expression, coupled with those mismatched eyes, harder to stare down than he'd expected. Impossible to dominate. Yet a perverse hope remained—any man *he* could cow wouldn't be likely to last five minutes with Kess. Symond knew his daughter.

Though he could not share their food, Leith had not been forbidden to share the family's company. He might have joined them within the cave at dusk, and sat in the fire's golden light, and taken some comfort from fellowship—but he chose not to. He thought it better to hold to the spirit of his fast, to keep his vigil alone, under his Lady's silver light. The night air, cool but never uncomfortable, always sweet, was better than food or wine.

He sat with his head tilted back, his mismated eyes fixed on his Lady's serene white disc. Her visage was still nearly perfect, though of course no longer entirely full. Leith wished he could be sure She was smiling, approving all he had done to win this far, offering him hope for success on the morrow. He did not wish to think of Her face as only blank, impassive. Or worse, beginning to turn away from him, a servant She had no further interest in.

When the moon had crossed the whole of the sky, Leith moved at last, rather stiffly, and found a sandy spot by the stream to lie down upon. The thick grass would be soaked with dew already, cold and uncomfortable, but the stream was warm where it issued out of the cave, and the dry sand a soft enough bed. He was used to worse. Leith rolled up in his gray cloak, closed his still moon-dazzled eyes, and gave himself up to sleep.

That sleep lasted perhaps a quarter of an hour, for Leith was hardly certain he had slept at all. He opened his eyes and Kess was standing over him, her feet planted wide apart, a fist doubled on either hip. Leith raised up onto one elbow.

"What is it?" he asked politely, though he had some suspicion in the matter.

"You think my mother's going to help you," Kess whispered harshly. "But you're wrong, and you'd better know it. I know what my father promised you, and what you promised him—"

"Kess—" She couldn't know unless the duke had told her, and the man might have said anything, Leith thought. Given her as fact whatever he wished was true.

"My sight was perfectly adequate—we're all on the same island, you couldn't hide something like that from me if I was blind!" Kess spat. "My mother won't see me sold into marriage, traded off like a cow! She'll help *me*, not you—"

Leith was beginning to feel distinctly sick. "So what do you suggest I do?" he asked wearily, resting his head in his hands. It had started to ache again, right at the back of his neck. His beestung finger throbbed, too, for the first time in many hours.

"Take your horse and get out of here! By dawn you'll be too far gone to track—don't think I haven't guessed how you caught up to me that time! Valadan was fathered by the wind, and he runs with his sire's speed! You could—"

"And go where? To seek some other witch who'll help me?

How will I do that?" Leith stared into her narrow eyes, seeking some shred of mercy. "Kess, can't you understand what it's like? You've seen how this curse works, what it's capable of. This is my chance to be rid of it. Probably my only one. If I can't shed the curse, I'll be condemned to wander forever—I won't dare stay long enough anywhere for it to strike everyone around me. I can't live like that any longer. I'll take whatever chance I have to!"

There was no mercy for him, it seemed. "You'll be taking a chance, all right," Kess hissed. "Magic costs dear. Just you remember that."

Leith did, the rest of a sleepless night.

Ere the sun had raised its face over the rim of the lake's bowl, Leith had been down to the water and had bathed. In the first brightening of the day, when the grass was a dew-jeweled carpet under his feet, he presented himself, chilled but clean within and without, at the cave entrance. A voice bid him enter; he did so. To his great relief, there was no sign of Kess there, nor of the duke.

Raichim wore a mantle of black wool, with flames picked out about its full hem in threads that shone like red gold. Save that they flickered with far more life than dead metal and firelight could answer for—did she spin the thread from her chimera's hair? Leith wondered. Could such a marvel be done? If so, then surely she could lift his curse from his shoulders.

If she chose to do so. Now that Kess had put the poisonous doubt into his ear, there was always that to consider. He could not avoid it, no matter how he schooled himself. Leith was not especially grateful for the fresh worry to add to his bountiful store of such.

The queen gestured for Leith to sit facing her, and she took his two hands into her own—which were tiny and clever, very like her daughter's, and felt quite dry. Leith's own palms were damp, though no longer with lakewater.

For a long while she simply sat, staring into his face, until Leith ceased to be uncomfortable about the scrutiny. The queen gazed into his eyes, and it would have been either impolite or cowardly to look away, so Leith stared back, and the black of her eyes became the black of the night sky, or the womb he had swum in, before his mismatched eyes knew any light at all.

When he came back to himself, Raichim had a hand resting lightly on each of his temples. Her own perilous eyes were lightly closed. Her right thumb gently rubbed the crescent of the scar under his left eye, and her lips moved, but the only sound Leith could hear was the bubbling of the hot water in the spring, somewhere at his back.

Later, she pressed a piece of black crystal—or perchance volcanic glass—to his forehead, and murmured strange words whilst the sharp cold edges dug into his skin. She poked up the fire, and flung bundles of dried herbs upon it, and bade Leith take the smoke into his mouth, and either hold it or let it out, at her pleasure.

The activity made Leith more than a little dizzy, after all the fasting. Happily he was not ordered to rise, but was suffered to kneel in his place till the fumes dissipated and his head cleared. He tried to judge the passage of time, but it proved impossible—within the cave day and night were one. He had no sense even of his Lady's position relative to his own. He could see daylight through the cave mouth if he turned his head, but he was sternly corrected when the witch caught him glancing that way, and he did it no more thereafter.

He felt a prick on the tip of his first finger, and Leith saw the witch holding his left hand over a bowl, whilst she pressed the point of an obsidian blade against the complaining finger. Three drops of blood fell down, no more, and then she took the bowl away, and stirred powders into it, and peered closely at the result. She herself inhaled fumes from the fire, deeply, repeatedly. She plucked hairs from Leith's head, and tied complex knots in them, and laid them on the fire, watching how they writhed about, burning, as if the scorched shapes they took were words, clues to the curse, solutions. She chanted, and the flames crackled in accompaniment, and made the sort of hissing one might expect of chimera cubs.

Leith noticed suddenly that the only light came from the fire—the cave's mouth showed naught but darkness. Kess was seated on the far side of the fire, her father by her side. He had never heard them enter, settle themselves, ask for or receive permission. It was as if they had risen up from the floor, like mushrooms after a deluge of rain.

He must, in fact, have either slept or been left sitting tranced, for the witch queen had exchanged her divining garb for a more sober robe of undyed gray wool, and her dark hair had been brushed back from her face and loosely braided into the sort of plait Kess commonly chose. Leith blinked, and the simple action seemed to take an hour. He would have been frightened at that, but emotion seemed as sluggish as his eyelids.

The queen's small hand drew back from his face, the palm leaving him first, then her fingers. Lastly, the warmth of her touch, and time seemed to resume its march.

"I have sought all this day," Raichim said. "With crystal, with the holy smoke, with dream-trace. I am still at a loss to declare why you should bear this curse, Prince of the Isles. It may even be that it was an accident, never meant to fall upon you."

Somehow, Leith could take no comfort at the information. He waited. She resumed.

"Your people were wrong to call you a demon—but they were right about your eyes. You have noticed, I think, that they do not each see the same world, in quite the same way?"

Kess made a tiny, surprised sound, maybe realizing how Leith had always found her so unerringly, no matter how determinedly she'd covered her trail.

"Your eyes are an anomaly," the queen explained. "There should be a firm wall between what is seen and what lies unseen—but for you, there is not. The rift in that wall acts upon what we call chance—luck. The effect ripples out around you—if any unchancy thing is likely to happen, it *does*, when you pass by. You do not cause it, but your presence hastens it."

Kess made another faint sound, impossible to decipher. It might have been amazement, that the curse she scoffed at actually existed, was somehow kin to her own visions.

Her mother had said nothing of any cure. "Can anything be done?" Leith asked, staring into the queen's narrow black eyes with some desperation.

"Yes—"

"*Hold.*"

Raichim stared at her husband, her nostrils flaring. Leith tensed for an explosion of some sort—a breath of chimera-flame, perhaps. He could feel the fury singing in the hand that rested so lightly upon his forearm. When she answered, her tone was calm, which seemed not reassuring at all, but the more deadly.

"Symond, this is none of your business. He is not yours, to decide what he shall hear, or not hear."

"I have a thing to say to him, before you tell him, Raichim." He did not rest a hand on his sword hilt, but the effect was the same.

Kess stared from one of her parents to the other, as if she had lost track of loyalties and had no least idea what to expect next.

Raichim tossed her braid back over her shoulder. "Speak, then, and be done."

The duke grunted, knowing full well she had conceded nothing. "When I came in search of you, Raichim, 'twas my intent to beg you to return to Keverne with me. I know now that you will never do that. You have your reasons, good ones. You tasked me that I knew nothing of love, but I tell you again that I lost my heart to you when you were younger than Kess is now. So I will prove with deeds what the words you distrust cannot—I will remain here with you."

"No!" Kess protested. She had unswervingly assumed that both her parents would come home with her, and cast about for some lure, some choice or duty, and settled on a duty as most likely to succeed. "Esdragon—"

"Esdragon I give to you, my heir," the duke said, smiling. He pulled his signet from his finger.

"But I don't want to go home without you!" Kess backed away from the ring, as if she had been offered a serpent.

"Yet you will," Symond said, and Kess recognized with a shiver of despair the firm hand that he had showed her but seldom—but never failed to employ at need. There was no appeal. "I did my duty by my people, these long years. Now it is your turn, daughter." He put the ring on her finger, frowned as the heavy gold circle turned loose upon it. "And Leith is going with you."

"Only to see you safely there," Leith hastened to amend. Kess' eyes had gone to slits, her hands to fists. "I gave you my word," he assured her.

"You pledged to trade the prize you had won for having your curse lifted. If that curse be *not* lifted, then Kess must abide by what she pledged, and so must you," Symond insisted.

"You think I'd choose to stay cursed, in order to force Kess to wed me?" Leith asked, bewildered. *Were* there such men, who'd seize a dukedom at the cost of a curse?

"Tell him how you propose to lift his curse, Raichim," Symond rumbled.

The queen hesitated, then raised her face to Leith's. "I can lift your curse," she said reluctantly. "But it will mean putting out one of your eyes."

A Curse Is Laid

THE FIRELIGHT SWAM before Leith's sight, through a thin screen of tears. "One of my *eyes?*" he repeated in a whisper, his face white as a hailstone. He had been prepared—had *thought* himself prepared—to face some unpleasant procedure, a stronger version of the day's testing, but this went so far beyond it that he could not take it in. *To lose one of his eyes? Deliberately?*

"You may choose," Raichim was saying, as if she spoke of goods available in the market. "Keep the right, and you will be as other folk, seeing only that which can ordinarily be seen, with ordinary sight. If you keep the left, it is likely you could become a wizard, able to see hidden things, act upon them."

Yet another choice? Was it any choice at all?

It was not, Leith decided. Not truly. It certainly wasn't a temptation. He had been given quite enough of magic for one lifetime—he could not imagine that being a wizard would be so much different from remaining cursed. He didn't think he wanted to spend the remainder of his life as he'd spent the first twenty years of it.

"You don't need to do this, lad," the duke pressed urgently.

Leith looked at Kess' mother, wondering where her wishes lay, what she might or might not tell him, to shape his decision. Despite the fire and the hot spring, he felt cold to his marrow. "Keep the curse, you mean?"

"It's *your* ill luck," Raichim agreed reluctantly. "Other folk aren't affected by it at once, however it has seemed to you. There are ways to shield them, to buffer the curse. You've always had the worst of it, that would not change. Those close to you—"

"Like Kess, when she marries me?" If they were trying—

either or both of them—to tempt him into a bad decision, Leith couldn't see how they hoped to succeed at it. Did they even have the same purpose in mind? He felt like a mutton bone worried between two determined dogs.

He looked at Kess, her face pale as his Lady's, full lips pressed together into a single colorless line, eyes ringed round with shadows of distress, dark as bruises. He did not need to wonder why she looked so. He knew how terrified she was of being forced into marriage, knew what she had risked to find her parents, to avoid being given away like a hide of land in her father's absence. She had never anticipated having to keep her word—just his luck that he, who had come to care for her, should be the only one who could hold her to it . . .

Beside that dreaded fate, Kess might not care if his curse fell upon her, too. But *he* would. Every mischance, every unhappiness that she ever suffered, he would know for his fault. And what Leith could bear himself, he would never wish upon another, not even if the price of freedom had been his death instead of an eye.

"Take the left one," Leith said, his lips trembling. He bit down hard on the lower one, till the mutiny was quelled. "Sir, will you do it?"

The duke stared at him, dumfounded. Plainly, he had expected that Leith would choose his daughter and his dukedom over cold-blooded maiming. Stunned, he nodded his acceptance of the task, duped into it by courtesy's dictates before he realized what was afoot.

"Best be done with it, then," Leith said, and knelt down before the duke.

All Symond could think to do then was to stall for time. He slowly unsheathed his dagger, made a great show of locating his whetstone and honing the point. The activity would surely prompt the lad to better consider his decision. The scrape of stone against metal alone . . .

Leith watched—and listened—with horrified fascination as oiled sandstone was applied to steel. He had made up his mind, and was determined not to shy back from his decision—but he could not help sickly contemplating what lay just ahead for him. That point, sharp enough to cut a thread falling through the air, was very shortly going to pierce his flesh. Nothing his curse had ever sent his way—not even the chimera—had prepared him for that sort of deliberate pain. Burns, sickness, near drowning, scrapes and sprains and blows—always he had been trying to escape them. Now there was no escape, except in the long term, if this butchery could indeed cure him of the curse. Also, Leith was well aware that pain anticipated always exceeds pain come unexpectedly—every nerve in his body was flinching already, though he had not yet been hurt in the slightest.

"I think I had better tie you down—" The duke's words knifed through Leith's reverie. Symond was removing his stout leather belt as he spoke. "Raichim, have you any rope? Or even strips of strong cloth?"

Leith was looking most alarmed. He had not arisen from his knees, but that had been his instinct, the moment binding was mentioned. He took hold of his terror, as he would have held tight to a shying horse, to calm it. "You won't need to do that, sir."

Symond raised a brow. Had it worked, then? Was the lad repenting? "I know you're set on this, and I am not doubting your courage. But this business is going to *hurt*." He held the belt in his hands. "No matter how pure your intentions, when that point goes in, you're going to move." No harm hammering the reality home.

"I won't move," Leith said, dashing Symond's hopes for his regained sanity. The duke frowned, displeased.

"You'll move. You won't be able to stop yourself. And if you start thrashing around on me, you could lose a good chunk of the rest of your face, which I think isn't what you want."

Leith swallowed hard. "I won't move," he repeated stubbornly. He didn't say anything more—his jaw was trembling, his teeth almost knocking against one another. That would be misunderstood.

Symond sighed, accepting one defeat while rejecting the other. What he *ought* to do was hit the young fool over the head with something, stun him long enough to get the job done. Or better still, to give the boy time to come to his right senses. The dagger in his hand had a nice, heavy knob for a pommel—one sharp rap behind the ear with that, and there'd be no more of this nonsense. He'd probably never even see it coming, state he was in.

The duke's hand was arrested before it had traveled two inches, his wrist seized in a steely grip that took him aback, considering how tiny was the hand doing the gripping.

"Symond, he has made his choice," Raichim said coldly.

"*Your* only choice was to help him—or not—and your word was given."

"If he wants to throw himself off one of your cliffs, do I have to help him with that, too?" Symond hissed.

A dangerous silence stretched. Kess still said nothing, but her face looked like a skull, save for her lips hiding her teeth behind quivers.

"Sir," Leith said—calmly, all things considered, "I know very well that there will be pain, but my Lady will give me the strength to bear what I must, as She always has. She has given Her priesthood disciplines, meditations that are taught to us . . . if I must not move, then I *will* not, no matter the pain. Only please don't tie me, as if I cannot be trusted. That would be harder to bear than the pain."

"It would be for your own good!"

"I am not unmindful of that." Leith tried to smile. His lips moved, but he didn't achieve the effect he sought, and he abandoned the attempt. "I thank you for the kindness, sir—but could we get on with this?"

How if I refuse? the duke wondered. But he was trapped by his pledged word and his good intentions—the lad was possibly just mad enough to try the business on his own if he was refused help, and that was surely a worse course to permit. Symond shut his eyes tight, opened them again. "You'd better lie down." That at least would limit his range of motion.

Leith looked startled again. Flat on his back, as if his sacrifice had to be torn from him by force when he would not freely give it? He shook his head angrily.

The duke's jaw clenched. "Have it your own way, then. Makes no difference to me."

Leith, satisfied, remained where he was, a slight tremor troubling his balance until he sat back upon his heels—a more stable stance. He was determined that a lack of food and sleep should not betray him into anything resembling cowardice. He calmed his breathing with care as he would before saying his nightly greeting to his Lady, cleansed his thoughts painstakingly, followed all of the ritual. He still felt cold, but his heartbeat was steadier, less frantic. He was nearly ready. Best the task were over with swiftly. He would do nothing to delay it—or worse, to his thoughts, postpone it.

The queen began to gather up cloths, chose herbs from her store of remedies, clinking jars and bottles. The duke scraped the blade lightly over the oiled stone. Kess stared from one tense face to the other—but said no word.

Leith looked past the knife into the candleflame, holding both his eyes wide open so that they were dazzled, all but blind. Pretending the light was the full moon, his Lady's light shining into his soul—the last time, Leith thought sadly, through one particular window. He wished he could have looked upon Her face once more, but that would havè meant leaving the cave, and he would have seemed irresolute. Probably he'd have needed to convince the duke all over again. Anyway, She would not rise for close to an hour, and waiting longer would be cruelest torture. He wanted his curse put to rest, no more delays. So, he gazed upon Her face with his mind's eye and let the trance deepen. His Lady—golden or silver, set against black, set against blue, always beautiful, beyond his powers of description . . .

The duke cleared his throat, a surprisingly loud sound. "Shouldn't you dose him with one or two of those simples beforetime, Raichim?" he asked his wife testily.

The queen folded a handful of dried herbs into a cloth, for a healing poultice. She put the bundle into a pan of hot water from the spring, to steep. "He has consented to this, Symond," she replied calmly. "Being drugged or drunken would taint—"

The duke growled and tightened his grip on the sharpened dagger's hilt, ready for the worst task he had set his hand to in a long career full of difficult matters.

At least, he thought, *I can be quick. I can show him that mercy.* But he bespoke Leith with a trace of desperation nonetheless.

"I'll ask you one last time—you're *sure* you want this done? It's your own choice? Never mind any of the rest of it—"

Leith nodded, and opened both eyes so wide that the candles certainly blinded him to everything else. The pupil of his left eye shrank to a black speck, afloat in a pale green sea. The right must be doing the same, though against that dark, dark brown 'twas less easy to see.

The duke shifted his dagger to a grip meant for delicate point-work. He moved his hand toward Leith's face. Leith stared frozenly past both knife and hand, thinking only of his Lady dancing a stately measure across a floor of stars . . .

"No!" Kess beat her father's hand away. The dagger's point nicked Leith's cheek just above the old scar and the newer

bruises. Blood spattered as Kess then slapped him across the face with all the force she could put behind her arm.

Had he been on his feet, Leith would have gone down like a felled ox, instead of only rocking back. Kess' small hand left a perfect imprint of itself—white first, then bright scarlet—across his cheek.

Kess stood poised, wrist cocked, in case Leith should be slow to come back to his senses, should require another treatment from her.

Leith did not, actually, react much to the blow, but he did shift focus to Kess as flame-dazzle and trance receded. Tears ran down his cheeks, mingling with the twisting scarlet trickle of blood.

"Why did you stop me?" he whispered, betrayed.

"Why did I stop you? *Why did I stop you!*" Kess almost hit him again, just for spite. "You were going to have an eye put out, and you don't even know that it would help! That's why I stopped you!"

"You're just making it harder," Leith told her sadly. The knife had fallen within his reach. He discovered it, picked it up, and passed it back to the duke, who received it with nerveless fingers. "Go outside," Leith suggested to Kess.

"I will not! I—"

"Kessallia."

Kess turned to face her mother, unfazed by the imperious tone. "You can't do this to him!" she spat. "I know what you're doing, but you can't—"

"Because you love him?" the queen asked curiously.

"I don't love him—"

Raichim lifted both her hands, brought them down in a gesture of command, and the air about the two men became solid as winter's ice. The magic had the effect of freezing them in their places, immune to any sensation—perchance even to thought. Certainly blind and deaf. The queen faced her daughter once more, in privacy. "Don't you?"

Kess stared at Leith, who was staring right back, obviously unseeing. A drop of blood stood out on his cheek, like a ruby, pendant beneath the moon's crescent. It did not fall, fat though it was.

"He doesn't need to hear you trying to make up your mind," Raichim said. "There may be things you need to say—but they would cut him deeper than any knife, cost him more than an eye. This is best."

Kess continued to stare, fascinated. She watched for Leith's chest to rise. It never did, but she saw no sign that he was in any distress from the lack of air.

"I cannot leave him so indefinitely, but he will take no harm from it," Raichim said impatiently. "Harken to me, Kessallia."

Kess turned her head, tilting it.

"Perhaps you have not learned to love. I was certainly unskilled enough, when I had only your years. I am not much better at it now." She put a hand on her daughter's arm. "Kess, don't do what I did! Don't run from something you think you hate—run *to* something you love."

Kess frowned. "What do you mean?"

"Keep you word. Or let him keep his. Look into your heart, and choose which it is to be."

Kess' expression became suddenly desperate as the meaning of her mother's command sank in. *"I can't!"*

"Only you can, Kessallia."

Kess had no notion how to go about examining her own heart—she suspected there was something more involved than shrieking *I won't!* whenever she received an order or an unpleasant request. So, she looked into Leith's face instead—so thin, with his hair raggedly shorn about it and falling into his eyes ever and anon, the green and the black one impartially. She traced with a glance the bruises he had gathered, staying by her side no matter how determinedly she drove him away. There was still a dark mark on his forehead, where he'd run into the mine prop she had purposely not warned him of. Blisters showed how the chimera's deadly flame had brushed him. She noted again the pale, twisted scar that he bore so proudly as a mark of his Lady's favor, despite all proofs that such favor counted for less than nothing under the sun's light.

If she let him proceed with his insane decision to follow her mother's remedy, then he *would* go out of her life once he'd conducted her back to Keverne. Leith would keep his word, to her and to her father—the one did not exclude the other. He'd take her home, then take himself away. Thereupon she'd be safe—and certain never to pledge a word again that would bind her into any man's hands. She'd rule Esdragon, and no one could force her to wed, not if she reigned for a thousand years. Not the silly young men, eager for the power she represented, not her aunt who had other sons to take Challoner's empty place—no one.

What was one eye, traded for all that? Leith was *willing* to do it, he wanted his curse lifted, more than anything—he had proved that to the point of tedium. She'd even allow him to take Valadan, make him a gift of her father's stallion, so that he could ride away in style.

And she would never see him again.

Never be wakened out of sleep by another of those silly moonrise chants. Never argue another crumb of pointless philosophy. Never see him stub a toe and bear it with good grace, turning about to actually *thank* his Lady for all Her goodness in keeping his life from being even more miserable than it was . . .

Never to see him again? The one man who didn't seem to regard her as a necessary curse by which a dukedom might be got? Kess stared at Leith's face, as if to fix it into her brain, for some future need, after he was gone.

She saw the green eye blink, and Kess sat back with a squeak.

"Damn," Raichim said, to Leith. "I forgot you'd be able to do that!" She flicked a finger, releasing him from her enchantment while she still held the duke immobile. "Lip-read every word, I don't doubt?"

Leith shook his head, but his troubled expression gave a lie to the gesture of denial.

He had certainly seen Kess' struggle, her distress. Kess knew he had, and the shame of the knowledge was unbearable, like trying to carry firecoals in bare fingers. She sprang to her feet and ran out, into the night.

"There's no ill fortune would *dare* come near that girl," the queen murmured, as Leith scrambled to his own feet.

He stared at her, green eye and black, unsure of the hope in what he heard.

Raichim nodded. "It's not a cure, but it's one worry the less. And she'd see any trouble coming."

He had knelt so long, both his feet were numbed from the ankles down and seemed outside his control, but Leith held onto the rough wall and stayed upright till he exited the cave. The feet awakened, and then his steps were as if taken on unsheathed knives, bladed with shards of glass. Leith ignored the nasty sensation, having felt worse, and caught up to Kess. She had halted between Valadan and the stream, as if unable to decide whether to wet her boots or risk trying to shift the stallion

Valadan's eyes glowed with rainbow sparks and gave Kess pause.

She heard Leith's stumbling footsteps behind her and whirled to face him—Kess had never in her life chosen to run from peril, except that once, from the chimera. Leith put a hand out, stopped just short of touching her face.

"Please stop crying."

"I never cry," Kess said. And her face was, on the instant, in the new-risen moonlight, dry as dust.

Leith tilted his head, squinted his right eye closed. "Yes, you do," he said, and touched her cheek. A moth's wings could not have brushed her tears away more delicately.

"I don't love you," Kess declared.

Leith closed his right eye again, like a wink. "Yes, you do," Kess heard him repeat—heard with a relief that spilled through her heart like moonlight through a casement.

Departure

TECHNICALLY, HE STILL bore his curse, Leith knew. But 'twas hard to hold that worry long in mind at the end of a month spent watching Kess studiously conning every spell of good fortune her mother could devise. Not that Kess had learned patience—Leith doubted she ever would—but the first fortnight's work had taught her the virtues of self-control, and she had made steady progress since. If any in Esdragon thought to profit from the mare's nest Brychan had left behind him, their new duchess would lesson them as to their error in very short order. And her marriage partner would stand firm by her side, willing and wanted and no more beset by fortune than any other man. So Kess swore, and so Leith utterly trusted.

And it was a good day for travel—the air chill but not to the point of discomfort, the wind negligible. Valadan approved.

"You are welcome here whenever you choose, Kessallia. With such a steed at your disposal, even this journey will never be arduous."

"Yet no one riding a lesser beast is like to trouble us," the duke whispered, pleased, into his wife's ear. He had his arms about her shoulders, though her woolen cloak was more than shield enough against the yet-sparse flakes of the winter's first snowfall.

Valadan danced and played eagerly with his bit, remembering the broad moors of Esdragon, anxious to try his speed upon them once more. Leith gathered up the reins, laughing at his enthusiasm.

His luck waved once more to her parents with a hand that flashed gold from one finger, then laid her moon-pale head upon his shoulder.